Abundance

Michael Fine

PM PRESS
2019
★

Abundance
Michael Fine © 2019
This edition © 2019 PM Press

ISBN: 978-1-62963-644-3
LCCN: 2018948938

PM Press
P.O. Box 23912
Oakland, CA 94623
pmpress.org

10 9 8 7 6 5 4 3 2 1

Cover: John Yates/Stealworks.com
Layout: Jonathan Rowland

Praise for

Abundance

"Much like Norman Maclean's later-in-life masterpiece, *A River Runs through It*, Michael Fine's *Abundance*, written after a distinguished career of medical practice here in the U.S. and in Africa, is a powerful first novel, an epic stretching from the civil wars of Liberia to the streets of Rhode Island. It's about the violence we practice on each other and the power of humanity to overcome it. A joy to read."
   —Paul J. Stekler, Emmy-winning documentary filmmaker

"*Abundance* is a riveting, suspenseful tale of love, violence, adventure, idealism, sometimes-comic cynicism, class conflict, and crime—especially war crimes. Dr. Fine expertly moves his narrative back and forth between Liberia and America (mostly New England), using his medical experience—especially in serving the poor—psychological insight, and deep knowledge of West Africa to craft a story that displays both the deep disconnect between the First and Third Worlds and our commonalities. I should add that the rescue mission that's at the heart of the story would make one hell of a movie."
   —Robert Whitcomb, former finance editor of the *International Herald Tribune* and former editorial page editor of *The Providence Journal*

"Michael Fine takes us into the heart of a country at war with itself. But our journey in battered Land Rovers along potholed red dirt roads is propelled by love not hate. That love offers hope for Liberia, our often forgotten sister country, and for anyone who confronts despair. Read *Abundance*. Reignite your own search for a life worth living."
   —Martha Bebinger, WBUR

"Michael Fine has eloquently captured the expanse of emotions as well as the variety of motivations of those volunteers working in Liberia. An excellent documentary."

—James Tomarken, MD

"Michael Fine has brought his lifetime of experience as a doctor concerned with community health in our country and Africa and his considerable writing skills to bear on the great question of our time: How do we heal a broken world? He makes you care about what happens to the people living their answers."

—Bill Harley, author, two time Grammy Award–winning singer-
   storyteller, and NPR commentator

In Memory of Adell Phyllis Gross Fine (1927–2014)

To Gabriel Fine and Rosie Fine

When you have eaten your fill, and have built fine houses to live in, and your herds and flocks have multiplied, and your silver and gold have increased, and everything you own has prospered, beware lest your heart grow haughty and you forget the Lord your God—who freed you from the land of Egypt, the house of bondage; who led you through the great and terrible wilderness with its seraph serpents and scorpions, a parched land with no water in it, who brought forth water for you from the flinty rock; who fed you in the wilderness with manna, which your fathers had never known, in order to test you by hardships only to benefit you in the end—and you say to yourselves, "My own power and the might of my own hand have won this wealth for me." Remember that it is the Lord your God who gives you the power to get wealth, in fulfillment of the covenant that He made on oath with your fathers, as is still the case.

—Dvorim (Deuteronomy) 8:12–18

Contents

Preface

LIBERIA, A NATION OF FOUR TO FOUR AND A HALF MILLION PEOPLE IN WEST AFRICA, IS about the same size as the U.S. state of Tennessee. It is a place of many languages and many communities.

Liberia was created in 1820, when a private organization called the American Colonization Society began transporting freed slaves from the U.S. to a small area of West Africa in an attempt to solve the problem of slavery for the United States without emancipating those slaves still held in bondage. Some of the settlers were from families that had lived as slaves in the United States for two hundred years. Other settlers were recently freed or had purchased their freedom themselves. Others came from families that had been free for generations. Few, if any, came from families that originated in the area they were coming to colonize. Few spoke the languages spoken by the people and communities then living in that place.

The American Colonization Society counted among its members people we now regard as some of the most decent and forward-thinking Americans of their time: James Madison, Henry Clay, Daniel Webster, Paul Cuffee, and Francis Scott Key. Even Abraham Lincoln was a member for a time. Some of these people believed that African Americans would never be able to have free and equal lives in the United States. Others believed that it was impossible, or immoral, for people of different races to live together.

The American Colonization Society brought about 13,000 free African Americans to West Africa between 1820 and 1847. (In 1820, the U.S. population was 9,638,453, of whom 1,538,022 were slaves.) The free African Americans created a colony of their own in Africa that was modeled on the United States. Plantations, schools, towns, language, culture, and even conservative politics were all copied from the southern United States the freed slaves had left behind—the only culture that the freed slaves themselves shared. Those people and their descendants, who would call themselves Americo-Liberians and are called Congo people by their compatriots, comprise a very small but politically and economically elite segment of the Liberian population.

Most people in Liberia today are descended from the indigenous population. Although English is the official language in Liberia, most people grow up speaking another language, which is the language of their ethnic community. Many people also speak Liberian Kreyol, also called Liberian Pidgin, which is a trading language based on English and Portuguese that has been used for three hundred years. Trading languages are common on the coast of Africa. At first, trading languages allowed traders and indigenous people to speak to one another. Then those languages were used by indigenous people from different cultures and communities to speak among themselves.

Bassa, Gao, Krahn, and Kpelle are four of the thirty languages spoken in Liberia. Kru is one of the four language groups.

The music of Liberian Kreyol often sounds familiar to American ears, but Kreyol itself is difficult for most Americans to understand. Articles, conjunctives, and final consonants are often omitted; adjectives are repeated for emphasis and many words are used in archaic forms. Thus "na" means "not", "ma" means "my" or "mother" depending on context. "Ga ca" means "good car"; "sma-sma (small-small)" means "very small"; and "De ro. I yaw wais' ma' ti, I weh sureleh blow yaw mouf o wais yaw fa" means "I'm the badass (a rouge). You are a waste of my time. I will surely slam your mouth and lay waste to your face."

In 1989, Liberia entered a period of brutal civil wars. The civil wars were fomented by Charles Taylor, who would become Liberia's president, but Taylor was aided and abetted by many people and nations. The wars lasted until 2003. The years between 1989 and 2003 were filled with unimaginable cruelty in Liberia; years of murder, rape, dismemberments, and chaos.

The recent history of Liberia is discussed in more detail in the appendix.

Chapter One
Julia Richmond. District #4 Health Center.
Grand Bassa County, Liberia. July 15, 2003

THE TOO SWEET CALLS OF THE PEPPER-BIRDS WOKE HER BEFORE DAWN. ASLEEP, JULIA HALF heard the chattering and whistling of the other birds, of course, but it was the fluty, chirping, melodic pepper-bird call that Julia recognized as she lay on her cot in the District #4 Health Center consulting room. She had come out with Sister Martha, her favorite nurse, and with her driver and guard, the previous day just before dark, twenty miles down a rutted one-track road into the middle of nowhere, across bridges that were unstable, and through miles of thick dark jungle. There was a war on, and although it was said to be far away, people like Julia moved about only during the daytime, and even then only with a driver and a guard, because of what was said to happen in the bush at night.

Of all the places she loved and the ideas that moved her, the grand romantic notions about healing the world and making it a safe place for all its children, Julia Richmond loved the District #4 Health Center most. She had only just come to Liberia, after stints in Haiti, Rwanda, and Bangladesh. She came to Liberia when Bill Levin, her friend and mentor in the U.S., forwarded an e-mail describing the position and the need. Liberia, after fourteen years of civil war, was among the most desperate places Julia had been and its people the most distant and afraid. Julia loved desperate places, the places where there was nothing and where the people had no one, so they took her for who she was, as she was, and didn't ask her the questions she couldn't answer for herself.

Julia also loved the softness of the light—the muddy browns, tans, and ochres of a place where you couldn't really see the corners or down the halls, where you could hear and smell people and things before you saw them. There was no electricity in the health center, so the light filtered in through the larger windows, one per room. If you wanted to read or see clearly, you stood or sat by a window, even at midday. Inside, the hallways and the larger waiting rooms were shrouded and warm. When you walked from room to room, the hidden life of the place was revealed, so it felt like you were discovering an unknown truth just by moving about.

The health center was in a village without a name. It was built on a rise. Rows of wooden benches lined its broad porch, benches that had been polished over many years by the bottoms of people who came shortly after sunrise and might sit there most of the day waiting for a doctor, a physician's assistant, or a nurse. The red dirt road emerged out of the jungle on the far side of a field that lay next to the health center, which meant if you were sitting on the porch you could see who was coming down the road from the jungle and who was going away. There were two clusters of huts near the health center—one behind, a little further up and over the rise, and one further down the road. Julia heard voices among the huts, murmuring and indistinct except when a baby cried or a child called out. She heard the crowing of cocks and the clucking of chickens, and she smelled the warm bitter smell of wood and charcoal fires, which reminded her of Arab coffee and burnt toast.

The first morning light fell on the health center before it came to the village on the other side of the rise.

Julia had been awake for a moment in the middle of the night. She heard muffled moans and then a cry. A newborn. They hadn't called her. The child must have been okay. The labor room was at the far end of the health center, and the nurse and the community health workers assisted at births.

Torwon and Charles, her driver and guard, slept in the village. Sister Martha, a Carmelite nursing sister from Burundi, slept on a cot in the dispensary. Yesterday they did a vaccination clinic and the big belly clinic as soon as they arrived, working until they lost the light.

Today there was a sick clinic. Then they would hurry home down twenty kilometers of one-track road that led to another twenty kilometers of county road that was wider but not better, scarred by potholes and ruts cut by runoff water from the evening rains. They would be back in Buchanan before dark. They had to be back in Buchanan before dark.

The six-bed infirmary had four overnight patients—two malarias, a dehydration, and a typhoid. The nurses and community health workers cared for those people without Julia's help. Some nights they awakened her when there was a crisis, but by the time they called her it was usually too late. So Julia had taken to seeing each patient just before dusk. It didn't matter. There were still often empty beds in the morning where there had been a sick patient the night before.

There was a latrine out back, built with Julia's patient instruction over many months, but no one else in the health center or village ever used it. Water came from the village. Each day they filled two ten-gallon jugs and carried them up the rise from the village pump.

Julia Richmond was thirty-two. She was from Mill Valley, and then Stanford and Brown, and could have worked anywhere, so God only knew why she loved this godforsaken place so much. She was trained in both Pediatrics and Emergency Medicine. She had green eyes, black hair, and pale skin that had tanned in the equatorial sun. In her own mind, Julia was awkward and insubstantial despite the letters after her name and what everyone said about her looks. Here she never had to judge herself against the standard of too many others like her, and here there wasn't a crowd of people just like her, so she didn't have to look at herself reflected in the hollowness of the culture that stamped out people who were all alike, again and again.

Julia heard footsteps. Then she heard murmuring and the creaking of wood as people climbed the stairs and settled themselves on the polished half-log benches. They came from the village and from the bush, one or two at a time.

She went into the clinic room to wash. The water jug was near empty.

I'll go to the village, she thought, *to the pump, and wash myself properly. And check on Carl's pump at the same time.*

She did not think about Carl himself but didn't not think about him either. She thought about Carl's pump and thought about how the water would gush from the spigot when she pushed down on the handle and about how she would splash the cool, clear water over her neck and face and use it to wash her eyes, and she thought about how alive she would feel as the water flowed over her and brought her from sleep to life.

They started the sick clinic just after eight. Sister Martha, a short, proper woman with dark skin, who dressed every day in the same white blouse, brown jacket, and brown skirt despite the heat, came to the consulting room just after Julia arrived. Sister Martha walked out to the porch to see who was waiting for them and to see if any of the clinic staff were walking from the village to the health center. Julia sat at an old wooden desk with a window behind it.

The first patient was a young man with a cut on his leg. He sat in front of the window in the pale yellow light of early morning. He was about nineteen, thin and wiry, with dark brown skin and brown eyes. Sister Martha stood next to the window.

There was an open cut in the man's calf the size of Julia's hand that ran deep into the muscle and was covered with white-green pus.

Julia held out her hand. "I'm Dr. Richmond. Let's look at that leg."

"Halloo," the young man said. He took Julia's hand. His grasp was warm but weak. "Sundaygar," he said.

"When did you get that cut, Sundaygar?" Julia asked.

Sister Martha waited a few moments. When Sundaygar did not reply, she began to speak in Kreyol. When Sundaygar did not look at her, Sister Martha switched to Bassa and began again.

The man now looked at Sister Martha, not Julia, and answered her.

"He got it in a palm tree. One week," Sister Martha said.

"How did you cut it?" Julia asked.

Sister Martha translated the question. Sundaygar answered in several long sentences. Sister Martha asked more questions, which the young man answered as well.

Julia dropped to one knee. She took Sundaygar's leg in her hands and turned it from side to side in the light.

"It cuts with machete. He is cutting palm nuts in the tree," Sister Martha said.

"When was your last tetanus shot?" Julia asked.

"He has not tetanus. The clinic has not tetanus," Sister Martha said, without translating the question.

"Let's get some Betadine and water and debride a little. I want to see the tissue," Julia said.

"The clinic has not Betadine today," Sister Martha said. "He wants to sew, to make stitches."

"I can't sew it. It needed to be sewn within twenty-four hours," Julia said.

"He is two days walk."

"Do we have Silvadene?"

"The clinic has not Silvadene," Sister Martha said.

"Any antibiotic cream?"

"Not cream today. Bottles amoxicillin liquid and pills, Bactrim."

Julia bit her bottom lip.

"There is no indication for oral antibiotics," Julia said. "He needs a tetanus shot and surgical debridement. Otherwise it's going to leave a big scar. Or get infected, in which case he loses the leg or dies. Maybe he can get by with a good topical antibiotic and twice a day wound care. Maybe."

Sister Martha did not answer.

Julia turned to the patient.

"You should go to Buchanan, to the hospital. Otherwise big big scar or infection. Okay?"

Sundaygar looked at Sister Martha, but Sister Martha did not speak.

Julia bit her lip once more, and then continued. "Maybe it's too late to sew," Julia said. "You need good wound care. Dressing changes twice a day. Infection is starting to creep in. If this gets infected, you could lose the leg. Or you could die."

She paused, waiting for Sister Martha. Sister Martha still did not speak.

"Let's do this," Julia said. "There are no signs of bad infection yet. Just surface infection. Take the pills that Sister Martha will give you. Keep the wound clean. Try to wait a few days before you walk far or work, and let it heal. It will take three or four weeks to heal—maybe longer. Come back if there are streaks of redness on the leg, if it gets more tender instead of less tender over time, or if you get a fever, the hotness of the body. Bactrim BID for ten days."

Sister Martha translated.

Sundaygar stood. He said something to Sister Martha, while Julia made a note on one of the dog-eared green cards, and Sister Martha walked Sundaygar to the dispensary.

"He is walking to his village now. He is climbing tomorrow," Sister Martha said, when she returned.

"Let's bring tetanus and Silvadene next trip. For the physician's assistant to have when we are not here," Julia said.

"Buchanan Hospital has not Silvadene. The health center has not refrigerator," Sister Martha said.

Julia looked away for a moment. Then she turned to see who was next.

The next patient was a twenty-three-year-old with burning on urination (an antibiotic and a talk about safe sex, perhaps translated, but probably not.) Then an eight-month-old with a cough for two days (clear lungs, normal weight for age, no fever—watch and wait, and come back for difficulty breathing, loss of appetite, or if the cough isn't gone in a few days. Perhaps translated. Perhaps not.)

Then Sister Martha brought in a young woman carrying a baby. A limp baby. Eyes open but dull. Breathing fast. Way too fast.

This was trouble. Julia didn't need a stethoscope, a thermometer, or a blood test. Bad trouble. Respiratory distress secondary to severe anemia. Anemia caused by malaria. Goddamn malaria. All these kids had it. Julia could spot it from a hundred miles away. Sick. Incredibly sick. Could die at any moment sick. Drop everything and run for cover sick.

The child would die soon—in an hour or in a day—if somebody didn't do something. Do something fast. Will die. If Julia didn't do something now.

The baby was a girl, six months old but barely eight pounds. She was not moving anything other than her chest. She didn't whimper. Her chest moved in and out twice as fast as a person's heart beats; in and out, in and out, in and out, the breathing without sound or obstruction but so fast that the skin between her ribs was pulled in with each breath. The mucous membranes were dry. There was no wheezing. The chest was clear. The fontanel was closed. The muscle tone was not good. The baby was breathing way too fast.

The child's mother was in her early twenties, a country girl. She was small, bony, and Bassa-speaking. The mom wasn't frightened enough. Her matted hair was wrapped in plain mud-stained green cloth. She had a small nose and mouth, and she looked away as Julia looked at her baby in the soft morning light.

Sister Martha spoke. There were four other children at home. The mother carried this baby for three hours. She walked with another woman, her mother or an aunt. They must have known how sick this child was. They had to know. The baby had been sick for days, maybe for weeks.

Julia pulled the child's lower eyelid down with her thumb. The conjunctiva, the red-pink lining of the eyelid, was white, not pink. To Julia, eyelids that pale meant severe anemia. The child didn't have enough red blood cells in her veins and arteries to sustain life. Malaria attacks and destroys red blood cells. This was malaria, as severe as it gets.

The child in front of Julia had severe malaria complicated by severe anemia and her heart was beginning to fail. Severe malaria in the bush, where most severe malaria occurs, kills a million African children a year. But maybe not this one. Maybe not.

"The child must to go to hospital. We leave now. Right now. We bring you and the child to Buchanan," Julia said.

Sister Martha translated into Bassa.

"Torwon. Charles. We are leaving," Julia said, loud and clear so her voice could be heard out of the room. Torwon and Charles were waiting in the main room, chatting up the ladies. "We are leaving. Now."

Torwon and Charles came to the door. Torwon was thin, young, and intense. Charles was a big dark-skinned man in his early forties, a big jovial man who loved to tease.

It was against the regulations to carry patients in the Land Cruiser. Sister Martha waited for Julia to change her mind, to vacillate as Julia often did. But Julia did not look at the faces of her colleagues. She stared only at the child, and the others could see that her mind was made up.

Then Sister Martha translated. They were leaving. Now.

The child's mother spoke in a quiet voice. She had other children. Buchanan was too far. She was afraid of the hospital fees. The child was not that sick. She needed only the pink medicine.

"Walk with me," Julia said. "Bring the baby to the Land Cruiser. Now."

Julia worried for an instant about blood for a transfusion. The hospital in Buchanan didn't have a blood bank. If you needed blood, you had to find a friend or relative to donate what is going to be transfused. Perhaps the mother would refuse. But Julia could give blood herself. This child would be dead by nightfall if she was not transfused.

The child's mother kept her seat.

"Tell her the baby will die in a day or two if we don't go to the hospital today. Tell her," Julia said, "that we have to go now. Today. She has to go today."

Sister Martha said a few words.

The mother stood. She went to get her mother or aunt, who waited outside on a worn wooden bench and wore a yellow Port Angeles

Dragons tee shirt over a green and blue lapa, a skirt made of brightly colored African cloth.

So it was they left the District #4 Health Center, breaking all regulations, and traveled twenty kilometers down a rutted one-track road through the bush in a Land Cruiser with a green Merlin insignia and the red silhouette of a machine gun with a red circle over it and the words "this vehicle carries no weapons" stenciled just beneath the silhouette of the gun on the driver's door and the back doors, with a child who was dying in her mother's arms.

In America, there would have been an ambulance, its lights flashing, its sirens blaring, driving seventy-five miles an hour in the left lane of a superhighway, as they called it in over the transponder, and the trauma center at the hospital emergency department would have assembled a team that would have been set up and ready to go the moment the baby was whisked through the ED doors. In Africa, in Liberia, there was a red dust–covered dented white Land Cruiser nosing through potholes still filled with the runoff from the previous night's rain, hoping against hope that the child might survive the trip, that the Land Cruiser wouldn't slide off the road or break down, that the hospital would have some blood on hand, that there was IV tubing to use to give the blood, and that the hospital hadn't run out of antimalarial medicine yet that week.

There is no malaria in America.

They drove as fast as the road would allow. They drove over an unusable log bridge that they should have gotten out and walked over. The Land Cruiser jolted into each pothole and sometimes bottomed out with a jarring bang.

At the end of the one-track road, they turned right, toward Buchanan, and climbed a hill.

They hit a rut. There was a jolt.

The Land Cruiser sagged to the left, and Torwon stopped it on the side of the road.

Chapter Two
Carl Goldman. Buchanan,
Liberia. July 15 and 16, 2003

THE MORNING OF JULY 15, 2003, WAS BRIGHT AND HOT BUT NOT INSUFFERABLE, BECAUSE a breeze was blowing in from the Atlantic. It was rainy season, so there were puddles of red water everywhere. Red runoff rainwater still coursed through the brooks and streams, which ran deep in the red earth, but the roads had dried somewhat overnight and were passable, to the extent any road in Liberia was ever passable in 2003.

The junction market next to the Bong County Road just east of Buchanan was already filling with people, even though it was early, just after 8:00. The market was a big open space in the red dirt where women came and built stalls out of wooden poles and sold anything they could carry—charcoal, pots, roasted corn, pineapples, dried fish, tiny bags of spices, palm oil, lapa cloth, and used motorbike parts—to one another. A shantytown had grown up around the market, in and around the walls of half-demolished concrete block houses, the remnants of a neighborhood that had been destroyed by shells and tanks the last time there had been chaos in the streets. Now the shantytown was jammed with refugees, with people who had come down from the countryside ahead of the fighting. The road and the marketplace filled with lorries, jitneys, and cars, with boys on motorcycles—sometimes three or four on a little 90cc Suzuki—and with people walking, the women balancing multicolored plastic tubs on their heads, the men carrying huge overstuffed cheap fabric suitcases, sometimes by a handle, sometimes on their backs.

A white Land Cruiser pulled into a shop next to the junction market. The Water for Power crew stopped there to buy water and rolls for lunch on the mornings they went north. The Land Cruiser had the silhouette of a machine gun stenciled on the driver's door, the passenger's door, and the back door. A black circle surrounded each machine gun and there was a black line drawn diagonally through the circle, and the words "this vehicle carries no weapons" was stenciled just beneath the silhouette of the gun—the same insignia that was on most of the NGO vehicles in Liberia whether they carried weapons or not.

Then three white Land Cruisers with the blue insignia of the local steel mill stenciled on their doors burst into the intersection from the Bong County Road, their horns blaring. They forced their way into the line of jitneys, goods lorries, cars, and motorbikes that were headed into the middle of the town, weaving in and out. A few minutes later two blue Liberian National police pickups, each carrying five or six armed men and a rear-mounted machine gun flew into the junction, also racing toward Buchanan.

"Hot time in the old town tonight," said David Wenang, the driver, who was dark, short, thin, and quick.

"They're going the wrong way," said Carl Goldman. He was in his late twenties, a thin, tall, brown man with an American accent. He sat next to the driver and was trying to be the person in charge. "I thought the government guys are in Buchanan to protect the north. So why are the Land Cruisers headed south?"

"MODEL move quick-quick," David said. "Good fighters. Trained in France. Armed by France and U.S. Maybe six days out. Maybe one. Maybe here tonight."

"So, if the army and Taylor's police are off the north road, that means the road should be clear and we should have an easy time. For once," Carl said. "Let's move."

"Sooner we gone, the sooner we back," David said. "The sooner we're back, the better I like it. No clear in Buchanan when we get back. Too many people. Too many refugee."

"We have a long day, David," Carl said. "Better to have those boys in Buchanan than in the north."

"Better for there to be no war again and no war in Buchanan. How many places today? Five? Six? Eight? If I was boss we sleep late and wait for the soldier-boys to come, shoot each other up, and go away," David said.

"Six places," said Carl. "Maybe seven. We make a chlorine run to Godeh, a drop and switch. Then we check wells on the way back. Just in and out. We quick-quick today."

"Quick-quick," David said. He put the truck into gear. They lurched forward through the red dust on the red road.

David drove even faster than usual on the red dirt. There were no other cars on the road. All the life had emptied out of the north, as if it were a sink from which someone had pulled the plug.

First there were a few people. Then there were no people.

They passed groups of three or four huts, each group arrayed around an outdoor kitchen shanty—an open cooking fire in the center of a roofed space lined with wooden benches. But there was no fire and no people in the huts. The huts were made of poles and plastered with red mud to make walls that were solid and plumb, with roofs made of palm thatch laid over a precise lattice of poles. The red walls of the houses were marked with repeating patterns in white paint—handprints, footprints, or silhouettes or stripes that looked, in its way, like wallpaper, or war paint.

People know war is coming again, Carl thought, *and they have gone to find shelter in Buchanan, or gone deep into the bush to hide.*

After a few miles, they began to see people again, but these people looked lost, like people standing outside as rainclouds thickened, not sure if it was time to head for cover. A few stood in one or two of the cooking shanties. Some squatted in front of the fires. Others lay on the benches. Still others walked between the houses, going somewhere and not going anywhere at all, all at the same time.

There were men with machetes walking on the side of the road. These men did not turn to look as the white Land Cruiser drove by and raised red dust.

But the land was otherwise empty. No animals, no goats or pigs, only a few scrawny African chickens. War was coming. Everyone was afraid of the war, and everyone was afraid of one another.

Carl saw Julia before he recognized her. Julia was standing on the roof of a Land Cruiser with her hands on her hips. The Land Cruiser was at the top of a rise to the left of the road.

David took his foot off the gas. The Land Cruiser lurched as it hit a rain-cut ditch and started to slow.

Torwon and Charles, Julia's driver and guard, knelt next to truck, positioning a jack in front of a flat tire. Julia lifted the spare tire off the roof, and then lowered it over the side of the truck, her ponytail moving from side to side over her shoulders. Torwon stood and caught the tire.

Another woman sat on top of the embankment next to the road. She held a baby in a green lapa fabric sling. Two other women sat with her. They sweated in the hot late morning sun.

"Stop or go, boss?" David said.

"Stop," Carl said.

David pulled the Land Cruiser to the right shoulder, but he did not turn off the engine. He opened his window. The hot moist air of the day embraced them. Carl got out.

"Ok?" Carl said.

"Damn road," Julia said. "Lucky we didn't crack an axle. Just a blinkin' flat."

"Need anything?" Carl said.

"Just decent roads. We've got it covered. We'll be up and running in a few," Julia said.

Charles, who was squatting on the ground next to the flat tire, grunted as he jerked a lug wrench. The truck groaned as the lug nut came loose.

Then there was a crack and the car settled, sinking to the side and back, like a boat that had taken on water listing to starboard just before it flipped over and sank.

"You were saying something about a cracked axle," Carl said.

"Damned axle. Damned road. Damned country," Julia said. She lowered herself off the roof of her Land Cruiser, knelt in the dirt next to Charles, put her hands on the wheel and tried to turn it. Then she wiped her brow with the back of her hand.

"The effing thing *is* cracked. We cracked one last week. Goddamned roads. I got a really sick kid here. I got to get to town."

Julia paused.

"Hey Carl, can you run that woman there into Buchanan for me? The one with the kid. We need to get her moved."

"I can't carry passengers. You know the drill," Carl said.

"I'm asking for a one-time exception. This kid is really sick. Like could die today sick. You'll beat me by two hours if you go now. Maybe three. It takes them forever to get a rescue truck up here. They don't know I have a sick kid, and they don't know to hurry their asses. I don't do passengers either. This one is different. This kid is really bad," Julia said.

"I'm headed north to Godeh. Maybe I can swing back and lift her in when we're headed home if your rescue truck hasn't shown yet," Carl said.

"I need you to run them to Buchanan now. This kiddo is going to die if she doesn't get transfused."

"Let's go boss," David said.

"The bush is full of dying kids. It's also full of boy soldiers," Carl said. "I've got to get this chlorine up to Godeh. They've got a bad well that'll kill a hundred of your kids if we don't get it treated. Let's do this. We run to Godeh without side trips. If the roads are good, we'll be back in an hour. We'll carry the kid in then."

"Carl, I have a kid dying from malaria," Julia said.

"And I have a village that will crash and burn without chlorine," Carl said. "Here's my best and last offer. I put the lady and the baby in the back with us, blast the AC up to Godeh, and keep everybody comfortable. Then we'll haul ass back to Buchanan as soon as we're done up north. It ain't perfect, but that's the best I can do."

"Nowhere near good enough. But it looks like the best I'm going to get out of you today. Just move ass. Super quick-quick. Please."

"Anything for you, Dr. Richmond," Carl said. "Almost."

Julia went to the three women sitting on the embankment. The youngest of the three held a limp baby.

"Sister Martha, please go with them," Julia said. "I'll wait for the crew. There's nothing more we can do for this kid until we get her to Buchanan. And Sister Martha pray or something, will you? We got this far. But now we are gonna need all the help we can get."

Carl helped each of the women into the back of his Land Cruiser. The limp child lay on its mother's lap. The two other women sat next to her on hard benches. Julia put one hand on Carl's shoulder as he latched the door, and then touched his waist.

Carl turned and put the flat of his hand on the small of Julia's back, "You drive a hard bargain. That's what I like about you."

"Just that?" Julia said.

"Nothing more for public consumption. Private is different," Carl said.

"Later for that. Now move," Julia said. "We don't have much time."

Carl got into the truck and David dropped it into gear. The Land Cruiser jerked forward.

They bounced and grunted and groaned down the hill, the Land Cruiser shuddering and thumping as it slid sideways and forward on the rutted red road.

At the bottom of the hill, the Land Cruiser fell into a deep washout and its undercarriage hit the road surface with a bang. Carl's head slammed down and back, jamming the bones of his neck. He turned to see if his new passengers were okay and his eyes followed the light through the back window.

Out the rear window, Carl saw a pickup, which could have been blue, coming across the hill from the right speeding down the District #4 Health Center road, speeding toward Julia and her disabled vehicle. The pickup raised a cloud of dust.

In the sun, next to the Land Cruiser, Carl could still see Julia, the sunlight catching wisps of hair that had shaken loose from her pony-tail.

It was better for Carl Goldman to be in Africa, better for him to fade into the background and let boundaries dissolve, better for him to become part of what is great and pulsing than to let the eyes of America cut Carl into a hundred thousand pieces. It was better to be in Africa than to be broken apart by false ideas about who he was and what he was. It was better to be here, despite the war, the danger, the poverty, and the madness, than to allow those eyes to reduce him to dust, to be just a shadow wearing clothing and not really a man. Africa was freedom, despite the war, the danger, the poverty, and the madness; the freedom to experience the world in all its complexity, the freedom to be whatever and whomever Carl wanted to be and to become whatever and whomever he wanted to become. Despite the madness and its chaos, Africa was life itself, while home sucks away your soul.

At home, they judge you and pigeonhole you the moment they see you, at the same time as they are studying your every move, recording everything you've ever bought or thought, so they can predict what you will want and maximize profit by selling you what they want you to buy. In Africa, Carl was part of a great complex human wave that pulled him under but that also lifted him. The wave spun him about but also carried him, part of a whole that was much greater than the sum of its parts.

In America, Carl Goldman was a black man and thus too often a mugger, a thief, a rapist, or a rapper or a pimp, though when they saw his name on paper they thought he was a Jew. In Africa he was just a man who was hard to place. In Liberia his cream-colored skin said he was not a countryman, but that he might be a Congoman or a South African, a Ghanaian or a Zimbabwean, or even perhaps an Arab. When they saw his name on paper in Africa before they saw his skin they thought he was a European, by which the Liberians meant anyone from Europe or America or Australia or Canada.

Carl Goldman was a thin man with cream-colored skin and dark wavy hair whose father was Jewish and whose mother came from Martinique, so what he looked like and what he was were not entirely the same. He was young, just twenty-seven, articulate, and well educated, despite what had happened long ago. He came to Africa to try his luck and to see if there might be freedom for him anywhere. He had a history that was complicated, but no one would know about that here. Wouldn't know. Wouldn't ask. Didn't matter. Here he could just be who he was and make a life for himself without thinking, knowing, or remembering. In America there was only one person Carl could trust. In Africa it was every man for himself, and the person you are is the person who acts, so the issue of trust or love was just never on the table.

Like every other expat in Buchanan Town, Carl Goldman lived in a compound. The Water for Power compound had walls made of bamboo poles that supported woven bamboo mats, each eight feet tall and eight feet long and so densely woven you couldn't see through them, so they looked like walls indeed. You couldn't see through those walls, but you could hear everything that was happening around the compound. You could hear the women walking on the lane that ran behind the compound on their way to the village pump. You could hear the boys teasing one another as they walked or ran in the gravel on their way to school, and you could hear the crunch of the gravel if and when a car inched its way down the dirt lane, but you couldn't see the women or the boys or the occasional dust-covered dented car— and the cars and the people walking couldn't see you.

The compound wall was topped with coils of razor wire, which marked it as an expat place. A massive motor-driven sliding solid metal gate kept everyone inside apart from the world outside. You could hear the power come on, a hum and a crunch, and then a clang, as the gate opened or closed whenever anyone came in or went out.

Walls made of bamboo weren't good for anything aside from shielding what was inside from local eyes. The walls wouldn't stop a bullet and provided no protection whatsoever from a tank or half-track. So when anarchy roamed the streets, when ten- and twelve- and thirteen-year-old boys high on uppers, riding in used four-wheel-drive trucks and SUVs and firing AK-47s swarmed over Buchanan like a runaway hive of bees, the compound didn't work as a place to hide. But they were between wars, or at least between battles, and for the moment Carl and his crew couldn't be seen and no one passing by knew what was waiting inside the bamboo walls under the razor wire. There could have been firepower, machetes, and hundreds of men hiding behind the bamboo and wire. You couldn't tell they were few, unarmed, and harmless.

Buchanan Town is the third largest city in Liberia, but there is nothing city-like about it. It is a just place with a port on the road from Monrovia to Maryland County; a place that is mainly Bassa-speaking, though there was plenty of Pele and Kru—a place of thirty thousand souls near the sea. The people of Buchanan Town live in small, one-story houses made of brick, with corrugated iron roofs, plastered with concrete that is painted in brilliant primary colors: white, red, blue, yellow, or green. The houses are all jumbled together. On the back-streets are solitary outdoor stalls that sell neighborhood essentials: phone cards, handmade brooms, gasoline and palm oil in jars by the liter, and spices wrapped in tiny plastic bags that hang from poles as if they were teardrops or dew.

Buchanan has a tiny port where Ghanaian fisherman landed their catch and a main street, Thomas Street, a dusty rutted road lined by shops that sell boldly-colored lapa cloth, pots and pans, machetes, palm nuts, big white canvas bags of charcoal, green, yellow, and red plastic bins and bowls of all sizes, and motorbikes. All the open spaces are filled with tiny market stalls where women in lapas sit on the ground selling pots and pans, handmade rusty metal charcoal stoves, corn roasted on a stick, pineapples and bananas, eggs, bush meat, dried fish, and spices. The air is filled with the smell of diesel fumes, charcoal smoke, and roasting corn.

Carl went into the bush every morning in a Land Cruiser, some-times with a driver and sometimes with a team of four, to plan, build, and check on the village pumps that brought clean water to people who lived in the bush. Carl made the schedule. David, his driver, knew the roads and the villages, even the villages that were a three-hour walk into the bush from the nearest road. David also knew the rutted one-track roads that crossed streams on log bridges and ran twenty kilometers through nowhere, and he knew the villages that you could only get to on the river, on the slow diesel paddleboat upstream.

In the compound, Carl was in charge. He had a mission, vision, values, and goals. In the bush, Carl was a passenger, an observer, with no way to exist or survive on his own, but he was also closer to the earth than he had ever been before. In the compound, Carl was all command and control. In the bush, they were just one wrong turn, one clogged fuel pump, or one broken axle away from the munching insects, the calling birds, the dark, and the undefined danger that lurked after dark. You live by your wits in the bush. You live each moment, each turn, each rut, and each bottoming out of the truck.

The road flattened as they drove north, which meant better going. They were not allowed to carry passengers.

"No change in plan," Carl said. "This is a dump and run. We got to be quick. In and out. Fifteen minutes. No more."

Carl looked at his passengers. He could see the baby on its mother's lap. The mother and the other women sat on one side of the Land Cruiser. Sister Martha nodded. The baby's chest was still moving in and out, in and out.

It did not look like word of the coming war had reached Godeh. Women and girls stood or sat together at the village pump, holding multicolored plastic tubs and basins or carrying buckets and tubs on their heads. Insects swarmed around the pump and around the women in the sunlight, and young boys, wearing only short pants or no pants, ran about in the yard in front of the pump, flitting like flies around the women and girls.

The pump master was waiting for them. He had kept good records, in pencil, in a notebook that was dog-eared and floppy because the pages had gotten wet and had dried, but which Carl could read when he needed to. David went to check the pump. Then Carl and David unloaded the chlorine and the water purification kits into a locked cabinet that was in a small cement block building with a thatched roof.

They turned and headed back south on the Bong County Road.

They were about a mile away from the District #4 Health Center turnoff when they saw smoke. A thin plume of black smoke no wider than a flag. Seconds later, they smelled the burning rubber and the fumes of spilled gasoline. The stink burned their eyes and into their nostrils, injecting itself under their cheekbones and into the back of their throats.

The Merlin Land Cruiser lay on fire on its left side enveloped in thick black smoke. The left wheel was in the red dirt, and the once white body of the truck was blackening, so you could only just make out the green Merlin insignia and the stenciled red silhouette of a machine gun with a blackening red circle over it.

Torwon lay on the grassy embankment where the two women had been sitting with the baby less than an hour before, his face and half his head blown off.

Charles lay in the red dust next to the wheel in a pool of blood larger than his body, a line of red and white flesh open from his thigh to his neck where a line of bullets had raked across him, his clothing and skin on fire, encased in flames from the truck.

No Julia.

"Stop or go, boss?" David said.

"Stop," Carl said.

"No time to stop. Dr. Richmond in Buchanan or Dr. Richmond dead. Stop now and we all dead if they close," David said.

"Go," Carl said. "Go fast."

Carl looked into the burning truck, and looked at the dry grasses on the side of the road. No more bodies.

"Go," Carl said. "Pedal to the metal."

Sister Martha started to speak, to beg them to stop and look for Julia. She stopped speaking when she saw what Carl and David saw.

No Julia. Julia was gone.

There was a checkpoint a mile down the road that hadn't been there when they came north that morning. A checkpoint and three soldier-boys standing in the middle of the road.

The soldier-boys had dropped two trees, one from each side of the road. The trees lay most of the way across the road and about five yards apart. The only way you could pass was to swing to the left to get around the tree that lay over the right side of the road, and then swing to the right to get around the tree that lay over the left side of the road.

The soldier-boys stood in between the trees, three man-boys dressed in fatigues, wearing red berets, smoking cigarettes, and carrying AK-47s. An RPG leaned against each tree loaded and ready so the boys could lift the RPG onto a fallen trunk, take aim at anything they didn't like, and fire; a nice clean shot at anything that came down the road.

A dented blue Ford Ranger, its rear window shot out, stood between the trees.

Carl knew the drill. Stop and search. Which meant anything and everything but not stop and search this far back in the bush.

Two hundred yards in front of the first dropped tree, David slowed to a crawl. Run up fast and you're RPG bait. Run up too slow and they start shooting, just for sport. Stop and get out and everyone dies after they rape the women. Carl was grateful that David drove quickly enough so it looked like they had a purpose, but not so quickly that they looked like they were coming for a fight.

David rolled his window down.

The soldier-boys grinned. They were smoking cigarettes as if waiting for target practice to start.

David began speaking as soon as they were in earshot. He spoke in Kreyol, and he spoke so simply that even Carl understood him.

"Si babi," David said as they rolled forward, his voice as loud as he could make it without shouting. *Sick baby.*

The truck rolled forward, faster than a quick walk, but not as quickly as a run.

"Docta he. Ta babi hospital. Baby dying. Ca stop," David said. *"There is a doctor in the car. We are taking a baby to the hospital. The baby is dying. I can't stop."*

The soldier-boys could see Carl who they took for a doctor in front, and the woman with the baby in the back. The Land Cruiser moved too quickly for them to ask any questions, or even give any commands. The Land Cruiser swung left, past the first tree. By the time the first fighter, the one who had actually thought to raise his gun, had taken his cigarette out of his mouth, the Land Cruiser passed him, and Carl could not hear whatever it was the soldier said.

Then the Land Cruiser swung right past the second tree. They were looking at open road.

For an instant or more, perhaps as much as a full minute, the Land Cruiser stayed in range of the guns and the RPGs. In that moment no one in the Land Cruiser knew whether they were going to live or die. They did not look back and did not listen for the ta-dump-dump of machine-gun fire or the crack and whoosh of the RPG. They were trying with every ounce of strength in their bodies not to hear anything at all.

And then they were out of range, alive and driving on the open road.

The few villages they had passed earlier that morning were now deserted or burning. Lines of bullet holes pockmarked the red and yellow mud-walled huts. The bodies of people who didn't get out of the way soon enough lay bleeding out by the cooking fires and the roadside.

"Taylor's boys," David said.

"The good guys," Carl said.

They saw smoke rising over Buchanan before they heard and felt the boom and the shake of explosions. As they got closer, they heard the bursts and rattle of small-arms fire.

"Coast road junction coming up," David said.

"Buckle your seatbelts people. It might get ugly for a while," Carl said. "I hope like hell Julia got back before Taylor's boys got to her. Sister Martha? You have any ideas?"

"She will be waiting at Buchanan Hospital for this child," Sister Martha said.

"She better be. This is no time for a nature walk," Carl said.

At the junction, there were three cars and two trucks on fire by the side of the road. There were more bodies in the market, and the torn blue and silver tarps that had covered the stalls flapped in the wind near the road where the market stalls used to be; where a truck or a half-track had driven through, crushing the stalls, the soldier-boys shooting everything that moved.

They heard sirens coming from Thomas Street. The sky was darkening with the late afternoon rain.

The earth rumbled again.

"Na thunder," David said. "*That's not thunder.*" He jerked the steering wheel. The Land Cruiser turned suddenly onto a narrow dirt road that ran toward the sea. They were off the main road, driving through backstreets and neighborhoods built around one-lane roads that few people knew. *Safer here,* Carl thought, *in the communities. The pickups and SUVs will go to the port, to Thomas Street, and to rail line and smelter at Mittal, and then to the road coming in from the east and south. They won't come here. Maybe we won't get shot at. Now. Today. For a few minutes.*

The air boomed and the earth rocked as they drove. "Heavy shit," David said. "I don't see planes."

"Taylor has friends all over," Carl said. "And enemies. You see planes and that means Nigeria or Europe or the U.S. is in. Or that Taylor's buddies have arrived—the boy scouts from South Africa, Russia, Israel, or France, the arms dealers and the mercenaries, the guys who drop barrel bombs from unmarked planes."

Carl looked back. Sister Martha nodded. The baby was still alive.

"David knows back roads through the communities," Carl said. "We'll get to the hospital quick-quick."

"MODEL in Buchanan now," David said.

"Live from Buchanan, it's Saturday night," Carl said. "Taylor must be pooping his pants. You get us in quick-quick?"

"Quick-quick," said David. "We float like butterfly, sting like bee."

The truck jerked and rocked as David steered around and through the potholes and the ruts. The ocean was on the other side of a single row of shanties and palm trees, each wave marking another moment that they weren't at the hospital yet, another moment that the baby was alive but still not treated, and another moment that they were still alive.

"They coming for Taylor," David said. "He bad before, but he strong and bad. Now he just bad. He kill anyone and everyone in his way, that Taylor."

"He kill my ma. He kill my pa. I will vote for him," Carl said. "That's what they're out there thinking, the guys with machetes and with guns. He's killing them and they're fighting for him. That's what we have to deal with."

A shell whistled overhead, fell into the sea, and exploded. The spray it sent up splashed onto the windshield.

People were gone from the neighborhood markets, the stalls, and the street. Carl didn't see men or boys with guns. The men and boys would choose one side or the other, which meant choosing one big man or the other, because this wasn't about ideas or freedom. This was about how big one big man could be, about who was strong and who was weak, about who would survive to hold ground for a little while and whose people would be slaughtered like sheep. The men and boys had already slipped away to the beach or into the bush where their guns and rusting hand grenades were hidden in boxes in the red dirt or in the sand, waiting to be dug up, wiped off, greased, and reloaded.

The hospital gate was jammed with bodies, with people standing, people being carried, people walking supported, and people with the hurt part wrapped in towels or bandages or just old shirts, holding the bad place that was oozing blood. Men and women squatted or lay on the grassy embankment across the road and milled about the court-yard, which was so thick with people that you couldn't walk from place to place without colliding with some part of someone else.

A line of trucks stood outside the closed gate.

"There," Carl said. He gestured to a bare spot of ground across the street; a place to stop the Land Cruiser. David pulled into the open place.

"Let's get this kid in. Dr. Richmond?" Carl said.

"She could be anywhere," Sister Martha said.

Carl opened the rear door. The baby was still breathing. "Come," he said to the women in the lapas in the back.

Sister Martha came out of the Land Cruiser first. The woman in the yellow Port Angeles Dragons tee shirt came out next. She and Sister Martha lifted the mother out of the truck. The baby was in her arms, still breathing.

The baby's eyes were open but dim.

"Come. Now," Carl said. They walked through the door next to the gate. Just then the evening rain began.

Carl moved the mother and baby and the other two women to a broad porch next to the gate that served as the waiting area for the outpatient clinics, out of the rain.

There were bodies everywhere—the wounded and the dead. But no Julia.

The clouds moved on. The rain stopped, and the sun appeared as it was setting.

In the courtyard, two PAs flitted from one person to the next, shouting orders to nurses who weren't listening. The PAs knelt next to people on the ground or listened to the chests of the few wounded people who were able to stand or felt bloody arms and legs or cut away cloth-ing where there was a wound so they might know who could be saved and who was already lost. They placed intravenous lines, gave pain shots, started whatever blood they had, and lined up the wounded on the ramp that led to the main building in the order they needed to go into the Operating Room, moving those who had died to the side, near the guard station. They paid no attention to Carl.

Carl searched the crowd. Still no Julia.

A doctor in a dirty white coat stood next to a young man on a litter, holding forceps and a curved needle with no more than five inches of thread or suture. The doctor holding the forceps was short and balding, with tan skin, black hair, and a black beard. Rivulets of sweat ran down his face and into his eyes. He squinted as a way to push the sweat out of his field of vision, and then wiped his forehead with the back of the hand that held the needle.

"Zig, it's me," Carl said. "Julia sent this kid in. Malaria I think. Julia here? She broke down on the Bong County Road."

"She hasn't come in yet. Maybe soon. Hot time in the old town tonight," Zig said.

"Can you look at this kiddo quick-quick? Do they teach surgeons about kids in Ethiopia?" Carl said.

"Tonight, I am kid expert. Until Julia comes. Let me look," Zig said. He turned to the baby, his gloved hands held high so as not to touch anything that wasn't sterile.

"Sister Martha, show me the conjunctiva," Zig said.

Sister Martha used her thumb to pull the lower left eyelid down.

"It is malaria. I see the problem. Sister Martha, we need to put you to work," Zig said. "Please take the child to Pediatrics. Draw a hemoglobin and a malaria smear and see that a line is placed. Then bring me the results as soon as they are ready. Ask the mother and her friend to give us some blood, yes? We have plenty of use for blood tonight. The baby will only need a little bit, perhaps a hundred ccs. Get them to give you a unit each. We can put the rest to good use. Where's Julia when I need her, anyway?"

Before anyone could answer, a man with a white lab coat started talking to the mother of the baby in Bassa. A second man spoke, also in Bassa, his voice raised and hard. It was David. The man in the white coat backed away, and then turned to sit at a desk, still talking to the baby's mother, almost under his breath.

"Tribal shit," David said. "He telling her how much cost. He telling her baby will die anyway, so the baby is better off dying in the bush. Damned PA. He know better than that. He want bed for someone he knows, someone who can pay, so he get his fucking cut. I tell her it free, but he got her jambled. It long night. We move, boss."

"What happened to Julia?" Zig said.

"They took out her jeep. Her guard and her driver are dead. She was gone when we got back. What the fuck am I going to do, Zig?" There was a close by machine-gun burst, and then the flash, shake, and shrapnel splash of an explosion. "We gotta go," Carl said.

"I'll let the ministry know," Zig said.

"You got your hands full," Carl said. "I'll make the call. The ministry, the embassy, and Merlin. And then the State Department and the president. I'm calling in the cavalry, brother, quick-quick. I just hope the goddamn cavalry is home to take my call."

"Just keep your head down and your pants dry," Zig said. "Julia's no idiot. If anyone can survive out there, she can. Fingers crossed. Everything crossed, okay? And just fucking pray that some of these poor bastards survive the night."

David drove slowly toward the Water for Power compound. The gunfire was behind them now. The streets were empty. The little backstreet stalls that sold gasoline for motor bikes, biscuits, little bags of spices, and phone cards were deserted and looked like skeletons on each street corner—four upright poles with shaggy thatched roofs standing in the dark.

The night supervisor threw the switch that opened the gate and waved them in, but he didn't call to them the way the day team always did, and he didn't come to help them unload. The two men who worked days were gone, the two mechanics were gone, and the kitchen staff was gone. The night supervisor and Grace, their Rwandan water engineer, were the only people left in the compound.

So even the Water for Power crew is in it now, Carl thought. Soon, all the men and all the boys in Buchanan would be gone, pulled back into this new war by someone who knew someone else; pulled back in by their brothers and cousins or what they knew about rank, team, and brotherhood. Most would be part of a ragtag band that would have been called a raiding party once; but now the bands and gangs and raiding parties had automatic weapons, hand grenades, and RPGs— and anything that could happen was going to happen as the known world collapsed into a world of blood, death, and dying.

The power shut down. The lights flickered and then the generator started up, a mechanical distant thrumming that kept Carl from hearing the other sounds of night. As the generators clicked on in the nearby compounds there was a weird symphony of sounds and smells—the drone of engines, the smell of diesel fuel, the sound of artillery, explosions, and small-arms fire, the smell of gunpowder, the sound of sirens, of people calling out, and the smell of charcoal fires, all mixed together.

Seven p.m. Three in the afternoon at home. Eight p.m. in London. They usually had enough gas to power the generator for about thirty-six hours, Carl thought. Carl's cell phone still worked, and he plugged it in quick-quick to recharge it while there was still power. They had one satellite phone stashed away in the main house for emergencies.

"Turn off the lights," Carl said. He walked back and forth in the office. There was a single desk lamp lit, a pinpoint of light in a large dark room. All the computers were turned off, their screens blank spaces where there should have been color and movement—mirrors in an empty room.

"She could be anywhere," Grace said.

"She hiding in village or in some health center," David said.

"She's not hiding anywhere. You saw that truck. Whoever shot up that truck has her," Carl said.

"Taylor. Probably Taylor," David said. "His men. Not MODEL. MODEL not north yet."

"I suppose that makes it easy," Carl said. "So all I have to do is to find out who has her and ask them to give her back? Anybody have

Charles Taylor's personal cell? Mosquito's home phone number? General Butt-Naked's e-mail address? Look, my first responsibility for the moment is to the two of you."

"We good," David said.

"You're not good. You're in the middle of another goddamn civil war. David, you've been through fourteen years of this, so maybe you know how to play it. I don't. Grace, we have to find a safe place for you. I need to hit the phones."

"I'll call Boston," Grace said.

"Good. David, what's safer for Grace? Being in the community or being here?"

"Being home in Rwanda. Or Accra. Or Lagos. Or Abuja. Not here. Not compound. They come to the compound. Not tonight. But soon. Maybe tomorrow. Maybe Thursday. Maybe Friday. But they come," David said.

"What's safe for you?"

"Na safe," David said. "I am Monrovia, but I'm not going to Monrovia now. I have woman here. I go to her community."

"Let's get you moving and Grace moving. Then I've got to find Julia, and I'll go out with her," Carl said.

"You not find Julia on your own," David said.

"I'm not going until I find her," Carl said. "I'm just not."

There was an explosion nearby, perhaps near the hospital, perhaps on Thomas Street, but close enough for the ground to rock and for pencils, pens, and coffee cups to fly off the desks, for the maps to slide off the wall, even for tall cabinets to fall over. Grace, who was on the phone to Boston, lost her call. When she called again the call did not go through. Then Carl tried his cell and that call did not go through.

"I'm going to the house to get the satellite phone," Carl said.

"Walk next to building," David said. "Don't take torch. Use torch only when you get to house. Don't turn on light."

When Carl returned with the satellite phone, David was gone.

There was no one at the ministry, and no one answered the phone at Merlin, but it was nearly 10:00 p.m. in London by the time Carl found a number to try.

Then Carl tried the good old U.S. of A. Vain hope but nothing to lose. It took an hour, but Carl got a duty officer in the State Department on the phone.

The USS *Iwo Jima* Amphibious Ready Group was off Monrovia, he was told, six to eight hours away. The duty officer listened to Carl's story. Then he took Julia's full name and occupation and asked lots of questions. Carl didn't know Julia's U.S. address or her passport number. The best he could do was to give rough directions to the place Julia's truck was hit. It sounded like the duty officer had a map up on his computer, because he was asking questions as though he knew Grand Bassa County.

"Before or after the road that runs east toward the LAC plantation? Before or after the turnoff into the bush that runs west? Before or after the village on the west side of the road . . . just south of that one-track road that goes west? Who had they seen on the road after passing the burning truck? What were the soldier-boys at the roadblock wearing?" Could Carl tell him anything about how they were armed? There was good intel about troop movements and factions on the ground in the zone around Buchanan, the duty officer said, where the situation was not as complex as the situation in Monrovia. They were evacuating Americans all over Liberia. Buchanan was a pretty easy in and out. But finding one person in the bush was hard, a needle in a haystack, no guarantees. They were landing in the morning. They'd send a squad. Carl needed to come out with the evac team so the guys on the ground could have accurate and up-to-the- minute information. They'd do their best.

Help was on its way. The duty officer wanted Carl to lay low, stay inside, keep the lights off and the vehicles hidden, and don't do anything, anything at all, to attract attention to himself or the compound. The best chance of getting Julia back was to work together, one team, no sudden moves and no surprises.

And hope that these woven bamboo walls topped by razor wire made anyone with a gun careful about coming after what was inside, Carl thought. *At least till morning. At least until the cavalry arrives.*

The gunfire quieted as the night wore on. Grace slept in a chair, her head on a desk, resting on her forearm. Carl did not sleep.

Julia was out there somewhere.

Carl's brain kept flipping back between two pictures. That image of Julia through the rear window of his truck, standing there on the hilltop next to her wounded vehicle. Then the smoke from the hilltop and her vehicle on its side and on fire, the bodies of two men on the ground.

They'd find her. They had to find her.

The marines came the following morning. A squadron of helicopters circled low over Buchanan and landed at the beach near Mittal and the UNMIL barracks where the Nibatt troops were bivouacked. After the helicopters, amphibious troop carriers landed on the beach, and the marines secured a perimeter. The moment the Americans showed up with an aircraft carrier and a destroyer offshore, Taylor's boys and MODEL both backed away, knowing they were outgunned. The big helicopters came next, disgorging vehicles onto the sand. A convoy formed and drove through the town. They went compound by compound, evacuating the expats, running them down to the beach, and then helicoptering them out to the ships that waited offshore.

When Carl saw daylight, he went to the house to pack a few things. Then he sent Grace to pack. They heard a nearby generator sputter and go dead. The sun became strong. They sat next to an open door and listened. No crunch of gravel under feet or tires and no talking as people walked from place to place. There was some small-arms fire in the distance and the sound of heavy trucks but no more explosions or artillery fire. The ocean breeze carried the smell of diesel fumes, burned rubber, and gunpowder. No charcoal now. People in the communities had faded into the countryside.

They heard a heavy truck outside the gate, and a man's voice on a bull-horn. "Carl Goldman. Carl Goldman. Water for Power compound. Water for Power compound. We are the United States Marines."

Carl opened the gate. There was a hum and a crunch and then a clang. Three Humvees and a half-track drove into the compound and turned around. A U.S. Marine sergeant lowered himself from the lead Humvee, stood, and saluted.

"Sergeant James McConnell, U.S. Marines 26th Expeditionary Force, sir. You rang?"

"We might need a lift," Carl said. "I think we have a flat."

"Oh, I think you have more than just a flat tire, sir. But let's give you a ride into town. You ready to go?"

"I'm waiting for news about an American doctor who is still up country," Carl said.

"I'm not the BBC," the marine said. "My orders are to find you and bring you in. We can check on other operations when we get you someplace safe and sound."

"Are you the only game in town?" Carl said.

"Four squads on the ground, sir, fanned out, covering the back-field."

"Give me ten, then. I need to shut down the generator and secure the premises. I have one more person with me," Carl said.

"You have five not ten, sir. This is an in and out. I have orders for one, not two, American citizens only," the marine said.

"Who else is here?" Carl said.

"I have USAID, AFSC, and Merlin in the half-track," the marine said.

"Brits, then."

"Our allies, sir. Courtesy to our NATO friends. Orders. All according to plan," the marine said.

"And the hospital?"

"Another unit, sir. We have four units on the ground in Buchanan, out rounding up the strays. We don't have much time. This is an in and out."

"Let's save one another time and hassle, sergeant. My colleague is from Rwanda. Which was once a German Colony. Then it was Belgian. So sometime in her life, maybe even today, my colleague might have had a Belgian Passport. Belgium is where NATO lives. I ain't going unless she goes. So let's call her Belgian, thank NATO for bestowing peace and blessings on all of us, put her in the half-track with me, and apologize if we have to but not get hung up on asking permission. I don't know who in this little village is going to survive the night," Carl said.

"I'm on a tight schedule, sir," the marine said. "Sounds like you got a plan. If you asked me, sir, I'd say your colleague is from the Bronx."

The helicopters came and went on the beach. Carl and Grace were dropped off at a roped off staging area, and then were moved from place to place as the wind from the helicopters flattened the flesh on their faces. One moment they were on the beach near the Nibatt compound, where there were guard towers at the perimeter, the ocean wind fresh, and the flags snapping, watching the Humvees and the helicopters come and go. The next minute they were in a helicopter, its throbbing engine and spinning blades surrounding them as it held them in midair, an intense, nauseating sensation, suspended a thousand feet in the air over the sea and moving at a hundred miles an hour. And then they were on the *Iwo Jima*, in waters just offshore, with two other U.S. Navy ships steaming close by.

No Julia.

The expats came out, one helicopter load at a time—people Carl knew from The Club and people he had never seen before. Katy, James, Suzanne, Jack, Tzippy, even Ahmed. One or two at a time, mixed in with people Carl didn't know. Some white South Africans, a mixed group of Americans and Europeans, a couple of Asian men—maybe Chinese. Not just American citizens. Not even close. Carl checked out each group as they trotted in from the helicopter deck, each person carrying one or two pieces of luggage—a suitcase, a backpack, and maybe a duffle.

Still no Julia.

The sailors let the expats mill about the mess where they had set up coffee and donuts, this being just like American soil. The ship swayed in the waves, back and forth, and the expats stumbled as they walked or stood still with their coffees, their feet wide apart for balance. Some went outside to smoke. There was a weather deck just off the mess set up for the convenience of the visitors.

Carl went back to the helicopter deck. The big cargo helicopter with front and back rotors lifted off from the beach, flew slowly toward them, and landed on the flight deck. No civilians came out. Nothing. No one Carl recognized.

There were two shorthaired marines in pressed uniforms, a man and a woman, sitting behind a table in the mess, processing the incoming expats, filling out forms and checking passports.

"How many more to come in?" Carl said.

"The mission is complete, sir," the woman said. "We've successfully evacuated the American citizens on the ground in Grand Bassa County."

"Where's Dr. Richmond? Not all American citizens. You're missing somebody really important," Carl said.

"Sir?"

"Julia Richmond. Dr. Julia Richmond," Carl said. "I was the guy who called the State Department last night and told them that Dr. Richmond had been abducted. Dr. Richmond isn't here. Is there another part of the operation? Could you have moved her out some other way?"

"This *is* the operation for Grand Bassa County, sir," the female marine said. She stood, and the second marine stood as well and came closer to Carl.

"Who is this Dr. Richmond?" the second marine said.

"Dr. Richmond is a pediatrician working for a British organization called Merlin, who was posted to the Liberian hospital in Buchanan. She's an American citizen. She was abducted yesterday, at about 1300 hours. Her driver and her guard were killed. She's out in Grand Bassa

County somewhere. Taylor or one of his goddamn militias has her. You need to go and find her. Like yesterday."

The male marine looked at his desk and began to shuffle through a file folder.

"I don't have any information about Dr. Richmond, sir," the male marine said.

"Look, the duty officer at the State Department last night said we have really good intel about who is on the ground and where they are," Carl said. "You know where she is. You have to know. You have to send out a squad and find her. She's an American. She's a goddamn American citizen."

"I just don't have any information about a Dr. Richmond, sir."

"You are going to leave an American civilian on the ground in the middle of this mess?" Carl said.

"I don't have any information about Dr. Richmond, sir," the man said. "All Americans were moved to the beach and transported here. All present and accounted for."

"The mission *is* complete, sir," the woman said. "We have successfully evacuated the American citizens on the ground in Grand Bassa County, Liberia."

"You haven't evacuated *every* American citizen. Go back in and get Dr. Richmond," Carl said, his voice loud and his back stiffening. "You have a commanding officer?" Carl said.

Carl's voice carried across the room. People stared. Some began to drift in from the table of coffee and donuts.

"Come with me," the man said.

"I have a satellite phone," Carl said.

"I have a commanding officer," the man said. "I also have a brig, sir. The operation is complete. I'm sorry. We're not going back in."

"You damn well better go back in. You have an American citizen that you have left stranded in the bush. I'm going to need both your commanding officer and your brig if you don't go back," Carl said. "Because I'm one step away from getting in that damn helicopter and going back myself. And I don't have a clue about how to fly the thing."

"Exactly why we have a brig. And a master-at-arms," the man said. "Understand your concern, sir, and happy to accommodate you in the brig if you can't take no for an answer."

"I can't take no for an answer," Carl said. "I can't believe somebody forgot to tell somebody else. You left her file on a desk somewhere. She's out there. You can't sail and leave her."

"The mission is complete, sir," the man said again. "We've successfully evacuated the American citizens on the ground in Grand Bassa County, Liberia."

"You have an American citizen on the ground in Liberia in the middle of a goddamned civil war," Carl said. His voice got louder, and more people began to move toward them.

"At the end of a civil war, sir," the man said. "Our information is that this war is over."

"You have an U.S. citizen missing," Carl said. "Her driver and her bodyguard were both killed and were left lying in the dirt. Her truck was set on fire. She could be anywhere, and she is in grave danger. And you are telling me the operation is complete?"

Now there was a crowd of people around them. Four men in uniform began to move through the crowd.

"Mission accomplished, sir," the woman said.

"We've heard that one before. I'm going to start dialing this satellite telephone. I'm going to call every senator and congressman in the Washington until you get on the phone and get someone back in there to get Dr. Richmond . . ."

A man in his late forties with graying hair and wearing a different uniform now stood in front of Carl, and four other men in uniform stood next to him.

"I understand you concern, sir," said the older man. "Feel free to make all the telephone calls you wish. But why don't you come with us now? We're going to take you to a place that is a little more private." Four sets of hands wrapped themselves around Carl's arms.

The brig of the USS *Iwo Jima* is a little room with barred windows in the door. They usually make you take off your shoes and belt. Carl was a civilian, so he got to keep his satellite phone. He worked the phone until the battery ran out.

In Monrovia, after the shelling started, people thought the Americans would come and save them all. Liberians stacked Liberian bodies in front of the American embassy, hoping that they would stimulate some thought, or guilt, or action. The helicopters came in and pulled the expats out. Just the expats. Americans saved Americans and Europeans. Liberians were left to save themselves.

Chapter Three
*William Levin. Providence, Rhode
Island. February 20 and 21, 2003*

THE MAYHEM STARTED JUST BEFORE MIDNIGHT WITH A VOICE ON THE RADIO. MASS CASU-alty call. The ward secretaries called in extra people. The chief of sur-gery showed up, began to move people out of the surgical ICU, and cooled the rooms, readying the place for burn victims.

A nightclub in West Warwick was on fire with a couple of hun-dred people trapped inside.

The ambulances rolled in unannounced, one after another, a third and a fourth after the second. Soon they were coming in waves, the firefighters and EMTs covered in soot, wan and trembling.

Levin heard the radio traffic, half listening to the scanner at the desk as he walked from place to place, so he had a sense of what was headed their way. He was in the main ED with an MVA when the first victim hit Trauma 2.

The first victim was a woman who was naked except for her shoes. Her hair was burned off and her scalp was black, her eyebrows gone, her face blistered; the skin on her arms and back hung loose like melt-ed cheese, and she was grunting, unconscious but still struggling to get air down her ruined, blackened, edematous trachea. Some second-year was asking questions, and Johnny G, the good trauma nurse who had been a medic in Iraq v1, was sticking the patient for a line.

"Do you take any . . ."

"Give me a tube," Levin said. He angled the resident out of the way and stood at the head of the bed. "We're going to knock you out, sweetheart, so we can get these burns fixed. You do the line," Levin said to the resident. "Johnny, hand me an intubation kit. Somebody get surgery here. Get Versed ready. Or Valium, if that's what's nearby. We need to snow her, so I can get her tubed. Let's move, people. You know you have pulmonary compromise when there is this much eschar. She was inside, in a room filled with hot gases. Let's get her tubed now and ask questions later. Get respiratory. She's going on a vent."

Levin snapped a laryngoscope open and turned its blade so he could see that it was lit. He opened the woman's mouth with his thumb and forefingers and leaned over so he could see inside. He lifted the laryngoscope with his left hand and leaned over the woman so he could see into her mouth. The tissues were all charred, but he could see what he needed to see. He slid the laryngoscope deep into the woman's mouth, lifting her upper face with his left hand as he reached for an endotracheal tube with his right.

"Seven up," Johnny said, and he unwrapped an endotracheal tube from its sterile paper and plastic envelope.

"Seven will do. She's not too big," Levin said. He threaded the tube into the woman's throat, following the light and the curve of the laryngoscope blade. He advanced the tube and closed his eyes as he felt for the smooth moment when an endotracheal tube slips into the trachea without resistance.

But the tube didn't pass. He opened his eyes, pulled the tube back a few inches, and then reinserted it. This time the tube passed. "Balloon," Levin said. He held the tube in place with one hand and withdrew the laryngoscope with the other.

Johnny attached a fluid-filled syringe to the small valve that hung from thin plastic tubing and pushed the plunger. Levin grabbed a green Ambu bag from the tray and attached it to the endotracheal tube and squeezed. There was a rush of air, and the patient's chest rose.

"Check breath sounds," Levin said, and he squeezed the Ambu bag again. "What's your name?" he said to the resident.

"Stacy."

The resident listened to the patient's chest left and right as Levin squeezed the bag a second and a third time.

"Good breath sounds left and right," the resident said.

"Ventilate, Stacy, until respiratory gets here with a portable vent," Levin said. Jacky Montequila, a friend and a surgeon who knew what she was doing, came into the room.

"Jacky, she's yours," Levin said. "Let's get her upstairs to your ICU, and you can make OR decisions later. We're going to need all the trauma rooms and every open ED bay we've got."

"I'm good," Jacky said. "Let's rock and roll. Bill's clearing out the SICU and getting all the ORs staffed. You keep them coming."

"It's going to be a long night. Listen," Levin said to the resident and the rest of the team and to a couple of medical students who had appeared and were standing at the edges of the room, "in a mass trauma you take your own pulse first. There's nothing to get excited about. Keep your wits about you. Listen and learn. Keep track of the numbers of victims and know your resources. Manage them. Triage saves lives. Tonight we have burns. Remember the rule of nines. Estimate total body surface area burn using multiples of nine. Nine percent for each arm. Nine percent for the front of each leg and the back of each leg and so on. We need the body surface area estimate for triage. So let's do one for every burn victim we see tonight. Any significant burn means the patient was inside that nightclub. So tube first, and ask questions later. Tube for any time inside, tube for likely inhalation trauma. Tube for any shortness of breath. Tube for hypotension. Jacky, sound right?"

"On the money. You tube. We debride. The raw excitement of the healing arts."

And then Levin went to Trauma 3, where there was a man whose skin was still wet from the water the fire guys had used to put out his shirt and pants, and he repeated the sequence. Tube 'em and move 'em.

Before long, fire victims overflowed the trauma rooms and filled into the big room of the main ED. Levin tubed seven. The big room stank. Levin and everyone else who worked that night all stank as well. The chairs, the gurneys, the curtains, the counters, the ceilings, and the lights all smelled of burnt hair, burned plastic, and charred flesh.

The curtains in the ED bays flapped as the ED docs, residents, and medical students hurried from place to place. They shouted orders, cut off clothing, drew blood, ran EKGs, intubated every other victim, talked to patients, and then moved patients upstairs lickety-split, first to the surgical ICU, then to the recovery room, and then to every ICU in the house as they filled every bed and needed more. The phones rang endlessly. The overhead page and their beepers didn't quit for a moment. People, the burned, screeched or moaned until they got morphinized and intubated.

The addressograph machines, which copied the patient's name and number from little blue cards onto the order sheets and the progress note sheets, thumped and rattled all night long. The floor was covered with wrappers from IV catheters, the wax paper backing of labels that went on tubes of blood, and the pale blue translucent plastic needle covers were everywhere, like confetti or shell casings.

The stink of burn is lipophilic. It likes fat and gets absorbed through your skin and through your nose and mouth and lungs, because it is in the air you breathe. It burns your eyes. The molecules—all those little roasted organic compounds—come in through your corneas. The stink gets deposited in your fat cells, liver, and brain, and it lives there for months, if not forever. You walk away, perhaps, but the stink of burn and smell of pain and the stench of dying always walks away with you.

Somehow, the ED staff managed to wrap it up by daylight. Sixty-three survivors. Forty-three admitted. Seventeen assessed, treated, and streeted. Three moved north to Boston by helicopter. Something like a hundred dead left on the ground in West Warwick, and then moved straight to the morgue. Hell of a night.

Levin tried sleep—and failed at it.

You don't really sleep after bad nights in the ED. You don't think about the dead and dying, but they are there anyway, looking at you. You don't speak about it either. Judy was long gone to work when Levin got home, which was just as well. You stumble home, make a cup of coffee to try to warm yourself, open the *Providence Journal*, then fall asleep sitting up. You wake up when your bent neck hurts enough. You stumble off to bed, and then don't sleep. The phone rings—someone selling something or a wrong number or the oil company calling to see if you want your oil burner cleaned. The bright late winter sunlight, reflecting into the room from the snow on the streets and on the roofs, wakes you. Someone backs up a utility truck, the burning beep beep beep wakes you next—in half sleep, and you think it's a monitor in the ICU or an IV pump or a beeper you've slept through. Then your beeper goes off—some nurse pulled your number off the chart and has no idea who the hell you are, that you are off call and don't admit to the floor anyway. You get a few hours of this, a half hour of obligatory unconsciousness, followed by some jackass knocking on your door, followed by obligatory unconsciousness again. Then you are sort of awake, your brain barely turning over. It's 12:45 p.m. You wanted to sleep until 4:00.

I should go to the garage, start Julia's car and back it up a foot to save the goddamn tires, Levin thought. *But not today. Not much is going to happen today.* Levin's body was running but his brain just wasn't engaged.

Shift starts again tonight at eleven, Levin thought. *Repair the world. Ha. Save one life and you save the world. Right. Bring the withdrawn light back to the world. Say what? Heal the wound one stitch at a time. Or not.*

What a mess. What a goddamn mess the world was.

What a mess, and too damned much work to do. Levin had to give his yearly talk at the medical school in four days—the role of emergency medicine in a country without a health care system—so there were slides for him to tune up and references to check. They needed the PowerPoint by e-mail in enough time to put it up on the website and make sure it was downloaded on the computer in the lecture hall. There was the Free Clinic executive board meeting at 6:00—no money, staff chaos, no continuity, too many patients, not enough people or time or purpose—but at least the clinic tried to take care of the illegals who no one else would see, and at least it was free.

There was the Peace Coalition meeting at 7:30 to plan a demo. Little Georgie Bush was getting ready to invade Iraq again.

Levin felt dead. All work and only work. He sometimes flashed on snippets of another existence, his life before he talked himself into med school. He was in the back of a U-Haul truck with thirty people who were about to occupy an air traffic control building in a desperate attempt to end a war, to stop the bombing of hospitals and the napalming of children. He was marching down the main street of a town in Mississippi, where the sidewalks were lined by angry white people. Sometimes he remembered Sarah before she went off the deep end and the intensity of being with her and talking to her for hours and hours. Sometimes he thought about walking in Muir Woods among the redwoods. Real life was an engaged life. This was sleepwalking. Might as well just keep working. That way Levin didn't have to think about the failures. Or feel. Or hope. Or remember.

Global health. Revolutionary justice. Repair the world. Use medical care as an organizing tool, creating solidarity through compassion. Build resilient communities. Say what?

Bill Levin was a thin man of sixty-seven who wore thick-lensed glasses and had thinning salt-and-pepper hair that he combed backward. When he talked you saw a prominent forehead and eyes that looked bigger than they were because of the thick lenses. He looked like an owl or a mathematician, and he was the workhorse of the ED, the guy who could treat 'em and street 'em and keep coming back for more. No one really understood what he was about or ever listened to his tirades, sitting at the ED desk, and no one even remotely suspected that he was a man with any kind of an inner life. He just showed up at the ED whenever they needed him, worked double shifts to give coworkers time off, and saw more patients than any other doctor. His snarky comments about capitalism, politics, or the hospital administration were easy enough to ignore as long as he kept seeing the patients and emptying the rooms, so that each empty room could be filled again with one more patient, over and over again.

Levin was a '60s leftover who washed up in Providence in 1979, after years of drifting from one demonstration to another, from one concert to the next, blown from place to place by pot smoke and unachievable dreams. He spent ten years in the International Socialist Organization, which sent its well-educated members into factories and warehouses to organize the revolution. Levin dug the work, the cab driving, the assembly line at a wire and cable factory, but he dug the people more—the hard-bitten, burned-out French Canadian dopers and the Azorean immigrant women who didn't talk much but sewed all day long so they could be with their kids at night, and the crazy Italian shop steward from West Warwick who was as corrupt as the day is long, who loved cars and beer more than women and wasn't shy about who he was, not ever. When the organizing yielded nothing—no class consciousness, no new unions, and no revolution, Levin finished college in Rhode Island and talked himself into medical school. That way he could still repair the world. Stitch up its wounds and open its airways.

Levin woke. It was 12:45. Computer time. He worked on his paper about emergency medicine in the developing world. He answered e-mails. Weekly e-mail from Julia. Pictures of clinics in the mountains. No electricity or piped in water. Smiling kids. Julia was in Africa doing real medicine. No CT scans. No MRIs. No consultants. She was in a place where they had real diseases—TB and HIV, meningitis, typhoid, malaria, rheumatic fever, and goddamn infant diarrhea; diseases that killed people in Africa by the hundreds. By the thousands. By the millions. Most of Levin's work was unnecessary, silly, or corrupt. His patients came in complaining of neck pain after a meaningless fender bender or back pain after carrying a dresser down a flight of stairs. Sometimes all they wanted was a record so the car insurance would pay them better or they could get worker's comp. Sometimes all they wanted was Vics or Oxys to sell on the street.

At 3:00 Levin went for a run. The sun had come back, early spring sun, bright but not strong. There was still snow on the ground but the air smelled of the sap that was moving in the maples that lined the streets. The light carried the hope that winter was finally over.

You have to run in the street, because no one ever shovels their walks anymore, so he stayed to side streets where there weren't many cars. He ran on Lafayette at first, up the hill to East, then right on Roberta. Left on Alfred Stone to the cemetery where they always plow the roads. A good mile around the cemetery, then down to the river, to hear the seabirds and look out over the marshland.

Levin imagined this place as it was in the time before people, when it was a high bluff over a beautiful river and estuary; the lime green grass and cattails waving in the breeze blowing north from Narragansett Bay. The river was beautiful, even in winter, even despite the squat brick buildings in the industrial park across the river in East Providence. Levin imagined this place again as a virgin estuary under a blue sky, the river teeming with fish, the deer, the beaver, and the fox coming to the river to drink at sunset.

Then Levin ran uphill, out on Pleasant, left on Ridge, left on Swan, then home again, pretending that the constant roar of traffic and the grinding of the trucks on Route I-95 just three blocks down the hill was also part of another world. About three miles altogether, maybe four, just enough to break a sweat and make you feel your skin and lungs but not so much as to put you down for the rest of the day.

He threw in a wash and made a salad for dinner.

Judy got in a few minutes after 6:00. They had been together for fifteen years. She had been abused when he met her, and he had talked her into a safe house, staying with it until she went. Now she worked in an abortion clinic counseling the kids. Good work. She talked, he listened. She was one life saved, which was a good thing. She liked to watch television. Levin spent his days and nights worrying about justice. You find out later that a saved life isn't the same thing as passionate company.

They ate in a hurry, and then he left for the first meeting in South Providence. The second meeting was at the Beneficent Church downtown. The Peace Coalition was planning the same demo that they'd been having for the last thirty-five years. Same groups. Same speakers. Same self-righteous and inclusive gobbledygook—rainbow this, peace and justice that, community this, environment that, but no focus, no program, and no impact. If Republicans had been running it, they would have been in and out in forty-five minutes. All these Peace Coalition types ever did was whine about what they couldn't change, concede defeat, and sit back to watch the bombs fall. Everyone knew that this invasion, like the shock and awe bombing of Baghdad, was already a done deal. More U.S. exceptionalism. Our version of the golden rule. He who has the gold makes the rules.

His shift started after the meeting. He walked out to the parking lot.

What Levin saw in the church parking lot didn't make sense. His car door was open. There were CDs and CD cases on the pavement, and a pair of legs hung out of an open door. For a few moments Levin was confused. That was his green Subaru wagon. It didn't make sense that someone's feet were hanging out of his car at 9:45 at night.

"Hey," Levin said.

A thin black man wearing sweatpants and a hooded sweatshirt wriggled out from under the steering wheel into a runner's crouch. There was a flat black box under his arm. A laptop. Levin's laptop. Just a kid, eighteen or nineteen. Dark skin. Bright eyes. Big forehead. Tiny ears. With a white coat, he could have been one of the hospital workers or community health center nurses Julia sent pictures of.

The thin black guy paused just long enough to decide Levin wasn't a cop. Then he threw something at Levin.

Levin, always quick with his hands, caught what the guy threw in midair. A screwdriver. He threw it back, hard as he could. There was a thud. Metal hit flesh and bone. A hand flew up to a skinny black head.

"Fock you," the thief said. Some kind of accent, maybe Jamaican. Then he was gone, running down Chester Street, Levin's goddamn laptop under his right arm.

Then Levin was running after him.

"Stop him!" Levin yelled. But there was no one on the street to hear him.

"Car thief!" Levin yelled next. A few people walked out of a wine bar two blocks away. They hurried to their own cars.

The thin black guy was quicker than he was. Levin was in shape, but he was not a sprinter. He was twenty yards behind and probably fifty years older. Levin pushed himself, gained a little, and then looked back to see if the people coming out of the wine bar were still there. They were gone.

The running man flew across Pine and then went under the I-195 overpass, where it was dark and deserted. Levin listened as he lunged forward. No sirens. The guy darted left toward the river, running as fast as Levin had ever seen anyone run. Levin pushed harder, but the car thief pulled away into the gloom.

And then Levin's breath failed him. He stopped, bent over, winded, and the car thief's footsteps pounded off toward the deserted river. *That boy is going to have one impressive black eye in the morning*, Levin thought. *The laptop's gone, but turnabout is fair play. An eye for an eye, actually and metaphorically. Maybe some justice was done.*

There were no people anywhere. Levin was old and slow. The thief was young and quick. What had Levin been thinking? It was just a laptop, just a thing, and it was pretty well backed up. He lost some PowerPoints and the drafts of a couple of papers, but no startling new ideas. What would have happened if he had caught the guy? Just not worth the risk.

Levin was halfway between Pine and Weybosset, almost back to his deeply disrespected automobile when he heard the sirens at last. At least *somebody* had called it in.

The lock on the driver's side door had been ripped out, so there was no way to close the car door. But it was just a couple of blocks to work. Why God invented duct tape. Levin found a roll under the pile of papers in the trunk. Chance favors the prepared mind.

He was duct taping the door closed when the cops showed. They looked into the car with a flashlight and offered to call an ambulance.

Police report available in five days at headquarters. No illusions about pursuing the perpetrator. Justice, such as it is now, would be found in an insurance settlement.

His goddamned car. And his goddamned laptop. Maybe this was some kind of a message from God. Perhaps Levin had just been repurified. Maybe. Levin had politics that didn't work, ideology that no one cared about, an emotional life that was a train wreck, and now, no laptop and a car with a door that was missing a lock and a steering column that was messed up. *You bang you head against the wall enough and your head splits open.* Maybe it *was* time to just start fuckin' over. Give up. Go to Cuba, sit on a beach, and look at the women.

Levin had a decent night. No drama. Just drunks and ODs. A bunch of people short of breath and a couple of schizophrenics out of control, the aftermath of the Station disaster, which got people who were already on the edge unhinged. Just dribs and drabs. A patient or two an hour. No beeping. No clamor. No ringing phones. At 2:00 in the morning, the nurses turned off the lights at the back end of the ED and pulled the curtains around a couple of the bays to let some of the drunks sleep. Sometimes you catch a break working the overnight. Huge change from the night before.

But then they needed him to pick up an extra shift. Betty Kidd, who was days, had a cousin who had died in the fire and needed to miss her shift for the funeral. They needed him until noon. Extra shifts suck, particularly after an overnight. Extra shifts after no sleep the day before suck double or triple.

He'd be done at noon. By 11:30 Levin was already in a landing pattern. He got a cup of hot coffee to warm his cold bones. He hit the head, relaxed his innards, and threw some cold water on his face and on the back of his neck. Then his brain started shutting down. No new thoughts. He imagined his bed. His warm bed. In his mind, he was already in his bed when Johnny G stuck a clipboard with one more chart in front of him.

"Bay 34," Johnny said.

Damn.

At least the guy in Bay 34 had a simple problem. A twenty-year-old with facial laceration. Just stitching. Great last patient. No previous medical history. Walked into a door. Pretty straight forward. Levin looked at the chart and the facial films before seeing the kid, ordered up a tetanus shot, and asked Johnny to put a suture tray together so he could breeze in, do the deed, and be gone. And then home to a nice warm bed.

Levin loved sewing. It was simple manual labor. He could sew in his sleep, which was a good thing because his brain was of questionable value after working for twelve hours straight. He'd offer the kid plastics but he hoped the kid would say just go ahead and do it, so Levin could finish his shift with something simple, and then get the hell out of there.

He blew through the curtain, headed for the packet of sterile white imitation latex surgical gloves, which were open on the procedure tray and lay awaiting his hands.

Thin dark-skinned black kid. Serious shiner about the right eye. Three-centimeter lac.

Something familiar. Levin woke up. What was it? Who was it?

The thief. The goddamn car thief. Laying there in Levin's ER. Turnabout *is* fair play.

"Hey," Levin said, as he turned away from the procedure tray. He expected the kid to bolt. But there wasn't even a hint of recognition on the kid's face. The kid just eyed him, some white guy in scrubs.

Levin waited. The kid did not have a clue. "I'm Dr. Levin," he said and extended his hand.

The kid took Levin's hand. He had a warm, formless hand, and it took all the energy Levin had left not to twist the bastard's hand and arm behind his back and push the arm up until the idiot cried for mercy. But Levin was a doctor, and you can't beat up on patients, even the ones who screw you, even the ones who fuck up your car and steal your blinking laptop.

"Ran into a door, huh?" Levin said, still one tiny wrong move away from jamming the kid's arm behind his back or calling a cop.

But the patient is the one with the disease. You got to pull yourself out of the equation whenever you walk into a patient's room. Medicine is unself-interested advocacy. All the crap that Levin had been saying all those years, everything he kept telling students and interns and residents and colleagues, all that preaching came back to him, right then. You got to put yourself aside. Patient care comes first.

The kid didn't answer.

"Got any allergies?" Levin said.

The kid didn't answer.

"You speak English?" Levin said.

"Small-small Inglis," the kid said.

"Anybody here with you?"

The kid didn't answer.

"Ma or Pa?" Levin said.

"Ma he," the kid said. "*Ma here.*"

Levin nodded, stood, and opened the curtain at the foot of the gurney.

"I need a translator," he said, in a voice that was louder than speaking but not a shout. "And see if this kid's mother is in the waiting room, will you?"

The kid's mother was there in five, a tired looking but well-dressed woman in a tan coat. The translator was a portly Liberian guy in his fifties who worked as a technician in the lab.

"Dr. Levin," Levin said, when Johnny G brought the mother in, and he extended his hand.

"Yvonne Evans-Smith," the mother said. She had a strong grip. "This is Terrance Evans-Smith," the mother said. "He injured himself on a door. He is a recent immigrant from Liberia, and his English isn't good yet."

The mother's English, on the other hand, was perfect; a formal, polite, British English that made Levin wonder what that story was—mother is a well-dressed black woman who talks like the Queen, kid who steals cars and barely knows the language. It wasn't all making sense yet.

"Thanks," Levin said to the translator. "I think we're good."

"Tell me about the door," Levin said. "When did you hit this . . . door?"

Levin pushed the kid's head back on the pillow. He was rough, even rougher than he intended to be. He held the kid's jaw between the thumb and forefingers of his right hand. He swung the overhead light around so it lit the kid's face but also so it went right into the kid's eyes. He moved the kid's jaw back and forth in the light, and turned the kid's head from side to side. The cut was three centimeters long, just over the right eyebrow, pretty clean, with a decent amount of swelling and ecchymosis at its base. The tissues around the wound and around the eye were a dusky purple black.

"Last night, after sundown," the mother said. "I noticed the wound this morning, when I saw blood on his pillow."

"Quite a shiner. Pretty dangerous door," Levin said. "This cut is gonna scar up good unless we sew it."

About sixteen hours had passed since Levin threw the tool at the kid. At least the kid told his mother the truth about the timing. You need to sew lacerations quickly, otherwise you risk infection. Inside eight hours is best. Sixteen hours is stretching it. Twenty-four is too long.

"Johnny, get me a Betadine soak, will you?" Levin said in a loud voice.

Johnny appeared a few moments later. He brought a bowl of gauze soaking in a brown liquid. Levin laid the gauze on the wound.

"And he needs tetanus," Levin said, loud, as though the person he was talking to was deaf. "No allergies, right?" he said, almost shouting and then he remembered that the mother spoke English.

"No known allergies, right?" Levin said again, quietly this time.

"No allergies," the mother said.

"What does he do for a living, besides interacting with doors?" Levin said. "He in school?"

"He's a night watchman."

"Look," Levin said, "It's a laceration on the face. I'm good at fixing them. I've done thousands, maybe two or three a day for the last ten years, but any laceration repair can cause a scar, and people are sensitive about scars on the face. Sixteen hours out, greater than usual risk of infection."

Levin paused, and looked at the kid and then back at the mother. "I'm supposed to tell you that I can get a plastic surgeon to sew the scar." Levin stopped. *What the hell am I doing?* He thought. *I have no business treating this kid.*

"But I'm *not* gonna sew this right now," Levin said. "I *am* going to stop bullshitting you. Your kid didn't get the damn laceration from a door. Your kid got the laceration from me. Terrance here got the laceration from a screwdriver I threw at him last night, after Terrance threw it at me when I caught him breaking into my car. My personal car. Terrance is a goddamn car thief, and he fucked up my car and stole my laptop. Forgive my French."

"Fock you," Terrance said. He reached up, brushed the packing away from the wound and he jumped up.

Levin turned to the kid. "So what's the story, Eddie? You got my laptop? You give me my laptop, I fix your face. Capiche?"

"Fock you," the kid said as he started to push past his mother. There wasn't enough space between the gurney and the next cubicle for two people. The kid's mother blocked his escape, her hands on her son's chest.

"Lay ba dan," the mother said. "De mon to zip de wou." *Lie back down. Let the man sew the wound.*

"Fock you," the kid said.

Then the mother slapped Terrance's face, hard enough that the sound of the slap rang out across the big room. People working at the desk and in other cubicles heard the voices and the noise. They turned toward the noise, a response that is natural to people who work in the ED whenever there is the sound of trouble.

The slap stopped the kid's forward motion. He shrank back, transformed from a thief who was quick on his feet into a misbehaving child.

"Lay ba dan. Quick-quick," the mother said. *Lie back down. Now.*

"Lie down. I got to repack the wound," Levin said.

"*He* will lie down," the mother said. "*I* will speak to him from this point forward. And I will speak *for* him."

The kid backed away from his mother and leaned on the edge of the gurney, glowering at Levin. The he laid back. He watched Levin, ready to jump and run.

"Why I am sewing this instead of calling a cop?" Levin said.

"Terrance is here illegally. He's overstayed his visitor's visa and is working under the table," the mother said.

"He's doing more than *working* under the table," Levin said.

Then Levin put his hands on the kid's face again. *I get it*, Levin thought. *Call a cop and the kid gets deported.* He gloved and opened a few packages of gauze that were sitting on the tray table next to him, soaked them in the pan of brown liquid, and laid the now brown and wet gauze on the kid's wound. *There's some kind of war on in Liberia. Or was.*

Later he would think, *Why did I do that?* The whole thing was crazy. He had been up all night, he was tired, his judgment was impaired, and his hands just did what they were trained to do. Your hands work even when your brain is not really there.

"Terrance was in the war in Liberia," the mother said to Levin.

"How is that my problem?" Levin said. Then he unfolded a paper drape from the treatment table.

"The war gang found him in 1993," the mother said. "He was ten. School ended for him forever on that day. They took him away to fight for Charles Taylor, our president. Taylor was a warlord then. Taylor's people put a gun to his head, and then another gun in his hands. They got him high on pills. They taught him how to kill, and they taught him how to maim and how to steal, but they didn't teach him how to read or think or work. Ten years old. There was no one there to teach him to listen, to know right from wrong."

"And that makes it okay for him to steal my car?" Levin said.

"A stolen car is nothing," the mother said. "People here don't understand the life this boy led. He was part of a pack of boys and girls who roamed the countryside with guns and machetes, involved in activities I don't care to think about. They killed and they stole and they raped and they maimed. Then they were cut loose and left to fend for themselves, which they did, until their ammunition ran out. Then they were hungry. Those boys came into a market where we used to live. My family found him and sent him here, to me."

"So I should just sew the cut and leave the police out of it?" Levin said.

"He is on a visitor's visa. I bought him a good used car so he could find a job, but who will hire him in America with no green card, no skills, no education, and no English? He is a night watchman. He will always be a night watchman, unless he is in jail or until he is deported. I am sorry for your car. I am sorry for your computer. I am sorry for my son, who everyone has abandoned. And I am sorry for my country, which has abandoned decency, and which the world ignores. He hates it here. He wants to be back home and roam the streets again, hopped up on who knows what. Right now, you and I are all that stands between him and *that*."

If he were back home, Levin thought, *I would be in my bed. What a goddamned stupid place to be. I want my bed. I've been up twenty-four hours straight, and I haven't had a good night's sleep for three days. I survived through all sorts of carnage the other night, and then the drunks, and now this. My brain isn't working. I want my bed, and I want my computer back. Maybe she's right, goddamn it. Maybe this kid didn't have a chance. Fuckin' American colonialism. We fucked up Africa. We fucked up Central America. We're fucking up the Middle East. This kid stole my computer and fucked up my car, and now he wants me to fix his face. Or she wants me to fix his face. Or something. And she imagines that if I can find the energy I need to fix his face, then I won't call the cops. Why is this my problem? I'm the completely wrong person to sew this lac. But it will take me ten years of explaining to get someone else to do it. Why can't we ever get anything right? Why can't we fix one little piece of a broken world? Just one little tiny piece without all these curveballs? Is there not one little place for justice in this mess?*

"Alright," Levin said. "I'm going to sew the goddamn laceration. I'm going to do it fast, and I'm going to do it perfectly, and I don't want one squeak out of you, kid. You hear me?"

"He hears you," the mother said.

"From him. I want to hear it from him," Levin said.

"Sew it," the kid said. "Please to sew it."

"That's better," Levin said. "Now keep still. Not a word. Not a peep. I'm going to numb it. The numbing will burn for a minute, and then you won't feel a thing."

Levin broke open a glass vial and drew the contents into a syringe. He changed the needles on the syringe, and then paused. Second thoughts. Always second thoughts. That's what they teach you in doctor school. Always second guess yourself. Before someone else does.

"Look, like I was saying, it's a laceration on the face. Any laceration repair can cause a scar, and people are sensitive about scars on the face. Sixteen hours out means greater than usual risk of infection. Some people *would* want a plastic surgeon to sew the laceration, and that is perfectly okay. I can call a plastic surgeon to the Emergency Department. It might take a couple more hours, but the plastic surgeon is specially trained to repair lacerations on the face and might be able to produce a better looking scar than . . ."

Levin paused.

". . . and you really don't want me fixing this cut. Terrance here just fucked up my car. He doesn't want me standing over his face with a needle in my hand."

"I want you to do this for us, please," the kid's mother said.

"Look lady, would you translate for your son. It's his face. His decision."

"Please proceed. It is fine for you to proceed. Better for it to be you," the mother said. "He will perhaps remember this day the next time he sees a car to snatch."

Levin waited, his gloved hands suspended in the air.

"Do it," the kid said, from under the drape. "Please to do it na." You could hear the bravado in his voice. He thought he was so tough he could stand anything. Which included Levin sewing his face, despite their mutual history. *Pretty tough after all, this kid*, Levin thought.

"It's going to sting, to burn," Levin said. You might feel a pinch. Tell him it's going to sting. For a minute. Then the stinging will disappear."

Then Levin took a breath, shrugged, and inserted the needle into the tissue underneath the torn skin and injected local anesthetic into the tissue. Then he pushed the needle deeper, and advanced the needle again. He pushed a little, advanced a little, pushed a little, advanced a little, injecting deeper or in a slightly different direction each time until the flesh beneath the wound was tense with local anesthetic.

The kid squirmed under the sheet. The mother put her hand on his shoulder under the sheet, and the kid quieted.

"Not a peep," Levin said. "I'm really good at this. You won't feel a thing from now on. Breathe normally. Just don't move." Then Levin leaned over the kid's face and the sterile field that covered it, and he began to sew.

You leave the world when you sew. Or the world becomes the wound and the wound becomes the world. The first stitch, in the middle of the wound, is the most important stitch because it brings the edges of the wound together. So the needle has to be exactly the same distance from the wound edge on both sides, which means you have to align the edges perfectly in your own mind. You have to visualize that wound with three-dimensional geometric precision, penetrate the skin with the needle in exactly the right place, twist the needle holder with exactly the right degree of torque and at exactly the right angle, find the underside of the opposing side in just the right place, feel your way through the tissue, and then penetrate the skin so the needle emerges on the other side of the wound, exactly the same distance from the edge on the opposing side as it is on the near side. Then you grab the needle just below the point with forceps, hold it in place as you squeeze the needle holder to release the needle and you pull it through the tissue, leaving enough suture so that you can tie a closing knot and bring the wound ends together.

"I know somebody in Liberia," Levin said, after the first stitch was placed. It ended up exactly where it needed to be.

"In Monrovia?" the kid's mother said.

"Some place else. I don't remember the name of the place. How big is Liberia, anyway?" Levin said. He was sewing, and he kept his mind on his work.

"Big, but not too big. Liberia is about the size of Tennessee," the kid's mother said.

"Bigger than Rhode Island. Which means my friend could be anywhere."

"What work does your friend do?" said the kid's mother.

"She's a doctor. She works in a little hospital and goes around to a bunch of health clinics in the countryside."

"My people are in Saint John's River," the kid's mother said. "Near a small city called Buchanan, which is a three- or four-hour drive from Monrovia, the capital. Liberia is not a safe place now, not for Liberians or Americans or anyone else. Your friend is a brave woman. Or a stupid one."

"Hey, I'm the guy with the needle in my hand, remember? Brave. And headstrong. Not stupid. It could be Buchanan, I'm not sure. What's the war about?" Levin said, as he placed one more stitch.

"What is any war about?" the mother said. "Greedy men who want more than they need. And poor people doing what they are told to do, who are slaughtered for their trouble."

"Which makes it okay for your kid to steal my laptop?" Levin said.

"I am ashamed about what happened, if you are correct and it was my son who broke into your car. I'm ashamed for my son. I'm ashamed for myself. And I'm ashamed for my country," the boy's mother said.

"Sounds like a different kind of place," Levin said.

"Different, yes, but also the same. In Liberia, there is nothing. Most people don't have electricity or running water. But we have children anyway, like you do."

The kid shifted under the drape, and Levin held his hands still. The kid's mother moved her hand under the drape.

"Okay?" Levin said. Then the kid settled, the drape rose and fell as he breathed in and out. Levin began another stitch.

She is a decent sort, this kid's mother, Levin thought. *Been through a lot. Dignified.* "Which means?" Levin said, as he was stitching.

"Which means life goes on despite the wars. Which means we have to feed ourselves and care for our children any way we can. Which means we have to live with people who have done terrible things. Which means we have to pretend to forget what no one should have to remember, but we remember anyway. Which means we put our faith in God, never in man. We believe in hope, and we believe in God, but we fear one another."

"Are we so different, here?" Levin said. "We've done some pretty terrible things to black people and Native Americans, and we pretend to forget those things."

"You can't be serious," the kid's mother said. "Don't you understand what you have? You all have enough to eat. Warm houses in the winter. Cool houses in the summer. Cars to drive in, and streets that are paved to drive those cars on. Schools for the children. Hospitals for the sick. Too many guns, yes, but no gunfire in the streets and no explosions in the night. Except in some places where people who look like me live. Your history is also difficult, yes. But you have a life and the time and space to try to make amends for the past. Each of you can hope to build a better life for yourself. Everyone in the rest of the world wants only to live like you live."

Levin was down to the last stitch.

She wants me to let the kid off the hook, Levin thought. *She wants me to let everyone off the hook. It's okay now. The sun is out, and no one is dying in the street, and that is justice? History composed by the victors. Rules made by people with money to suit themselves. Okay, she loves her kid, and he is no angel. But you can't just pretend it's all okay when it isn't. Property is theft*, Levin thought. *I know that. One little laptop doesn't count for a hill of beans in this world. So why am I so ticked off?*

Levin pulled the paper drape off the kid's face, bunched the paper into a ball, his right hand high and steadied by his left hand as if he were shooting a basket, and threw the balled paper into a wastepaper basket. Then he looked closely at the wound repair, seeing only the new suture line and not looking at the kid's actual face at all.

"Two points," he said. "Nailed it. We got us a perfect sculptural closure, with perfectly matched wound edge opposition, resorbable suture, and not a single unnecessary stitch. The Michelangelo of suture repair, if I don't say so myself."

Then Levin retrieved a small foil envelope from the suture tray, opened it, and squeezed a thick line of antibiotic ooze over the wound, covered it with gauze, and taped the gauze to the kid's skin with white surgical tape.

"The usual discharge instructions," Levin said. "Keep it clean and dry. Return for redness, tenderness, fever, or bleeding. Wound check in three days. I'll write you a script for Bactrim, which is maybe a little overkill, because we waited sixteen hours before sewing the wound. Suture removal in a week. Follow-up with a primary care physician in two weeks. They'll give you a list of community health centers and primary care doctors taking new patients at checkout."

"But what the hell," Levin said, as he stepped back from the gurney. "I'm not discharging you. I'm going to get a cop, and I'm gonna get my car fixed and my laptop back."

"And you are going to send my son back to Liberia where he will die in the next war?" the kid's mother said.

"I'm not sending this kid anywhere. The war in Liberia ain't my problem. I didn't break into a car. He did."

"And you have witnesses to this break in?" the kid's mother said.

"Lady, I don't need witnesses. I saw this with my own eyes. You have a lawyer?"

"I can get a lawyer."

"Oh come on. Are you trying to say your son didn't break into my car? I just fixed this kid's face."

"Dat ca shi. Da laptop shi," the kid, Terrance, said. *The car is shit. The laptop is shit.*

"Move yo mouh" the kid's mother said. *Stop talking.*

The kid jumped off the gurney and stood between his mother and the large open room. Then he was gone.

"Yo, security," Levin said, his voice loud enough that the whole room could hear. "I'm sorry for your trouble, lady, but this just isn't my fight."

It took half an hour for the cops to show, and by then the kid was long gone.

After security came and went, Levin went to the ED crash room to wash his face, stash his stethoscope in his locker, and get his coat. They weren't going to find the kid, at least not right away. There would be a police report ready in five days at the new Public Safety Complex on Washington Street. Which didn't matter for shit, because there already was a police report sitting there from when good old Terrance broke into the car in the first place. His car would cost more to fix than it was worth. No cop ever chases a car thief. They write it down and let you file for insurance. No one was ever going to Pawtucket to look for this kid. Let's be real.

Levin had no business repairing that lac. What had he been thinking? There was no way he could have been free of bias. If the tables were turned and a colleague or resident had asked him about doing the repair, Levin would have said, huge conflict of interest, patient with whom you've had an altercation—you recuse yourself right then and there and find someone else to be the suture jockey.

Working twelve hours without a break keeps you from thinking straight. Dealing with the kid at all was a huge mistake, and if anything had gone wrong Levin knew that the Medical Board would take his license away. Hell, should take his license away. But the lac repair went smooth as glass. God protects children and fools. And ER docs coming off call.

Levin walked out through the waiting room. He needed a shower and a night's sleep. The mother was standing near the main ED door.

"Sorry about all the fracas," Levin said.

"I am sorry for your trouble with the car," the mother said. "I'm Yvonne Evans-Smith."

"You told me," Levin said. "And you have a son named Terrance." They stood together. "And I bet your son Terrance took the car and left you stranded," Levin said, after his brain told him why the woman was standing there almost an hour after her son had fled.

"The car is here. He took the keys. It's his car. The keys were in his pocket," the woman said.

"He have a license? He's on a visitor's visa, right? So he's undocumented. And no license," Levin said. "But what does it matter. He's someplace else with the keys. And you're stuck here."

"I'm waiting for a cab," the woman said.

"What the hell, I'm headed out. I'll run you home," Levin said. "As long as you don't mind riding in a car that you have to start with a screw driver, that has a fucked-up steering column and a door held on by duct tape."

Where the hell did that come from? Levin thought. *Talk about no boundaries. Why the hell do I always have to try to fix everything myself? Another dumb idea on the long list of dumb ideas. Will I never learn?* Levin thought.

"I'm fine with a cab," the kid's mother said.

"The hell with the cab, Ms. Evans-Smith. Yvonne, right? This is Providence, Rhode Island. Deep in the middle of nowhere. You could wait an hour for a cab around here. I live up on the East Side, right on the border with Pawtucket. And you live where?"

"In Pawtucket, as well, just off Mineral Spring."

"Hell, that's one exit up 95 from me. And who knows, maybe we find your kid, and maybe I get my laptop back."

"I don't know what happened to your car or your laptop," Yvonne said.

"Lady, you can bullshit me all you want but don't bullshit yourself," Levin said. "It was your kid. But that's okay. It was your kid, but it wasn't you. Let's forget about the car and the laptop for a little while.

Just let me run you home, so I can get out of this place and go home and get some sleep."

"Thank you, then," Yvonne said. "Very kind, considering what we have just put you through. I can't make any promises about the laptop, though. We can only hope."

"Let's do a little more than hope," Levin said. "This way you'll know where and how to find me. In case the laptop happens to magically appear. Just in case."

It was cold on the other side of the revolving door. There had been a little bit of snow overnight, which remained on the ground as an icy crust. Still, the sun was back, and it was worth all the money in the world, even though the air was still cold. Spring was coming.

Chapter Four
Julia Richmond. Grand Bassa County,
Liberia. July 15 and 16, 2003

JULIA COULD NOT SEE WHAT WAS LEFT BEHIND WHEN THEY DROVE PAST THE VILLAGES. BUT she could hear. She heard automatic rifle fire and the taunts and the boasts of the boys in the back of the truck. She heard muffled voices calling out and screaming, which faded as they sped away.

Julia saw the mud-walled huts. In one village they were just build-ing a hut. There was a beautiful latticework of poles where the walls and roof would be, as if someone commanding the power of history had reached into the bush, found a collection of perfectly straight poles, and then assembled them, carving a safe space for human life out of air and elements.

One moment she had been on the roof of their Land Cruiser, low-ering a tire and getting a kiddo dying of malaria moved into Buchanan the quickest and best way she could manage. The next moment she watched Carl's car drive north with Sister Martha, the child, and its mother. Then she saw a pickup on the road from District #4 Health Center. They heard the rumbling bass of a stereo from the blue pickup. You could see that there were people in the back of the pickup as it came closer to the main road, but you couldn't see their faces or hear the sound of the pickup or their voices. Only the sexy grind of the music pulsing into the country air. The pickup turned right and climbed the small hill that was between the road it had come from and the hill they were on.

Julia had looked away, thinking to sit on the side of the road and wait for the relief truck from Buchanan. Then the pickup was on them. There were three boys in the front and five or six in the bed. The boy on the passenger side leaned out the window with a gun and began firing.

"No weapons!" Julia shouted, but all she could hear was the ripping and rattling of gunfire.

"Oh blessed God!" Torwon screamed. Blood burst from the right side of his head. He covered his face with his hands. Then he staggered to the side of the road and fell.

The boy in front kept firing until the blue pickup was next to their truck. The music from the pickup sizzled and whomped.

Charles, who had been squatting next to the rear wheel, stood as a line of redness crossed his belly and chest, and then he groaned and fell slowly into the road, face down.

Then the boys in the back started firing into the Land Cruiser. The bullets crunched and rang in the metal and the glass. The shattered windows collapsed, the shards hissing as they fell into the skeleton of the truck. Then there was a bright yellow flare, a roar, a hot wave, and then thick black smoke as the gas tank exploded. Suddenly there was acid in Julia's eyes. She felt her eyebrows sizzle and turn to ash. The stink of burning rubber choked her. Julia's throat closed. All she could see was orange and black, and all she could feel was burning. She bent under the smoke and backed away to find air she could breathe as her hair started to burn.

The boys in the back of the truck laughed and hooted. Then they jumped from the truck and surrounded her, all touching her at once. They touched Julia's breasts and butt and neck and crotch and face.

"Get the fuck off me," she said. "Who the fuck do you think you are?"

She stepped forward, swatting their hands with her hands. Someone grabbed her from behind, a sweaty arm around her neck, and sets of hands grabbed her thighs. They lifted her into the air as they spread her thighs apart. It felt like they were ripping her body in two.

Then one who was wearing a yellow bandanna and whose bare chest was crisscrossed by ammunition belts came and swatted the others away with the butt of his gun. They lowered her so she was standing. The man-boy wearing the yellow bandanna couldn't have been more than seventeen. He had dark skin, small red eyes, and a dark, humped up scar that ran from the right side of his face half way through his right nostril.

One of the others, off to Julia's right, shoved a gun barrel against her temple. And then the man-boy in the yellow bandanna slowly reached his hand behind Julia's neck, pulled her to him, and pushed his mouth and then his tongue into hers.

Then he jumped back, hit Julia across the face with the back of his hand, and put his hand on his bleeding tongue.

"Fock you!" he said. He swatted her away and yelled something in Kpelle that she didn't understand. He hit her face with the back of one hand again and punched her with the other, one-two. Julia's head snapped backward, the bones of her neck crunching together, and her nose began to bleed.

They bound her hands with a bloody rag and shoved her into the cab next to the driver, with two others—the one with the yellow bandanna right next to her, his gun resting on her thigh and pelvis, the steel from the stock pressing into her flank and its barrel under her breast. The beat of the music throbbed in the air, shaking Julia's thighs and back and keeping her from thinking.

She wasn't dead, and she hadn't been raped. Charles and Torwon were dead. They hadn't shot her when it would have been easy to, and they hadn't raped her right there in the road beside the truck.

Two blue police Land Cruisers were waiting for them at a road junction a mile or two toward Buchanan, where a road came in from the east. The truck carrying Julia slowed. One of the thin men-boys in the uniforms, who had RPGs standing in the red dust next to their dusty but pale blue vehicles, half lifted a rifle onto his shoulder, but it was not a serious threat or challenge. The driver stopped and the men talked in Kpelle, not Kreyol. Then some of the men-boys got into their Land Cruiser, and one of the Land Cruisers followed the pickup south.

The cold barrel of the gun jutted into the soft part of Julia's belly, just under her ribs. It jammed into her flesh and bone every time they hit a rut or the truck swerved, and it hurt her every time she took a breath. *Carl will see the burning truck,* Julia thought. *He'll be back from Godeh soon. He'll see the truck on fire and see Charles and Torwon dead on the road in the dirt. Whatever was true or not true about who we are to each other, Carl will get help.*

But there wasn't going to be any help. Carl would hit this checkpoint. Then Carl would also die. They carried no weapons. Carl and the kiddo and Sister Martha and Carl's driver and the mother and the mother's mother. They would all die. And there was nothing Julia could do to stop it. And then it would be hours or days before anyone knew that Charles and Torwon were dead and that Julia was gone.

The pickup turned onto a road that ran east and north. So they weren't going to Buchanan. They were taking her somewhere but not back to the hospital. To a place she didn't know. Where no one would ever be able to find her.

There is no privacy for NGO expats in Buchanan, so Carl and Julia met at Sparks Hotel. For a drink and dinner.

It was a Lebanese place that was trying to look American, so they had hung football jerseys on the walls. It had a jukebox that didn't take money that played disco and top ten music from the '80s and '90s, over and over. The rest of NGO life reminded Julia of the world of graduate students in a university town, where everyone goes to potlucks and drones on and on about their professors, their work, and about who is sleeping with whom. In Buchanan NGO staff ate at one another's compounds most nights. They had Liberian housekeepers and cooks to make the food and clean up afterward, but each NGO made a great show of using food they grew in the compound garden, of cooking together and helping to clean up, and of recycling the paper and the organic waste. The bedrooms in the compound houses were like dorm rooms at college only the walls were thinner, so you could hear the person in the next room as they walked, snored, or turned over in bed. In each bathroom were sheets of neatly typed rules about cleaning up after use and about the disposal of feminine hygiene products. The sheets of rules sat inside clear plastic envelopes and hung from the mirrors. The rules had lots of capital letters and exclamation points for emphasis.

They met at Sparks after the evening rain. They had their drivers drop them at the hotel. The drivers went back to the compounds and would return when they were texted. They could have come over in the same van, but they came separately, and the plan was for them to return separately, each to their own compound.

It was a hotel and restaurant. The customers were mostly white and Middle Eastern but anyone was welcome. Near the little harbor. The white South Africans and Rhodesians (because that was how they still thought of themselves, as Rhodesians, and not Zimbabweans) came with their girls or picked up Liberian girls at the bar—girls who made themselves up and sometimes dyed their hair blond or green or pink and sat on the laps of the white men while the fake jukebox cranked out the same music, over and over. Those white men looked like rugby players, stocky and blond, although there were also Ukrainians and Poles and Bulgarians—thin, very pale men in cheap suits who often brought made-up white women with big blond or platinum hair and bigger eyelashes.

Carl bought the first round. "Glad you could come," he said. "I wanted a place where we could talk."

"Thank you for asking," Julia said. "You never get a moment to yourself here."

"We can talk about Rhode Island," Carl said.

"Little place," Julia said. "Not much to say."

"Wait, I'm from there," Carl said.

"And I spent four years there. I still have friends there. My mentor is there. My car is there. Like I said, not much to say. I didn't like it much. I like you, though."

"You want to talk about your work?"

"Not really. Does your work matter?"

"It matters some. We get clean water to about one village a week. Keeps people from getting cholera and other dread diseases. Gets one person in each village a job. It matters more than anything I could do at home. Does anything in the U.S. matter?" Carl said.

"Not much. How many of your pumps are still working five years out?" Julia said.

"Not many, unless we swing by to check on them once a month. Supportive participatory development. Participatory development doesn't work. People aren't ready. Incremental cultural development. New development model. Whatever all that means," Carl said. "You take care of these cool little kids. Fun, no?"

"The kids are fun, yes," Julia said. "I love being in charge, being the one person who can fix it. Sounds strange, but I even love it when they call me in at 2:00 a.m. for a kid with a fever who needs a spinal tap. This won't mean anything to you, but I love being able to prance in half asleep, look at a baby, roll the kid over, and do a quick spinal tap. There is nothing quite like the feeling you get when you put a needle into the spine between the vertebrae at exactly the right place, feel the membrane around the spinal cord 'pop' as the needle goes through that membrane, and then see drops of crystal clear fluid come out through the hub of the needle. And then I start the kid on antibiotics, and sometimes I even get to save a life. At home, I might do two spinal taps a year, and then the kid goes to the Pediatric Mobile Intensive Care Unit, and I never see that kid again. Here, I do two or three taps a day. I do the tap, start the antibiotic, see the kid on rounds every day, get to know the mother and her sisters, and sometimes even the father and the other kids, and then I get to see the kid when she's better, when I'm out in the bush doing clinics at the health centers. As long as the kiddo doesn't die. So not very often, to tell the truth."

"So you do the bush as well," Carl said. "The bush is different. People at home will never understand it."

"I love the bush, the country places far away, where they need everything," Julia said. "You're right. No one in the U.S. knows or understands what goes on out there—the women with twenty children, all those complex relationships, different fathers, different mothers, kinship, the sharing and the control and the violence, the rituals, and the secret societies. Women in the bush die in childbirth all the time. That almost never happens at home."

"You miss being home?" Carl said.

"Naw," Julia said. "I don't miss the self-important fluffery. We have these great important lives in which nothing else matters besides work, while most of what we actually do is work ten hours a day, watch TV, wait in line, and fill out one stupid form after the next. I do miss having people I know and who know me to talk to. Don't get me wrong. I like my colleagues and all that. But talking to people about medicine and even the countries they come from is different. It's not personal. No one here knows anything about Stanley's Burgers in Central Falls or Ray's Pizza on Sixth Avenue in the Village or the Talking Heads or Will.i.am, and I'm betting you know all that stuff without even thinking about it. I miss people to talk to and people to be with. See? You can tell. I'm talking too much."

She wanted him to say, no, you're not, or something, but instead he just shrugged. She drained her gin and mostly tonic. "So what about you? You miss home?"

"It's different for me," Carl said. "I fit in here. Sort of. I'm not from here, but nobody knows that instantly just by looking at me. I miss Stanley's a little but not so much. Home is a hard place for me. Tough history. I can't see that ever changing. Here no one will ever know who I am, but at least here not everyone has already decided that I am who I'm not. I can make my own life here. Yeah, it's a little lonely from time to time, but things here will change. Have to change. No place to go but up."

"You—we—won't change things here, though," Julia said. "People have to want to change it, and they don't. At least not yet. They could learn how to make their world safer and cleaner, but they don't want to. They live the only life they know, and in its own way, it works for them. They live hard, and they die young, but they don't worry the way we worry, and they don't ever feel worthless or struggle with self-doubt. I'm trying to keep kids alive one at a time, when I can, but the odds are tiny, and it's a huge uphill battle. I could save a lot more kids if their mothers brought them in as soon as they got sick. Hell, I could save even more if everyone slept under a bed net. But I lose a lot of kids, and that's all on me. It really sucks to lose even one. I guess I hope to keep a few of these kids alive long enough so that they can grow up and change things. Bill Levin, my friend and teacher in Providence, has all this stuff about if you save one life, you save the world, about how each life brings the lost light back to the world. My work is nothing like that. Not much light. Too many kids dying in the bush. Sometimes we get lucky, that's all."

Julia put her hand on Carl's hand, which was holding his glass.

"You want dinner?" Carl said.

"Not necessarily. We can eat any time."

"I'm getting a room," Carl said, and he ran the inside of his calf against the inside of Julia's calf as he stood up.

One of the white Rhodesian guys sat down in Carl's chair as soon as he was out of sight. He must have been six foot three and 250 pounds. He had blond curls that hung down the back of his neck.

"You look lonely," the Rhodesian guy said.

"That chair is taken," Julia said.

"Pleased to make your acquaintance," the Rhodesian guy said. And he stood up and went away.

The room was a cheap room that claimed to have a view of the harbor. It had a bed with a mattress that sagged in the middle and a desk next to the window that had a chair in front of it and a bureau that didn't match on a far wall, a ceiling fixture with a bare bulb, and no television. The window had a blind but no curtains. An air-conditioner in the window rumbled and hummed. It produced a moist breeze but no cold air. Out the window you could see the floodlights from the steel plant floating over the blackness where the sea likely was and the headlights from occasional cars but nothing else.

Carl put his hands on Julia's hips as he kissed her after they came into the room. They were standing just at the point where the narrow entryway opened before the bed, and Carl hadn't closed the window blind yet. He knew how to kiss, and Julia discovered that she did too. She thought she had forgotten, but it was like remembering something she had never really known. He knew how to unbutton her. Carl was strong and he smelled like burnt orange—strong and sweet.

He undressed her in the light. She sat down on the bed. "Wait," she said.

"I can't wait," Carl said.

"We have to wait," Julia said. "I'm a doctor, remember? Always ready. Though maybe that makes me a marine." She reached for her shoulder bag and rummaged in it. Carl, sensing what she was about, reached for the wallet in his pants.

"I have one as well," Carl said. He took her hand and pulled her up and off the bed so he could pull off the bedspread and they could have cool sheets for their bodies. "And that puts you in the coast guard not that marines. Semper paratus. Always ready. The marines are semper fi, semper fidelis, always faithful, which does not appear the subject of our discussion of the moment."

He knew how to fuck too. As well. Better than that. Long and slow. Then deep, hot, everlasting, and explosive.

They made love a second time. Then they lay together side by side as they caught their breath.

"It doesn't get much better than that," Julia said. "Kind of a grand slam."

"A grand slam is four runs, three men on," Carl said. "That was just batting practice. Wake me in a few minutes if you're still awake." And he fell asleep.

Julia lay awake, staring at the ceiling. She hadn't fucked anyone in a long time, and this was better than she expected. He was sweet, and he was smart, and he was good in bed. *Damn*, she thought, *I'm falling for this guy. Not good.* He would find out, over time, how little she had to offer, how vapid and boring she was, and he would move on to someone hotter, or smarter, or richer, or famous. It had happened before.

She closed her eyes, looking for sleep. And it found her.

He woke her with an embrace, and they made love again. It was later, but how late there was no way to tell. He got up to look for his watch, but she pulled him back into bed.

"Hey," Julia said. "Talk to me."

"Oh, now you want to talk," Carl said. "What do you want to talk about? You probably also want dinner in a nice restaurant. And wine. Probably a fancy California Chardonnay."

"Stop. Just talk," Julia said. "Tell me stories about growing up. And I like good French wine not California crap. California wine is for Californians. Which I was, once. Now it's Côtes du Rhône. Dry, deep, and full of body."

"Stories about my youth," Carl said. "Back home in little Rhody, hot summer days, getting up when the rooster crows, feeding the cows before breakfast, working hard all day in the hayfields, fishin' in the fishin' hole, swimming in the swimming hole, that kind of stuff?" Carl lay flat on his back, looking at the ceiling.

"That kind of stuff," Julia said.

"It wasn't like that," Carl said. "I'm looking forward, not back. How about you?"

"How about me what? You're ducking the question."

"Not ducking. Just skillfully evading," Carl said. "My life is the opposite of an open book. Closed, sealed, and put away. What's past is past. That's a quote from a great ancient sage of my people."

"You are misquoting," Julia said. "What selfsame ancient sage said was, 'The past can hurt. You can either run from it or learn from it.'"

"Oooh," Carl said. "Your knowledge of ancient literature is deep and extensive. Getting a little personal, aren't we? The residency was pediatrics, yes? And not psychiatry."

"Residencies. Pediatrics *and* Emergency Medicine, if you please," Julia said. "And you are still ducking the question."

"You really don't want the details. I just don't go there anymore," Carl said, and he rolled on his side and began to caress the small of Julia's back, her butt, then he ran his hand deep inside her inner thigh.

"That's good," Julia said. "Very good. But it doesn't get you off the hook. So you were born in Rhode Island?"

"I was born in Rhode Island. In Pawtucket, Rhode Island, in a neighborhood called Fairlawn, which had no people of color then, other than in the housing projects closer to downtown. It gets pretty messy after that."

"You have siblings? Sisters and brothers?"

"One sister. Eighteen months younger. She's still in Rhode Island."

"And?"

"No ifs, ands, or buts, other than the very nice butt in my hand as we speak. That's all there is. More than enough."

"And your parents?"

"I had a mother and a father. My mother was from Martinique. Very Creole. Very dark and very beautiful. You just don't want to know all this. We have better things to talk about and better things to do," Carl said, and he pulled her to him.

"Ummm," Julia said. "Sweet. Very sweet. Tempting to be sure. Exceptionally tempting. But it still doesn't get you off the hook. What about your father?"

"Look, can you let it alone? I like fucking you. I like you. But my life is my life. Do what you want with my cock. Just leave my family out of it," Carl said.

"No push," Julia said. "I'm just interested. Sounds like your father wasn't easy."

"My father was a Jewish guy from Boston, all right? Very political. Pretty isolated. He got weird after we moved to West Virginia. This is all pretty messy. You just don't want to know," Carl said.

"I do want to know," Julia said. "How old were you when you moved to West Virginia?"

"I was five. My sister was three. We lived there for seven years. Then we came back to Pawtucket. Satisfied?" Carl said.

"What brought you all to West Virginia?" Julia said.

"The car. It was a Chevy. I don't know," Carl said. "My father was trying a back-to-the-land thing. He bought a cabin on a dirt road in the mountains. We grew our own food. He went hunting for meat, and he thought he could make living writing articles for left-wing newspapers and magazines about life off the grid. He had a little family money. My mother was a speech pathologist. She worked in the schools. We lived off her income."

"Sounds nice," Julia said.

"It wasn't nice," Carl said. "I was a black kid from the North in a white place, and I had a family that didn't get being black in America. So I looked a little black, but for sure black enough to make me black in West Virginia, and I thought white, which meant I didn't get how to go along and get along. And my father was convinced that the John Birch Society and the Ku Klux Klan were about to take over America, and that we had to be ready, so we could hold out until the Russians came. Crazy stuff. Crazy-crazy. He was probably schizophrenic. We were alone, back in the woods, where no one could see or hear."

"Yikes. What kept you sane?" Julia said.

"Who says I'm sane?" Carl said. "I found a black church, or they found me. Little place by the side of the road. Weirton, West Virginia. We lived about five miles out of town on a dirt road in the woods. Old steel town. There were a couple of old steelworkers, the guys who worked the coke ovens. Their families prayed together. I started hanging out there on Sundays. Rode my bike. I told my father I was fishing."

"And?" Julia said.

"No and . . ." Carl said. "My cover got blown in the weirdest way. There was also a little synagogue in Weirton. A couple of the store-owners and some of the doctors were Jewish, but by the time I was growing up, that community was in decline. Most of the families had come as immigrant peddlers a generation before. Their kids all moved to Pittsburgh, New York, Boston, Cleveland, or DC. My father, crazy as he was, would take us to that synagogue on the Jewish Holidays, and as much as we felt like outcasts every day, we felt really weird in *that* place. Anyway, the synagogue caretaker went to Bethel AME. I started talking to him at the synagogue, and my father got suspicious. My old man followed me the next Sunday. That was that. I got grounded for Sundays. We moved away about six months later."

"Where are your parents now?"

"My mother died before we left West Virginia. My father's in jail in Massachusetts. Long story."

"Your sister?"

"She's okay. She lives in Rhode Island. She went to Princeton, and she could have lived anywhere, but she's back home now. We talk. We're close. She's okay."

"Sounds complicated."

"It is complicated. Was complicated. Not complicated anymore."

"You want to talk about it?" Julia said, and she reached over and put her hand on Carl's cheek.

"I've talked way too much," Carl said. He took Julia's hand off his cheek and put it on the bed, away from him. He rolled over onto his side, his back to her.

He's angry, Julia thought.

He turned around again. "It's okay. You're okay," Carl said. "I haven't talked this much about myself in years. Pretty boring. Sorry I rambled on."

She's even smarter than she looks, Carl thought. *Why am I talking so much? Got to be careful now.*

"I'm sorry," Julia said.

"Nothing to be sorry about. The past is just the past." Then he fell asleep.

Julia lay quiet for a few minutes. *I shouldn't have gone there*, she thought. *I fucked up again. Who is this guy? What the hell has happened in his life? Why do I like being here so much? Why does wanting hurt, every time?* The ache in her shoulders, the strange sensation that was part pain, part rapid heartbeat returned.

Julia stood, went to pee, turned off the light, and came back to bed. She lay on her back, her eyes open.

The air-conditioner hummed. There was no light from behind the blinds yet. The nurses would be making middle of the night rounds at the hospital.

She woke just after dawn. Carl was gone.

A hard left turn. The lean of the truck shifted the gun barrel that was jammed into Julia's side, and she took a quick breath while she had the chance. The radio was pounding so loud she couldn't hear or think, so loud it hurt. Julia was sweating, but she couldn't wipe the sweat from her brow. It dripped into her eyes, and she had to squint so she could see. Sweat, not tears. They could all go fuck themselves. They might make her scream, but they wouldn't make her cry. The oily sweat of the man-boys on both sides of her smelled like spoiled butter and old leather, and she felt the grit on their slippery skin as the pickup swayed and jolted, taking them deeper into the middle of nowhere.

Yellow Bandanna yelled something in Kpelle, and the two others in the cab whooped. Julia jammed her elbows into the ribs of the driver and Yellow Bandanna. She twisted her wrists inside the cloth that bound them, but she couldn't tear free. The driver whooped and jabbed her with his elbow, hard and deep under her ribs. Yellow Bandanna let go of the stock of the gun, grabbed Julia's wrists in his hand, and twisted them, hard. They were young boys, but they were strong, and Yellow Bandanna's hand was big enough to hold both Julia's wrists at once.

"Fuck you," Julia said.

Yellow Bandanna laughed and said something in Kpelle. The boy next to the passenger door said something, and then the driver said something. Yellow Bandanna humped the air, rocking his pelvis in time with the blaring radio beat, jamming the gun barrel into Julia's ribs with each thrust.

"Goddamn it," Julia said. "Please go fuck yourself."

Yellow Bandanna looked at Julia for the first time.

"Stink-mouh! Na focked," he said. "Ya plenty-plenty fock-o," *Listen to the mouth on the woman! I'm not fucked. You are completely fucked, though.*

The pickup turned right, and the lean drove the gun barrel into Julia's chest. When the truck evened out, Julia saw the plantation sign and the guardhouse. She recognized the road. She knew where they were. It was the road to the clubhouse. They were going to The Club.

The Club sat on a hill from which you could see for miles; all the way, it seemed, to Sierra Leone, to Ivory Coast and Guinea, to the borders where there were iron and diamond mines and a railroad that in quiet times brought iron ore to a huge smelter that was perched on a harbor near the sea. Once Julia even saw a train.

Toward the end of day while the sun was still strong and bright and the hills were green and blue, you could see the clouds forming below the mountains, and you could see the thunderstorms in the distance—purple blue patches against the green of the mountainsides. As evening came, you could see the sky flaming orange and red. The wise deep light of the end of the day.

There was a TV over the bar, and the men at the bar cheered whenever someone on the television scored a goal—black men and white men cheering together, something Julia never saw anywhere else in Africa. But women never sat at the bar.

The expats gathered at The Club on Sunday afternoons. The hospital people came after brief work rounds. The NGO people came earlier and stayed later than the hospital people and spent most of their time talking politics. Julia wasn't sure that any of them did real work. The hospital people, on the other hand, worked. They worked hard—endlessly, incredibly hard. The hospital people were there to get a break from seeing people who were sicker than it was possible for human beings to be sick, and from losing little kids and young women, day in and day out, to get a break from living through hell and heartbreak all day long, every single day of the year.

The hustlers who usually hung out at the bar at the Sparks Hotel came to sit at the bar of The Club on Sundays. They never looked at the view. They watched soccer on the television and made a big noise when a goal was scored. The NGO people and hospital people sat together on the porch behind the club near a swimming pool with pale blue water, and together they watched the evening storms roll in. They watched the weaver birds making their colonies, which looked like apartment houses in the ironwood trees. The surgeons from the hospital who came from Ethiopia, Nigeria, and Slovenia played ping-pong, while the others drank beer and talked about the news from America, Europe, and the Middle East. About poverty. About social class and social chaos and the great divide between rich and poor. About the abundance they had left behind. And about Africa, where you see what happens to the lives of the poor in a world where everyone lives off his neighbor, and the poor and rich are always at war.

Looking out like that, sitting in a place that seemed like it was at the top of the world, with waiters to bring you drinks and a swimming pool at your feet and being with smart accomplished people, in a place and in a way where there was nothing pressing, no immediate anxiety, you could understand how colonists lived. You were living on someone else's land, living on someone else's back, the pain and the fear of the lives of others invisible to you, and yet while you were sitting in The Club it felt like you owned all of the known world, which existed only because you had built it and was real only because you were looking at it.

One Sunday in early April, late in the afternoon and soon after she had arrived in Liberia from Rwanda, Julia sat in that circle of people, in lawn chairs, watching the red sun setting over Sierra Leone.

Julia kept to herself. She had just lost another eighteen-month-old to meningitis—kid sick three days, the easiest spinal tap she had ever done; just roll the kid on his side, find the space between two vertebrae, insert the needle, and then pop, right into the spinal canal, and the beautiful clear fluid flowed freely from the hub of the needle, crystal clear drop after crystal clear drop. They had a good vein and had the antibiotic they needed and they got it started right away, but the kiddo died anyway in the middle of the night. No one called her. There was just an empty basinet in the morning when she made rounds. At home, the kid would have been in the PICU, and a whole team would have worked on him all night long. The whole bit. Here, just an empty basinet in the morning. Didn't matter now. What's done is done. Water under bridge.

Zig, the Ethiopian surgeon was there. So was Katy from Hampstead Heath who ran the Buchanan branch of Merlin. Sister Martha was there, and so was Grace, the Rwandan hydrologist who brought a new guy, a tall, tan-skinned American. The American sat next to Julia. He had just arrived from Sierra Leone.

Julia turned to talk to the new guy, who told her his name was Carl, and then turned away before she could introduce herself. He was more interested in listening to the others. The United States had just invaded Iraq after the shock and awe bombing of Baghdad. They were talking about Iraq, which was a continent away—but there was nothing any of them could do about Iraq. Bill Levin was probably worked up about it, and he was probably right, but he got worked up about every world crisis, real or imagined, and none of his demonstrations ever stopped even one little war. Julia was sitting in Liberia where there were people dying in the bush from preventable diseases all day long. These people just liked hearing themselves talk.

A bunch of white Irish and Zimbabwean guys were clustered around a football match on the television over the bar, and you could hear them shouting from time to time at a reversal or a goal. It was hard for Julia to listen to any of it.

The new guy signaled a waiter for a drink. He had a New England accent, hardly black at all. "That's the paradox of development," he was saying. "You do have to live to love. But to live you have to want, and have, and be willing to work to have, and compete to have, and separate yourself in the interest of having. And then you can't love. Families and the communities here create a place, a context in which people can love. Our job is to help families and communities change or to try to keep individuals alive while communities change. Good stuff, but few of us have that much unselfishness in us. And then look at what happens. Development brings more stuff, more goods, and more guns. More wanting. Wanting brings war. War is the triumph of having over loving. Our work gives people the tools they need to go to war with one another."

Huh? Julia didn't know what to say or think. *I'm a lightweight, she thought—one more white woman doctor, one more idealist, head in the sky, feet in Africa, doesn't stay in one place for more than a year or two.* This new guy Carl was apparently not so new after all. Julia heard something she liked in that voice—energy, intelligence, experience, pain, and recovery. *The substance I don't have,* she thought.

The talk moved on to other topics. Keynesian economics. Phenomenology. *The Pedagogy of the Oppressed.* The new guy seemed to know about all of it, and even so he was quiet when others were talking and always kept something in reserve. All Julia knew was how to match three medicines to four diseases and hope for the best.

The calling of the birds became louder, and there were now long whistles, interspaced between the calls. Carl, the new guy, spoke well. He knew who he was. *I'd take a little of that,* she thought. Not that he even noticed her. Julia was nothing. Nobody.

And then there was a long cheer from the bar, and the others went inside for the television and a beer, and Carl and Julia were left alone.

"Game?" Julia said, for the surgeons had abandoned the ping-pong table for soccer and beer with the rest. It was a weak hope.

"Sure," Carl said.

The daylight was fading. Julia put on the electric lights.

Carl had a strong forehand and an unstoppable slam, but no backhand and almost no serve. They traded points at first, feeling out each other's strengths and weaknesses.

And then they had a long volley. The white ball went faster and slower, popping and clicking like the clatter of horses' hooves on a cobblestone street, swinging from one side of the table to the other as they each danced alone behind the table. Julia could feel where Carl was going to hit the ball and was ready for it. Carl's arms were longer, but Julia was quicker. As the volley went on, they each bounced from side to side, seeing only the ball and one another.

Julia changed pace. She fed a simple but slow shot into Carl's backhand that he easily reached, and his return put a slow looping ball exactly where Julia wanted it, about three-quarters of the way down the table, with a moderately high bounce, right in her sweet spot. He couldn't know about her slam, which she had kept hidden from him.

She hit the ball hard. She nailed it. She barely looked as the ball flew across the table, fast and hard enough to be barely visible and bouncing far back on the table, landing at the very last moment, exactly where she wanted it to go.

But somehow Carl reached it, and the ball came back high and slow and so long it looked like the ball would certainly miss Julia's end of the table. But somehow the ball came down, and touched the table's edge.

The game was over. And Carl came around the table like a good sportsman, prepared to shake her hand. Then Julia did something she had never done before. She reached up and touched the cheek of this man she had just met. Then, on tiptoes, she kissed his cheek.

"I'm Julia," she said.

There was a dead black man in a green uniform that was too big for him slumped over the desk of the plantation guardhouse. His neck was red with blood, his silly policeman's hat lying at a strange angle on the table in front of him, leaning against his chest.

The guardhouse windows had been smashed, and there were jagged edges of glass hanging from the window frames, distorting the reflected light. The glass was spattered and streaked red, as if someone had started to paint the inside and then shook the excess paint off the brush.

Across the road was the large white sign of the Liberian Rubber Corporation, which in blue letters announced that this plantation was a collaboration between the Republic of Liberia and the people of the

United States, but Julia knew that wasn't true anymore. American-owned once. Chinese-owned now. The sign certainly didn't fool the Liberians, who knew it was owned and run by foreigners, who were all the same, present but not meaningful. Foreigners were people who lived in a different world, a tolerated burden living in their midst, living on their backs; nothing you could talk about but nothing that was ever going away.

The crossing gate, a thin yellow pole with black stripes, was in pieces on the road, where someone had smashed through and then run over it. The pickup ran over it as well.

The pickup sped down the plantation's main road. The road was paved and the going was smooth, so the gun barrel jammed under Julia's ribs didn't jab her in new ways. Yellow Bandanna and the driver and the boy near the window kept their eyes on the road and didn't look at Julia. Their faces were young faces, but their eyes were blood-shot and fixed.

The road was lined with rubber trees in perfect sixty-foot-tall rows. Each tree had a spiraling groove cut into its bark. The collection cups hanging at the bottom of the grooves were tipped askew, as if someone had forgotten them, and then forgot the rubber trees altogether.

The drive to The Club was longer than she remembered. The blacktop was still good, better by far than the red dirt roads of the county. The trees had been cut down in places and the stumps burned, the ground left empty and charred. There was a red barn on a hillside off to the right, a red barn that looked like it belonged in Vermont. Once upon a time, the rubber workers raised their own beef on the plantation, and there was a school for their children and a company doctor who visited each settlement of shacks once a week. Once upon a time.

That farm was nothing like the farm where Kim Terrell ended up, and the road through the plantation was nothing like the road Julia drove to try to rescue Kim.

Kim Terrell was a medical student from Iowa, a farm girl, big and strong and also blond and uncomplicated. University of Iowa, straight out of public school. She had shown up one Sunday morning in April the year before, in for two months, in a car she had hired at the airport, a beat-up old Suzuki taxi. No guard. She had written Merlin six months before to set up the clerkship, but the doctor she had written to, a family practitioner named Suki Thompson, was long gone. No one remembered Kim was coming, and no one knew what to do with her at first. God loves children, medical students, and fools, though Kim was only one of those. Perhaps, as it turned out, two.

They needed the help, so Julia put her to work right away. Kim wrote notes while they were on work rounds. Before long she was running the ward during the day while Julia was out in the villages. Some days when Zig's OR load was light and he felt like he could run the ward alone Julia took her along with her to the village health centers. Julia also let Kim make some village trips with Sister Martha when the village was close by, as long as there was cell phone service in that village so Kim could call in case of trouble. Good experience for her. Kim was always looking for more experience and for more responsibility. She hung out in the Emergency Department at night, helping the PA's work up new admissions. No one thought much about that. There was no better place for a medical student to hang out than in the Emergency Department and to see what came in from the villages at night, because everything came in—women in labor who had ruptured their membranes a week ago and had gone septic, kids with asthma, young men in comas from brain tumors or meningitis, women with ruptured ectopics who were bleeding out, people presenting for the first time with HIV, TB, malaria, typhoid—you name it, they saw it in that ED.

No one was that surprised when July came and Kim said how much she loved working at the hospital and put off her departure for six months. She got a leave from medical school, she said. She was learning more in Buchanan than she'd ever learn doing fourth-year electives. Everyone at home supported her decision. No one was surprised, but no one thought she was thinking very clearly, even then.

They knew Kim had been eating lunch at the hospital instead of in the compound. They just didn't know why.

There was a PA Kim worked with when she hung out in the Emergency Department at night, a smooth guy named Alex who was from a community about twenty miles out, from out toward Maryland County along the coast. Sometimes Kim ate her lunch with Alex. They would sit on a hillside near the hospital kitchen and talk. No one thought anything about that either.

Alex always had a story. When he presented his cases on morning rounds he presented them backwards, starting with the diagnosis and *then* detailing the history of present illness and the physical examination, as if he decided what the diagnosis was going to be first, and then chose details or made up findings to fit the diagnosis he wanted to give. That he was wrong more than he was right was one problem. That he started the wrong treatment more often than not and killed people by waiting when he needed to act was a more serious problem yet. You had to be kind and patient, because he was a Liberian PA, and they had too few Liberian clinical staff who were likely to stay. But most of rounds were devoted to fixing what Alex and the others had gotten wrong. A good day was the day that Julia and Zig could fix the mess in time, before the patient died.

One morning in October Kim didn't show for hospital rounds. They started on the surgical ward.

"The first patient is a seventeen-year-old woman from Buchanan who had presented in the middle of the night with vomiting and abdominal pain of four days duration and right lower quadrant tenderness," said Tiffany, the PA on duty the night before. "No recent vaginal bleeding. The temperature is 99.8. The blood pressure is 86 over 52. The pulse is 110. There is no rebound tenderness and the white blood count is normal. She is admitted to the surgical ward to rule out appendicitis."

The patient, a young woman, was thin and dark-skinned. The sheets on the bed were tan from washing and age and were wrinkled. The patient wore a thin light blue hospital gown and her hair was braided into tight beaded corn rows that hung to her shoulders and were scattered on both sides of her head as she lay sweating on her pillow. She looked scared and got more scared when the six people in jeans, tee shirts, and white coats surrounded her bed.

"Pregnancy test?" Zig said, as he walked to an orange ten-gallon water jug that sat on a table nearby and pressed the spigot at the bottom so he could wash his hands. There was a moment of silence.

"LMP?" Zig said.

Another moment of silence. Tiffany spoke to the young woman in Bassa. Zig put his hands on the young woman's abdomen, and she flinched. She twisted away as Zig pressed his fingers deep into her soft belly, and then she flinched again as he suddenly let go. He placed his left hand on the young woman's abdomen, without pushing, and tapped his third finger with the second and third finger of his right hand, moving his left hand as he tapped it. The young woman flinched again. Then Zig put his right hand on the girl's upper abdomen and pressed in with his second and third fingers, first on the left and then on the right.

"Tell her to take a deep breath," he said, and he pressed in deeper on the right as Tiffany translated and the girl breathed in deeply.

"The patient is not certain of the LMP. Four or five weeks. Not one or two," Tiffany said.

"Shit," Zig said. "Kim, get me a sterile prep kit and a sterile 20 cc syringe with a two-inch 18-gauge needle please."

The people on rounds looked at one another for a moment. Julia walked to the end of the ward, and brought back a package wrapped in green cloth, a syringe wrapped in plastic, and a brown bottle.

"We're in luck," Julia said. "No Kim, but it's a Betadine day."

"*You're* in luck," Zig said. "*I'm* on my way to the OR, where this kid should have been six or seven hours ago." He unwrapped the green cloth package on a table, spread out a green cloth sheet that was inside it, and opened the syringe package so the syringe fell on the cloth sheet. Then he scooped up and put on a pair of surgical gloves and with his gloved right hand held out a few gauze pads to Julia, who squeezed some of the brown liquid in the brown plastic bottle she was still holding into the gauze. Zig turned and wiped the girl's right side with the brown liquid, moving the gauze in an expanding circle, moving quickly.

"Lay her on the right side," Zig said. "Tell her this will hurt but only for a minute."

Tiffany translated and the girl turned to her right. Zig uncapped the syringe and put his left hand on the girl's abdomen, his thumb and first finger spread apart, marking a target. Then he slowly inserted the needle into the girl's abdomen, advanced it, and pulled back on the plunger with the thumb of his right hand as it advanced. After a moment, a spurt of thin red-pink fluid came into the syringe. Zig waited until the syringe was about one-third full. He pulled it out of the girl's belly and held it to the light.

The fluid was red tinged. Pink-red not blood-red. Watery, not thick and opaque.

Pink-red. Not blood. Zig swirled the syringe and waited.

"It's not clotting," Zig said. "Non-clotting blood in paracentesis fluid in a young woman with abdominal pain who missed her period and is getting shocky is a ruptured ectopic. She's got a tubal pregnancy that has burst open her fallopian tube and now she is bleeding into her belly. She'll bleed out if we don't get this fixed now. In Boston, you'd have a quantitative beta subunit HCG, an ultrasound, and maybe a laparoscopy, but it would take you two hours to get that done and another hour to have her in the OR. All I have is a healthy index of suspicion, a head on my shoulders, an 18-gauge needle, and a strong arm. We've got a ruptured ectopic. We can be in the OR in ten minutes. Wide open IV saline please, type her, see if you can find me a little blood to cross match, and let's get her to the OR. Now. Perhaps we can snatch one tiny victory out of the cold fingers of defeat."

"I'll do rounds," Julia said.

"Tiffany and Alex, you assist," Zig said. "Alex, you'll pass the gas. Tiffany, scrub with me. Julia, you take Kim today."

"Kim's not here," Julia said.

Zig looked around.

"I can round on my own," Julia said. "You take the others."

"Anyone know anything about Kim?" Zig said.

"Kim is not well today," Alex said.

"What do *you* know about Kim's health and well-being?" Zig said to Alex. Zig looked at Julia as he took his gloves off.

"Kim is not well today," Alex said.

Zig jerked the sterile drape off the table. He threw it into a bin for laundry, and then he flung his used gloves into a garbage pail.

"Perhaps Kim will return when her morning sickness improves," said Tiffany.

"We'll take care of Kim tomorrow," Julia said. "Get this kid to the OR now."

Julia went to Alex's village a week later.

The village was east and south of Buchanan, about five miles off the main road to Maryland County, close to the sea. The land was low and open, mostly grasslands and wetlands, with salt ponds and lime green grasses in the estuary that swayed in the least breeze and moved with the currents. *Malarial country*, Julia thought. Low and hot, though maybe the sea breezes kept the mosquitoes from settling and biting. *I hope she is using a damn bed net*, Julia thought. *I hope she learned that much from us before she came here.*

Kim was bent over, hoeing a garden plot with a girl of about fourteen. There were other women working in the village, one grinding a white paste in a wooden trough, one standing at a fire in the cooking hut, and one sitting on the ground, working with her hands. Five or six children were scattered about the village near the pump and in the garden. One old man slept on a bench in the kitchen hut, and two more men squatted in front of one of the huts. A few scrawny chickens darted from place to place, pecking once, twice, three times, and then running across the yard to stay near a hut or a tree in the shade.

The women heard the truck and turned to look when Julia's door thumped shut. "Stay here," Julia said. Torwon turned off the engine. Charles opened his window to catch the breeze and to listen for trouble.

Kim stood and put a hand to her forehead to shield her eyes from the sun. A short, round, plump, dark woman in a yellow and green lapa came to the door of the hut nearest to Kim, and then came out of the hut so that she stood between Julia and Kim.

"Good day," Julia said. "Hey Kim."

"G'day," said the plump woman.

"Hey, "said Kim.

Kim's hair was braided now and hung all to one side. She was wearing an orange tee shirt and a sky-blue lapa and black sandals made from the rubber of old tires. Her face was puffy, and her body had just begun to swell, so she was five months, maybe more. So much for the story about morning sickness. The pregnancy must have started early, just after she arrived, long before anyone noticed that she was spending any time with Alex. *That vulture*, Julia thought. *Alex hit on her right away, before Kim had a chance to get her bearings. You never know where it's coming from next. Alex always has an angle. I should have watched more closely. You can never turn your back, not for one single second.*

"Kim, is there anything you need?" Julia said.

"Kim ga. Kim okay," the plump woman said. *Kim is good. Kim is okay.*

"Let's walk together. Show me around the village," Julia said.

"Wait na. We walkabout da fa," the plump woman said. *Wait. We can explore the farm together.*

"I'd like to walk with Kim. Just me and Kim. To talk together," Julia said. "Alone."

"We can walk. It's a white thing," Kim said, but she looked at the plump woman, not at Julia when she spoke.

"Okay-okay," the plump woman said. "Quick-quick wa." *It's okay to take a quick walk.*

But the plump woman didn't move from between Kim and Julia. She put her hands on her hips and remained standing in the bright hot sun. Kim leaned her hoe against a fence made from branches and walked behind the plump woman toward the cooking tent. Julia met her there. Then they walked to the Land Cruiser.

"It's a village" Kim said. "Alex's farm. A good place. Not really much to show. I've helped keep the garden in shape. That's Mallie, Alex's head wife. She looks out when Alex is in Buchanan."

"You want to talk about it?" Julia said.

"There's nothing to talk about. This is my life now," Kim said.

"And your family back home, medical school and residency, and everything else?" Julia said. "You're ready to write all that off? All that hard work?"

"All that hard work, which were preparing me for more hard work?" Kim said. "Always feeling like I don't know enough. Always feeling like I'm never good enough. I never felt the way Alex makes me feel. He makes me feel smart. He even makes me feel beautiful. Mallie makes me feel like I belong here. I'm going to have a baby. That baby will belong here. At home if I want to have a baby I have to beg for time off from work and apologize for taking the time. Then I'm supposed to act like I want to be back in a hurry. And then I have a baby and am a doctor at the same time, always rushing to be everything to everybody, no time to think. No one's rushing me here. I can breathe."

"You know that women in Liberia are valued mostly for their ability to produce children," Julia said.

"I *can* produce children!" Kim said. "Solid Iowa farming stock. Good teeth and a strong back. Maybe I can have fifteen."

"That's not what I mean," Julia said. "Alex will have other women. You know how it goes in Liberia. Women he's married to. Women he's not. Some women have other men."

"I know about that," Kim said. "Doesn't matter. Alex makes me feel alive. Liberia makes me feel alive. I'm part of something here. At home you are always alone. At home they make you feel like property, like you are only good for taking tests, getting grades, and maybe someday earning money. To show the neighbors."

"Are you safe? No one's forcing you? There isn't anyone here you can call in the middle of the night. Remember you still have options. We can get into that Land Cruiser, have you back in Buchanan in an hour and to Monrovia by nightfall. Back in Iowa on Thursday," Julia said.

"My own free will," Kim said. "This is my choice. I'm here for the duration. Mallie isn't standing there to force me to stay. She's there to make sure you don't try to force me to leave. I know you are looking out for me too. But I'm an adult, and I can make my own decisions. So thanks for coming. I'll pass on that ride back to town."

"Alex isn't our most trusted or reliable PA," Julia said.

"I know who Alex is. And who he isn't," Kim said.

"You get to big belly clinic then. You take your vitamins. Use a bed net. You know the drill. We can always get you home if anything changes. You take care of that baby, you hear?" Julia said.

Julia leaned against the car door most of the way home, her head on the window.

"Talk sweet to her. Right thin," Torwon said. *You were kind to her. That was the right thing to do.*

"Alex yona boy," Charles said. "He rascal. She comes home soon sorry on one-cent car." *Alex is just a street peddler. Kim will come walking back in a bad way.*

"Wait now ad stink moot," Torwon said. *Don't talk badly about these people.*

Julia shook her head and didn't speak.

Kim was right and wrong at the same time. She was an adult, responsible for her own choices, and she had talked herself into this one, big time. But Charles was also right. Nothing good could come of this. Julia should have made Kim get into the car with her and she should have taken her home. She should have been tougher, more in control. Or gotten Torwon and Charles to pick Kim up and just put her in the car. You don't let people who are insane make their own choices. And love, or whatever this was, was making Kim insane. The average life expectancy in Liberia is about forty. Kim didn't have the life skills you need to survive. Julia hadn't been tough enough. She let everyone down.

But maybe it would be okay. Maybe Kim knew what she was doing and it was Julia who was confused.

Then two weeks later Julia heard one of the community health workers say that she had been out to Alex's village, that Kim's face was black and blue. And that Kim was talking to the traditional midwives, and not doing big belly clinic at all.

So Julia asked Carl to go out and take Zig with him. Maybe Carl could do for Kim what Julia had failed to do. Perhaps Carl was the person Julia wasn't.

They went out, and they came back. They took four men from Carl's team just in case. Julia had been clear. Get her back. Don't take no for an answer. Just put her in the car and bring her home. And then we'll ship her back to Iowa for safekeeping.

Julia was doing the ward and she saw the Land Cruiser pull into the courtyard of hospital compound where the hospital cars parked at the end of the day, and she went out to meet them.

Zig got out of the back. Carl was sitting in the front seat. He pulled down his window when Julia walked down the ramp from the ward.

No Kim.

"Where is she?" Julia said.

"She's in the bush," Zig said. "She isn't going anywhere."

"I thought we said you would just put her in the car," Julia said.

"She was gone. They must have known we were coming," Carl said. "Alex works here. News travels fast. She wasn't there."

"Did you look?" Julia said.

"There isn't much to see. You've been there. Four or five huts, a cooking hut, and a garden. No we didn't walk into every hut. We didn't exactly have a warrant for her arrest. They didn't want us there. That woman you met, Alex's head wife, she was there. She said Kim's not here. She made it pretty plain we weren't welcome," Carl said.

"So you didn't see her," Julia said.

"No we didn't see her," Zig said.

"You should have checked the huts," Julia said. She turned her head away.

"Julia you are over the top on this," Carl said. "She's of age. Maybe not thinking straight but of age. You don't go marching into people's houses, regardless of how right you think you are. This is a place with its own culture and its own rules. We have to respect that. You want to find her, you come with us next time, and you do the dirty work. Even then I don't think we can bring her back against her will."

"She's going to die out there. This is suicide. She's all alone," Julia said.

"Then she's no different than a hundred thousand Liberian women. No different than African women from any of the fifty-plus nations. Everyone lives this life," Zig said. "People make their own choices, even when they make choices that they can't survive."

"You can't make different choices if you're dead. We're going back," Julia said. "I'm going with you. We can't leave her out there alone."

"Let it settle for a few weeks," Carl said. "Then maybe we'll all go back together. But I don't think she's coming in. This is the life she wants."

"You didn't do what you needed to do," Julia said. "I'm going to try to find someone else to go. The church people might go. They know what they believe."

"Suit yourself," Carl said. "You are way over your skis. And there ain't no snow on this ground, and there ain't going to be snow in Liberia anytime soon."

Later, back in her room, Julia threw a book against the wall. Carl was not the man she wanted him to be. Kim was lost. Julia was not the person she needed to be.

Three weeks later, Julia was awakened by a car honking in the middle of the night, and a few minutes later there was a loud knock on her door. There was a pregnant woman in labor. In trouble. Big-big trouble.

It was Kim. Her face was waxy, blue-white, and wet. Her braids were pulled back behind her head so her forehead and features stood out. Her eyes had glazed over. She was breathing in big, deep agonal breaths. Sister Martha was there. So was Alex.

"Vitals?" Julia said, as she put her hands on Kim's belly.

"Sixty over palp," Sister Martha said. "Pulse 140 and thready."

There was a horizontal blue line on the upper part of the abdomen. The abdomen was tense. There was no uterine fundus, no smooth firm dome, and no capsule to hold and protect the baby. Fetal parts were easily palpable beneath the skin. Julia felt a flexed leg, then a bent arm, a shoulder and the child's nose and mouth just beneath the cool white skin of Kim's belly. There was no fetal movement. The baby wasn't moving. The child was dead.

"She's in shock. She's ruptured her uterus. Get the OR ready. Get Zig. Get the lab. Get me two 18-gauge catheters and two bags of normal saline and as much blood as we can find. Type-specific to start. Cross-matched if we get that far. Was she in labor?" Julia said. She walked over to a treatment table and pulled two wrapped catheters from a jar.

"The patient commenced labor at zero three hundred hours three days ago," Alex said. "She failed to progress."

"Fuck you," Julia said. Then she scooped a few wet white gauze pads from a metal tin, turned back to Kim's side, wiped the skin on the back of Kim's hand with gauze, opened one of the catheters and slipped it under Kim's skin. Sister Martha connected tubing to a bottle of IV fluid, ran the fluid through the line, and handed the end of the tubing to Julia as she probed with the catheter until a spot of blood showed in the hub of the catheter. Then Julia pulled the metal stylus, the needle, out of the catheter and connected the tubing.

"Open it wide. Run it as fast as it will run. We're on borrowed time," Julia said, and she walked around the foot of the gurney, slapped the back of Kim's other hand, wiped the back of it, and jerked off the plastic and paper covering of the second catheter.

"Zig's scrubbing," Sister Martha said.

"Who was managing her labor?" Julia said as she inserted the catheter under the skin of Kim's left hand. "And let's get an intubation set up please. I'm going to tube her as soon as the IVs are running, on her way to the OR."

Kim's breathing grew suddenly shallower. Julia looked at Kim's face and shook her head.

"We don't have much time. Not any time. Let's move people," Julia said.

"The patient was attended by a traditional midwife," Sister Martha said. She punctured a second bottle of IV fluid and began to run it through the tubing. "She ruptured her membranes three days ago. When her labor failed to progress, the midwife placed a wooden plank on the uterine fundus and pressed on the plank with both hands, hoping to expel the fetus through the cervix and vagina and deliver the child naturally. When the labor still failed to progress, the midwife stood on the plank, one foot on each side."

"So somebody put a board on the belly of a pregnant woman in labor and stood on it?" Julia said.

Then Kim's breathing stopped.

"The respirations have ceased," Alex said.

"Fuck you, Alex. Fuck, fuck, fuck you. I need that tube right now!" Julia screamed. She left the catheter under the skin of Kim's left hand and moved around the gurney so she stood over Kim's head."

"There is no pulse," Sister Martha said.

"Get Zig, Alex. Tell him to break scrub. Tell him I need him now," Julia said. "Sister Martha, start chest compressions. I'm going to tube Kim now," Julia said, and she picked up a laryngoscope from a table and snapped its head open so the tiny light went on.

"There is no tube," Sister Martha said.

"Give me a seven," Julia said. "A six and a half will do if that's all you have."

"There is no need to tube," Sister Martha said. "There is exsanguination. There is no blood to transfuse. There is no operation to repair the damage now. The baby has died. The girl has died. We will pray for these souls and ask for their forgiveness," Sister Martha said.

"A seven and a half then," Julia said. "Please give me a tube."

Kim lay on the gurney, blue-white and still, her waxy eyes still open but without life in them, a sheet over her big still belly, and an IV catheter in the back of each hand.

When Zig came in, Julia was standing over Kim, the laryngoscope in her hand, its tiny light still on.

Zig took the laryngoscope form Julia and closed it. The light went off when the blade snapped shut. Then Zig reached over and closed Kim's eyes.

They passed a small lake that lay next to a hill. The steel stitch in Julia's side hurt less. Yellow Bandanna was awake, but his face was flatter and his eyes were dull, and he must have relaxed his grip on the gun. They were moving fast, fifty, perhaps sixty miles an hour, and there was a stiff breeze on Julia's face from the open windows. The stereo was still booming, BOOMCHA BOOMCHA BOOMCHA, the bass shaking Julia in her seat. It would have rattled windows in buildings along the side of the road if there had been windows or buildings.

The road ran between the lakeshore and a grove of rubber trees that were tall enough for the angled grooves in the pale green bark and the towering darker green leafy tops to be reflected in the water.

Still water. No waves.

One Sunday in the dry season they went to Roberts Beach. It was hard for Julia to believe that there can be places as beautiful as Roberts Beach in a country as bereft as Liberia.

The beach was a little more than a sand bar curling into the ocean with a cliff on one end that boys use for diving and a spine of palm trees on a low hill with ocean with surf beyond the hill. There was a good breeze off the ocean and a crashing surf.

Six of them went for an outing in two cars—Julia, Zig, Carl, Grace, and Rashid, the community health guy from Pakistan, as well as two visitors, both women from Britain, who rode with Carl and Grace.

They sat at a rickety refreshment stand made out of odd-sized boards and driftwood painted bright yellow and bright green and white, in the shade of a patio made of poles and thatched with banana leaves. A thin wizened man with a white three-day beard brought them drinks. They sat and watched the surf breaking and watched the white and green Ghanaian boats, pirogues, fishing a few hundred yards off-shore. Bent signs near the water said you shouldn't swim because of the riptide, but there were people, mostly boys from town, standing in water as high as their chests.

They sat in the shade and talked about the foolish police, who wore hot uniforms and big blue-visored hats that didn't fit and ran checkpoints that existed only to extract payoffs. They laughed about the castoff four-wheel drive pickups and SUVs imported from the U.S. that roared through the streets of Buchanan without mufflers, their exhaust noise shaking the windows, so loud that you'd look for a semi or freight train and all you'd see was a little red Honda CRV. They talked about the signs on the back of taxis or in the small shops: Lord's Blessing Taxi; God have Mercy and Kindness Car Service; God's Blessing Tailor; God is in Control Business Center; All Thanks to God Medicine Shop; We Are Here to Serve God Shoes Doctor. Then they talked about the news, about the rumors of Charles Taylor getting indicted in Sierra Leone, about the rebel group in Loma County and how the British were behind them, about 9/11 and the Israelis and the Palestinians and the war in Iraq and the looting of Baghdad.

How wonderful was that day for Julia, who didn't think much about the news, to be sitting on a beautiful beach and to hear the perspective of people from other places. Julia believed that people from around the world hated the U.S., and through that hatred those people also hated her and burned our flag and our president in effigy every chance they got. But that was not what these people thought. They did not think Julia was the enemy, or even an enemy. They seemed to like the U.S., to respect it, and even to like and respect Julia and her work. They were puzzled about our choices. Respectful of our power. Curious about our democracy. And hopeful that we'd eventually get it right, after trying all the other options.

Carl, the other American, was listening and looking out to sea when he got bored. They were still not an item. They had been together twice. That was good, really good. She throbbed when he left. Ached. And thought too much about him later.

But Carl acted like he barely knew she existed. Days and sometimes a week would go by without her hearing from him. He didn't stop by or come to the hospital to see her. They had chance meetings. Dinner at Zig's. They'd see one another at the Bong County Road crossing in the morning, when her crew and Carl's crew were on their way to the bush. She saw him at The Club on Sunday afternoons.

She was a lightweight and Carl knew it. No theory. No Marx, Marcuse, Friere, Habermas, Foucault, Rawls, or even Paul Farmer. She tried to listen sometimes, but none of it had any weight, any reality. There were little kids in the bush dying of measles and malaria and of simple dehydration after diarrhea and that was about all Julia knew. Carl needed someone who could think like he thought, who could understand the big picture, who could quote the Old Testament and Shakespeare and was also good in bed.

That wasn't her. Julia was just not that much about being an item anyway. She was about her work. Kiddos dying in the bush. Good prenatal care. Bed nets. She was awkward and she wasn't good at relationships and she wasn't really that smart. And she'd be gone in a few months, so what was the point? It was good while it lasted. What little there was of it. Just between them. Two consenting adults.

While the others talked Julia went alone into the surf. The furious tide crashed around her legs and belly and tried to suck her legs out from under her as she walked into deeper water. When she bodysurfed, the waves twisted and turned her and beat her up good until she fought back and ached with the exhilaration of being alive. The hell with Carl. The hell with Africa. The surf was as good as it gets. She swam until she started to get cold, swam hard, across the waves, and then she body-surfed back to shore. She let the riptide twist her and toss her and roll her into the pebbles, seaweed, and sand.

Then Carl walked into the surf to where Julia was, half kneeling, half floating in water that was not quite waist deep where a wave had dumped her, still a little short of breath, after a long rough ride, and he held out his hand and arm for Julia to hold as she stood. It was a strong hand.

Then a wave hit them, and Carl reached around Julia's waist so he could hold her, his feet spread wide apart and planted in the sand. Carl and the wave together lifted Julia, so her feet floated toward shore, and the wave poured over her neck and chest and back and abdomen, but Carl's arm kept her head out of the water, and she held her side and chest tightly against him, against his chest and flank, which was warm and strong. The next wave knocked them both over. The next wave after that sent Julia twisting toward shore, spinning her about so she didn't know which way was up.

Then the surf paused. Julia had enough time to plant her feet and turn around and look for Carl.

And suddenly the tide reversed, and sucked her back under and out to sea, sucking her out fast and hard. Her body twisted in the current. She felt the exhilaration of force and speed at first. Then everything was out of control. The shore was suddenly distant, the little refreshment stand just a speck of color on the beach. Her arms ached.

And she was way too far out. She swam hard across the current but she couldn't break the rip. She swam harder. Suddenly she felt fear. *Can't panic*, she thought. *But maybe I really can't. Can't swim. That far. Alone.*

Then there wasn't enough air. Julia was swimming with everything she had in her arms and upper body and legs. But struggling. Tired and short of breath. Then cold. Then very short of breath.

And then Julia felt herself dying.

It was a strange, sad sensation. Carl was far away. The world was far away. Julia's life was not her own. It had never been her life. Now it was vanishing. She was glad for having lived. But so sad to lose the world that would now never be hers.

There wasn't much breath left. Weak, she thrashed about with her elbows and arms, watching the sky disappear. There was only a cold chill and the water around her.

And then Carl was there. He put his arm around Julia's waist. She threw both arms around his neck. Her head came out of the water and she took a deep breath. And then another deep breath. And then the world came back, and she was holding onto Carl, whose body was still warm and strong.

"Go limp," Carl said. "Hold my chest, not my neck. I'll swim for both of us."

Julia molded herself to Carl's body. She began to shiver, even to shake, and the only way she could get warm was to fold herself into him. She wrapped her arms around his chest.

Carl started swimming at right angles to the current. The current continued to carry them out to sea but Carl swam to where the water wasn't moving so fast. And then he swam a little further, to a place where the waves broke but the water was quiet between the waves. And then he stopped swimming and rose out of the water.

"You can stand," he said. "Sand bar."

Julia was shivering and breathless, but she stood, her legs weak and her body shaking. She wrapped her arms around Carl, and pushed her chest into his to stop the shivering and the dying. But it was more than not dying. Julia felt something she had never felt before. Carl was the body part Julia lacked. The missing piece had been found. Julia had never been whole before.

No one on shore could see or would know. They had gone for a swim. But had come back different. Really different.

"Oh man," Julia said. "You just . . ."

"Shhh," Carl said. "You gotta do what the sign says. You can't go swimming here alone."

He kissed her forehead first, and then he kissed her closed eyes and kissed her cheeks and nose and mouth, and he held her to him, and he didn't let her go.

But they were still not an item. Not yet.

Chapter Five

Carl Goldman. July 16 to 18, 2003

FIRST THEY FLEW HIM TO A STAGING AREA IN SENEGAL. THEN THEY FLEW HIM TO Wiesbaden. He landed about 10:00 at night. Carl called Naomi at about 6:00 in the evening, her time. That way he wouldn't have to wake her when he got to Boston.

It took them most of the night to process his paperwork and ferry him over to the civilian airport. Evening flight from Frankfurt, westbound so you land a little after you left, according to the clock.

He cleared Boston customs about 1:00 in the morning. Naomi would have come to the airport but she had to work the next day. They were used to this—his coming in early in the morning and driving himself to Lincoln. Carl rented a car in Boston and got to Naomi's house at about 3:00 a.m. He found the key under a fake rock in a landscape bed near the front door and let himself in. He slept in Naomi's spare bedroom. She got up and went to work without waking him. Naomi would be home at 6:30.

Carl didn't sleep. He was unconscious, perhaps, but he spent the night tossing and turning. There were men coming out of the walls. The cars in the garage were on fire. There was a naked woman with him, her hands around his cock and balls, her head thrown back, her face ashen and soft, like it was made of putty, so she was all eyes and mouth with no nose. She was moaning, but her eyes were closed, and she was in unimaginable pain. The face of a bearded man came in and out of these dreams, a face he remembered but couldn't place. Sometimes he thought he saw Julia, sitting in the middle of the burning Land Cruiser, her flesh melting, her hair and her eyelids on fire. Other times

RPG shells rained in through the wall, the rockets homing in on Carl's chest and naked groin as he lay in bed. And then there were moments of peace, sitting at Robert's Beach, drinking a beer with Julia, watching the pelicans fly up the coast as the sun was setting.

Carl woke up to birds, their chirps and clattering—a wall of sound before dawn. There are also birds in Buchanan, but the dawn is later. There, you hear one call over and over, twceet–tcheapup-cheap, twceet–tcheapup-cheap, the pepper-birds singing from high in the dahoma trees, so their songs sound much farther away. Here, Carl heard a chorus of birds near dawn, and the birds forced him awake. And then he was unconscious again, waking and falling asleep in the bright light of midmorning.

Here. Lincoln, Rhode Island. Not Buchanan. Not Liberia. With his eyes closed Carl heard the whop whop whop of helicopters blotting out the endless popping of automatic weapons and he saw black smoke pouring out of buildings and trucks that had been hit by RPG fire.

With his eyes open Carl saw four plumb white walls and heard the birds, the hum of air-conditioners, and the whisper of the refrigerator compressor from the kitchen, clicking on and off according to narrow parameters set by a thermostat.

You don't think when the marines come knocking. You just do what they say. You assume they are going to find everyone and get everyone out.

There was an oval picture of a woman on Naomi's wall—a silhouette in black and white, but suddenly in this silhouette there was sun on the woman's golden skin, and Carl could make out wisps of hair against the sky. His mother as a girl. Then she was Julia, floating above the ground, catching thermals as she soared from place to place, inhaling the air that was thick with the sweet smell of plowed earth, the green smell of just-cut hay, and the tall airy smell of the pine forests beneath her, as insects whirred and cavorted in the setting sun, and birds of all colors.

Julia was lying next to him. Then she wasn't.

Julia. The awkward, smart, sexy doctor girl. Fucked him before she really talked to him. It took balls to do that. She thought she didn't have anything to say, so she fucked him first, and that way she didn't have to talk, but she could still get close. Then she talked to him anyway. Then she made him talk. When he wasn't looking. When his guard was down. Very strange to hear himself talking. Who the hell did she think she was?

One day they walked to Thomas Street at noon. They had slept together twice, and they already knew war was coming. Carl's truck was broken down so the team couldn't go out. He worked on logistics all morning, reviewing maps with his team and working at the computer, developing spread sheets and timelines. His concentration was blown from just sitting there for three hours. He thought, *What the hell, I'll take a walk and surprise her.*

Julia was in the hospital that day. She was surprised and happy to see him. Happy but guarded, as if she didn't quite believe he had come on his own, so she was on the lookout for a hustle or a hidden agenda. Julia took off her white coat before they left. She was wearing a purple tank-top. Her neck was thin and graceful and her shoulders, which had already started to brown in the equatorial sun, were slender but also muscled.

The sun was strong at noon. It made you squint and sweat just from standing in it. You could feel the burn the instant you stepped out of the shade. You walked a little fast hoping to get quickly to shade but not too fast, otherwise you'd sweat profusely. *Beautiful, fragile, and tough all at the same time,* Carl thought when he glanced over at Julia.

There was a beggar on Thomas Street with no legs. He was a bald guy with very dark skin and a short scraggly beard who walked on his hands, that is, walked by using his arms as if they were crutches. He had thick dirty brown pads that he slipped his hands into and that covered the back of his fingers and his knuckles. When he wanted to move, the beggar would rock forward from his buttocks and stand, if you wanted to call it that, on the stumps of his legs, put his fists on the ground in front of him, lock his arms and shift his weight onto his elbows and hands, bend the stumps of his legs at the waist, lift his torso off the ground, and then swing his body forward between his arms, so his torso came to rest on his buttocks in front of his hands. Then he would bring his hands in front of him again and repeat the process. That way he could move along the street, slower than walking, but faster than you might think, moving at perhaps half or three-quarters the speed of an adult walking unhurriedly but deliberately in the hot midday sun.

The beggar with no legs usually sat under the awning of the Lebanese hardware store in the morning so he could appeal to the market ladies and the street kids as they walked by. He had shade until the sun reached its apex. In the afternoon the sun fell on that part of the sidewalk, and then the legless beggar would take himself to the market, or, if he could, he'd cross Thomas Street and sit in the shade of the stores on the other side, since people tended to walk on the shady side and the legless beggar preferred the shade himself.

Of course, the traffic on Thomas Street was endless at that time of the day, with one lane stacked up in either direction, and motorbikes, carts, white jitneys loaded with fifteen people in a space meant for eight; with repurposed U.S. school buses that had been painted red and purple and had air horns stuck on the front just over the driver's window; with lorries covered with blue tarps rumbling in the street, waiting for traffic to clear. All the vehicles, even the lorries, darted into the middle of the street to pass one another the moment there was a break in the oncoming traffic, though there wasn't room for three cars across. So there was a cacophony of movement, honking horns, cars, and motorbikes weaving in and around one another or coming to sudden screeching stops.

That meant no one other than boys on motorbikes could see the legless beggar when he swung himself to the edge of traffic, looking to cross the street, and no one was looking at the legless beggar when he swung himself forward to cross in front of traffic as he made his way to the other side.

So he waited each day at noon until someone on a motorbike or a taxicab noticed him, until a person of normal height came over and walked into the street or, if they were driving, parked and got out of their car, jumped in front of traffic, and stopped the flow of traffic by holding his hands outstretched, fingers apart, waving his arms and shouting. The cars and buses and trucks and motorcycles could see a man like that so they stopped. Then, they would notice the legless beggar and would wait until he rocked himself across the street. After he was across the temporary traffic cop would continue on his way or return to his vehicle, and traffic would resume its normal frenetic motion, the legless beggar now safe in the shade on the other side of the street.

As Julia and Carl turned from Hospital Street onto Thomas Street, a dusty red Honda motorbike pulled to the side of the road just past where the legless beggar was waiting to cross, and the four boys riding on it jumped off, laying the motorbike on its side as they walked into the street, their hands raised and their fingers apart.

The legless beggar scowled. He knew these boys and their tricks.

Still, the traffic stopped. The legless beggar looked right and left. If he waited, the people in the cars and trucks would grow angry at him because they did not know what he knew, and then there might not be anyone else who would stop to help for a very long time, and he would grow hot and even more thirsty in the hot sun.

So the legless man launched himself into the street, moving as fast as he could, in a legless man's imitation of running.

As soon as he entered the street the four boys waved their arms in unison, as if to say good-bye and then they ran back to the side of the street, righted their motorbike, and rode off, laughing, high-fiving, and slapping one another on the back, leaving the legless man in the middle of traffic on his own. The cars just adjacent to where the legless man had been stayed put, as they could see him clearly.

"Oh shit," Julia said. She ran into the street.

A bright orange taxicab swung into the middle of the street where a center lane might have been if there was room for it. The taxi had been stopped two cars behind the goods lorry that was stopped on the far side of the street waiting for the legless man to cross. The taxi was aimed directly at legless man who the driver still did not see, as the legless man swung himself into the taxi's path, rocking forward as fast as he possibly could and not looking left or right now, but only moving, his version of running for his life.

Julia raised one hand as she ran. She swooped down and lifted the legless beggar by the arm pits. The legless beggar threw his arms around Julia's shoulders. His torso, hanging from her neck like that, was almost as tall as Julia was, and so his legs hung just above the road surface. The orange taxicab's horn blared and the driver jammed on his breaks and skidded to a halt, just past where it would have hit and likely decapitated the legless beggar. Julia carried him back to his starting place and lowered him to the sidewalk. The driver of the orange cab raised his hand and pointed a finger as he swore, yelling at Julia although he was swearing mostly at himself. And then he merged back into his lane of traffic and drove off.

Carl raised his hands, fingers outstretched, and stood in front of the goods lorry that was still waiting for the legless beggar to pass. Julia went back into the street and raised her hands in front of the cars on her side of Thomas Street. The legless beggar entered the road and Julia walked next to him, hands outraised so everyone could see her. She walked with him until he was safely across the road.

"Jesus," Carl said when he joined Julia on the side road, "What were you thinking?

"I spent four years of residency learning not to think, and four more years of medical school learning what not to think about," Julia said. "Sometimes you shoot first and ask questions later."

"But . . ." Carl said.

"No buts," Julia said. "It's part of the package. Unself-interested advocacy. Sucks in a partnership. Sucks worse in a lover. You're never quite first even when you are. Full disclosure. I'll understand if that doesn't work for you."

"Just get better at ping-pong," Carl said.

"Don't confuse luck and skill," Julia said. "Turnabout is fair play."

Then there was a man with a beard and a white coat, his collar open, pens in the pocket of his shirt coming through a window or a door. That man knew something he didn't know.

Carl's body was picked up by a huge wave and then the wave slammed him into the rocks. Julia was swimming nearby. The wave was lifting her. And then Carl was drowning. Deep under. Needing air. No air. Some light but no air. No way to know what was up. And then another wave lifted him and slammed him into the rocks again, breaking all his ribs.

He did what the marines had told him to do. If they knew about him and they knew about the others, they had to know about Julia. Who she was and where she was. How to find her. He got suckered. He followed their orders even after he kicked up a fuss. Carl let them leave Julia. He had let them bring him home without her. He let them leave Julia behind.

Carl didn't know if she was dead or if she was alive. Maybe they didn't go after her because they knew she was dead. He was in and out of sleep. Julia, only Julia. He wanted to be thinking about a hundred other things. Check in with London. Check on David and Grace. Think about the next placement.

But Julia was everywhere, and Julia kept coming back.

The morning July sun now burst through the east-facing windows. This was America, not Africa. America, where the air-conditioning keeps you from feeling the sun's heat, but the light was undeniable.

Carl woke with a start. A part of him was missing, a part he hadn't quite yet known was there.

Carl turned on the radio, and then went to the computer. LURD was in Monrovia. MODEL was at Firestone, and there was heavy fighting in the plantation, as they both closed in on the airport from different directions. Taylor was on the run. It was only a matter of days, maybe even hours, before Taylor fled or was killed. And then there would be further descent into endless chaos, more likely than not.

He hadn't been thinking about Julia when he had been with her in Liberia. She was a diversion. Entertainment. A fact, an option, not a person. A lightweight. Good enough, from time to time. Convenient. Relief. Pretty enough, not settled in herself, lots of bad choices, good company, no real focus, someone to see after work, a break from the routine. Mutual consenting adults. Love the one you're with.

But here she was again. She was pushing him to take that kid with malaria to Buchanan. She was standing on the roof of the Land Cruiser. The way her skin looked at The Club as she talked about her work and its difficulties in the red light of the setting sun.

Julia was alone. Out there somewhere alone. Julia was scared, but she wasn't giving up, not for one single second. Somehow Carl sensed Julia's fear and isolation, which didn't make any sense. Julia was five thousand miles away, sitting in a truck between two armed men. Carl got a little short of breath, as if there was a gun stuck in his own ribs. He was waking up in a bed in Lincoln, Rhode Island. What kind of sense does that make?

There Julia was whenever Carl lifted his eyes or turned his head or stood to get a glass of water or to make coffee.

She had entered *him*. She had become part of *him*. No one asked her to come in. But there she was. He hadn't even known she was there.

And now she was gone. Someone had vacuumed up Carl's insides, and he was collapsing, his outside falling into where his inside had been.

Carl didn't think they were leaving her behind. He thought they had her too. He just went when they said go. He had called it in. They said they'd find her. They found everyone in Buchanan. But they didn't find Julia. They didn't look for her. They didn't even look. They just marched in and scooped up the people they could find, and they forgot to look for Julia. It was an accident. A drunk man hits a pedestrian he didn't see on a dark country road at night and thinks he had just hit a pothole. Julia had been left behind.

All Carl cared about was that Julia got home safe. *I want Julia home safe*, Carl thought. *I want Julia.* Carl wanted Julia. There it was. It hadn't been clear to him before. *I want Julia*. He always made damned sure he never wanted anything or anyone.

Carl wanted Julia. Simple as that. Which made everything else complicated.

Naomi had come home, to the extent Lincoln, Rhode Island, could ever count as home to anyone. They had no family left in Rhode Island. Their mother was dead. Their father was in jail in Massachusetts. West Virginia was ready to extradite him for another trial should Massachusetts ever decide to let him go. Their mother's parents had died of natural causes in Martinique in their sixties—but they were never close once their daughter had married this man they didn't understand, once she disappeared into a different world, and then just disappeared. Their father's parents were in assisted living in Brocton, near their son, whom they visited. In spite of everything. Naomi went to see them every few months. Carl never went there. Other than Naomi, he could not go near anything or anyone that had anything to do with that time or that place. Brenda, even Brenda fled back to the panhandle of Florida where her people were.

But Naomi had come back here like a homing pigeon, as if she had imprinted herself on the place instead of on people and relationships. Naomi didn't do relationships either. You form yourself around what you know. When they were small Naomi followed Carl around, playing at what Carl wanted to play at. Carl survived by detaching himself from people and places. Naomi survived by attaching herself to Carl and to this place. Carl remembered their mother better, so he could remember what love was. Naomi had somehow used her attachment to this place as their home to remember that love matters, if only someone could teach her how.

Now Naomi worked in a hospital, running a diversity program. So-called. Her life was her work. She submerged herself and went to work every day, doing work that didn't matter in a culture where nothing was real. Diversity program. We name things the opposite of what they are, but we don't fool everyone. The way they call subdivisions

"Flowing Waters Creek" or "Sky View Farms," but they aren't farms or creeks, they're subdivisions filled with tract houses. Diversity? Now sometimes the white guys in suits are gay Asian women. Our version of progress. You say the word inclusive, but the only people we include are people we know already. You change the package but the product always remains the same, as long as there is return on investment and the business model works. The rich get richer, the poor stay poor, and the shop windows get all decked out for Christmas. The common man is entertained, and no one notices who owns what, who keeps what, and who calls the shots.

She was a beauty, his sister. Present. Always present. Hiding in plain sight. His damn little sister was quite the grownup. Quite the knockout. Not as tall, darker than he was, and damn was Naomi well put together. Long hard brown hair. A business suit. And pearls. She looked just like him, they said, only she looked like she was ready to run the world.

And she brought dinner.

"Oh God," Carl said. "Pizza strips and Del's Lemonade. You trying to kill me with bad food? Finish what Charles Taylor started and failed at?"

"Could have worse," Naomi said. "I could have brought dough-boys from Iggy's. Pizza is a vegetable. Comfort food. Good for the soul. Bad for the body. The body is temporary. The soul is forever."

They sat on the deck behind Naomi's kitchen and living room next to a stream that ran in a low place, a fold in the hillside where the builders couldn't put more condos because the ground was too uneven. It was summer. The stream was reduced to a trickle, and the water was green with algae in the brackish pools. Scrub trees, black locusts, and buckeyes, with the occasional white birch and maple, grew along the stream, all spindly and with more branches than leaves. But they made enough of a screen that you couldn't quite see into the windows of the condos across the divide. You couldn't hear the breeze in the leaves, though you could imagine it. There was the constant hum of air-conditioners. Each unit had an air-conditioner that looked exactly alike and they all emitted a pitched hum that had a high and a low note that was both irritating because it was there and calming because it was so damned constant.

"Pretty crazy in Liberia?" Naomi said.

"Crazy enough," Carl said. "What's happening here?"

"That what goes around keeps coming around. Different day, same stuff, same struggle," Naomi said.

"Your love life got flares and rockets yet?" Carl said.

"I am waiting for the ultimate black man to appear in Providence, Rhode Island, take me out to dinner, and then sweep me off my feet. Or the ultimate white man," Naomi said. "And it is quiet around here."

"That's good," Carl said. "There is enough craziness in Liberia to fill the globe. We don't need no more of that craziness here."

"So what happened in Liberia? You ducked that question," Naomi said.

"I duck a lot of questions. You read the news. They got a little war on. Nasty guy running the country, which is filled with other nasty guys. Rebels from the north moving south. Rebels from the south moving north. All sorts of people with guns working both sides against the middle. They don't care who is in the way. I was in between, in the right place at exactly the wrong time. Ergo, the U.S. Marines and semper fi. I got pulled out when the going got rough. Easy for Americans. Much harder for Liberians," Carl said.

"What's next for you?"

"Maybe stay with Water for Power and head south to Central America or the Caribbean. Maybe head to someplace else, back to Africa or Asia. It's July. Too late for the GREs or the LSATs. I don't have the energy for graduate school or law school. Anyway, when you get done with school like that you have to be a college professor or a lawyer. Can you see me teaching at Brown and hitting on the sopho-mores? Not my gig."

"You could stay in Rhode Island and make some trouble here. I could use a little real family close by just because or in case of the other kind of trouble," Naomi said.

"Rhode Island? I don't think so," Carl said. "Too white. Too suburban. Too good old boy Italian and Irish for me. Though a little color and a little attitude might be good for this place. But too much history for me, Naomi. I have full faith and trust in the Plymouth County Correctional Facility, may they lock the door and throw away the key. I don't know how you do it. Stay so close by. I'm not expecting any trouble. I just don't want to be anywhere near here. Cursed ground. More for you than for me. You're what brings me back. Nothing else. What keeps *you* here?" Carl said.

"This is not about me," Naomi said. "You're welcome to stay as long as you want. If you want to drive me to work and pick me up, you can have the BMW and lose the rental."

"Now who's ducking questions?" Carl said. "Naomi, I'm going back."

"Going back where?"

"To Liberia."

"Oh, give me a break," Naomi said. "You can go back in six months when their little war is over. It took a battle group of the U.S. Navy and a landing party of the U.S. Marines to get you out. Give George Bush his due. Give it a rest."

"I don't think so. Somebody got left behind," Carl said.

"Somebody isn't your problem. That's what the State Department is for. Besides, how are you going to get there? I doubt Delta is ready when you are. Airlines don't fly into war zones. Their planes get shot down. U.S. citizens can't go there now," Naomi said.

"People get in. It's not hard to cross borders," Carl said.

"And what do you do when you get there? Assuming you can find your way across a border. Hitchhike? No rental car counter at the river you have to wade across in the middle of the night," Naomi said. "And who is somebody?"

"Just somebody," Carl said.

"Tell me more about that somebody, please. Do you have a wife and a kid stashed in a village? Or four wives?" Naomi said.

"No. It's not like that. There's a doctor. She got lifted by a militia the last day I was there. The marines left her behind. I thought they were going to get her, but then she wasn't with us at the end, when they brought everyone on board ship, and it's driving me crazy," Carl said.

"You were crazy already. This doctor is a woman, yes?" Naomi said.

"This doctor is a woman, yes," Carl said.

"And there is more to it than that?" Naomi said.

"Not much more. Some more. Very little more," Carl said.

"But enough more that you want to trade a safe, cool, dry house in Lincoln, Rhode Island, for a war zone in Liberia where you have no place being and risk you ass and your life with no viable plan and no reasonable hope of doing anything other than getting yourself killed?"

"At least nothing has changed," Carl said. "I'm the same guy. Not corrupted by success or fame."

"Change is good," Naomi said. "Especially changing away from doing things that are just stupid and dangerous. Tell me more about this doctor."

"Not much to tell. She actually spent some time in Rhode Island, at your very own hospital. Pretty pie in the sky. She likes saving little kids in the bush from dread diseases. She's good in bed. What more do you need to know?" Carl said.

"A lot of women like saving little kids. Some are even good in bed. What's her name? I like calling women by their names. Particularly women my only brother is talking about risking his life for," Naomi said.

"Julia. Julia Richmond," Carl said.

"Never heard of her."

"She was a resident."

"I never remember the residents. Big egos. Little impact. They think they are important. And color-blind. But that's another story. Why Dr. Richmond?" Naomi said.

"No why. I didn't think this was anything," Carl said. "I was thinking of it as convenient. Situational."

"Some not anything if my brother is thinking about this woman at all ten minutes after she's out of his sight. And?" Naomi said.

"No *and* either. Look, I told her some of it," Carl said.

"*We* don't even talk about it," Naomi said. "Maybe it's better she stays in Liberia."

"Not the whole thing. Not your part. I didn't say anything about you," Carl said. "We keep talking around it. My part *and* your part, I'm not sure that's so smart."

"Speak for yourself," Naomi said.

"I live in abstractions. I live in ideas, in movements, in vaguely promoting change in the lives of others halfway around the globe," Carl said. "I duck my own life."

"Get more therapy. Therapy is cheap. They threw enough at us. Liberia in the middle of a war is idiocy, not therapy," Naomi said.

"I'm done with that kind of talking," Carl said. "No one else can live your life."

"So are you in love with Dr. Richmond?"

"I don't know what love is," Carl said. "I know I love you. I loved your mother. Maybe I even loved him once, though it tears me up to admit it. This is different. I talked to her, Naomi. I can't even really talk to myself. I can't just leave her out there," Carl said.

"Let's go into the house," Naomi said. "Thank God there is no way for you to get to Liberia. I hate doctors and their egos and their stupid institutional racism. And Liberia. And things the way they are. And changing."

"Change is good, remember?" Carl said. He stood up and piled his glass and silverware on a plate. "Somebody taught me to clean up after myself."

"Change is just change," Naomi said. She opened the door. "That was your mother and your grandmother who taught you to clean up after yourself. Women who knew about cleaning and who believed that God is good."

"The god of cleaning up after yourself is good," Carl said. "My mother and my grandmother taught me that women are good, and that you better listen to them or the god of cleaning up after yourself might strike you down."

Naomi closed the sliding glass door behind them and locked it.

The air-conditioners hummed in the evening air, though they could only hear Naomi's air-conditioner now. The sun had set. Bats were emerging from corners, attics, and the crawl spaces of storage sheds. They swooped and twisted, barely visible against the dark sky. The water trickled from pool to pool, and a barn owl hooted in one of the black locust trees that lined the stream.

Chapter Six

Julia Richmond. Grand Bassa County,
Liberia. July 15, 16, and 17, 2003

THE PICKUP CLIMBED A HILL. THE GUN BARREL PUSHED DEEPER INTO JULIA'S RIBS, BUT THE pain and pressure shifted. It still hurt to breathe, but it hurt differently.

The sign at the side of the road said "Members Only." It was a small sign, near to the ground, painted in gold cursive lettering that looked elegant. There was a checkpoint at the top of the hill where the road opened into a parking lot, and two soldiers with AK-47s in fatigues and wearing red berets stood between green barriers—the ping-pong tables pulled out from near the swimming pool lay on their sides.

They were waved through the checkpoint. Two helicopters sat on the tarmac, one blue and one camouflage green. The pickup drove through the crowded parking lot, through camouflage green Hummers and troop transports, Toyota pickups, Jeep Commandos, beat-up Toyota and Honda SUVs, the pale blue Land Cruisers of the Liberian Police, and a few white UN Land Cruisers, so Julia couldn't tell who ran this place. They parked next to the building.

"You come now," Yellow Bandanna said.

The driver got out. Julia leaned away from the gun barrel. The cold steel touched her skin but wasn't jammed under her ribs now.

Then Yellow Bandanna thrust the barrel into her ribs again.

"You. Now," he said.

Julia slid her legs under the steering wheel. She used her bound hands to push herself out of the truck. Yellow Bandanna followed and closed the truck door behind him.

The boys in the truck whistled and hooted.

"Missy, missy, missy. Be my missy now," said a boy wearing pajamas, a print of little bears from a story book.

Then the boy raised his rifle and sighted down its barrel at Julia, who was three or four inches from the muzzle of the gun.

One slightest movement and it ended. Julia's heart pounded. She couldn't see the boy's face. All she could see was dark hole in the center of the barrel of that gun.

The boys in the back of the truck all stood and called to her. They leaned over the truck and put their hands all over her.

But Yellow Bandanna grabbed Julia by the collar and pushed her in front of him so that he was standing between Julia and the gun. It didn't matter. The boy kept her in his sights. Julia saw the gun aimed at her head follow her.

As Yellow Bandanna pushed her forward, Julia saw the explosion that would drive a bullet toward her. She imagined the bullet. She heard the crack of the gunshot. She saw the bullet leaving the barrel of the gun, the brief burst of flame from the end of the barrel as the bullet spewed forward, and imagined the bullet's entry through the back of her skull. Then she pictured the bullet's path as it tore through brain tissue and blood vessels until that bullet was flattened by hitting the inside of her skull, and then Julia saw the hot flattened lead destroy more brain tissue yet before it came to rest.

She stopped at the door. Her hands were bound. Yellow Bandanna pulled the metal and glass door open for her. He shoved her through with his bent right knee and another hard push at the back of her neck.

Julia saw her reflection in the glass door. Her face and arms were black from grease and ash, and her eyebrows had been singed off. Her shirt and shorts were covered with red dust. Her dirty black hair had come loose, so she looked like a hiker after two months in the woods.

Yellow Bandanna opened another door and pushed Julia inside.

Once there had been a bar, a lounge, and a television set, a place where men would come to watch the World Cup, where people sat together, drinking, talking, sometimes singing, and cheering a goal or a great defensive play. Now there were armed boys standing at the bar, armed boys lying on the floor, and a stack of gray ammunition boxes lettered with languages not English stacked next to the bar. Girls with short cropped hair but also dressed in fatigues flitted between the boys. A boom box cranked, the bass rattling the windows. The room stank of gun grease, gunpowder, sweat, beer, cigarette and pot-smoke, all mixed together. More boxes were stacked on the patio where the ping-pong table used to be. Bigger, longer boxes, painted olive green.

Someone had strung camouflage netting across a rope hung from the ceiling and that divided the big club room in half. The furniture had been pushed to one corner, to the back and left, and was all jammed together next to the big window that looked out on the swimming pool and the distant grey-green hills.

A big man in green fatigues with very dark skin, a broad face, and a broad hooked nose stood in the center of the room with a knot of men and boys around him, waiting their turn to talk.

The big man was six-two or six-three and heavyset. He was bald, dark-skinned, and self-assured, with large hands and powerful shoulders—big, not trim. He smiled when he talked—a coy, controlled smile that kept you from knowing what he was thinking. He was in charge and he knew it. He wanted to make sure that everyone else knew that as well.

They waited their turn.

The big man spoke to each soldier-boy, each of whom peeled off from the group as soon as the big man was finished. Julia thought she heard American English, but the voices ran together and she couldn't be sure.

Then the big man turned to Julia and Yellow Bandana.

"What treasure have you brought me today, Daniweil?" the big man said. American English. Midwest accent. He moved his eyes from Yellow Bandanna to Julia, looking her up and down.

"Surprised?" the big man said.

"Chicago?" Julia said.

"Well done. St. Paul first. Then Chicago. My parents are Liberian. Born here. Grew up in the States," the big man said. "Make yourself comfortable. You aren't going anywhere quick-quick."

The big man reached into Julia's top pocket and pulled out her cell phone. He laid the cell phone in his palm as if he were holding a bug that he wanted to inspect. He closed his fist around the cell phone and crushed it. When he opened his hand the pieces fell one by one to the ground.

Then he pulled a hunting knife with the word "Winchester" engraved on its blade from his belt. He lifted Julia's hands and jabbed the blade between them. Then he cut the cloth that bound her hands together with a single swift jerk, all while looking straight into her eyes, from which she did not turn away.

He held both her hands in one of his. His hand was twice the size of hers, warm and powerful. He dropped her left hand but kept her right hand in his grip.

"Dr. Richmond, I presume?" the big man said. "The cell phone wasn't much good anyway. No service here. No service in Buchanan either, anymore."

"Who are *you*? What am I doing *here*?" Julia said.

"Sorry about your men and the Land Cruiser. War sucks. But it sucks worse if you lose."

"What are you doing here? Who are you?" Julia said.

"Call me Jonathan. I'm the reason you're still alive. You are a pediatrician working at Buchanan Hospital for Merlin. From California. Trained at Brown. I know everything about you, but you don't even know my name or who is who in this war."

"I don't pay a lot of attention to politics."

Jonathan turned Julia's hand over in his, and then pulled her forward, twisting as he did so, so that her hand and arm were under his. Then he walked with Julia to the bay windows, walking arm in arm like a couple coming onto the dance floor for the next dance at a charity ball.

"What am I doing here?" Julia said. "I need to be in Buchanan. They need me at the hospital now."

"You were in the wrong place at the wrong time. I'm now figuring out how to turn lemons into lemonade. You're the lemon. I'm the lemonade."

"And Chicago?"

"Forget about Chicago. Don't let the accent fool you. Maybe you noticed. I'm not Uncle Sam," Jonathan said. "Or Uncle Tom." He stretched his arm out in the light and turned it from side to side.

"I'm not your friend or your babysitter. I've got a war to win, and I've got to figure out how I can use your inconvenient presence here to win it. At the moment, I'm wondering if a battalion of your marines are going to appear at my doorstep looking for you. Your marines will land on the beach in Buchanan tomorrow and evacuate Americans and Europeans who are here with NGOs. They just might come looking for you. I'd much rather they didn't arrive on my doorstep unannounced. But I don't think they know you're here."

"I need to be back in Buchanan," Julia said.

"Don't you worry about Buchanan," Jonathan said. "There's nothing you can do in Buchanan now. Buchanan is overrun. Your hospital isn't a hospital now, or won't be one soon. Nothing pretty will happen there."

"Can you get me to the beach?"

"Can but won't. I'm not here for your convenience. You aren't of any use to me on the beach or with those marines. You may be of some use to me here later. Deal with it, missy. You are not in charge anymore, and the sooner you understand that the simpler your life will be. This is Liberia. Liberia, Africa. Not Liberia, New York, LA, Chicago, or Providence, Rhode Island."

A helicopter drowned out all speech as it landed. The wind from its rotor shook the roof and the ground. Its engine whistled and then shut down.

"Plenty-plenty woman palaver," Jonathan said "Daniweil, pu she upstairs." *Too much talking to a woman. Put her out of the way someplace.*

"I'll be back," Jonathan said. He walked out a side door. Julia heard him shout and then curse. Yellow-Bandanna, Daniweil, was standing behind her.

Now Julia was alone.

It had once been a linen closet.

Daniweil pushed Julia down the hall from the bar to the kitchen. There was a door just past the kitchen, between the men's and the women's changing rooms, big enough to walk into. But not big enough to lay down in. The shelves were empty. There were no windows. No chair. Nothing. It looked for a moment like Daniweil was going to leave Julia's hands untied. Then he thought the better of it, turned her toward him, and retied her hands in front of her, loosely enough so she could move them against one another but tightly enough that any movement made the cloth tight on the wrist she moved.

He shoved Julia inside and her flank hit the shelving. She grasped a shelf with one hand to keep herself from falling over.

Then Daniweil closed and locked the door. And disappeared.

Only darkness. A line of light peeked under the door, and there were thinner lines of light around the door.

It was a few steps to the door. A cold metal handle. There was no play in the handle, but there were a few millimeters of give in the door, front and back. You could make it rattle. Pushing hard down on the handle didn't move it. Slamming it with the back of your hand didn't move it either. It wasn't going to break off. The mechanism wasn't cheap Chinese metal that would break just from her weight.

The room slowly developed a hint of dimension. Julia began to see the sides of the lower shelving. The light seeped three or four feet back.

The door opened inward, so it wouldn't pop, even if she was big enough to burst the frame and she just wasn't close to big enough for that.

Carl was dead. He had been killed at that checkpoint. Carl, Sister Martha, the kiddo, the kiddo's mother, her mother, and Carl's driver. All dead. One RPG shell. Zig might hear by bush telegram even if no one made it out. Someone in a village saw the smoke from the Land Cruiser. The word goes village to village, cell phone to cell phone. Person to person when the cell phones are dead. Word travels in the bush. There are eyes. Maybe Zig had time to call the ministry or Merlin. Maybe.

Sounds. Voices. Distant. From above and through the door. The voices from above were louder, which meant the closet had a dropped ceiling, Sound travels better in the space above a ceiling than it does through the walls. A shaking. A bigger truck coming or going. But no tire sounds, no crunching or hissing. The parking lot and trucks weren't close. Distant slammed car or truck doors. Clear enough but distant. Across doors and through walls. Perhaps a window in the kitchen. The window in the women's changing room looked out to the side. The window in the men's looked out the back. Soft engine clatter and buzz. A single engine, droning.

Bill Levin might eventually figure she was gone, but that might take weeks and he wouldn't know what to do or who to call. Her mother and everyone in California had written her off the moment she set foot in Africa. If they got a ransom demand it would occur to them that Julia was missing but not until then. *I'm alone,* Julia thought. *How did it all go south so fast?*

She had value. She had to have value. Otherwise they wouldn't have kept her alive. Something to trade.

Carl was dead and Sister Martha, the baby, the baby's mother, Carl's driver, and the mother's mother were all dead. There wasn't time to mourn. Julia had to focus, the way she did when a code came in to the ED. You can't let what you might feel stand in the way of your thought process or choices. *I'm trained to focus in a crisis. To take my own pulse first. To keep my head,* Julia thought. *I can think my way out. Bad things happen. You can't let yourself get distracted.*

The smell of sweat. Her sweat. Dank, bitter, and sweet all at once. Old tennis shoe moldy.

They were not an item. Julia was never going to get to be an item. Relationships weren't her thing. She didn't know how to listen. She had nothing interesting to say. When someone got close they could see her for who she was. They could see she was empty, that she had no compass, no drive, and no new ideas. They could see how she drifted from place to place, how all she ever did was follow directions, how all she ever had to do was stand in line, and how she got promoted by just for taking tests and waiting her turn.

She was an American doctor so it was risky to keep her. She'd attract attention. But she was also a bargaining chip. The big man, that Jonathan, had said it. The marines were coming. They might come for her. They also might not come.

Footsteps. Sudden, dull, and then gone. Concrete floor. Wood vibrates. No vibration.

The very faint rumble and hiss of a jet, high up.

Carl had changed, was changing. They were not an item, but he had turned to her in an interesting way in the last few days, as if he saw something in her and felt something, as if he was starting to feel what she felt. Not when they slept together the first time. She had felt it then, but there was always a huge distance between what she felt and how she acted, as if the world wasn't ready for her to feel like that. She had frightened him away, doing what she always did, missing the cues and trying to get to close too soon. She had fucked him too soon. She always did that. She slept with men who she thought would never like her right away before they figured out that there was nothing much there besides a body to be pummeled. She never mastered the art of getting close to someone. A little talking. A little kissing. A little bit at a time, slowly getting closer and closer, testing each other, asking, is this someone I can like? Is this someone I can trust? Is this someone who can be part of me? She jumped into bed with Carl because she didn't think she could ever be close to anyone. But it happened anyway. They were getting close. In spite of her emotional clumsiness. The real closeness had just begun. They were the only option for one another in Buchanan, but it was more than that. He started to come by on his own. He was sweet, very sweet. And strong. And smart. And able. He was starting to let his guard down and be with her when he was with her. And now he was gone. Julia would never get it right.

She turned and measured by putting one foot in front of the other, her tied hands in front of her. Nine of her feet to the back wall of shelving. When her hands touched the back wall, her forearms rested on a shelf, in almost to her elbow. Maybe sixteen inches of shelving. Six shelves. Floor to ceiling. Six of her feet from side to side.

Rape crisis training, years ago: California, outside, in Palo Alto, in the sunshine. Lock your arms. Raise one hip. Twist out to the side. Put your feet on his hips and then kick into his face, under the chin, and into his groin, and then run.

She walked from back to front, and then turned and walked from front to back, marching in a tiny oval, eight of her normal steps around.

She counted steps. At 40, Torwon and Charles and the Land Cruiser on fire. At 110, the popping and rattling of the guns as they went through villages after that. At 157, Carl, his face when she pushed him about the malaria kid. Then his face close to hers when he was on top of her, when she could feel him and how he condensed into his body, driving into her, but how she couldn't see him. Then his face and his eyebrows when he lay next to her in bed, talking. His eyebrows had suddenly become large and hard, and shaded his eyes, so she couldn't see them as clearly as she wanted to. Then Sister Martha and the kiddo in the Health Center, the soft brown light from the window on the brown still face of that child, breathing so fast, the child's whole self condensed into its breathing in just the same way as Carl had condensed into his body. Two hundred and thirty steps.

You get away first. She'd get shot if they saw her run.

Somewhere between seven and eight hundred steps she lost count. She had counted to fifty too many times. Seven hundred and forty-nine. Seven hundred and fifty. Seven hundred and fifty-one. Seven hundred and forty-two. Seven hundred and fifty.

Who knows I'm missing? Julia thought. *Carl might know if Carl is alive, but he is dead. Sister Martha is dead if Carl is dead. Zig will know if Zig survives the night, but then what? How long will the phones work? Zig could get the satellite phone at Merlin, if Zig lives and can get to Merlin before Merlin is overrun.*

How can I make a life for myself that lets me love and be loved and also build a world in which others can love and be loved, all at the same time? Julia thought. *Assuming I ever get out of this mess.*

The light under the door began to fade. Julia sat on the floor against the rear wall of the linen closet, her back resting on the first shelf, her arms around her drawn-up knees, and her head resting on them. The light became very dim and red. It was the light from an illuminated exit sign in the hall—battery run. The batteries ran down after the generator was shut off.

Julia slept.

Then she had to pee. She stood. The light was still faint and red under the door.

No voices. No car doors. No engine clatter. The generator was off for the night. The red lights from the exit signs would fade before dawn as the batteries ran low. There might be flashlights.

She walked the oval. Urgent now. She squeezed her pelvis in. Then she counted. A hundred and fifty-seven steps. Then she just walked. Waiting was useless. They were not going to arrive at a rest stop on the highway. You might wait for a rest stop. You might wait until you go into a building and find a ladies' room. There was nothing to wait for here.

She pounded on the door. *Why does nothing in Africa ever work?* Julia thought. *What am I doing here? Why can't I ever, ever get it right? They are all dead, Carl and Sister Martha and that child. It is God's will, which is what they say in Liberia and all across Africa whenever tragedy strikes. We must put our faith in God.*

"Hey, hello!" Julia yelled. She pounded on the door, and rattled it, and pounded again, and cried, "Hey, Hello! Hello! Anybody there?" over and over.

No one came.

I can't trust my body, Julia thought. *I can't trust my mind. I can't trust anybody. What good is trying?*

Then finally, desperate to pee, she called out, "Pee-pee! Hey Hello! Pee-pee." She called again and again.

A weak, inconstant yellow light faded in under the door. Footsteps. The door opened. A weak yellow flashlight exploded into her eyes. She backed away. A thud. The door closed and locked. When she went to grab the door handle and rattle it again, she tripped on something new at her feet, which thudded and rattled as it fell. It was a bucket, a plastic bucket with a cold metal wire handle.

She stood it up, fumbled with her pants, and used the bucket. It wasn't perfect. It was dark. Nothing to wipe with. But her body let her be.

I want to live, Julia thought, *and I want to love someone, and I want someone to love me, and I want to try to make a world in which people can love and be loved, because without that kind of world no one can love at all. I don't know how to do any of this. Without us all together, men with guns will come and destroy the possibility of love itself. And love makes life real.*

She slid the bucket with her feet, slowly and carefully, under the shelving on the right side of the closet, so she wouldn't trip on it when she paced.

Now the closet smelled of urine, sweet and sharp at once, and of sweat.

Then Julia sat and wrapped her arms around her knees again and laid her head on her knees. The floor was hard. Too hard. She wept quietly. No one could see.

She slept again, in and out.

Chapter Seven

Terrance Evans-Smith. Kingston, Pawtucket,
and Providence, Rhode Island. July 18, 2003

THE WIND FROM THE OCEAN WHISTLED AS IT RATTLED THE METAL WALLS OF THE CAVERNOUS building. Terrance felt the breeze. It cooled Terrance's skin. It was hot here too in summer. The moist air felt something like the moist air coming off the ocean at home, but the days here were almost twice as long, and long days meant there wasn't as much time for the air to cool in darkness. The hot nights wear you down, because all you can do all night is walk. Walk the perimeter with a flashlight looking at the fence. Walk the buildings first outside and then inside. Clock in and clock out. Sit at the desk in the gatehouse in the morning. Raise and lower the crossing gate for each car as they show their ID. No matter how many weeks he had been doing this job, his mind still shut down in the middle of the night. He slept for an hour in the bathroom, his chin on his chest, sitting on the toilet.

It was just a night watchman job. Ma thought it was the moon. She thought he came home and slept all day.

Terrance took off his silly hat and put it on the top shelf of his locker. The he took off his uniform, which was too big for him, and hung it beneath the hat. Stupid hat. He only wore it in the morning when he was sitting in the gatehouse. Stupid uniform. The uniform made him meaningless, made him just like everyone else. Meaningless. No man. Nowhere. Not strong.

No one here understood the power of the early morning, when you can see but not be seen. Invisible. Invincible.

The white people watch at dusk. Their police cars prowl the quiet streets at night. People listen just after dusk, some on their porches taking in the cool evening air. Most sit in front of their TV sets, the colors from the TV washing the rooms, the people in their living rooms mesmerized, decapitated, paraplegic, comatose but still awake enough to hear.

But no one is awake in the morning just after dawn. No one sees anything just after dawn. They stumble out of bed, shower, and get their coffee, but all they think about is getting themselves and their kids out of the house. You are invisible. Powerful. And back, ready to roam again.

Terrance had an old Ford Taurus, mostly red, with one green fender off another car. Ma gave him the ninety-nine dollar down payment, and then he made the loan payments out of his pay envelope. The car cost thirty-nine dollars a week. There was no chance that the car would outlive the car payment. Too much white smoke came out of the tailpipe when he drove on 95. The engine rattled when he accelerated, but the damn thing got him back and forth, and it had lasted two months. It wasn't an invisible car, not among the quiet houses, so the car went back and forth from the house to work and from work to the house again, evidence of his regular life.

But regular wasn't much. He had once been king. They owned the streets. People begged and whimpered when they stood in a house or drove an SUV off the road and into the middle of a village, smashing the market stalls as they came on. There was blood. Plenty-plenty blood. Bodies ripped apart. Blood made him invisible. *Invincible.*

Terrance drove slowly on Davisville Road. He passed acres of houses. First the old base housing—grey, shingled, and needing paint. Then he passed some two- and three-story barracks and some ramshackle single-story houses that no one arranged into a neighborhood, scattered on the land like grass seed thrown down on dark earth. Then you come to the developments that were just outside where the base used to be, the squat brick- and stone-faced ranch houses, with bushes lining the sidewalks and pickups that had ladder racks in the driveways and delivery trucks parked on the streets at night. There were brown people mixed in among the white people in the cars on

Davisville Road and mowing the lawns, and those people meant he didn't completely stand out—except that he was even darker and the car was old and so beat-up.

Some of the cars in the driveways or parked on the street were good enough to take. They were money. But Quonset was just two miles away to his work and too close for comfort.

Terrance turned onto Post Road. He drove for about a mile and then turned to cruise the big old colonial houses that sit on the hill overlooking the harbor in East Greenwich. Doctors' houses. Lawyers' houses. Bankers' houses. Financial planners' houses. Houses with impeccable paint, with three- or five-car garages, with gatehouses and swimming pools and tennis courts. You study these places, the people who come in and out in the mornings, the painted vans that bring workmen—the landscapers and the plumbers and the electricians, the painters and the plasterers and the pest-control people, the lumberyard trucks, FedEx and UPS trucks, garbage trucks, recycling trucks, cable TV trucks, and the tree trimmers, their large green trucks pulling orange chippers. The men driving the trucks wear uniforms or baseball hats or hard hats, and there is often a pair of thick leather gloves wedged on the windshield on the driver's side. The men in the trucks are mostly white men, but some are brown. The brown men often look uncertain, as though they are waiting for someone to tell them they have come to the wrong place or are here at the wrong time.

Ma didn't know his life. She dressed nice, she went to work every day, she came home to her place with the screen door hanging off and cleaned it. Every other Saturday she went to the fish market on Lonsdale Avenue where they do Western Union, and from there she sent money home. She had her job and her world where they tell her what to do and how to do it. She existed by following the rules. Just existed.

But Terrance had lived. Lived large. Ranged free. When you live large you do what you want when you want to do it. When you live large you take what you want. When you live large you are who you want to be. They don't tell you what you can't do, they tell you to do more and to take more, and they tell you ways to be bigger and stronger. Old ways. Secret ways. Things people here don't know anything about. You put a red thread around each wrist and a blue thread around your neck. You never eat pumpkin and fuck three times every day, right at dawn and noon and nightfall. You tattoo your right arm with the picture of a black monkey, just below the shoulder. You take a small bone from a dead man's hand and hang it from your belt. You always carry the claw of a leopard. You drink the cane wine and take all the pills they give you, because pills make strength. When you go out, if there is enemy you dress like a woman, so you disappear and the bullets can't find you. You take your women and smear them with leh, with white clay, from the face to the waist and that lifts them above the earth, so the bullets can't find them. You find a big man who is strong enough to cut out the hearts of the living and brave enough to eat that heart while it is still beating. The big man is so strong that nothing ever comes near you, so no harm will ever come to you. You fly above the earth, and the enemy runs away, because they know you are coming, and they are afraid.

Terrance swung left, back onto Post Road above the water to his right, behind a line of condominiums and expensive-looking apartment houses, next to the railroad tracks. Then the houses started coming closer together, the sides of the road clogged with small stores and doctors' offices, and the ocean disappeared as he climbed a hill. The road dropped into a congested place stuffed with buildings and stores, and then split, shunting him off to the right. He followed the new road, which was straight and flat and ran through miles of fast-food joints and dry cleaners—as ticky-tacky as the houses on the hill were polished and elegant. Then he turned off to drive among the acres of ranch houses and split-levels, some of which had RVs parked outside, on streets that all looked the same. There were school buses and crossing guards and many straight roads, but these were roads no one walked on. They were streets that had cars parked on the side of the road. You could park a car on one street, and no one would notice you if it was dark, but by day you would stand out just by walking on the street, even if it was early morning.

The streets took him back to the larger road. The larger road took him to the airport. Then he drove slowly north on the highway, nursing the car in the right-hand lane. Then home to the place with the broken screen door.

Terrance slept for an hour, maybe two.

When he woke, he put on a clean orange tee shirt, a Patriots cap turned backward, and big sunglasses with orange brown lenses, and then put headphones around his neck. Tool belt under the tee shirt. The hat and the glasses and the headphones, they made him invisible. Strong. He put the leopard's claw in his pocket and closed the torn screen door behind him.

The man who bought the cars was off Broad near the port, in an old brick mill that had a parking lot littered with bent soda cans and used diapers, used condoms, old needles, and broken glass.

Terrance's mother's people were from St. John's River. They were Bassa people who lived on the east bank of the river. They fished for tilapia, which they dried and put away in storehouses, and which kept them nourished in the rainy season. They grew bananas, cassava, pineapples, and yams. In St. John's River mangoes grew wild and fell from the trees just before the rainy season. Or you could climb the trees and shake the mangoes down, but the trunks were fat and the bark was slimy, particularly after it rained, and once one of the cousins fell from the tree and did not get up.

He lived next to the river for four seasons. His mother finished college and had come home to Buchanan after the first man sent her away, because the first three were girls and they all died. He came to live with his mother and the new man in Buchanan. The new man had three women and twelve children, and Terrance's mother walked proudly with him on Thomas Street when he was small, haggling with the cloth merchant and the Lebanese hardware man and the stalls where they sold pots and pans. His mother walked slowly and haggled slowly, without buying, to show him and her new belly to the world.

Then the war that killed Doe came, and his mother sent him to be with her people on the river, and she went off to America. He was on the river a few years and started school.

His mother sent money for his school fees and sent him school books and school clothes—brown pants and a bright yellow shirt. The students walked many miles to the school, so in the morning the paths and roads were dotted with brown pants and yellow shirts, as all the students walked to the school, which was painted white with blue trim and had a white and blue wall around it and a field to play football. There were many children in each form. They sat on the ground or on seats made from the trunks of rubber trees. You could see the river from the school, and you could also see the people in the dugout boats pulling in the nets that caught the fish they dried in the hot midday sun.

Then the war came back. Terrance was smaller than the others, so when they came through the school they took the others first. They came back a few months later and took him. They cut away his school clothes, and gave him pink and blue pajamas to wear. They taught him the things he needed to know to be a fighter, a man, the commander of the streets, and the ruler of the bush.

Ma was in America. Then there was no war again, and they, the people who ruled the world, had no more enemy to kill, and they were hungry. ECOMOG was running Buchanan then, and ECOMOG kept them from taking what they needed. He camped with his unit on the river delta near the iron smelter. They lived on what ECOMOG was letting the UN bring them, which was not living at all. His mother's second man came and found him with his crew in Buchanan, between the battles, when they were hungry, laying around and waiting for more war.

One day the second man brought him jeans and a tee shirt and a thin, blue plastic grocery bag of mangoes that were bruised and soft, the kind of mangoes that the wind shakes from the trees in St. John's

River, the kind he used to leave for the insects and the skinks. But you could still eat these. His mother's second man came back three days later and brought a cell phone. His ma said come. He was hungry, so he came. The others had started to vanish, to go back to their people in the bush. He went to his people first. They got him clothes and papers and put him on an airplane that he flew in the sky.

In America he slept all day and roamed at night, remembering. Then his ma find him a place to be at night, and then he sit at a desk wearing a blue monkey suit that was too big for him and walked the grounds with a flashlight all night.

Terrance opened the door of the Taurus, and then thought the better of it.

There was a bus into Providence and another bus that ran down Broad Street into Cranston. If he got off on Broad just past 95, no one would see him at all. Dark skin, young and thin, another kid hanging around the high school. Didn't matter that it was summer and ninety-five degrees at 11:00 a.m. The streets over there were filled with thin black kids with backwards baseball hats, sunglasses, and lots of bling.

The thing about a bus is, you sit high over the street, like you own it, like you can fly, and if you sit in the back and stretch yourself out you stay above the earth where the bullets can't find you. One little way to be strong and invisible in America. Almost. Not really strong. Mostly invisible.

He swung out of the second bus about an hour later. The bus hissed as he left it, the air coming out of the hydraulic system that raised and lowered the street side of the bus for people who were old and couldn't climb the steps. The bus hissed even though Terrance was the only person getting out or coming on. He was off and walking before the side of the bus dropped to the level of the curb, only to rise again as it pulled away.

On Broad was a good place. He had trouble here once when he couldn't see who was on the street, when that man chased him. He had outrun trouble that time. Now he was quicker, and he knew to go in the middle of the day, when he could see who was coming. He was quick-quick. Invisible. Powerful. Invincible.

There were cars in the parking lot at Classical and cars in the parking lot just across the street. One or two SUVs but mostly small old Hondas and Fords and banged up Toyota Corollas.

He walked south on Westminster. There was an old office building across the street and a restaurant supply store at street level, its windows filled with stacks of pots and pans and steam tables. The police headquarters were a few blocks away, but the police paid little attention to these streets. They seemed to think their very presence was enough to keep people like Terrance away.

Too much traffic on Westminster itself. He was quick-quick and could be in and gone in a moment but better to be in and out in a place where nobody was driving on the street.

He walked west on Westminster down a hot long block thinking to walk away from the police headquarters. Then he crossed the street and doubled back.

There was a red RAV on a side street.

He would be quick-quick. It was a cheap RAV, with nothing fancy on it—no power windows, no power seats, and no electronic locking ignition, but it had those letters. 4WD. The letters he needed. Money in the bank.

The lock was the old kind, the kind you could pull out as a unit with a one-hand yank if you had a lever. Once the lock was out, the door opened, and you either popped the ignition off the column and crossed the wires or fished the wires under the dash and crossed them. Fishing the wires was a neater job, because then you could get keys made later once you had the car off the street. That way no one would have to rebuild the steering column, and that was the way to go if the car was staying in the U.S.

But popping the lock was okay if the car was going out of the country or was being parted out. It's easier to pop the lock if you are working in daylight, because you can pop it while you sit in the driver's seat. If you sit in the driver's seat you look like you belong there. Anyone walking or driving by would think it was your car and you were just getting ready to put the key in the ignition. In order to fish the wires, you have to lay on your back under the steering wheel, so fishing the wires is better to do at night in a parking lot or a driveway where someone driving by isn't going to see your feet hanging out in the street.

There was a car alarm though. There were always car alarms. No one pays attention to them. You can pop the hood and pull the wire of a car alarm in about ten seconds if you know what you are doing, and by then everyone thinks it is someone else's alarm regardless of which car you hit.

He stood sideways and pressed his body against the back door, so you couldn't see his hands if you made the right turn from Cranston Street and were driving by. The lock was out of the door in a half second, the door opened and he was inside, as the DOO-IPPP, DOO-IPPP from the car alarm shattered the street. He popped the hood using the lever next to the seat, hopped out, went to the front of the car, pulled a wire cutter from his belt, and cut the wires going to the car alarm with two quick jerks.

The alarm fell silent after just five or six DOOO-IPPPs, about as much time as it takes a guy in a business suit to find his keys in his pocket and remember the right button to hit.

Then he was sitting in the driver's seat with the door closed, and no one walking by could tell he was anyone other than a man in a car sitting in the driver's seat.

He popped the ignition lock on the column, using a bezel, a tool that slips into the slot where the key goes, locks itself from the inside, and settles two bars against the steering column, far enough away from the key cylinder to keep from blocking its movement out of the steering column, but close enough to give you leverage. Once the bezel is in place, one hard twist of the handle and the key cylinder pops out. It's a hard, twisting motion, all in the wrist, like gutting a fish or breaking the neck of a chicken.

There was a red and a blue wire soldered to the lock cylinder. He cut the wires with a wire cutter, stripped their ends with a flick of his wrist, crossed the wires, and hit the gas with his right foot.

The car started.

He gunned the engine and dropped it into gear, and then gunned it again as he swung it around, a quick u-ey back to Cranston Street.

The light was red, but there was no traffic going west, so he paused for just another instant and gunned the engine once more. Flying high. Invincible.

The RAV made a smooth screeching right turn onto Cranston Street, and then he hit the gas.

It hadn't taken sixty seconds from the moment Terrance saw the car to the moment he was in it and driving west on Cranston Street. There was no one in America and no one in the world who could tell he was any different from any other black man in his twenties driving a car down a road in the middle of the day.

He was invisible. Invincible. Invulnerable. Able to leap over tall buildings in a single bound.

Chapter Eight

Carl Goldman. Lincoln and Providence,
Rhode Island. July 18, 2003

THE PHONES FIRST.

Merlin was useless. They knew nothing. The compound in Buchanan had been overrun. The home office in London was trying to raise anyone who might still be in Buchanan but the cell phones weren't working—and there had never been any landlines. The hospital had been overrun as well, and pillaged. It wasn't clear who was in control of what. They knew it wasn't safe to move around. They believed MODEL was the dominant force in Buchanan, but Taylor's men—and boys—were still active in pockets across Grand Bassa and Bong Counties, fighting for territory, shooting up the villages, raping and maiming and pillaging as they went. No one knew who was where. No one knew who was alive and who was dead. No one knew what was going to happen next. There was nothing to do. Eventually one big man would emerge and quiet the countryside. Then the guns and RPGs would go back into the wooden boxes and be buried again in the bush or at the beach, ready for the next round.

Carl tried the resources he knew in country. The U.S. embassy in Monrovia was worthless. USAID, less than worthless—they'd all left with the marines. Carl tried the few cell phone numbers he had in the memory of his phone—Zig and David, a few people at the Ministry of Health, a couple at USAID in country, others at the embassy, but it was the same all over. Nothing. The person you are trying to reach is unavailable. Or the repeating buzz of a busy signal, with each pulse hitting like the shock from an electric fence. Or the sound of a ring, over and over and over again, as if there was one telephone, set on a table in the middle of a huge empty auditorium or soccer stadium—the phone ringing alone, with no one to answer.

The ocean was now a brick wall. Carl couldn't see over it. Julia was a grain of sand on a beach in a hurricane.

Carl was sitting in Lincoln, Rhode Island, in a condominium complex, listening to the birds, the chattering of the lawnmowers, and the whine of the leaf blowers.

Julia was alone in Liberia, stranded someplace in the middle of hell.

The State Department next. Dial one if. Dial two if. He got an automated attendant at the Bureau of Consular Affairs and then got the Africa Desk. Same drill as three days ago over the satellite phone. Very different tone. She was still missing? There had been a military evacuation in that area. The Privacy Act prohibits us from sharing information about U.S. citizens. We hope she is safe and will contact you soon. You were with her in Liberia? The military operation has been successfully completed. All U.S. citizens in that area have been evacuated. I will make a note of the information you are offering for the file. One of our analysts may contact you at a later date for further information. Thank you for calling the State Department of the United States of America.

But there was a guy. Julia talked about a guy. A teacher. A mentor. Something like that. A guy who kept Julia's car for her while she was overseas. In Providence, Rhode Island. She e-mailed with him. Maybe he had news.

He was a doctor at a hospital. Robert something. Jewish kind of name. Maybe. Julia did kids. Maybe a pediatrician. Julia did the emergency room. Maybe in the emergency room. There are hundreds of doctors in Rhode Island. Maybe a thousand or two. But not hundreds of thousands. Should be findable.

Carl sat at Naomi's computer and opened the Yellow Pages in the phone book. He looked back and forth from one to the other. There were about ten pages of doctors in the Yellow Pages. About half a page of pediatricians. Emergency rooms. No emergency room doctors. Six Roberts in pediatricians. Four with Jewish sounding names. Pretty thin.

The hospital's website was better. Pictures and bios and e-mail addresses. In Pediatrics, lots of women. Four Roberts. Nothing for sure. In Emergency Medicine, fewer women. Williams and Roberts, Lawrences and a Dan and a Gary and a Francis and a couple of Brians. None of the Roberts fit though. Mostly young guys or guys with Irish names. A couple of the Williams, a Gary and a Dan had Jewish names. Those were all pretty young as well. But then there was an older William; William Levin. Pediatric Emergency Medicine. Global Health. Guy in his sixties.

William Levin. Old guy with white hair. Phone number. E-mail address. Long shot. A long shot is better than no shot at all.

Carl called. Voice mail of a secretary. He left a message. Then he sent an e-mail. Maybe this Dr. William Levin had news.

Then he called Delta. And Lufthansa. Kenya Airlines and South Africa Air. No they weren't flying into Liberia. Air Morocco—not flying into Liberia either. Service temporarily suspended. There were flights to Accra, Conakry, and a twice-a-week flight into Abidjan. Freetown was still too crazy, and even Conakry was a crapshoot. The roads to the border were anything goes roads. You could talk yourself to the border, and you could walk across a border. But a guy alone on that frontier is not smart. Not smart at all, even if you are desperate. Desperate does not equal stupid. Or suicidal. It didn't add up yet.

He checked his e-mail again. You never know. Maybe the Levin guy would get back to him. Maybe Julia had found some way out.

Médecins Sans Frontières. The Doctors Without Borders guys. They were in Africa. They were in Liberia. Maybe they knew something.

Carl checked his e-mail again.

It was 7:00 p.m. in Paris. The Médecins Sans Frontières website was for fundraising—pictures of kids and villages and white people in white tee shirts with their backs to the camera. Carl knew that drill. He sent an e-mail and would call Paris in the morning.

He needed to clear his head. None of this made sense. *Maybe I'll take a walk*. He got halfway through the kitchen before he turned back. And then he started to pace. Kitchen to the computer in the dining room. Dining room back to the kitchen.

It was past midday and hot outside. The air-conditioners were buzzing away. He walked into the living room. The red rental car was across the parking lot. The air was shimmering above the asphalt.

The computer pinged.

There was an e-mail.

Chapter Nine

Julia Richmond. Grand Bassa
County, Liberia. July 18, 2003

THEN THERE WAS LIGHT UNDER THE DOOR AGAIN. DISTANT VOICES. THE RATTLE OF AN engine. Car doors thudding closed. Another plane overhead.

Julia's mouth was dry. She stood and paced. And counted. And lost the count after about 250-something steps. The numbers always disappeared after 50, jumbling together. She needed to pay more attention, to keep her focus.

She needed to eat. Were they going to bring something to eat? To bring something to drink? If it was morning she had last eaten a day ago, at the health center. A cup of muddy coffee and some trail mix.

They might remember. You need to drink to live. She pounded on the door. No one came.

Julia imagined Carl, sitting at a computer in his compound, looking for news of her. Calling people. Trying to get help.

That was silly. Carl was dead. Sister Martha was dead. The kid with malaria was dead. She rattled the door and tried to jam the handle down again, but it didn't break.

No one came.

She pounded on the door again.

No one came.

"Feed me! I need water!" Julia yelled. "Daniweil! Jonathan! Water!" Julia yelled again. "Daniweil! Jonathan! Fuck you all!"

No one came.

They owed her water. She deserved water. No one should be treated like this. Then she sat down next to the bucket of her urine and wrapped her arms around her knees. There might not be water.

Every day of her life there had been people around. Good people and bad people. Mostly pretty average people who never quite lived up to Julia's expectations. Those people had lives that were pretty average. Lots of compromises. People who lived together and didn't love one another. People who were crappy to their kids. People who had inappropriate expectations of one another. Maybe they didn't pay attention. Maybe they had crappy values. Maybe they just wanted stuff—houses and cars and prestige, to be popular, whatever that was. To make money. People who spent their days in meetings where nothing was accomplished. People who sucked up to their bosses and tried to intimidate their co-workers. Some guy wanted a corner office, and that was his whole life. Some secretary wanted to fuck a manager, because she thought people would think she was brazen and free, and then she talked herself into believing the manager would leave his wife and kids for her, and she'd get the house with the swimming pool. Sometimes a guy who was a manager would leave his wife and kids, because he liked fucking his secretary and wanted to be able to fuck her whenever he felt like it, even at lunch. None of that mattered. It was all okay. It was all better than dying in a linen closet in the middle of Liberia—a place no one knew existed. The people at home were all people, and even if they were stupid and crass, they were around enough to keep one another from dying of thirst, from starving, from getting raped or slashed open by drug crazed man-boys who were hopped up by stupid African warlords, themselves made insane by impossible dreams of lust, power, money, and sex.

"Water! I need water!" Julia yelled. "Daniweil! Jonathan! Water!" Julia yelled. She yelled again and again. The light under the door was grey and strong, not red and weak. It was daytime. They could hear her, damn them.

If I'm going to die here, I'm going to die on my feet, not on my knees, Julia thought. *I'm going to be dead a long time. I'm going to die fighting to live.*

She rattled the door again and she kept rattling it, rattling, and then yelling. She took breaks to walk. Three paces up. One to the side. Three paces back. One to the side.

It wasn't working. Julia felt alone and she felt abandoned and she felt impotent. *Now it is coming out,* she told herself. *How I don't really have what it takes. How I'm not really as smart as they always said. How I'm not really able. If I were smarter, if I had better skills, I could break out of this trap. But I'm not that smart, not really. All I'm good at is standing on line and taking tests.*

What would Carl do if he were here? she wondered. *He would talk his way out. He'd engage Jonathan, rather than confront him.* Maybe.

And then sadness about Carl overwhelmed her. So close. Now lost.

Got to put yourself aside if you are going to think clearly, she told herself. *That's what they teach you in doctor school. Put the self aside. What did Bill Levin call it? Unself-interested advocacy?*

That shit got me locked up, Julia suddenly thought. *All that unself-interested crap. That was what brought me to Africa, and that is what led me here. That crap is going to kill me. I'm locked up in Africa, a zillion miles from home. They just killed a guy I loved. And people I loved. I'll never have a life for myself this way. I'm going to get out of this place, even if I have to tear down this door with my teeth and fingernails.*

Julia rattled the door so hard she thought the handle might break, and she pounded on it with her fists.

"Water! Water! Water!" she yelled.

Finally, there were footsteps and a voice to shush her, and a key scraped in the lock.

A flashlight exploded into Julia's eyes. The room flooded with light. Another bucket thrust into her chest.

The door slammed shut again. Julia let the bucket slip between her elbows and guided it by pressing it between her inner arms and her chest, and then pelvis and legs, and squatted to bring the bucket to the floor. Then she felt the inside of the bucket. There was a large plastic bottle and a pot that had a soft warm lump that felt like a foam pillow or a breast and four cool lumpy cylinders that each had broken fibrous covers—likely four ears of roast corn.

Julia's hands were tied, so she lifted the bottle with her hands, and then trapped it at waist level between her body and the shelving. She used the bottom of both sides of her hands to twist off the bottle cap, which fell onto the floor in the darkness. She was able to reach her tied hands around the bottle, and then she drank.

The water was stale, metallic, and brackish, and tasted like it had been standing outside in a rusty pot. It was warm. But it wet Julia's lips.

The bottle dropped as Julia lowered it. It bock-bocked two or three times. She felt the water splash onto her feet before she found it with her hands, stood it up, and then lifted it into the new bucket, wedging it against the side with the corn and soft lumpy material.

She pulled off a moist piece of the lumpy material and put it in her mouth. It was spongy and smooth and tasteless—fufu—a soft starchy ball of cassava that filled you and soothed you as you ate it, and when you ate enough lulled you to sleep. She picked up one of the ears of corn, pulled the husk back, and bit into it. It was soft and mealy, taste-less and thick, and had she not been hungry, she would have spit it out. But she swallowed the corn and put the ear back into the bucket for later. Nothing to look forward to. Enough to keep functioning. Until whatever came next.

Chance favors the prepared mind, Julia thought. *I'm ready.*

Chapter Ten
William Levin. Providence,
Rhode Island. July 18, 2003

It was 10:00 a.m. Levin showered, changed, and drove home. You can taste the sweetness of sleep before you lose yourself in it. The paper was on the porch. No mail yet. Levin sat at the kitchen table and opened the paper. A few minutes of the *Times* was a glorious way to decompress.

Some Liberia news on page five. Levin remembered reading that things in Liberia were heating up. An indictment. Presidents moving back and forth. Rebel armies on borders. Shelling. Boy soldiers again. It was hard to keep track of what country was falling apart when, which African president was in power, and who was about to be overthrown or had just been overthrown, and who had declared themselves president for life. Africa was a little like Rhode Island, full of political drama of uncertain consequence. Hard to keep track of all the good old boys, and who was doing what to whom or taking what from whom at each moment.

Now there was a map with a curved arrow that had a broad base to show the movement of troops and control, an arrow that came up from the lower right corner of the map of Liberia and stopped about a third of the way across. A third of the way across, at a town called Buchanan. Stopped at Buchanan. That was where Julia was. Not cool. Uncomfortable. Not cool at all.

You read the *New York Times*. You skim the headlines. You file away the facts. You rarely ever associate those facts with the lives and fortunes of people you know and love.

Levin sent an e-mail.

It often took a week for Julia to respond to Levin's e-mails. If he didn't write, he'd hear from Julia once every month or two. If he wrote, she'd respond. She was busy. He didn't have very much to say.

His student. His only real student. The rest became orthopedists in California, plastic surgeons in New Jersey, or neurologists in New York. But Julia was different. They met when Julia was a medical student. She asked questions when Levin gave his yearly lecture—a pert young woman with green eyes and black hair who took herself way too seriously. She followed up the lecture with a series of e-mails, wanting to know more about various aspects of what Levin presented. No one had ever done that before. *Leave it alone*, Levin thought to himself. *None of this material is going to be on the test.* Then she showed up in the ED for an elective month and hung around most nights after her shift was done. What could Levin tell her about electives in the developing world, in Nicaragua, Honduras, Haiti, and Kenya? Which was a better experience? Could she get scholarship support to travel?

And then she stayed for residency.

In the ED, Levin became Julia's mentor. He steered her through internship (it gets better. I promise.) He got her gigs at WHO and CDC to keep her sane, a month at a time, and together they hooked her up a three-month stay in Kenya.

Julia wanted to work in the developing world. Most of the time, her head was in the clouds, stuck on romantic notions about the role of medicine in international relations and how better health could create peace and make a more just society and all that.

But Julia got tougher, as a resident. Levin had seen her fix and focus in the middle of the night when a gunshot victim was bleeding out. He had seen her put her hands on a tense belly, know what she was dealing with, tube the guy and open the belly down in the department, not waiting for the surgeon or the OR, because there just was no time to wait.

They became friends as her mind and her skills developed. Julia finished residency and joined the ED staff. Then she began traveling to the developing world to do things Levin himself only dreamed of. He kept her car in his spare garage when she was away, and she had her mail come to his house.

She sent pictures. Beautiful pictures of kids posed in front of rural clinics, of pregnant women standing on the porch of a health center, of a new latrine that everyone in a community was digging. He made a screen saver out of those pictures so everyone in his office could see them, one picture of smiling little kids after the next, whether he was in the office or not.

Julia was the real thing. Julia *was* repairing the world, saving lives, using her brain and the cunning in her hands and fingers, listening to people, speaking clearly so she would be heard despite not having the language of the place, understanding complex problems, making difficult diagnoses without fancy tests and tools, and improvising. Three billion people living on a dollar a day. Levin had a warm house and a TV to watch. The world was going to hell in a handbasket. Julia was out there fixing it. Levin was sitting on his duff, an imposter.

He wouldn't get a reply for a week or two if he e-mailed. That wasn't good enough. He tried Julia's cell. It was six or seven at night over there. She should still be awake.

Different ring tone. Quick repetitive buzzing. Very loud. No answer.

Levin looked online, at the BBC, and at the State Department website, and at al-Jezeera, where you could sometimes get unfiltered news. What he read was worrying. There was fighting in Buchanan. They had sent in the U.S. Marines and pulled Americans and EU nationals out. There was a travel warning. U.S. citizens cautioned. Unstable military situation. Don't travel there. If you are there, don't go out. Avoid crowds.

He called the State Department and got connected to the Bureau of Consular Affairs, Africa Desk. They couldn't provide any information. Privacy laws. They could record data for the file. There was already a report in the file. All American citizens had been evacuated. The mission was complete.

Those words made him sick to his stomach. If Julia had been evacuated, she would have come back to Providence or called or e-mailed. Levin checked his e-mail again. There was nothing.

He called Julia's mother in Mill Valley, who was just back from playing tennis, chipper but completely clueless. She didn't even know there was a war on in Liberia, or even that Liberia was a country in Africa. She hadn't heard from Julia in a few weeks. Nothing out of the ordinary.

The Liberian embassy in Washington didn't answer their phone.

Levin got Jack Reed's office on the phone and badgered a nice young legislative assistant into making a call. Senator Reed's office put him in contact with someone at the State Department, who said exactly what the last person said—privacy laws again. All she could do was take down Julia's name and last known address. Open a case file.

Levin hadn't thought much about Julia in months. But he couldn't stop thinking about her now. Levin could hear her voice—impetuous, smart, and unrealistic, the voice of someone who was barely thirty, who has this stupid, blind hope, this belief in doing the right thing because it was right, this commitment to unself-interested advocacy, to unconditional love, the light that had almost gone out in himself. Repair the world. Right. As the world spun out of control, as the rich got richer, and the poor got poorer. How much good had those beliefs done *him*? Or the world or anybody else?

Who was Julia to him? Probably just a faint hope, a distant fantasy, a last gasp; not a student, not a lover, but somehow more than a friend. A voice. There was a line from somewhere that described it. He pieced the line together, word leading slowly to word. "Neither ... father ... nor ... lover." It was Theodore Roethke, a poet from the northwest he'd read in college. "Neither father nor lover." That phrase described it perfectly, described who he was to Julia and who Julia was to him.

The poem was called *Elegy for Jane*, and as soon as the line came back, his brain stopped short. "Neither father nor lover." It was an elegy for a young woman who had been killed, thrown from a horse.

The thought of Julia dying, of Julia's body lying crumpled on the ground, her head snapped backward and her face that ghastly blue-white was too much for Levin to bear. But there it was. They had evacuated all American citizens, and Levin hadn't heard from Julia. She could have been caught up in this mess, and she could be dead. There was already a report in her file.

I'm a coward, Levin thought. *I'm sitting here in America, going to work every day, just plugging up the holes people shoot in each other, treating headaches with Percocet, and ordering MRIs. We pay agribusiness to grow corn, and then sell the corn syrup to food processors, who sell it on TV; and we get diabetes and heart disease from eating all that crap, and then big pharma and the hospitals and the device manufacturers sell us more stuff to fix it all, and the insurance companies line up to pay for it so that a bunch of rich guys can line their pockets while we fatten ourselves like turkeys, ready to be cooked and eaten on Thanksgiving Day. I am wasting my life*, Levin thought, *pissing away my days and nights to repair the damage done by a for-profit culture that is out of control. This is "finger in the dike" stuff. I'm one more cog in the machine that is destroying the communities that make us human. My life isn't about repairing the world or about bringing the lost light back into the universe. It isn't about kindness or goodness or justice or even about love. My life is complicity, not action.*

There was a ping from Levin's computer, which was on a desk in the next room. He needed sleep.

One more e-mail. Just one. Probably junk.

Chapter Eleven
Julia Richmond. Grand Bassa
County, Liberia. July 18, 2003

THE LIGHT UNDER THE DOOR DIMMED, BECAME FAINT RED, AND THEN WENT OUT BEFORE IT came back.

Julia worked at slipping her hands out of the cloth tie that held them together. She reached back with her fingers, stretching them to the point of dislocation, but she could not even put the third finger of either hand, which reached furthest when she flexed her fingers as far as they would go, onto the knot. The cloth tightened against her wrists when she moved her hands, which made them tingle and then go numb.

She stood and paced when she was awake. She rubbed the cloth on the edge of the shelving, hoping to fray it or wear it away. The light wasn't good enough to see if it worked, when there was any light at all.

Or she sat, and she dreamed.

Her hips began to ache from the hard floor. She could picture the anatomy—the femoral head as it entered the acetabulum of the hip joint, the greater trochanter rotated out and up as she flexed the hip and the knee. That meant she was sitting on bone, the ridges and grooves of the acetabulum pressed into the muscular gluteus and its ligamentous attachment to the bone, where there was no fatty cushion. She tried to change positions when she was sitting or laying back. Sometimes she sat with her knees drawn up to her chest. Sometimes she lay on her back on the floor with her hands under her head. Sometimes she lay on her side, her clasped hands as a pillow, her knees drawn up.

Then she was kissing someone, a man who might or might not have been Carl, and was absorbed by the kiss. *Some people talk when they make love*, she thought. *I like kissing. I like believing that the other person is feeling exactly what I am feeling and is totally there with me. Talking, explaining, asking, offering, and calling out—all that takes you away from being drawn up together, from that place that makes you feel like you are out of yourself; all present and all gone at once.*

Then she woke.

The dreams came and went. Carl, Torwon, Charles, Sister Martha, crowds of little kids saying "How are YOU?" her mother in a tennis jumper, her father, a thin man from long ago, cars and jet bombers and machine guns, all jumbled together. The smoke and the man behind her. The gun jammed into her ribs.

The light under the door began to dim again.

Then steps on the concrete. A crunch. Metal on metal in the door, in the lock. A wash of light. Bright white light, blinding her.

Julia was yanked to her feet.

Chapter Twelve
Carl Goldman and William Levin.
Providence, Rhode Island. July 18, 2003

CARL STEPPED ON THE GAS OF THE RENTED RED RAV4, ONLY HALF SURE OF WHERE HE WAS going. Hot day, good AC. What do they call it? Ice cold air.

Hard to imagine that this is one planet. Here, driving down Route 146 on a hot day in July, the air-conditioning keeping his skin cool. There, used RAV4s and CRVs are strike vehicles. They come in to the villages after the motorbikes have come through, loaded with small boys and small girls popping pills. Taylor's boys liked the four-wheel drive pickups better, because you can jam six or eight of the boys into the back, but the RAV4 would be good enough for one of the militias. It was four-wheel drive, perfect for rutted red dirt roads that had potholes as big as lakes. Its high undercarriage let you go places you couldn't get to otherwise. They burned through RAVs like this one in a couple of months over there. Drive it hard. Burn it out. Abandon it, all shot up, in the jungle or just off the Monrovia road, and then find yourself another one.

Off the highway on Atwells, and then a right on Westminster. He passed Classical High School, and then found himself on Cranston Street, which meant he'd gone too far. He drove a couple of blocks, looking for a place to turn, made a left after a cemetery, and then made another left to come back on Elmwood Street.

Elmwood and Cranston Streets and the places to their south and west were where the immigrant communities lived—the Guatemalans, Dominicans, Hondurans, Hmong, Liberians, Gambians, Nigerians, and the Ghanaians. They lived all together in a colorful part of town between Elmwood, Cranston Street, Broad, and Broadway, near the armory and the parade grounds, their churches and restaurants the only way an outsider could tell each community was there.

South and West Providence had once been the richest part of the city. The grand old Victorians near the armory and on Parade Street and Princeton Street had once been the homes of rich manufacturers. Then a hundred years ago, the old WASP mill owners, bankers, and merchants moved to the East Side, and their houses became the second or third steps for Irish factory workers, Italian restaurant owners, and Jewish merchant junk dealers after the immigrants started to succeed. Those grand old houses were crumbling now. There were fire escapes and paved parking lots where stained glass and grand lawns used to be.

In South Providence were now acres and acres of old wooden houses that needed paint, punctuated by squat brick buildings put up by social agencies that had walls covered in graffiti and storefronts that had signs painted in bright colors right on the glass; storefronts with metal gates that would pull down over the windows at night. The grand old churches and synagogues had been sold years ago. Now they were Pentecostal churches and mosques, with new neon crosses or crescents and bright colored banners and flags. The side streets seemed deserted. There were houses and parked cars but almost nobody in the street.

Carl drove past the restaurant he was looking for twice before he recognized it. He parked out front. Sally's Liberian Restaurant. It was in an old VFW hall. There was a handwritten sign on the door. They were open from noon to seven but closed Sundays, Mondays, and Wednesdays.

Bells over the door jangled when he opened it and jangled a second time when he slammed the door shut.

There was a big red white and blue Lone Star flag on the wall next to the kitchen, plastic flowers in vases on each table, and a menu written in red magic marker on a white board propped up on a chair near the door. The menu listed three items but had no prices. The place felt deserted, but, hell, the door was open, so Carl took a table in front of a window and made himself at home.

After a few minutes, a big woman wearing a yellow apron came out of a back room with a plate of fried plantains as if she had been expecting him.

"You waitin' on somebody?" she said and laughed.

"Ya Mama. Waitin on one. Lookin for another. Just home," Carl said.

"Le me fee ya. Ga stew. Ga jollof rice," the waitress said. *Let me feed you. We have goat stew and jollof rice.*

"Okay, okay, jollof rice then. And more plantains. Love plantains. And a coke," Carl said.

The bells over the front door jangled again. A white man with a beard came in and looked around. The bells jangled a second time as he closed the door. He looked past Carl, expecting someone else. *Oh yeah*, Carl thought. *America. I'm invisible again.*

Carl raised his hand in a half-wave and started to stand.

"Dr. Levin?" he said, when the man didn't acknowledge him.

"Carl Goldman?" Levin said, catching himself. "Sorry to be late."

He shook Carl's hand and pulled up a chair. He had a real grip, though. Carl wasn't expecting that.

Levin was older than Carl expected. He was wearing jeans and a Hawaiian shirt. He had stringy swept-back white hair and big glasses with thick lenses that made his eyes look large and bulging.

Levin ordered. "You Liberian?" he asked.

"Me? Not Liberian. Not African either. Just plain old African American—a little African, a lot of everything else—a little French, a little Spanish, a little Jew," Carl said.

"How did *you* get out?" Levin said.

"Your friendly U.S. Marines. They landed Saturday. Two days ago. Seems like a hundred years ago. Picked up the USAID and State Department folks. Grabbed a few NGO people while they were at it. I'm NGO. That's what Uncle Sam's helicopters and Humvees are for, I guess. Semper fi."

"What were you doing there?" Levin said.

"NGO stuff. Hydrology. Building village pumps," Carl said.

"Good stuff. Sounds crazy over there, though," Levin said

"Crazy enough," Carl said. "You're Julia's mentor, right? She looked up to you. Talked about you."

"Teacher once, a long time ago. Friend and colleague now. I have her car in my spare garage. Start it once a month and try to drive it once in a while. When I remember," Levin said. "Now she's the shining star. I'm just a guy with a telescope, looking for her in the sky from a hundred million miles away."

They fell silent.

"It's not good," Carl said. "She got caught in a fight between Charles Taylor's people and a group of rebels moving up from the south. Taylor is the president, so-called. Taylor's men burned her vehicle. They killed her driver and her guard. No way to know what happened next. I saw her maybe forty-five minutes before all that. Her vehicle had broken down. She was waiting on the side of the road for a repair truck. She was fine when we left her. When we came back, her truck was on fire, her guys were dead. And she was gone."

"Damn," Levin said. "Damn. Damn, damn, damn. No word from her?"

"Nothing," Carl said. "I called the State Department. Next morning the marines showed up to evacuate Americans. But Julia wasn't there. I called them. I was worried about Julia, not for the rest of us. The rest of us were okay."

"Damn. Where is bloody goddamn American imperialism when you need it most?" Levin said.

"When the marines landed. I thought they would go for Julia first," Carl said. "I thought she'd be there on the beach when they came to airlift us out. But she wasn't there. It all happened fast. I can't believe they left her."

"It's a war zone. Shit happens. Where the hell is she?" Levin said.

"Anybody's guess," Carl said. "Liberia is the size of Tennessee. She could be anywhere. She's probably in Grand Bassa or Bong County, just north of Buchanan," Carl said. "Short of an air force or an amphibious assault, it's not possible to move around in Liberia right now."

"Anything we can do?" Levin said. "Strings to pull? Chains to yank? This is Rhode Island. We always know a guy who knows a guy."

"I don't know. I don't know who has her. Or where she is. No way to know if she's alive," Carl said.

"She's alive," Levin said. "There's real grit underneath all that privileged white girl crap, all that insecurity and self-doubt. She's a street fighter, that girl, and don't you ever forget it."

"That's the sense I got from the State Department. That she's alive," Carl said. "They aren't confirming or denying. I think maybe they got some wires crossed. I think they thought she was out. What we've got now is just some kind of cover-up. But it sounds like they know where she is and who has her."

"I got the same bullshit," Levin said. "They know. They just ain't talking."

The food came.

"So are you going in to get her?" Levin said.

"You can't get to Liberia now," Carl said. "I checked all the airlines. Even the little African ones. You can't move around in Grand Bassa County, where she got nabbed. There are roadblocks and militia everywhere—bridges out, trees across the road, checkpoints, you name it. But I'm open to any and all bright ideas. Yes, I want to go in and get her. I just don't know how."

"How well do you know Julia?" Levin said.

"Just from Buchanan," Carl said. "There are about thirty expats in Buchanan, give or take. We'd hang out nights and weekends. Have dinner together. That kind of thing. Potlucks. Drive out to the beach on Sundays."

"Answer the question. You an item?" Levin said.

"Not exactly yes, not exactly no," Carl said. He paused. "More yes than no. Maybe more than that."

"Got it. More yes than no. Enough to be here. Not enough to stay there. Okay, no way in and no plan. So why the email?" Levin said.

"Misery loves company, I guess, "Carl said. "And I'm looking for ideas. I need an army. And an air force and marines. I need help. I need a strategy, and I need a plan. You got any of that?"

"I barely have the clothes on my back. But its sounds like you got religion, brother. Kind of a day late and a dollar short, though," Levin said. "Anyway, I'm a different kind of guy. I'm a peacenik, not Rambo. And this isn't about me."

DOOO-IPPP, DOOO-IPPP, DOOO-IPPP.

The sound was sudden, brilliant and piercing. Painful. Right outside. Close by car alarm.

DOOO-IPPP, DOOO-IPPP, DOOO-IPPP.

Not my problem, Levin thought. No car alarm on his fucked up old car. Barely any car.

Carl turned his head away from the noise. DOOO-IPPP, DOOO-IPPP, DOOO-IPPP. He pulled the keys out of his pocket and looked out the window. Then he jumped up, went to the door, and pulled it open. The bells on the door jangled. Levin felt a blast of hot air. The bells snapped as the door slapped shut and the DOOO-IPPP, DOOO-IPPP, DOOO-IPPP blasted out again, dying out halfway through its cycle.

Suddenly Levin felt ashamed. Ashamed of himself. Ashamed of his life. A great big empty life filled with pot smoke in which nothing was accomplished. He hadn't really ever loved anyone. All those stupid big ideas signifying nothing. Julia was lost in Africa and nothing anyone, Levin or anyone else, could do to help. This Carl seemed like the real thing, but Carl didn't have a clue either. Nothing was working. Levin couldn't do one thing to help the one person in this life he loved and wanted to protect. Nothing else mattered. He was useless.

Then Levin heard a shout from the street.

Chapter Thirteen

Julia Richmond. Grand Bassa
County, Liberia. July 18, 2003

So much light! Everything was yellow, white and grey. Then something grabbed Julia by the back of the neck. It tugged under her arms. He had her shirt. He yanked Julia to her feet. She couldn't see anything. Couldn't see him. He dragged her into the hall, spun her around, and pushed, so she stumbled and tried to walk, the bones of her bottom aching, her legs and knees spasmed, cramping and stiff.

He shoved her back toward the big room. The light still hurt. Julia stumbled down the hall, her hands tied in front of her. The man at her back pushed her, one hand on her right shoulder, the cold flat side of a gun between her shoulder blades, in the small of her back.

Julia couldn't see the man. Every time she tried to look back he jammed her forward with the gun. The pushing came straight across, not down. He wasn't much taller than she was. There was light in the kitchen windows but not streaming-in light. Kitchen on the east side. So it wasn't early morning.

The big room had men and boys standing and men and boys lying on the floor, mostly against the walls. Some sat. Some squatted. Some slept. That smell of sweat, beer, gun grease, and pot smoke again, like old wet leather. Guns and ammunition belts lay on the men and boys or just next to them. A few RPG launchers leaned against the wall. Yellow Bandanna was in the room near the front door. Jonathan was standing behind him.

The wooden crates that Julia had seen when she arrived had been rearranged. Some were set up against the wall, doubling as benches and tables. Others were stacked high so as to divide the space, to make rooms and sections. The sun was streaming in the bay window in the back, so it was late in the day. There were thunderclouds low on the horizon, and the sun was just above them. The clouds were orange red, blue, and purple, and rays of light spread over the vista as if the sunlight was the top of a pot or a crown, covering the green and purple earth. It was early evening. The evening rains were moving in.

"My friend who we've kept on ice," Jonathan said. "It's Madam Orange Juice joining us again. Bring her here. 'Orange Juice on ice is nice,'" Jonathan sang, his bass voice rumbling across the room. "Orange Juice on ice. Drink real Flo-ri-d-a Or-ange Juice. Orange Juice on ice."

Yellow Bandanna grabbed Julia's arm and yanked her forward.

"I'm glad you had time to sit and think," Jonathan said. "Don't forget who is keeping you alive." He took his knife off his belt, and cut the cloth that held Julia's wrists.

"Sorry about the closet. At least we kept you out of the midday sun. Now I am going to need some help from you. Tell me, what are you hearing from your friends and colleagues in Buchanan?"

"I don't know what the hell you're talking about," Julia said. "I've been in a closet, remember. You crushed my cell phone. I haven't exactly been Miss Chatty Cathy."

"Why did they leave you here? I was expecting a return phone call and a deal by now. I get angry when people don't return my calls," Jonathan said.

"I have no idea what you mean. Get me back to Buchanan," Julia said.

"Your marines landed yesterday," Jonathan said, "They cleaned out the Americans and the Brits. And some others. They didn't leave a beachhead. Or any units on the ground. Good of them. Now I need to know why there is no deal for you."

"I have been sitting in a closet for two days, thank you very much. I don't know anything about deals or marines," Julia said.

"Why aren't you worth the price of a couple of helicopters and a few RPGs?" Jonathan said. "Why has your government abandoned you?"

"Who *are* you?" Julia asked.

"I'm your worst nightmare, lady," Jonathan said. "And your ticket to ride. But I can't keep you for more than a few days. Then we have to move on. So prove yourself, missy. Show me what you are worth. There is some kind of family back there, in California, yes? And eventually that family will find a senator or a congressman and your State Department, yes? And then your government may discover it is ready to work with us. Perhaps. If we are all still here. If you survive that long. USA. USA. What bullshit."

"Wait a fucking second, Julia said. "You're the one that's stuck; otherwise you'd be on the move already. You're boxed in. Completely surrounded. Out of options. You have no way out, other than trading little old me for safe passage. Only that's not working. One of these days someone bigger and stronger, someone with more guns and real soldiers is going to land on your doorstep, and then you're mincemeat. A smudge on a canyon wall. So you are quaking in your fuckin' boots, despite all the big talk. Do your soldier-boys know that you've led them into a blind alley? That they're sitting ducks?"

"Who do you think *you* are?" Jonathan said. "All your friends have abandoned *you*. They don't care one whit about your high ideals and self-righteous passions. All they care about is what everyone cares about, about who owns what, where the firepower is, and who is fucking over whom. Maybe they just misplaced you. Maybe someone forgot to tell someone else, and now that someone is covering their tracks. Or maybe they are sending people like you a message: that this is our world, not yours, and the do-gooders and bleeding hearts should stay the hell out of Africa. I bet they are saying you're already dead."

"Fuck *you*," Julia said. "I need to get to Buchanan. They need me there, now more than ever."

"You don't know anything, do you?" Jonathan said. "No one needs you. Your hospital has been overrun. It's barracks and an ammo dump now. The hospital staff did what the rest of Buchanan did, which is to disappear into the bush. That's what we do here when there's a war on. Anyone who can disappears. Quick-quick. No one comes to see the doctor. Our children don't need to get your shots right now. They need to keep from *getting* shot. Our people know how to survive. Just like your bureaucrats."

"I'm still your only ticket out of here," Julia said. "You need to treat me a little better than this."

"You ain't nothin'," Jonathan said. "And you gonna stay nothing until somebody who knows their ass from a hole in the wall calls me back."

"I don't want to vegetate," Julia said. "Put me to work. Let me look at your soldiers when they get sick or if they get hurt. Then get me south."

"What makes you think I care about what you do? You think I have time to worry about the sick or wounded? You don't understand what's happening here, do you?"

"I understand that you're in way over your head," Julia said. "That you are only smart enough to know that you're not smart enough to get out of here alive without me. And that you just might have to dump all these nice people just to save your own worthless skin."

Jonathan jerked one arm and smacked Julia with the back of his hand. She fell into a club chair that had boxes stacked on top of it.

Julia stood up and shook her head to clear it.

"You don't have a clue, do you?" Jonathan said. "You do what I tell you to do. Nothing more and nothing less. I own you. For the moment, you're alive. That's more than you deserve."

"You know who I am, and you know what I'm worth," Julia said. "Get me to Buchanan."

"Take her away, Daniweil. I don't care to babysit some spoiled California princess," Jonathan said.

He turned to go and then turned again. He raised his hand.

"You don't have the stomach for Africa," he said.

Then he hit Julia again.

This time, Julia's head snapped backward, but she didn't fall. She planted her feet, leaned in and punched, quick and hard. She swung from her back foot and put all her weight behind the swing. She hit Jonathan in the middle of the neck.

"You little white bitch," Jonathan said. He grabbed Julia's right arm with his big left hand and with one motion, swung her arm behind her back, spinning her so she was facing away from him, and then the blade engraved "Winchester" was on her neck. Jonathan's heavy warm thumb pressed into Julia's neck, all that was between her skin and the knife's blade.

"There are no wounded," Jonathan said. "There won't be any wounded. You are useless to me. Just useless."

He pulled her left arm toward her right shoulder to hurt her. But Julia didn't cry out. Jonathan loosened his grip on her left hand.

"I'm staying here until morning," she said. "Then you are going to get me to the hospital in Buchanan so I can get back to work."

"Talk is cheap," Jonathan said. "I own you. Not the other way around."

Then he let Julia go. He reached into a pocket, pulled out a red bandanna that was moist with his sweat and tossed it to Julia.

"Think what you want," Jonathan said. "Just don't bleed on the upholstery. Danu, she's yours tonight," he said, looking straight at Julia, "after I'm done."

He turned and was gone, out the door to where the helicopters were parked on the tarmac.

Julia put pressure on her nose and stopped the bleeding, as Daniweil wrapped his hand around her left arm, his fingers digging into the muscle. He pushed her through the back door.

The ping-pong table and pool tables were gone.

There was no one around the swimming pool now. Just stacked crates. An empty place where no one would see. The old ping-pong paddles lay on one of the crates, and there was a pool cue still leaning against the wall.

Daniweil pushed Julia over one of the crates and jerked the back of her jeans from behind as he unbuttoned his pants.

"You asshole," Julia said, and turned so she was looking at Daniweil.

Daniweil caught both Julia's hands and shoved her down on the crate. Then he pulled her to the ground. Julia arched her back. She kicked Daniweil as she went down, her knee catching him in the stomach, and he hit her in the face with the back of his hand, hard enough to turn her face to the side and make her nose bleed again. *This is what they taught me to do,* Julia said to herself. *I can do this. I can beat this asshole to a pulp.*

And then she was on the ground on her back and Daniweil was on his knees between her legs, his hands pinning her arms and hands to the ground.

He leaned over her to put his body on her chest so he could keep her flat while he pulled her jeans down. But Julia found Daniweil's left shoulder with her right hand. She pushed hard, locking her elbow and throwing all her weight behind her arm. She threw Daniweil back, and then she twisted to the right. She tucked in her left shoulder, raised her left knee, locked her left foot, and then pushed hard against the ground with it, twisting her body out from under Daniweil as he lunged for her throat.

Before Daniweil's hands reached her, Julia pushed again, harder, away from him, bent her knees, put one foot on each of Daniweil's hips, and pushed him back again, throwing him off balance, backward, which gave Julia enough time to kick. Right leg. Hard. Left leg. Harder. She missed his groin the first time, but she found his belly with the kick and he groaned and reached out for her blindly. The second kick landed, hard, under his chin, and it threw him backward. The third kick, harder yet, found his groin.

And then Julia had the pool cue in her right hand. She slammed the cue into Daniweil's groin, which left him bent over on his right side, protecting himself. Then Julia knelt over Daniweil's head. She held the pool cue in both hands in front of her. Daniweil rolled to his left, into the untrimmed boxwood hedge.

But Julia was on him before he could turn over. She caught his neck with the pool cue, her hands on either side of his head. She pulled the pool cue into her knee, which was behind his neck, as hard as she could.

Daniweil gagged, struggled for a moment, bucking, and then he went limp. The yellow bandanna came come off his head and was lying crumpled in the dirt. Blood from Julia's nose dripped onto his forehead and eyes.

Julia released her grip. She could have pulled harder, right then, and collapsed Daniweil's windpipe, and maybe could have broken the bones of his neck. She knew how it felt to break bones, the sound and feel of the crunch bone makes as it collapses under pressure, from all the times she had beaten on the chests of dying little old people who got CPR when all they wanted to do was die.

She backed off, breathing hard and sat for a moment to catch her breath. She took the yellow bandanna from where it lay on the ground, and wiped the blood dripping from a cut on her face and still dripping from her nose and then jammed it into a back pocket.

Then she stood and walked into the clubhouse.

It was dusk. The evening rain had come and gone, and the ground was wet. The trucks were coming and going in the front of the clubhouse. Men were shouting and calling out. Daniweil would recover, once he got his breath back. But he sure has hell wasn't going to try any of that shit again, and, she guessed, neither was Jonathan or any of his man-boys.

They needed each other, Julia and Jonathan. But Julia was going to do this on her own terms.

Live free or die, indeed.

Chapter Fourteen
Carl Goldman and William Levin.
Providence, Rhode Island. July 18, 2003

CARL RAN OUT OF THE RESTAURANT AS THE RAV WAS MAKING A U-TURN. HE LOOKED AT the other cars in the street and at the space that was where he had left a car. Then he saw the RAV moving away. There was a parking space where his rental car had been. He'd seen the RAV moving from the restaurant window. It didn't add up. Then it did. "They stole . . . someone's taking . . . that's my car," Carl said, almost to himself.

"THAT'S MY CAR!!!" he shouted.

The RAV sped toward the corner as Carl walked into and then out of the parking spot where it had been.

Levin came through the door of the restaurant, smashing the bells together as he jerked the door open.

"THAT'S MY CAR!" Carl shouted again. "He stole my car!" He started to run after the RAV, which was now at the stop light, but the RAV didn't stop—it screeched around to the right.

"POLICE! Call the police!" Carl shouted.

"Fuck the police. They're useless. Which car?" Levin said.

Levin ripped off the duct tape holding the door of his banged-up Subaru, threw himself inside, jammed the key into the ignition, gunned the engine, and spun the car around. "The red car. At the corner."

"Get in. This one's mine. We'll run that motherfucker down," Levin said.

Carl was running down the street in the direction of the RAV, which had just turned the corner. Levin hit the gas, reached over as he drove, and threw the passenger side door open.

"Come on!" he said.

Carl looked at the open door and at the red RAV disappearing down Cranston Street. He caught the roof of the Subaru with his right hand and swung himself into the car as Levin hit the gas and turned the corner. Carl slammed his door shut at the same time as Levin's door swung closed, pulled closed by the force of the right turn.

The traffic light at the next corner went yellow just as the RAV went through it. Levin hit the gas again. They sped through the intersection but they didn't get any closer to the RAV, which also sped up as it hit a stretch of road that ran next to a baseball field where there were no traffic lights.

"They hit *this* car a couple of months ago," Levin said. "I should have dumped it. But you can't buy a used four-wheel drive in Rhode Island anymore. They're all getting bought up and shipped to Africa. That bastard. He doesn't know we're here. I'll catch that sucker. He won't ever steal a car again."

The RAV turned left.

"He turned," Carl said.

"I'm on it," Levin said.

They went through another yellow light and swung onto a broad but quiet street lined by big trees and low brick garden apartments.

It was summer and hot. People sat on lawn chairs next to the street or on the hoods of cars, some of which were missing wheels or had windows smashed. Some cars had their hoods open as men in tee shirts worked on them.

The street curved left, and they lost sight of the RAV. Levin sped up, and they saw the RAV turn.

"Made him," Levin said, as the car spun around the corner.

They were on Broad Street going south. They passed a cemetery and tried to pick up speed but there were cars in their way.

The RAV was almost two blocks ahead of them. Levin passed one car and hit the gas. They passed a bus. Then they were just a block behind, stuck at a light.

The light changed. Levin hit the gas again. They gained on the RAV, passing a truck loaded with fruit and a bus. Then they were behind the RAV, only four or five car lengths back.

But another bus swerved into their lane, stopping in front of them to pick up passengers. Levin had to break for the bus and let the truck go by him. He paused, swung behind the truck after it passed, went around the bus, and then swung back into the right lane to pass the truck on the right.

The RAV was gone.

Levin wheeled the car around, making a quick U-turn in the middle of the block, and then made a right at the first street.

No RAV.

"Let's prowl," Carl said. "Let's go down to the waterfront. You said something. No four-wheel drives in Rhode Island. Everything getting bought up and shipped to Africa. I know something you don't know, which is the bush in Liberia is crawling with old four-wheel drives without mufflers. They come from somewhere. They can only get to Liberia by sea, right?"

"And Providence has a port, right?" Levin said. "And the port is half a mile from here, and that RAV is a four-wheel drive, right?"

"So my rental car with four-wheel drive got pinched so it could be shipped to Africa," Carl said. "And somebody in Providence, Rhode Island, has a racket, stealing four-wheel drives and sending them to Africa from the Port of Providence. So if we want to find that car, we find the wise guys who are running this racket before that car gets on a boat."

"I'm on it," Levin said. "Eyes peeled. Look for a courtyard or a parking lot. They'll have to stash your car out of the way until a boat docks. There are only so many streets in South Providence and only so many little parking lots. We'll nail that bastard in no time. At least we can get you your *car* back."

"We've got to do way more than that, brother," Carl said. "She's out there. We've got to go out there to get her, and we've got to bring her back."

"Let's see if we can get your car back first," Levin said.

"We're going to find a way to get the car and *Julia* back," Carl said. "Find a way or make one."

The port was just a few blocks away. It smelled of grease and diesel fumes. They drove between mountains of metal scrap. They heard the crunch and roar of front-end loaders and cranes scooping the scrap and dropping it into the hold of a freighter. Every time Levin saw taillights turning a corner, he hit the gas.

They didn't see anything. They left the port and nosed down Public Street, behind the Blue Bug, a sculpture of a giant termite that sits on the roof of a building next to a highway—the sign for an exterminator. Then Levin made a right onto Allens Avenue and drove past the sign for the Russian Submarine, a decommissioned Russian sub docked improbably in Providence as a tourist attraction. They made a left on Terminal Drive, drove almost to the water, and then swung right on Shipyard Street.

They made a right on Harborside, drove up next to an old hotel that had been made over into a college dorm, climbed a hill, and then they were in Edgewood, where the streets were straight and the lots were perfect rectangles—the homes of working people and junior faculty.

They swung right and left and right again and drifted through a neighborhood of old brick factories and older mill houses. Levin drove slowly enough that they could see into the driveways and yards. They looked down each side street as they drifted by.

The houses were tired, with rotting porches or peeling paint. Many were boarded up. Most of the cars were burned out. There was broken glass and beer cans everywhere. The streets were full of potholes, so the Subaru shuttered and groaned as they traveled.

Then they were on Broad again, again drifting north.

That was when they saw him. On Broad. Almost to the middle of the block. Headed south. Just as they sped up to go through a yellow light.

They saw the RAV at the same moment.

Levin wheeled the car around.

"The . . ." was all Carl said. He was thrown against the passenger door by the force of the spinning car.

The light was red. Levin stopped and looked and went through it. Then he hit the gas.

The RAV was in the middle of the next block, in the left lane, and they lost sight of it for a moment when a bus pulled between them. They passed the bus, sailed through a few lights, and gained ground.

They crossed the highway on an overpass. There was a park on their right, with streets and no traffic out of the park, so Levin hit the accelerator and they jolted forward. They were six car lengths behind. The light at the corner turned red with the RAV on the other side of it.

Levin stopped, checked the side street, and went through the light.

The RAV turned left.

Chapter Fifteen
Thomas Johnson. Providence,
Rhode Island. July 18, 2003

THOMAS WAS NOW IN THE EXPORT BUSINESS, AND HE WAS GOOD AT IT. IMPORT IS HARDER. They check everything coming in, and you need false compartments and a double set of books. You have to remember who is just a little corrupt, how they are corrupt, and who is just asleep at the wheel, if you want to do import. Every once in a while you are going to get caught so you have to have a sharp lawyer who is likely to be a bigger crook than all of them. Unless you want to run drugs. But that is a more dangerous game. You can make import work if you do your homework and follow the golden rule—he who has the gold makes the rules. Even so it is a lot of work. You have to stay on your toes and always look over your shoulder, always watch your own back.

Export is easier, particularly to Africa. No one cares about Africa. Ships leave the ports at Providence and Davisville empty since no one in the U.S. makes anything anymore, and because no one in Africa can afford the grain and corn, the beef, pork, and chicken, the fruits and vegetables that America's factory farms produce. The ships go back empty unless you fill them with things America doesn't want or need—old cars, used clothes, or hazardous waste that is too expensive to dump in the USA. Thomas knew, someplace in the back of his mind, that a different kind of export had happened once before, two and three hundred years before—sugarcane from the Caribbean to Rhode Island to be made into rum. Rum to Africa. Africans slaves to the Caribbean, and then sugarcane picked by slaves back to the Port of Providence—and that trade had made some men in Rhode Island rich—but that was hundreds of years ago, and this was different.

Export was now just a way to make a living, a way to find use for what America didn't need, things that people back home could use. Mostly it was a way to make a living. Easier than import. But still, you have to be quick on your feet.

Thomas had come to the U.S. early, in 1980. He escaped Liberia by the skin of his teeth. He came first as a student. USAID sent him to Wyoming. Two years as a black man in Wyoming was an education all by itself. An associate degree in accounting from Cheyenne Community College wasn't good for much in the U.S. but was good for something in Monrovia, so he went back and got himself a good job in the Ministry of Trade; a job where he didn't have to do much and that let him buy and sell American cars on the side, bringing in "lightly used" Lincolns, Thunderbirds, and Cadillacs. He was well placed to ensure that customers did not have to pay the ridiculous import duties. Very well placed.

The ministry job had almost cost him his life, though. Doe came in and started executing big Congomen on the street. Thomas came from Congo people, though when Doe came in Thomas was not that big yet. Thomas was willing to be bigger and was waiting to be bigger, but then he was plenty-plenty happy that he wasn't big enough for Doe to want to find him in the first few days when they were tying Congomen to telephone poles and disemboweling them. But Thomas was just big enough for Doe's men to come looking for him a few days later, so he got small-small in a hurry, for a few days and nights, and then he got just big enough again to be on an airplane to Accra, and then just big enough to start over in Providence, where he had a sister, but where his associate degree in accounting wasn't good for much at all.

In Providence everyone and their brother is an AA and a BA and a PhD. Or a JD from Suffolk or New England School of Law. Thanks be to God Thomas knew cars. Before long, he learned to fix cars, and to do that you had to learn how to take cars apart. It didn't take much to learn how to take hot cars apart fast, and from there he built his little empire. Small-small empire. Big enough to be good and to be getting rich. Small enough that no one saw and no one had come after him. Yet.

The ships come from Lebanon. They fly Liberian or Panamanian flags. They carry raw materials—lumber or salt from Egypt, China, Chile, or Canada, concrete from China, Canada, Columbia, Mexico, and Korea. Manufactured goods and clothing from China, Bangladesh, the Dominican Republic, or Honduras. The ships left empty unless Thomas filled them, so the haulage was cheap and he filled them with anything he could mark up. Room for 750 cars, or fewer cars and a couple of hundred bales of old clothes. He did okay with old clothes, which gullible American people thought they were giving to the poor. He bought them for pennies a pound. They could be sold anywhere in Africa for ten times what he paid.

The old clothes covered his overhead. He made his money on the cars. Thomas spent his days collecting those cars, buying them at auction or processing the cars that came in from his boys on the street—cars with catalytic converters that had burned out, cars off lease, high mileage cars from dealerships that weren't worth fixing up to sell, cars that came in with bad steering columns, their driver's side door locks and the ignition locks popped.

The profit margin was lower on the cars he bought legally, but they gave him paperwork cover for all the rest. The legal cars were parked at the pier, a thousand or two thousand cars all parked together at the port in a big lot that no one could see from the road, back behind the yards that stored chlorine, salt, scrap metal, and cement. The cars were far from the street but close enough to the pier that you could start them up and drive them right onto the ship when the ship was in and the ramp was down.

The hot cars, where the real money is, were stashed in a number of places—some in his garage off Broad Street, some hidden in plain sight in the used car lots of South Providence, Olneyville, the West End, Elmwood, and Washington Park—the places poor people lived and no one ever thought to look for cars that had been lifted. They were stashed one or two in each little used car lot so the stupid state police couldn't see the pattern if they happened on one or two in a chop shop raid. Still, no car was more than a mile or so from the port—and all the cars were close enough that the boys could load them in one night, after the sun was down.

The red RAV pulled in off the street one Monday afternoon in July. The boy was a country boy, still a little green, thinking he was still somebody, having ravaged the streets like boys and girls do back home. He came by once or twice a week.

Business was good. Thomas gave $2,500 for a good Japanese or German car—a Prelude or an Integra or an Acura, and $3,000 for any Mercedes or a BMW that he could part out. You can get $3,000 for the engine, $2,000 for the transmission, $1,000 for the air bags, and $1,000 for the catalytic converter, and that's even before you take the body apart; so there is probably $10,000 clear in each one, after you pay the boys and after you figure in the time of the chop—but they have good security systems and are hard for the boys to get their hands on. He paid $2,000 for a late model American SUV or truck—easy to get, easy to take apart, but parts bring less, because there are plenty of wrecks around. He paid $1,500 for anything that was a four-wheel drive. The four-wheel drives all went on the boat and he could make out good with them—$500 to the shipping, $200 to people at home. They were going for $7,500 to $10,000 right off the boat in Monrovia—even the old ones—all bought up by one penny-ante warlord or another—so he cleared a little less for each one, but there was less work and no risk. Warehouse them until the boat comes in, drive them over at night, run them right on deck, and the job is done.

Terrance drove into the one open garage bay. Thomas stood up at his desk behind the office window when he saw the boy drive in. Each four-wheeler was ten thousand dollars and a beautiful little sight to behold. Thomas raised his fat eyebrows. It would be boat night soon. He needed a little extra from this boy. This boy would do more if he wanted his copper. He would come when he was called back and drive with the others when the boat came. There were seven hundred vehicles to move, so he needed fifty drivers, all his boys and then some, all hands on deck. They'd load seven hundred cars in twelve hours.

Thomas opened the office door as the country boy opened the door of the RAV.

"Ga ca," Terrance said. *This is a good car.*

"Maybe ga ca. Plenty-plenty ca na," Thomas said. *Maybe it's good. I have plenty of cars now.*

"Coppa?" Terrance asked. *Pay me now.*

Thomas pulled a thick wad of folded bills from his pocket, and counted out seven hundreds and handed them to Terrance.

"Sma-sma coppa," Terrance said. *The money is too little.*

"You drive two days," Thomas said." All boys drive two days. Rest of the money in the then. No room here for this car. Take it to the port. Boy there will drive you back."

Terrance scowled. The big Congoman watched the boy as Terrance got into the car, shaking with disgust, and as Terrance slammed the car door and backed the RAV into the street.

That boy will come back when I need him, Thomas thought. *He wants his money. They all want their money. That's all they want.*

I once flew above the earth, taking whatever I wanted, Terrance thought as he drove away. *I don't have to eat this Congoman's shit.*

Terrance drove and he drove and he drove, circling the neighborhood, turning it over again and again in his mind. *I want my money now,* Terrance thought. *I go back.*

Chapter Sixteen
Thomas Johnson, Carl Goldman,
Terrance Evans-Smith, and William Levin.
Providence, Rhode Island. July 18, 2003

THE BOY WAS TOLD TO TAKE CAR TO THE PIER, AND THEN RIDE BACK. THE BOY WAS NOT told to bring the car back.

The car, a red RAV, pulled into the garage. The boy sat in the car, summoning his courage. A beat-up green Subaru pulled in behind the RAV.

A white man with a beard and a thin black man jumped out of the Subaru. The boy was sitting in the RAV. The white man and the thin black man didn't look like cops. Not packing or carrying from what Thomas could see.

Thomas stood up, grabbed the baseball bat he left next to the door for emergencies and walked through the door of his office. The boy was looking at him, at Thomas, eyes simmering. The boy wasn't looking at the men in the Subaru. Terrance opened the door of the RAV slowly.

The white man wore a flowery shirt and looked uncertain. White people, in Thomas's experience, were impossible to read. They were meaningless, disorganized, and confusing. But then they bring the world down on your head when you least expect it.

It was the black man who came around the front of the Subaru and stood up square.

"Not your car," Carl said to the boy in the RAV.

Thomas wrapped his right hand around the handle of the baseball bat.

"Who you?" Thomas said to Carl.

Terrance got out of the RAV, closed the door and stood with his back to the car. "Shit Terrance, don't you *ever* quit?" Levin said.

Carl heard Thomas's question and made his accent at the same time. He looked at Terrance.

"Who *you*?" Carl said.

"De ro," Terrance said. "I' yaw wais' ma' ti, I weh sureleh blow yaw mouf o wais yaw fa." *I'm a badass. You are a waste of my time. I will surely slam your mouth and lay waste to your face.*

"He's a kid who's in over his head," Levin said.

"Ma ca," Carl said. "Wa na trouble. Wa ca. Ma ca." *My car. I don't want any trouble. I just want my car back.*

Then, looking at Thomas, Carl said, "Who are *you*?"

Terrance saw the Congoman's face change when Carl flipped back to American English. Whoever this thin black man was and wherever he was from, he knew to stand up.

"Bidness ma," Thomas said. "Who da?" he was looking at Levin.

Terrance saw a white man, and then he saw the doctor who sewed his face, gave him shit, and then came to his house to talk him into going to school. One Congoman asking him to eat shit. One black man acting in charge. One white man doctor who had no idea which way was up. This was one place Terrance didn't want to be.

"Worry about *me*," Carl said. "Tell me about the car."

"Who wants to know?" Thomas said.

"It's not your car," Levin said.

"No?" Thomas said, and turned to Terrance.

"Where you from?" Carl said.

"From Sinkor. Before, Congotown. He' twent-two yea," Thomas said. *I've lived here 22 years.*

"That my car. It rental. Need to come back," Carl said. He looked around the shop again. He let his eyes and then his head move, so the other could see him looking.

There was a long pause as Carl processed where he was, what he saw, and sorted out who was who.

"You move cars?" Carl asked.

"Ay budniss ma," Thomas said. *I'm a business man.*

"You ship cars?"

"Export bidniss," Thomas said.

"Where cars go?"

"Whe ca se," Thomas said. *Where there are buyers for cars.*

"Go to Africa?"

"Go whe buy ca. Libya, Tunisia, Morocco, Sierra Leone, Ghana, Nigeria, Liberia, Ivory Coast . . ." Thomas said. *The cars go to wherever there are buyers.*

"By ship?"

"Na drive," Thomas said. *You don't drive cars to Africa.*

Another long pause. *What the hell is Carl thinking?* Levin wondered. *Let's get your car back and get out of here. This can turn ugly fast. What Terrance is going to do is run away, but I know where to find him. The big guy with the baseball bat is a wild card.*

Cover blown, Terrance thought. *Ma knows now or will. More shit. That Levin man has a one-track mind. Get in school. Get you in ESL classes in Providence, and get you a GED. Just like the church people. Show up here, sign up there, and you get a ticket to heaven. Levin didn't have a clue. But the black guy who looks like a professor knows his shit.* All Terrance wanted was to be out of there and get his life back.

"When boat come?" Carl said.

"Boat soon," Thomas said.

"You get me on the boat? You get me to Liberia? To Buchanan?" Carl said.

Carl's crazy, Levin thought. *He thinking about a boat? We need to get that RAV back, and then get the hell out of here. He's going to get us both killed. I should have stayed in the restaurant when that damn car alarm went off. Now I'm in way over my head. I'm a doctor. Not a cop.*

"Who sa ga Liberia?" Thomas said. *Who said the boat goes to Liberia?*

"Liberia is in Africa last time I checked," Carl said. "And I'm pretty sure you know people there."

"That boat car bidness. Not cruise ship," Thomas said.

Liberia. Buchanan. The boat goes home, Terrance thought. In all the time he had put cars on the boat for Thomas, Terrance had never thought about where the boat goes. There it was. The boat goes to Liberia. *The boat goes home. That skinny black guy figured it out. That skinny black guy badass.*

Holy shit, Levin thought. *Carl's got himself a way to get back to Liberia.* A door that had been closed and locked suddenly opened.

"You get this man on your boat," Levin said.

"Boat go Monrovia. Na Buchanan," Thomas said. "What you wa go Buchanan for? Liberia crazy. Buchanan crazy-crazy now. Money good. But drop cars Monrovia and get out quick-quick." *The boat goes to Monrovia, not Buchanan. Why would you want to go to Buchanan now? Things are crazy in Liberia. More crazy in Buchanan. We ship cars to Monrovia, because there is good money in it. We drop them in Monrovia and get out quickly so no one gets hurt.*

"Better no one knows what you do here," Levin said. "You know who I am?"

Going to Liberia can't work, unless it does, Levin thought. *You get there. You look and you listen and you wheel and deal. Chance favors the prepared mind.*

"Put the RAV on the boat with me," Carl said. "I'll get myself to Buchanan."

So you can drive from Monrovia to Buchanan, Levin thought. *Where Julia is. Give the man his due. Julia,* Levin thought, *he's going to come find you. This Carl has balls.*

Woo hoo! Terrance thought. *Boat go to Monrovia! That skinny guy a badass!*

"You dead meat in Liberia alone," Thomas said. "Big big trouble for me when you get yourself killed."

"Bigger trouble for you now if he stays here," Levin said.

Thomas paused, weighing the odds.

"I need men to run cars when boat come," Thomas said, in American. "Run cars, maybe we put you on boat. Load for twelve hours. Then sail. Why you wa go Liberia for?"

Woo hoo! Terrance thought. *Ride that boat! Drive that boat! Back home quick-quick! Be wild in the streets again! Invisible! Invincible! That skinny guy with Dr. Levin a badass!*

"The U.S. Marines pulled me out of Buchanan. I left something behind. Something I need to go back and get," Carl said.

"Something or someone?" Thomas said.

"Not your problem," Carl said. "I want on that boat, with the RAV, and I want to be in Buchanan yesterday."

"Good luck with that," Thomas said. "You got an army?"

"I got an attitude," Carl said. "That should be plenty. What's it gonna take to get me and this vehicle on that boat?"

"Give me $7,500 for my trouble and we good," Thomas said. "This boy needs his piece. And I need mine."

"Five," Carl said. "I got five. Five and no trouble from us. I need a car to drive for two days, so I can get around after I report this one stolen."

Thomas paused again, a businessman's pause. Carl waited.

"Six." Thomas said.

"Done," Carl said. "When boat?"

"Two days. We load cars all night. Boat sails when loaded. Come ready."

Carl looked from man to man. *I've got two days to report the car stolen, round up cash and supplies, and then I'm good,* he thought.

"Everybody good?" Carl said.

Carl looked at Terrance to see if there was going to be more trouble from him.

Terrance looked Carl up and down. Carl talked American talk. He talked some Kreyol. He dressed good. But he was a badass in his soul. He looked at Levin, who wasn't any kind of badass at all. Crazy-crazy people. There is a boat and it goes home. In two days! "I drive wi you. I sail with boat," Terrance said. "Me Buchanan. I get you Buchanan. Tha on you own. Another five."

Thomas raised his eyebrows, but the rest of his face and body didn't move.

Neither father nor lover. My life is done, Levin thought, *and it was all for nothing. This Carl is the real thing. Julia deserves a real life, even if I'm not the man to give it to her. If you have to dance in the apocalypse, you might as well be dancing with people you love.*

"Two," Levin said to Terrance. "I'm in for two. Two if you stay in Buchanan. Five if you come back home with us when we're done and try school."

"Three na," Terrance said. "Fo mo i ba. I mi ba." *Three now. Four more if I come back. If I come back.*

"Done," Levine said. "My dime," he said to Carl. "I got a little money stashed away for emergencies. Which this is. And I'm in. I'm coming too," he said. "Better to die on your feet than live on your knees."

Thomas lowered the baseball bat. But he didn't put it down.

Carl had a car, and he had a crew.

"Two days. You got three drivers," Carl said. "Watch out, Liberia, we're coming."

"Ain't no mountain high enough," Levin sang, "ain't no ocean wide enough, to keep me from getting to you."

"To keep me from getting to you," Carl sang back.

Terrance shook his head. Dr. Levin and the skinny black dude were crazy-crazy.

But he'd be home soon, and invincible again.

Chapter Seventeen

Terrance Evans-Smith, Carl Goldman,
and William Levin. Monrovia Port,
Monrovia, Liberia. August 15, 2003

ON THE MORNING OF FRIDAY, AUGUST 15, 2003, THE 4,400-TON FREIGHTER *BRIGHT Moments* steamed into the Freeport of Monrovia, captained by a Liberian pilot of Scottish birth who had come aboard just beyond the breakwater where the *Bright Moments* lay at anchor, awaiting a pilot and anchorage while the complex political situation in the Republic of Liberia sorted itself out. The *Bright Moments* had visited ports in Nigeria, Ghana, and Ivory Coast before arriving in Monrovia. Carl hadn't slept during the voyage. He spent his days searching the shortwave and, when there was a satellite link, checking the internet for news and his nights pacing back and forth on the deck, even when the weather was lousy and the ship was tossed around by the surf.

Four days before, Charles Taylor, president of the Republic of Liberia, stood in front of stained red curtains at the Mansion, the supposedly haunted presidential palace of Liberia, with the presidents of South Africa, Mozambique, and Ghana. Those men had come, Taylor said, to give the proceedings an air of importance, but he knew and they knew they had come to ease Taylor out of power, because no one believed that he would actually resign and leave the country, but he couldn't back down once the other presidents were there.

Taylor compared himself to Jesus Christ, handed the green presidential sash to Moses Blah, his vice president and an ally from the days they trained together in guerilla warfare in Libya, and then he was helicoptered off to the Robertsfield Airport. Nigerian troops and U.S. security people in plain clothes escorted him through territory held by MODEL, the Movement for Democracy in Liberia, which at that moment held the airport and most of the south and east of the country, to the extent anyone ever holds territory in Liberia. At the airport he was put on Nigeria 001, the personal plane of Olusẹgun Obasanjo, once a military dictator and at that moment the elected president of Nigeria, and flown to Abuja, Nigeria, with all three presidents in tow, and was welcomed by President Obasanjo, with all the pomp and circumstance befitting a head of state. Taylor would live in splendor for three years in a private compound in Calabar, Nigeria, under virtual house arrest while Nigeria provided him with immunity from arrest by the international criminal court.

LURD, Liberians United for Reconciliation and Democracy, held most of Monrovia including the port where the *Bright Moments* would land. On August 14, 2006, at 11:30 in the morning, the day before the *Bright Moments* docked, a convoy of Nigerian troops under UNMIL's command moved in to occupy the port once LURD withdrew.

There was a rumor about rice in the warehouses. People gathered. They waited for rice.

Two U.S. Navy helicopters from the USS *Iwo Jima* circled overhead and a single U.S. Marine Humvee, which held three men from the 26th Marine Expeditionary Unit, joined the Nigerian convoy.

There was a ceremony as the UN and UNMIL flags were raised over the port. LURD withdrew. The people who came for rice swarmed over the warehouses, stripping them. One of the U.S. helicopters landed on the pier. A unit of munitions experts who were U.S. Navy Seals deployed throughout the port and searched for mines, depth charges, other hidden explosives, and booby traps, and then returned to the helicopter, which took off over the ocean. The sky was grey. A light rain had begun to fall.

By nightfall, most of the Nigerian troops withdrew, leaving only a small guard unit at the gate. Everyone was relieved that the day had passed without bloodshed. The Nigerians drank themselves silly. By the following morning all was quiet in this land God had abandoned.

The *Bright Moments* slipped into port without a tug at 10:30 in the morning on the incoming tide when the sun was already bright and the air was hot and thick with the sea's moisture. Knowing something—but still not enough—about the situation on the ground, the captain dropped a launch with four armed crew members. The Scottish harbor pilot eased the *Bright Moments* up against the third pier as the landing crew tied her fast to her berth, moving as quickly as they could, since all the harbor men had vanished and the stevedores and longshoremen had become militia or had been killed long ago. The AK-47s strapped over the shoulders of the landing crew were a wise but that day unnecessary precaution.

Then the *Bright Moments* dropped a ramp. A few minutes later, seventy battered white vans full of wiry, thin, dark-skinned men drove in from the Monrovia road and parked near the ramp. The captain of the *Bright Moments* walked down the ramp and met a man from one of the vans. The captain and the man then got into that van, which gunned its engine and drove onto the ship. That van came down the ramp again a few moments later, and the wiry men left the vans, swarmed up the ramp and into the waiting ship.

The cars on the *Bright Moments* started. They came off the ramp, one after the next, and were parked in seventy rows of ten cars each, seven hundred pickups and SUVs, all different.

Carl, Levin, and Terrance were in the very last SUV, a red Toyota RAV with Massachusetts plates and a U.S. flag over the hood, a U.S. flag tied to the antenna, two U.S. flags flapping from poles that they had duct-taped behind the rear windows, and a U.S. flag tied to the back door over the spare tire. Terrance drove. Carl was in the passenger seat. Levin was in the back, so it looked like there were two soldiers escorting a U.S. diplomat or other dignitary. Maybe the red Toyota RAV looked like a diplomatic vehicle. Maybe. Maybe. But only if you didn't know what the vehicles of U.S. dignitaries actually look like. If you didn't look too close.

The ramp rose off the pier and was pulled onto the ship. The lines were cast off. The men with AK-47s jumped off the pier into the launch, which pulled alongside of the ship. Cables were attached. The men in the launch climbed rope ladders up to the deck and the launch was hoisted onto the deck and secured. Then *Bright Moments* set sail.

The vehicles on the pier restarted their engines. They drove off single file, a strange convoy of vans, SUVs, and four-wheel drive pick-up trucks wending their way out of a destroyed port in a destroyed country before the so-called peacekeepers were even awake, passing only the two bribed soldiers at the gate, lounging on white plastic lawn chairs, their legs apart, and smoking cigarettes. When one of the men driving a pickup waved to them, one of the Nigerians waved back.

A red RAV came roaring past the convoy to its left.

Terrance hit the gas. He pulled to the left and passed the convoy the second he saw that they were using only one lane. The RAV whipped past the SUVs and pickups, moving so quickly that the air between them made a whooping sound, like the sound a train makes as it rattles over the crossties of the track.

Now Terrance was free. Back home. Unchained. Terrance was a bird in a cage on board ship. There was no place for him there. There was nothing for him to do. The sailors were from all over the world—Filipinos, Malays, Indonesians, Somalis, Ethiopians, Cape Verdeans, and couple of Lebanese. When they weren't working they huddled in groups of two or three who spoke the same language. They didn't know what to make of Levin and Carl, and they looked at Terrance like he was from another planet. In the USA Terrance was invisible. On board ship they looked like they were afraid of him, as though he was going to bring them bad luck.

Free at last. *Oh man*, Terrance thought. *There is life after death.* Driving this car. Important. Driving two big men. Flying past the convoy. Home. His own country. He never thought he would survive that place with the couch and broken screen door. His ma was good to him but not good like this.

They flew past wrecked warehouses—one-story concrete build-ings pockmarked by bullet holes with rusting metal roofs and weeds growing out of the cracks in the walls and near the roofline. Some of the warehouses were missing a wall. Others were missing a piece of roof, so a there was now a pile of rubble where a wall and a roof used to be. Still others were missing corners or sides, and there was underbrush growing out of the rubble where the walls had fallen in and the roof had collapsed.

Carl, the thin black man, was on edge the whole time they were on the ship and maybe was less of a badass when he was on the ship, waiting to arrive. He sat on the computer, paced, used the ship to shore when they let him, and looked at maps. Once in a while he talked to Terrance, though, talked about Liberia, about who was who among the big men, about who Terrance knew around Buchanan, about the roads and the villages in the bush, like he was looking for that woman doctor in his mind's eye every second. Terrance knew the villages and roads around Buchanan, but he didn't know what places were called or how close or far apart they were in miles. He knew in time. Carl knew the country. He showed Terrance maps. Terrance had never seen maps before. You could see the badass come back into Carl when he looked at those maps. You could see him planning, measuring hours and days, pissed as hell that the boat was taking long, pissed more that they weren't in Liberia yet, pissed when they got stuck at anchor waiting for a pilot and a place to berth. He paced and he talked to himself. He looked through you, not at you. That Carl. Terrance didn't think he ever slept.

But now Terrance was home. His land. His own country. His talk. Wild and free.

They drove past old shipping containers that were torn open and lay on their sides, and they passed rusting trucks with their windshields smashed and their hoods raised.

My place, Terrance thought. *My life*.

Levin also turned out to be different than Terrance thought. Terrance knew Levin as the big doctor-man, big important man with a white coat who his ma put up on a pedestal. Levin was just an old preacher man. Those moves in the hospital that day when Levin busted him for breaking into his old car were bullshit moves. Levin didn't have the whatfor to make any of that stick. Go to school. Read a book. Talky-talky about this and that. Not real life. Not the real world. A big man only in his own mind.

On board ship, Levin read and walked around the deck, dressed up like he was going for a hike. And walked. Ten, twenty, thirty, fifty times around. He talked to Terrance, though. Pie in the sky shit. The history of Liberia. Slaves from Africa. Rum to someplace else. About colonies and rich people getting richer. The man did not seem to understand that everyone wants to be richer, that nothing happens if you just sit still. He didn't get that if you ever want something in this life, you got to take it, that no one is going to be giving you whatever you want just because you want it. All he talked about was people and villages, like there is anything special about being dirt poor and stuck in the middle of no place, a sitting duck for the next badass with a gun.

All crazy-crazy talk. But Levin talked so much that some of the talk stayed in Terrance's head. Liberia was a country, like the USA. You got to wonder why they have cars and television sets in the USA, and nobody in Liberia has nothing. You start thinking things that you didn't plan to think.

But you sure can make a preacher man like Levin grin if you ask him a question while he babbles on. He gets juiced if you say anything about what he was babbling about yesterday or the day before that.

Terrance wanted to be in Buchanan already so he could grab the cash. You know what two thousand dollars is in LD? He would do right by them, by Carl and Levin, anyway. His ma would be proud. They were real people, big men in their own way. He and they were doing something righteous together, however crazy-crazy it was.

The RAV turned right onto a larger road, and suddenly there were people everywhere. Women in red, yellow, blue, and green lapas carrying big multicolored bins on their heads. Men wearing tattered tee shirts. Children just milling about on the road. Tiny shops built out of tree branches lashed together, covered with rusted metal roofing scavenged from buildings that had collapsed, shops that sold roasted corn and bottles of yellow liquid and pots and pans.

God is good, Terrance thought. *People back on the street. My people. Alive again. Wild and free. Life after death.*

"How are we gonna get to Buchanan like this?" Carl said. "It's gonna take a month."

"Dri tro pepl. Fla tro pepl. Na stop us na," Terrance said. He shifted from second to third gear, and then shifted back to second again. *Drive through people. Fly through people. No one is going to stop us.*

"You are one crazy motherfucker," Levin said.

"Crazy mutherfucka. Crazy, crazy, crazy," Terrance said. The RAV swayed and jerked as Terrance steered around people and potholes.

"Where are all these people from?" Levin said.

"This Liberia. This Monrovia. Plenty-plenty people," Terrance said.

"There are always people in the street during the day," Carl said. "People walk. Do business. Hang out. Walk to school. This is a people culture, not a car culture. Liberia is made of six-year-olds. These kids are everywhere and spend their days in the street."

"How long are we going to be in Monrovia?" Levin said.

"Quick-quick," Terrance said.

All of a sudden Terrance realized that Levin and Carl had no idea what Liberia was really like and how hard it was going to be to get to Buchanan, find that woman doctor, and bring her home. Carl, maybe some idea. But Levin didn't have a clue. All of a sudden Terrance realized that he was their teacher now, and that they needed him way more than he needed them.

"Only as long as it takes to drive through," Carl said. "Too long, if some of these damned people don't get out of the road."

"Where are we headed?" Levin said.

"Buchanan!" Terrance said. "Quick-quick. Got a missy to find and free-up."

"There's a hotel a few miles down the road," Carl said. "First stop. We might learn something there, if we get that far today."

"Damn. Is there a bar at this hotel?" Levin said. "I could use a beer. And I don't like beer."

"There's a bar," Carl said. "And woman, usually."

"That's a surprise, coming from the man who launched a thousand ships," Levin said.

"I'm good. We were on the boat four weeks. I got my eyes on the prize. But I'm not traveling alone."

"I'm staying with beer," Levin said. "Or a good whiskey if they have it. What I really want is a stand-up shower and hot water that stays hot. What about the rogue?"

Terrance grinned. "De badass rogue. Plenty-plenty women Buchanan," he said. "We go Buchanan na." *I'm still a badass trouble maker. There are plenty of women in Buchanan. We are headed to Buchanan now.*

"Terrance you are a changed man," Levin said. "That sea air must have done you some good."

"Na chan. Different. Ha ta fli. Go to ler ya. Ge ya ready. Ma ya meh. Ge ya invisible. Strong-strong. Invincible," Terrance said. *Not changed. Different. I have to fly. I have to teach you. I have to make you both men. Invisible. Strong. Invincible.*

"For today I'll take invisible," Levin said.

"Strong-strong wouldn't be bad," Carl said. "And invincible. There is a lot of Africa between here and Julia, and a lot of Liberia between Julia and home."

They drove onto a bridge and saw a city on the other side of the river. Red roofs on low houses everywhere. The roofs looked like rice paddies seen from the air, red patches with trees poking out between them. Smoke rose over the houses and the streets. Some gray-green concrete buildings that were two, three, five, or ten stories tall pushed up between the red roofs.

They crossed a broad brown river. A green hill covered with houses and buildings stood over the sea. White seabirds floated in the air under the bridge and glided over the river. Green sea grasses on the tidal flats waved in the sea breeze blowing in from the ocean. The air smelled dank, like wet earth, and bitter, of charcoal cooking fires. There were no boats on the river.

The bridge was blocked by people, many of whom carried bundles and bowls on their head. They were making a mile an hour, maybe two. They would have made more progress walking.

"Checkpoint," Terrance said as soon as they crossed the bridge.

Four concrete cubes set in the middle of the road. A blue pickup was parked to one side. Two soldiers stood on either side of the cars and trucks that threaded through an opening between the concrete blocks. The soldiers each carried a machine gun strapped over a shoulder. Each car in front of them rolled forward and stopped. The windows next to each passenger rolled down. Sometimes the soldiers leaned into the windows. Sometimes they opened the doors, or the driver got out to open the car's trunk.

"I got no papers," Levin said. "I got a passport, but it's expired."

"Day stop," Terrance said. "Dey just checkin to pay de bill. Small-small bill. Na trouble." *This is a routine traffic stop. They just want a little money.*

"Gimme dash," Terrance said. *Give me small bills for a little bribe*

Carl reached into his pocket. "U.S. or LD?" *American Dollars or Liberian Dollars?*

"U.S.," Terrance said.

Carl gave Terrance a dollar.

"Na one. Gi fi. Coppa ta," Terrance said. *Not a one. Give me five. Money will talk.*

"I hope they buy the American flags," Levin said. "This looks like a lousy place to get shot."

"Gi te. Quick-quick," Terrance said. *Give me a ten.*

Carl handed Terrance a ten-dollar bill as space opened in front of them. Terrance put the bill in the top pocket of his shirt and opened his window.

The soldier on Carl's side of the car let the barrel of his gun drag against the car window as the car slid forward, making a faint line in the red dust on the surface of the glass. Carl opened it. The soldier leaned over so he could see inside. The soldier next to Terrance also leaned into the car. His hand was on the grip and trigger of his gun, which he slid forward so the barrel, which had been strapped across his chest, was now pointing at Terrance.

"USA," Terrance said. "All ga. USA." *It's all good. USA.*

"USA shit," the soldier next to Terrance said.

"Na tra ta," Terrance said. "Bi ma he. Respe." *Stop talking trash. I'm driving an important man. He deserves your respect.*

'Respe earn. Sha respe Liberia," the soldier said. *Respect is earned. Please show some respect for the Republic of Liberia.*

The soldier on Carl's side opened the rear door next to Levin. He leaned inside so he and Levin were face to face, and he pointed a finger at Levin.

"Ya na USA. Ya boo-goo-man. Ya tricky." The soldier next to Levin said. *You're not USA. You are a boogeyman, trying to trick us.* Terrance felt the RAV sink a little to one side with the soldier's weight. He could smell liquor on the man's breath.

"Thank God. He bi man. Take time in life. Sha respe. He white heart," Terrance said. *Thank God (I'm telling the truth). He really is a big man. Be careful. Show respect. He is big enough to forgive you.*

"Who he?" the soldier next to Terrance said.

"He Doctor Bill Levin, bi docta USA. Ya ga me. He pres from USA," Terrance said. *He is Doctor Bill Levin, and important Doctor from the USA. You are good men. Here is a present from the USA.*

He handed a bill out the window.

The soldier on Terrance's side took the bill with his left hand and let go of the gun so it hung from its shoulder strap. He reached over so he held the bill in both hands and pulled it tight, so the bill snapped in the sunlight.

"You may go," the soldier said in careful school English. He slammed the palm of his hand on the roof of the RAV, and the soldier leaning through the rear door backed out of the car, stood and closed the door. It clicked shut.

Terrance moved the RAV forward, and then shifted into second gear. They were able to drive without obstruction for about a hundred yards before the crowd overwhelmed the street again.

"Hot damn, Terrance, you blew through that like it was nothing," Levin said.

Terrance grinned. "Da stop. Easy. Dash goo," Terrance said. *It was a day stop. Easy. We gave them enough money.*

"Terrance, you are the *man*," Carl said.

"Tanky ya. Ha ways. Too tricky way. Sa easy. Sa ha. Fear ti wha wickit boy on da ga," Terrance said. *Thanks. I know how to do this and have some pretty crafty ideas about how to deal. Some are easy. Some hard. I think there will be way tougher people in other checkpoints in front of us.*

Carl and Levin don't know anything about Liberia, Terrance thought. *They are my crew now. I'm in charge.*

"Now get us to Buchanan by nightfall," Carl said.

"No problem nightfall," Terrance said. "Problem get to Buchanan alive and nightfall what day."

"Plenty-plenty crazy stuff ahead," Carl said. "Small-boy units. The ATU. A couple of rebel armies, armed by the CIA. We gonna fly like a butterfly, sting like a bee. Get in. Get out. Get gone."

"My boys in the bush," Terrance said. "Crazy-crazy."

"You help us with them, you earned your keep," Carl said.

"I ga my boys," Terrance said. *I got my boys.* "You find docta and then get home."

"Good," Levin said. "Terrance, you run the road. Carl, you find Julia and then get us the hell out of here. I'll be in charge of yelling 'duck' when somebody shoots at us and ruining bad jokes."

"All *you* gotta do is sit back there and act like the bossman," Carl said. "But don't let that shit go to your head. And all *we* gotta to do is to make a hundred miles of really bad road into a superhighway."

"We're probably screwed whatever we do," Levin said. "You two are the brains. I'm the brawn. Which means we are in really deep shit."

They turned south and east, onto Haile Selassie Avenue and into Monrovia itself, where the street was jammed with more people yet.

The houses and small apartment building were made of grey-white concrete block covered with white, green, or yellow stucco. But the stucco had fallen off or been shot away from most of the walls, and the concrete was pockmarked by bullet holes. There was black and grey mold growing on the concrete, which made the buildings look rusted and crumbling. Their rusted red metal roofs were patched with white, tan, and black metal panels and by blue tarps that flapped in the seacoast wind—a worn-out quilt with lots of holes. Many of the larger buildings were unfinished, just eight or ten stories of poured cement, surrounded by wooden scaffolding that was partially torn away; just concrete shells standing in the midmorning sun. Big tombstones. Monuments to nothing. Big ideas gone bad. Empty promises exposed for the world to see.

After four hours of inching forward in the hot sun, they found themselves in the center of government. The throng in the street disappeared for a few hundred yards. Monrovia is the capital city of the oldest republic in Africa and full of government buildings. They drove past the Capitol Building, the Supreme Court, the Old Executive Mansion, the Ministry of Foreign Affairs and the University of Liberia, which were all deserted. No cars out front. No people walking in and out. No lights on behind the windows. The statues and monuments in front of the buildings were all damaged, the figures missing heads or limbs, bullet marked, or covered in graffiti. People walked in the street in ones and twos, but no one walked near the buildings. Tattered flags flew from a few flagpoles. Machine gun emplacements stood at the entrances. No one going in or coming out. It was like driving among the pyramids. Stone and cement, surrounded by a desert. Only the desert in Monrovia was green, the sky was overcast, and the sea was everywhere around them.

They passed City Hall, where Haile Selassie Avenue turns into Tubman Boulevard—a district of houses and stores. People crowded the streets again, and the RAV could barely move forward. The signs on the squat grey and yellow buildings had been shot away or were hanging from one corner or by one side. The shops were empty, boarded up or deserted, their windows shattered, leaving shards of broken glass; the manikins from the displays lay on their sides. They were missing arms, legs, wigs, and clothing and were covered with dust and spider webs. There were rows of palm trees. Most of the palm trunks were broken off ten or fifteen feet above the ground, so the trees looked like broken off teeth. The moist air from the sea was hot and thick. The salty sea air mixed with the warm bitter smell of charcoal smoke and the sweet putrid smell of sewage but also of the sweet green smell of the remaining palms, so it was hard to know what to make of the air.

Then Terrance spun the wheel and hit the gas. The RAV screeched into a side street that ran to the ocean.

Terrance turned hard again and pulled the RAV between a shipping container that was parked on the street, its top half ripped off, and a small apartment block with half a wall collapsed, so you couldn't see the RAV from the street, although the street was only half a block away.

"Sink," Terrance said. "Sink now." He pulled his knees to his chest and dropped low in his seat, so his head was below the level of the dash.

Carl and Levin dropped in their seats. As they did, they saw the people on the street scatter.

They heard boom and a rhythm, a rattling set of bass notes that was coming toward them: BOOM, BOOM CHA BOOM, BOOM, BOOM, BOOM CHA BOOM, BOOM, BOOM, BOOM CHA BOOM, BOOM, loud enough to make the RAV shake and their teeth vibrate. Then they heard bursts of automatic weapon fire. They were just a block from the ocean, so the booming and the rattle of gunfire was set against the crashing of the surf, a weird, almost musical, counterpoint.

Two boy-soldiers on foot came into view. They were half-naked and wore aviator sunglasses. They carried AK-47s which they waved as they walked. They walked in time to the music. BOOM, BOOM CHA BOOM, BOOM, BOOM, BOOM CHA BOOM, BOOM, BOOM, BOOM CHA BOOM, BOOM. One was bare-chested, wore camouflage pants and carried a knapsack made out of a teddy bear. The other wore a woman's yellow coat with a faux fur collar that belonged in New York in the fall over an ammunition belt and ragged blue jeans. Both boys wore flip-flops on their feet. They were small and slight, perhaps twelve or thirteen, but they walked like they were bigger than they were, strutting like they owned everything they could see.

Then two more boy-soldiers walked past, one closer and one further away as they walked the street. BOOM, BOOM CHA BOOM, BOOM, BOOM, BOOM CHA BOOM, BOOM, BOOM, BOOM CHA BOOM, BOOM. The boy who was closer was wearing jeans and a tee shirt and was bigger and a few years older than the first two boys. He carried a bigger machine gun in one hand without a shoulder strap, and he turned from side to side as he walked, bouncing to the rhythm, high-stepping and bebopping. He twisted his head from side to side, looking about, the way a gliding hawk tips its head as it flies, searching for prey. The boy pointed the gun where he looked, so when he saw the world he saw it from the perspective of the muzzle of the gun, looking at where the hot lead would spray the moment he pulled the trigger.

Then a beat-up red pickup came into view, and the beat got even louder, loud enough to hurt. BOOM, BOOM CHA BOOM, BOOM, BOOM, BOOM CHA BOOM, BOOM, BOOM, BOOM CHA BOOM, BOOM. There was one boy-soldier driving, another in the seat next to him, and one more on the standing roof of the cab. The boy on the cab was wearing short pants that came down to his knees. His feet were spread far apart. He had a purple bandanna on his head and two ammunition belts draped over his shoulders.

The bed of the truck was filled with cardboard boxes, and there was a glistening yellow tubular mass hanging from the antenna.

"Intestines," Levin said. "Who butchered a pig?"

"Na pig," Terrance said.

The boy on the roof of the truck took aim at a window above the street. The machine gun popped and spit, jerking in the boy's arms. There was a crack. Glass rained into the street. The shards hissed as they showered the ground.

"Damn," Terrance said. "Be still now. Dead still."

Two more boy-soldiers came into view, one near and one on the other side of the street, both strutting and dancing. As he passed them, the boy-soldier who was closest spun around and looked directly at the RAV, which he could suddenly see, just for a moment. He raised his gun. The windshield of the RAV caught the sunlight. It was the only unbroken glass on the street.

The boy was about fourteen. His eyes were red, and he looked tired. He was also naked from the waist up. He wore a Boston Red Sox baseball cap that was on sideways and a white and blue necktie around his bare neck.

He badass, Terrance thought. *He me.*

Levin and Carl sank deeper into their seats. Terrance closed his eyes and waited for the hot lead to hit.

They heard the pop and rattle of a burst.

And at the same time, plink, plink, plink, plink, plink, plink, plink, plink.

Bullets hitting the dumpster.

Missed the RAV. Missed it completely.

We invisible, Terrance thought. *Strong power.* And then he looked at Carl and at Levin to make sure they were okay.

And then the BOOM, BOOM CHA BOOM, BOOM, BOOM, BOOM CHA BOOM, BOOM, BOOM, BOOM CHA BOOM, BOOM faded. The pickup moved down the street.

When Carl and Levin opened their eyes again the boy soldier who had drawn a bead on them had turned and was walking down the street again in time to the beat. On his back was a small blue and red knapsack that had a picture of a Mickey Mouse on it—the kind first graders take to school on their first day.

"Damn," Levin said. "What the hell was that?"

"SBU. A small boy unit," Carl said. "Charles Taylor's vision of peacekeeping. Terrance, you saved the day. They would have blasted us to kingdom come if we had been on that street."

"And the guts hanging from the antenna?" Levin said.

"Big me e d ha a enemy. Ma'm strong. Bult ca hu'r im. Le gu fa boys to ler," Terrance said. *The big men eat the hearts of their enemies. It makes them strong. Bullets can't hurt them. They leave the guts for the boys so the boys can learn fear and courage.*

Terrance started the RAV and backed it out of their hiding place.

People were coming back onto the street. The three men could still hear the booming rhythm but it was fading. The crash of the waves became fainter as the noise of the street and the engine rumbled and hummed.

There was rubble everywhere. Rubble and people. After four blocks they came on a body lying in the street—a man in fatigues with his chest and belly slit open. People stood off from the body, not looking at it, aware but not wanting or willing to approach it.

The RAV nosed through that crowd. Then the throng closed in behind them, so the three men couldn't see the body once they had driven past.

This is my life, Terrance thought. *I can move. I can operate here. I can breathe. I'm strong here. I'm free here. These are good men. Carl and Dr. Levin. We can do this thing, find this woman. The bush is a hard place, but it is a good place if you just stay close to the earth. Get beyond these people and this road. Go to the bush. Find this woman if she can be found. We can move better in the bush.*

And I can live this life or have a different life. I can be here at home, find my boys, and live again, strong-strong in Liberia. Or I can choose. I can be what ma says and Levin says. Strong-strong in America. Do school and know or do the bush and live. I with Carl and Dr. Levin now. They are men like me. I can live this life or their life or go back and forth. I know both peoples. Both places. Both lives. I fly above the earth.

Terrance looked in his rearview mirror and could still see the crew vanishing down the street. "Crazy-crazy boys," Terrance said, almost under his breath." Crazy-crazy."

They inched.

The sea of people became a movie or a dream state, each person coming into view for a moment, and then disappearing as they inched past, sometimes leaving a track on the dust of the window or the fender where the person touch or just rubbed against the car. One old woman banged her fist against the window. Hollow-eyed young men and impossibly thin women with close-cropped but still matted hair—all of whom looked like they hadn't slept in weeks—just stood in the street and barely moved to make way. Clouds of doe-eyed six-year-olds. Sometimes the kids waved at them. But most of them were too weak, too timid, or too tired to wave or beg. Many people pounded on the windows. At first, the three men thought those people wanted something or were angry. But their faces were flat, so the three men accepted the banging and thought to themselves, that's just people saying I'm here, I exist, I've survived. So far.

American flags. Massachusetts plates. They were ignored. They could have been driving the Batmobile. They would have been ignored in that.

Late in the afternoon the sky grew dark. Thunder shook the streets. The sky opened and rain fell in sheets. Some people took cover. Others remained in the streets, standing still in their ragged clothing, the water running through their hair and down their faces and shoulders in sheets.

Then here was a hotel sign and a compound wall on the left side of the street.

"It's getting dark," Carl said. "We're for the night. Turn here."

He mad we ain't there yet, Terrance thought. *All Carl sees is that woman.*

The hotel guards saw the U.S. flags and Levin in the back. They raised the gate.

The guards didn't matter, though. The hotel's walls were pockmarked by bullet holes, just like every building in Monrovia. A big generator in the parking lot clattered and smoked. The parking lot was filled with UN Land Cruisers and big black cars that had been recently washed.

Carl took the one room left. He paid for it in cash, and they headed to the restaurant.

The halls were hot and dimly lit. They smelled of mold, human sweat, and sexual juices.

Terrance had never been in a place with so much light, so much talky-talky and click thump noise. The restaurant was filled with men and women dressed up for a show and UN soldiers from all over. The bar was crowded with loud-talking people in uniforms, men wearing business suits but no ties, and Liberian women in short skirts and tight tops, with straightened hair. One dark-skinned woman had dyed her hair blond. Another pink. Another sky blue. Each woman had two or three men clustered around her. *Who are these people?* Terrance thought. *They think they are USA, that they are so strong, so invisible, so different from people in the street, who only eat and die.*

"Who are all these people?" Levin said.

"What you see is what you get," Carl said. "UN, CIA, military intelligence, and embassy guys. Ours, British, and French. China is in Liberia big time, but they don't drink here. They have a hotel about a half mile down the road. The Chinese drink like fish. Boy are they hard on the Liberian women. Don't ask. Israelis and South Africans here as well. Belgians and East Europeans—gunrunners and diamond traders. The gunrunners drink with the peacekeepers, military intelligence, and the state department types. Chicken at a fish place. That's why I love this country."

"The uniforms?" Levin said.

"Peacekeepers. So-called. The UN doesn't have its own troops. Ghanaians, Finns, Canadians, Nepalese, Pakistanis, Cameroonians, and Nigerians. Lots of Nigerians. Nigeria is the big power in West Africa. Most of the UN troops are Nigerian. Sometimes the Nigerians keep the peace. Sometimes they run their own little war. They grab and hold territory themselves. Loot and rape. The Nigerians are even harder on the Liberian women. You ever run into Nibatt, Terrance?"

Carl and Levin are okay here, Terrance thought, *so I can be okay here as well. Carl has no idea what it's like to walk the streets or roam the bush locked and loaded. The Nigerians are pompous fools. They hide behind their guns and uniforms, but they stick out like a sore thumb and everyone laughs at them. Levin doesn't even know he's in Africa.*

"Nibatt stay Buchanan. Le country alone. Na strong in de bush. Bi in ta. Bi, na stra," Terrance said. *Nibatt stays in Buchanan. They leave the countryside alone. They aren't strong in the countryside. They are big as long as they are in town, but they are not strong in the bush.*

"What does it mean to be strong in Liberia?" Levin said. "The big men who think they are strong are shooting this country up, while Liberia is on its knees, bleeding out. Is that strong?"

"Strong ma wa thru he na blink. Strong ma crew strong, wa thru bullet," Terrance said. *A strong man can walk through hell without blinking. A strong man makes his crew strong so they can walk through bullets with him.*

"Juju. Nonsense," Carl said. "Terrance, no one walks through bullets. We all die the same way."

Carl is smart-smart, but he doesn't know my people, Terrance thought. *Levin is smart-dumb, but he doesn't know who rules Liberia. I will teach them. They have only me now.*

"Strong ma li before he dies," Terrance said. "A we ma dies before he li. Strong cru li together foevaa." *A strong man lives before he dies. A weak man dies before he lives. A strong crew lives together forever.*

"None of that crap is real, Terrance," Carl said. "All the dressing up, the bones and the hats and the dresses—all bullshit. The big men who eat the hearts of their enemies die the same way that everyone else dies. They take a bullet and they go down. Guns don't kill people. Bullets kill people. Your crew is out there dying like the rest."

You don't know what is real, Terrance thought. *You haven't lived yet.*

"We crew now," Terrance said. "We live and die together."

"We lived through one day. That makes us strong. At least for today," Levin said.

"Holy Moses," Carl said.

A man and a woman in uniform who had just come in found places at the bar. They were standing just behind Terrance, waiting to order.

"Remember me?" Carl said.

The man looked at the woman. "Can't say I do."

Carl stood. Terrance stood as well.

"I was the guy on the *Iwo Jima* who bugged you about a woman doctor when you evacuated the expats from Buchanan," Carl said.

"Oh yeah, the guy who wanted to try out the brig for the night," the man said. "The guy with the satellite phone. What the hell are you doing here? You people all got moved stateside."

"Dr. Richmond never appeared," Carl said.

"Sorry about that. The mission . . ."

". . . was successfully concluded. I remember. But I'm back. With reinforcements. Looks like we have to finish the job for the marines. Looks like we get to go find Dr. Richmond ourselves."

"Good luck with that," the woman said. "You'll never get to Buchanan. People running from LURD are jammed on the road south. People running from MODEL are moving north and west. The already wonderful Liberian roads are blocked by people on foot. You can't get around without a helicopter. The copters are getting shot at when they're up. Shot at by everybody with a slingshot."

"Happy to accept the loan of a helicopter," Carl said.

"Only in your dreams," the man said. "Helicopters cost money. And they break. Walk if you want. You already got the best ride of your life when we lifted you out of here."

"You're putting three more Americans in harm's way," Carl said.

"Bullshit. *You* are putting three more American's in harm's way. Or four," the man said. "Don't expect the cavalry to come to the rescue a second time."

"I'm going to be absolutely clear," the woman said. "We can't guarantee your safety. Not even a little. Not in Monrovia, not in Buchanan, not in the bush, and not even here. Your government doesn't think you belong anywhere near the Republic of Liberia. You're going to get yourself and your so-called reinforcements killed, and if you don't watch your ass, you're going to get Dr. Richmond killed as well. Dr. Richmond is okay. You can only make things worse for her. She's as good as she can be, given the situation. You, however, are totally fucked if you don't turn yourself around and head home *today*, whichever way you got yourself here. Capiche?"

"The hell with that," Carl said. "We're going to Buchanan. And we can use all the help we can get."

"Help you?" the woman said. "We don't even know you exist. You getting yourselves killed is your problem. No one in their right mind is going to put more American lives at risk to protect this little field trip."

"Thanks for the brass band and the red carpet. It's nice to know the U.S. government is taking care of business," Carl said. "I promise we'll call only if we really need you."

"You can call all you want." The man said. "Nobody's home. Mission accomplished. We're outta here. Packing up and heading home. You oughta do the same."

"We'll join you when we have Dr. Richmond in tow."

"Good luck with that too. By which I mean nice to know you. And you should live and be well. By which I mean don't call me, I'll call you," the man said.

"Appreciate the warm welcome and support," Carl said. "Semper fi."

The man and the woman turned to face the bar. Carl and Terrance looked at Levin.

"What's the scoop?" Levin said.

"Julia is alive," Carl said. "And they know where she is."

Levin wasn't sure where he was when he awoke in the middle of the night. They had turned the generator off at midnight. There was no AC, so the room was hot and sticky, and the moist air smelled of mold and sweat. It was pitch black, inside and outside. Levin heard occasional voices calling one another in the dark; not close, blocks away, not feet away, and further off as well. Then random gunfire, single shots and short bursts in the distance, mixed in with the voices far away in the dark.

He turned over and felt the hard floor. Hard and cool.

A hotel. They were in a hotel. In Liberia. Levin remembered the plink, plink, plink, plink of the burst of machine-gun fire hitting the dumpster next to the RAV. The strutting kid with the sunglasses and gun. The red pickup parading down the street, rap booming and intestines hanging from the antenna. Levin was sleeping on the floor, on cushions from the single chair in the room. Carl and Terrance were snoring on the bed. The bathroom. Where the hell was the bathroom? How did this hotel room lay out? Damned old man bladder. This would have been a good night to sleep through. But not tonight.

He knelt, and then stood, his hand on a wall. And waited. He had a little flashlight on his key ring, but that was in the pocket of his pants, and he didn't want to go back looking for it. Maybe there was some light that his eyes could find if he waited for them to get used to the dark. Maybe a night-light of some kind in the bathroom or the seepage of light from under the door.

But nothing. Dark as a dungeon.

Levin felt his way along the wall. Where was the damned bathroom door? A doorknob. A window. Some lights in the distance, from the few places that had generators and enough firepower to risk being seen. He felt around in the dark. The toilet. Close the door. Sit. Better.

Up to my neck in it this time, Levin thought. *How does anyone let a place get like this? Yeah, yeah, yeah, the usual explanations—colonialism and U.S. imperialism and globalization and consumer capitalism, all true and all lies, each in their own way. There were kids on the street with automatic weapons, shooting each other and everything in sight. Dead men whose hearts had been cut out and eaten raw. Where are the decent people who should have been able to stop this? Where were the mothers of these kids and the grandmothers who keep the world on its track?*

I could die here, Levin thought. *Probably will die here. That's okay. My work is done. I had my run. Passed on some of what I learned. Julia can carry it forward if she survives. Maybe we'll find her and get her out. Maybe she'll survive on her own. She's tough, that kid. She'll probably outlive the three of us, Africa or no Africa, war or no war.*

I didn't defeat global capitalism, Levin thought. *Or greed. Or stupidity. Or colonialism—all different ways of saying the same thing. But it's been a good ride. Saw a lot. Thought a lot. Did a lot. Even fought for justice a little, but God knows we are far off that mark. And how cool it is to be here. Riding around a war zone with these two cowboys. We got this far. No one would have thought it. Everybody dies of something. Might as damn well go out in a blaze of glory. Finding Julia and getting her to Carl—that's a story they can tell their kids. That's more than enough glory for one man, for one lifetime. Sure beats running in a cemetery.*

Levin stood. He could see his sleeping comrades now by the faint light from the window.

They weren't snoring, Carl and Terrance. They were out deep and breathing heavy. Human beings. Good men, even Terrance, the rogue. There is goodness in people. Maybe greatness. *I'm lucky to be alive. I'm lucky to be here*, Levin thought.

One body. No demonstration ever sets you free. But being together does.

He found his pillows on the floor, lined them up and lay on them. And slept.

Chapter Eighteen

Terrance Evans-Smith, Carl
Goldman, and William Levin.
Monrovia and Samuel Kanyon Doe Stadium,
Paynesville, Liberia. August 16, 2003

CARL WOKE THEM BEFORE DAWN. THERE WERE TOO MANY PEOPLE ON THE STREET TO DRIVE fast even then.

People cooked in the road, sat in the road, and slept on the street. Women with boxes and bundles. Men bent double with big fake-leather suitcases held together by belted circles of silver duct tape on their backs. Shanties made of scavenged metal roofing and blue and silver tarps, built right on the broken tarmac.

Terrance nosed through the crowd, which parted before them and closed in after them, as if people were water.

They barely made one mile an hour. Walking would have been faster, only you couldn't get through the throng any better on foot. Carl stared out the window, tense and angry.

The throng got thicker outside JFK Hospital. Gaunt men in camouflage stood at the wrought iron fence in front of the hospital. Blue jeeps and pickups were parked inside the gates. The soldiers pointed their guns at the people in the street. People walked in front of the guns but kept their distance, ready to run for cover the moment one of the soldiers lost his nerve and started firing.

They drove up a hill that overlooked the ocean. Then they drove through Congo Town, where most of the buildings along the road were wrecked—a wall gone here, the windows shot out there, another building falling in on itself where a tank or half-track had pushed through it. *Somebody had themselves a good little battle in here,* Terrance

thought. *One wild time. Really messed it up.* Someone cut all the telephone and electric wires off the telephone poles that ran along the
street. The short wire ends looped around each pole, running every
which way. Telephone poles with bad hair, but there was no wire
from pole to pole. Nothing was connected any more. Everything was
ruined. Life was fried. Frazzled. Gone.

Nothing moved. Nothing worked. Hope was a memory. A dream.
A hallucination. A mirage.

The evening rains and dusk came. The sky became yellow, orange,
purple, and red.

A crowd gathered at a soccer stadium in front of two tents flying
white and red flags. One more army, Terrance thought, and turned
south to get away, expecting another check-point.

But Carl pointed to the tents.

"Médecins Sans Frontières; Doctors without Borders," Carl said.
"We'll stop here. Three goddamn miles today. Maybe four."

Men and woman dressed in white coats and blue jeans moved
through the throng, some dispensing water in tiny paper cups, others
with clipboards and stethoscopes. They checked with each person on
the line and sent people off to different queues.

"My crew," Levin said. "I'll go to parley."

Terrance and Carl opened their doors when Levin did and stood to
stretch, leaning against the RAV as Levin walked into one of the tents.

They were surrounded by Liberian people, lost inside their
clothes, covered with red dust. An old man who looked something
like his ma's second man, only older and shrunken, and who couldn't
look up. Young women, some carrying babies, others standing alone,
but all who looked away the second he caught their eye, the second he
saw the fear and disappointment, afraid and ashamed of the lives they
had and had lost, afraid of Terrance who was washed and fed, afraid
for themselves and of themselves, as if they knew their bodies had
betrayed them by giving birth to boys and men like Terrance, afraid
of the hotness that brought men and women together. Old women,

just waiting, without any hope or expectation, waiting for God in his mercy to make known his plan. Children hiding behind their mother's lapas, confused about where they were. Terrance checked each person, looking for the eyes of someone he knew and who knew him among the shells of people who stood on line.

These were the people Terrance had raided when he was strong-strong, invisible, and flying above the earth. Here, standing on the same ground, waiting with Liberian people, Terrance discovered the war at last. He wasn't raiding or taking what he wanted. He couldn't fly above the earth, invisible and invincible. He also wasn't just driving through a shapeless mass, dodging a throng of the abject and the walking dead. Now Terrance saw the war and felt the war and suddenly discovered how the war he made had reduced Liberian people to ghosts, to shells, to victims, to the weak and helpless and a people without a home or a purpose in their own country. Suddenly Terrance saw himself as a Liberian for the first time, as one more victim, even though, for Terrance, to be a victim—to be wounded or dead—was to be less than nothing, subhuman, a woman who licked your boots begging, a severed head, its mouth tasting the red dirt.

They are my people, Terrance thought.

The men and women in white coats and jeans walking among the others were different from the people they walked among. They were now the only people who appeared to be alive, who walked and talked and acted like they belonged.

Levin found Logistics.

The Médecins Sans Frontières people had been in country since May, they said—and they were up to their eyeballs. Yes, they had heard that Merlin and the County Hospital in Buchanan had been overrun. Nothing they could do about Buchanan now. They had teams in Bong, Grand Cape, Mount, Bomi, Gbarpolu, Grand Bassa, Margibi, and Grand Gedeh Counties, and those teams needed all the help they could get. The supply chain wasn't working. MSF was trying to negotiate air drops of supplies with UNMIL, but have you ever tried to talk to anyone at the UN? Try getting a coherent answer in anything under six months. They knew about the burned-out vehicle of the Norwegian and the two Liberians who disappeared in Toe County in the spring. They had heard that Julia had disappeared north of Buchanan, her car found burned out, and that two men with her had been found dead. There was a website that listed missing and dead health workers around the world. They hadn't heard anything else. They didn't have a reliable internet connection yet. The three men could park the RAV next to the tents, and there were cots they could use for one night and breakfast in the morning, just tea or coffee and a hard roll wrapped in plastic.

Levin asked about who was here doing kids and emergency assessments and where they were here from. It took him two minutes to ferret out a connection. Seconds to find somebody who knew somebody else. Two degrees of separation. Global health, emergency response, and stabilization. Maybe one degree. University of Indiana folk at Eldoret. The group in Burma. Partners in Haiti. The torture assessment project run by PHR out of NYU.

They could use Levin's help in the Pedi tent overnight. I know he isn't properly credentialed. He's here and he speaks kids. We know people in common. Someone had read a paper. Pedigree works. The hell with credentialing. Let's put you to work.

The football pitch was purple and covered with bodies and tarps. It had once been green and flat with white chalk lines marking the boundaries of the playing field. Now the air above the pitch was gray from charcoal smoke and the stink of too many bodies in not enough space.

Terrance and Carl got dinner in the volunteers' mess.

Levin reappeared at about midnight when the generators shut down and the camp quieted. He paced while Carl and Terrance slept on bedrolls next to the RAV. He was snoring at sunrise, when he awoke with a start. Then he fell back to sleep. They let him sleep and snore until the sun rose over the tree line.

Chapter Nineteen
Terrance Evans-Smith, Carl
Goldman, and William Levin.
Paynesville and Harbel, Liberia. August 17, 2003

THE AIR WAS ALREADY HOT IN THE SHADE WHEN THEY SET OUT THE NEXT DAY. A DULL
yellow haze hung in front of the early morning sun. They were about a
mile from the stadium when they hit their first stretch of open road—
fewer people, no cars, and no checkpoints. Terrance got the car up to
thirty miles an hour.

The cement block houses and the shops lining the road had all
been destroyed. They passed groups of traditional houses made from
poles with mud walls and layered palm leaf roofs arranged around
outside cooking shanties. A few people sat or stood beside the fires.

They passed a bombed-out gasoline station. The pumps were
gone and the bright red canopy that once stood over the pumps had
collapsed. There was red dust on the bright green, blue, and red painted
walls—paint and brightness that had once beckoned to travelers on
this important road, which connected Monrovia, capital of the oldest
democracy in Africa, to the international airport and to the Firestone
plantation, the largest rubber plantation in the world.

"Check the tank," Carl said. "Long trip. I don't know if there's any
gas between here and Buchanan. If we get to Buchanan."

"Ha ta," Terrance said. *Half a tank.*

"Stop when you can. Next open gas station," Carl said.

But there weren't any open gas stations. Instead there were
destroyed gas stations, one after the next.

Then Terrance noticed something. There were rickety tables in
front of destroyed gas stations where the gasoline pumps used to be.

On the tables sat five-gallon jugs filled with amber liquid, and next to each jug were one or two smaller bottles and sometimes a large white funnel. Terrance knew these jugs from little shops in the small villages he raided. Now the jugs were on the main airport road. Next to the table, as often as not, sat a man or a woman in a white plastic chair, holding an umbrella as a shield from the sun.

They passed one or two of these people before Terrance realized that Carl and Levin didn't know what they were seeing.

"Petrol," Terrance said. "Na gas station. De se petrol ju ba ju." *These aren't gas stations. They are selling gas by the jug.*

"You're right," Carl said. "Those guys with jugs are all that's left. That's a gas station now."

"Sure there ain't something more solid up ahead?" Levin said. "Who knows what's really in those jugs."

"I wouldn't count on it," Carl said.

They passed a third and a fourth rickety table, but the large glass jug on each table was almost empty.

Then they passed a table with a full jug.

"Stop here," Carl said. "Let us avail ourselves of what God's provided."

Terrance pulled the RAV off the road.

A man in an orange tee shirt and cut off jeans who was missing his left foot and ankle sat in a chair next to a table that held one of the large amber jugs, a smaller one-liter plastic soda bottle, and a white plastic funnel. The one-legged man rose on a pair of handmade crutches whittled from the branch of a tree. He hobbled over to the window of the RAV.

"Wha co?" Terrance said. *How much?*

"U.S.? LD?" the man said.

"U.S.," Terrance said. "Quick-quick."

"Two dolla liter, U.S.," the man said.

"Wha co jug?"

"Eighty dolla U.S. jug."

"All jug. Quick-quick," Terrance said.

Carl handed Terrance four twenty-dollar bills, and Terrance handed them to the man on crutches.

The man balanced on his one good leg, leaned one of his crutches against the car, inspected the bills, folded them and put them into his pocket. He hobbled back to the table, put the one-liter plastic soda bottle on the ground and put the funnel in the mouth of the soda bottle. Then he lifted and tipped the large glass jug to one side so that a thin rivulet of gasoline spilled out of the jug through the funnel and into the bottle on the ground.

When the one-liter soda bottle was three-quarters full, the one-footed gasoline seller righted the large gas jug, leaving the soda bottle on the ground but removing the funnel from its mouth. Then he hobbled toward the back of the RAV, opened the gas cap and put the funnel into the tank. He hobbled back to where the full bottle stood on the ground. He bent and lifted the three-quarters full soda bottle, nestling it under his arm. Then, leaning on the car, he hobbled to the back of the car and carefully poured gas through the funnel into the gas tank. Then he put the one-liter soda bottle under his arm again, and hobbled back to the table that held the larger glass jug as he got ready to repeat the procedure.

"It's a ten-gallon jug," Carl said. "This is going to take all day."

Terrance shook his head. "Slow-slow," Terrance said.

Levin started to open the door, but then he stopped himself. He was trapped by the crutch that was leaning against his door.

"Me," Terrance said. He opened his door, stepped into the sun and stood for a moment while his eyes adjusted to the light. He was the man in charge now. He was in his own country.

Terrance stood next to the one-legged man as he poured gas into the one-liter plastic soda bottle on the ground for a second time.

"Me," Terrance said. He lifted the bottle and the funnel while the one-egged man watched, walked to the back of car and emptied the bottle into the gas tank. Then he brought the bottle back to the table.

"Na ga," he said. "Wa me. Betta wa." *No good. Watch me.*

He lifted the jug, which was still mostly full.

"Whew," Carl said from inside the car. "Terrance is gonna make magic happen, Terrance and our new friend. American time. Not glacial time. Not that there are any glaciers in these parts."

Terrance lifted the jug and carried it to the gas tank. The one-legged man followed. Terrance tasted gas in his nostrils and felt it burn his eyes. The one-legged man hobbled close to the car. He put the funnel in the gas tank and steadied it, balancing himself by holding onto the car.

"Very cool," Carl said. "Team work. Ya'll are reading my mind."

Terrance tipped the jug. Gasoline splashed in the funnel and flowed into the tank. One smooth pour. Clockwork. Cake. Easy. All in this together. Sweet as pie.

The jug was almost empty when a white Toyota pickup roared past in the direction of the airport, its bed filled with soldiers in camouflage uniforms, "ECOMIL" stenciled in blue block letters on its doors. The pickup slowed, stopped, and swung around. It pulled into the gas station. It drove up just perpendicular to the RAV so that the doors were just beyond the RAV's nose, its cab abutting the small raised island that had once held gas pumps and now held only a rickety table and an empty plastic one-liter soda bottle, and stopped so it was blocking the RAV's escape.

"USA!!!" said one of the soldiers. The rest of the soldiers in the bed of the truck joined him. "USA!!! USA!!!" they said together. The soldiers wore camouflage helmets and had folded sky-blue berets under the epaulets of their shirts.

The driver, a dark-skinned soldier with spit-polished black boots and a blue beret got out of the truck. He looked at Terrance. He wasn't smiling.

Terrance finished pouring the last of the gasoline. He straightened and set the now empty but still heavy ten-gallon glass jug on the rickety table.

The soldier in the blue beret, who Terrance, Carl, and Levin took to be an officer, assessed the facts of the case. American flags.

No identifying information on the vehicle. Not a Humvee. No uniforms—just men, could be Agency, could be anyone.

A well-fed man in clean clothing was pouring gasoline, while a one-legged poor man watched. There was a white man in the back of the vehicle.

"Have you paid for the gasoline, sir?" the soldier said.

"Wha?" Terrance said.

"Have you purchased the petrol, sir?"said the soldier. The soldier spoke a stiff African accented British English so he sounded more like a diplomat than he did a soldier. He stood square—his shoulders thrown back, his feet spread wide apart, his hands on his hips. In command of the situation.

"We pa," Terrance said, turning to face the soldier. *We paid.*

It doesn't matter that this is Liberia, not Nigeria, Terrance thought. *It doesn't matter that NiBatt is fat, stupid, and afraid of its own shadow, that they will never go out into the bush. It doesn't matter the Carl and Levin are big men, each in his own way. All that matters now is that armed men in the truck are locked and loaded. And that there are seven of them.*

The soldier looked at the one-legged man.

"No pa," the one-legged man said.

The soldier pulled his gun out of its holster and pointed it at Terrance.

Then the one-legged man reached for but knocked over the second crutch, the one that had been leaning against Levin's door. The second crutch thudded as it hit the ground.

The soldier, seeing the sudden movement, swept his gun toward the falling crutch and then jerked the gun up just as quickly, keeping Terrance in his sights.

Behind them, the men in the truck sprung into position—the near row kneeling, their guns trained on the RAV—and the back row standing, their guns shouldered and trained on Terrance, the guns held over the heads of the men in the near row.

Carl and Levin froze in their seats.

The soldier with the gun turned left and pointed the gun at Levin. "Out of the truck, sir," the soldier said. "Slowly. Hands on head."

Levin opened his door slowly. Carl started to open his door and stopped when he realized that only Levin had been ordered to move.

"One side. One side only," the soldier shouted. His voice echoed in the empty space in front of the dusty cinder block walls that had once been bright blue.

The one-legged man put his left hand back on the car for support and rocked backward, closer to Terrance, who shifted to make room. With the crutch on the ground and the one-legged man in the way, there was no place for Levin to stand.

The soldier looked from Levin to the one-legged man to Terrance and to Carl.

"I pi crutch just na," Terrance said. "Na fea." *I'm going to pick up the crutch now. I'm not trying to hurt or frighten anyone.*

Terrance bent and found the crutch with his hand. He kept his eyes on the soldier in the blue beret. Then he slowly lifted the crutch and handed it to the one-legged man, keeping his eyes on the soldier with the blue beret. The one-legged man took crutch, Terrance's simple kindness giving lie to the claim of no pay. He hobbled back to the table and Levin stood, his hands on his head.

The soldier now pointed his weapon at Carl.

"Out. Out of the car. Now," the soldier said.

Carl opened the passenger door and stood, moving very slowly. He put his hands on his head, and Terrance did so as well. The one-legged man kept his hands on his crutches and leaned slowly into them now that he had two. He rocked back and forth, shifting his weight between his one leg and the crutches, his version of being ready to run.

The soldier with the blue beret kept the gun trained on Terrance, but he straightened his knees, coming out of his shooter's crouch. Carl, Terrance, Levin, the one-legged man, and the soldier in the blue beret all let go of a breath together.

Then another soldier in a blue beret, an officer, older and heavier, came around the front from the passenger side of the pickup.

"Report," he said. The second soldier stood at attention next to the soldier in the blue beret holding the gun and looked only at the man with the gun.

"Looters, sir," said the first soldier.

"You know your orders," said the officer.

The second soldier turned to the men in the truck.

"Aim," he said.

The soldiers in the truck with their guns shouldered tightened their grips. They focused on their gunsights, aiming at Carl and Terrance.

"Papers?" said the officer, who Carl, Levin, and Terrance now took to be in charge. "You have checked their papers?"

"No, sir," said the second in command. "Not yet, sir."

The second in command turned to the soldiers in the truck and raised his left hand, spreading his fingers and stretching out his palm as if he was a policeman at a busy intersection, stopping traffic.

The sun was still bright and strong, and there was a hot breeze from the ocean, which was just a mile away over a bluff that was across the road. The morning smoke had cleared, but the smell of the charcoal fires still hung in the air.

The second in command pointed his gun at Levin.

"Papers!" he said.

Terrance noticed that all the other guns were aimed at Carl and himself, not at Levin.

These soldiers are Africans, Terrance thought, *who have come to show the world that Africa can solve Africa's problems. But these men, who are as likely to kill us as they are to talk to us, are still looking at this white man as the only source of power and looking to that white man for instruction and redemption as ineffective and disorganized as this white man is, however decent his intentions.*

"We go Buchanan," Terrance said. "Who dere na?" *We going to Buchanan. Who is there now?*

The second in command stepped closer to Terrance and looked at him full in the face. "Papers!" he demanded. "Papers *now. Now!*"

"Ya ho he foo. So-so bi ma. We pa petro. Sear de cru ma. Fi a-ee dolla U.S. No papers. Taw i sorry," Terrance said. *You should hold his foot (be ashamed). This is a very important man. We paid for the gas we bought. Search that man on crutches. You'll find eighty U.S. dollars. You don't need our papers. You apologize to this man.*

The second-in-command pointed his gun at Terrance's chest. The guns in the truck swung a few inches, so they were now all aimed at Terrance's head.

There was a crash. The gasoline jar fell over. The one-legged man was running away. He hit the table with a crutch as he backed away and toppled the jar. He swung between his crutches, springing forward with his one knee, the crutches out in front of him as far as he could reach with each stride, like an oarsman on sculling shell.

All the guns in the truck pointed at the one-legged man.

"Stand down!" the commanding officer said.

"Let him go," Carl said.

"Le he be," Terrance said. *Leave him alone.*

"At ease," the second in command said, and he holstered his pistol. The men in the truck lowered their guns.

"I've got papers," Levin said suddenly. He reached around and pulled his wallet from his pants and slowly removed his driver's license. He held it out for inspection.

"Nigeria good," Terrance said. "Nigeria and Liberia good together. Nigeria, Liberia, and U.S. all good."

"Papers," Carl said. He pulled his wallet and took out his own driver's license, as well as a wad of bills, and walked carefully around the car.

Then Carl handed his driver's license and ten more twenties to the commanding officer. The commanding officer glared at Carl and the muscles on the back of his neck tightened, pulling his head back and stiffening his neck.

The commanding officer took the twenties and the license. He paused. He looked the license over, handed it back to Carl, and put the twenties in his top pocket to give to his men later.

All at once, Carl felt the pressure of cold steel on his temple on the right side of his face, and felt a man's hot breath on his neck, as his nostrils tasted the stale burnt paper smell of cigarette smoke. The sergeant was standing next to him, holding his gun to Carl's head.

"America thinks it can buy the world," the commanding officer said.

For one brief moment, the commanding officer, weighing the space between simplicity and complexity, between threat and risk, between emotion and opportunity, moved his head almost imperceptibly from one American to the next.

"You plenty-plenty trouble," said the commanding officer, and he almost smiled. Then the muscles of his neck smoothed.

"Nigeria good. Africa good. America good," Terrance said.

"Your ships off Mamba Point give us cover," the commanding officer said. "Your marines are with us at the airport. Nigeria and U.S. will bring peace to Liberia together. America takes care of Nigeria, and Nigeria takes care of Africa. Together we bring peace to Liberia and order to Africa. Together."

The sergeant lowered his gun. The lieutenant glanced at the camouflage helmeted soldiers in the back of the pickup. He nodded, and his men lowered their weapons as well.

"Together," Carl said. "Peace to Liberia. Honor to Nigeria. Nibatt, we salute you." Carl took half a step backward, and Terrance and Levin did the same.

The lieutenant and the sergeant stepped backward. The sergeant holstered his gun. The one-legged men hobbled over the hill behind the RAV, looking smaller and weaker than he had looked a moment before.

"Safe journey," said the lieutenant. He and his sergeant watched as Carl, Levin, and Terrance opened and then slammed shut the doors of the RAV.

Terrance started the RAV, backed it up a car-length, and pulled onto the airport road, headed south and east.

Chapter Twenty
Carl Goldman, William Levin, and
Terrance Evans-Smith. Robertsfield
Airport, Harbel, and St John's River,
Liberia. August 17–19, 2003

PEOPLE FILLED THE ROAD AGAIN, SLOWING THEM. BUT BY MID-AFTERNOON THE THREE MEN were at the airport.

On a rise near the sea they saw the rows of white tents, white vehicles, and white transport helicopters. A compound. A large compound with high fences topped by razor wire, with guard towers at the corners and along its length. Then they saw the army barracks—long rectangular cement block buildings with tiny windows. Soldiers with machine guns stood in the guard towers, looking down on the throng of people walking and driving on the seacoast road. A sign on the largest building said *A med Forc s of Li eria. First Ba talion.* The Lone Star flag was flying. But so was the UN flag, as well as a few flags they didn't recognize, and at the end of a role of flagpoles was the flag of the good old USA.

The UN was at the army barracks and the airport, along with a small American marine encampment. UN and U.S. vehicles drove too fast back and forth on the airport road. There were naked children in the yards of the houses and compounds across the street from the barracks, naked children who wandered onto the busiest road in the country. The ruins of cement block houses stood across the street from the barracks. New jungle was already growing in their foundations.

Progress, Carl thought. *Almost half way to Buchanan. Maybe two days. Maybe a day. Not a week.*

Army, Terrance thought. No easy escape. Good to have the flags and the men beside him. He sat straight up in his seat. There was a bead of sweat on his upper lip.

Order, Levin thought. *We can come here if we need help. Americans. The UN. Stability. Strength. Good old American imperialism saving the day again.*

They turned just after the airport. There was a UN checkpoint there manned by Thais, who stood in front of a sandbagged machine gun emplacement and waved them through. Americans, maybe. But no threat.

Then they found themselves driving through a rubber plantation where the road was paved and smooth, though still jammed with people. There were straight rows of trees on both sides of the road, tall slim trees with smooth green bark and branches or leaves only at the treetops, so you could see the rows of trees lining the hillside and far into the distance. The trees had spiral grooves cut into the bark that ended about three feet above the ground, where small white buckets hung from the trunk of each tree. They were driving through the Firestone plantation, one of the largest producers of the sap used to make natural rubber in the world. A million acres of Liberia leased for ninety-nine years to a U.S. corporation for six cents an acre.

The line of people on the road walked five and six deep on each side, strangely silent. The road itself was straight and level with a white line painted down the middle. At the top of the hill was a green concrete block warehouse, and just below it a row of oblong black tanks laying sideways, each as large as a house. A huge white letter was painted on the end of each tank, spelling out F-I-R-E-S-T-O-N-E.

The road forked at Harbel. They turned south and east again.

The road surface disintegrated once more.

Their moment to moment existence became bouncing and jerking again. Terrance steered them around the potholes, zigzagging from one side of the road to the other to make use of the short stretches of good pavement, and then braking so as not to bottom out when the pavement suddenly disappeared.

But the potholes were the easy part.

The endless sea of people everywhere made the going dead slow. Dusty walkers, carrying everything they owned on their backs and heads.

"Woodstock," Levin said, though neither Carl nor Terrance knew what he was talking about. But not Woodstock. Not people going to. People running from.

Where they going? Terrance thought. *Same-same all over. No place to run. No way to hide.*

An airplane or helicopter would fly over every few hours, and then all the people on the road dove for cover. Then you might make five or ten miles an hour for a moment. When the people came back and covered the road again, you were back to dead slow.

It was amazing, despite the chaos, how easy it was to eat and drink as they traveled. Women and old men carrying woven trays or baskets of food and drink for sale walked among the throng, sometimes shouting out but mostly just walking, sad-eyed and without hope or energy, but always able to drop the tray or bin from the heads and negotiate a deal. Plastic bags of water or ground nuts, oranges that were much more green than orange but still had a sweet taste and enough moisture to wet your mouth, overripe mangoes, dried river fish, and roast field corn that tasted like cardboard or paste. The vendors quoted prices in Liberian Dollars, but came flocking when Levin or Carl made a purchase in U.S. currency, one single dollar at a time. What they bought wasn't good, and it probably wasn't really safe to eat, but it kept them alive and gave them a little fluid to sweat out as the RAV nosed its way toward Buchanan.

They slept the third night in the car. They parked the RAV just far enough off the road so it wouldn't be hit by a bus or a goods lorry. Terrance put the passenger seat back as far as it would go and slept curled on his side, a rolled up pair of Carl's jeans under his head for a pillow. Levin and Carl slept side by side in the back, the rear seat dropped to make a flat cargo space, their knees drawn up almost to their chests.

It wasn't a good sleep. Levin snored. The RAV rocked whenever Levin or Carl shifted, so it was easy to imagine yourself sleeping on a boat, rocked and lifted by the waves and rubbing against the dock, again and again.

Terrance lay on his back, listening to the others breathing. He drifted in and out of sleep. There were birds calling before dawn. Then it was morning and footsteps in the gravel and voices, cars, trucks, and buses moved on the road.

And light. Glorious light.

It took two more days to make St. John's River, a trip you can do in under an hour when there is no war on. They were thrown from side to side, jolted again and again under the hot bright sun. They arrived in the late afternoon.

At St. John's River there is a village of twenty huts and a road-side market on a hill overlooking the river. The market is tiny in peacetime—perhaps ten stalls, stretched out along the road, where old women sell mangoes, dried tilapia, and bags of charcoal, oranges, bananas, and red and yellow oil palm nuts. The air is kept fresh by the breezes that follow the river, but the charred woody smell of the cooking fires, as thick as coffee, percolates amongst the thatched huts, the women with babies on their backs, the boys playing in front of the village pump, and a few toothless squatting old men.

Now thousands of people camped on the hilly clearing above the river—a mass of human bodies as far as the eye could see—and the air was full of human noises, of murmurs, chatter, grunts, and children's squeals, of the thump and thud of running footsteps, of the crackle of the cooking fires and the clang of pots; a herd that had been brought to a river to bed down for the night.

It was late afternoon. The sun was moving behind dark rainclouds.

Home now. My place. Ma's people, Terrance thought. *My people. We almost Buchanan. My boys close.*

The afternoon rain began, pouring down in sheets.

Terrance parked near the gnarled trunk of a huge mango tree, under a canopy of waxy, broad, dark green leaves. The three men opened their windows a little so they could breathe in cool air while they were waiting for the rain to pass. Then they all fell asleep where they sat, their heads angled on their necks and their sweating arms akimbo.

It was almost dark when Terrance awoke.

They were in the middle of a sea of people. There were coals glowing red in the tiny handmade sheet metal cook stoves that sat in middle of the clusters of bodies. The air was thick with charcoal smoke. Carl stretched, the RAV rocked, and before he knew where he was or what day or time it was, Terrance raised his flopped-over head and turned to look at the back seat.

"No Levin," Terrance said.

"Shoot. Where are the keys?" Carl said. Carl sat up. Terrance turned to look.

"Keys heah in ashtray. Levin no' far, na ru way." *The keys are here, in the ashtray. Levin isn't far. He didn't run away.*

"He shouldn't be out alone," Carl said.

Terrance turned and scanned the clearing. They could see the little market from where the RAV was parked and a sea of bodies between them and the market.

"He gou. He fine. Na trouble." *He's good. He's fine. There is no trouble.*

"Let's find him. He's walking alone with cash in his pocket."

They locked the RAV and began to pick their way across the clearing, steering around people scattered on the ground and their bulging cheap suitcases, around their bags and bundles.

Terrance's memory flashed with each step. He had lived here with his mother's people on the river before the war found him. He had run on this field and climbed the mango trees at its edge. He remembered being a boy who played in front of the village pump. He remembered the fishy smell of the drying tilapia, suspended on drying nets in the sun next to the river and the flies that buzzed over the fish until they dried. Each step was a different memory.

Terrance searched the crowd, but he did not see people or faces he knew. Those people, if they still lived, would be in the houses he was approaching.

He was different now. Older, taller, calmer, fleshier from sleeping late on his mother's couch and from the four weeks on that ship, sleeping late and doing nothing. It was not possible to know anything about these people in rain-soaked lapas, torn tee shirts, and mud encrusted torn designer jeans who squatted or lay on the ground, spread out over a clearing on a hillside over a river in the waning light near sunset. It was not possible to know who was kin and who was not kin, who had once been friend and who had once been enemy, or if anyone remembered him as the schoolboy who walked to school in a white shirt, brown pants, and yellow sweater, the primary school uniform that his ma sent money for from America when she paid his school fees, or if anyone else remembered him as the hopped up boy-soldier he had been, raging through the compounds, the marketplaces, and the villages.

He was walking with Carl. They were looking for Levin. They were here together. Everything else was long ago.

They were thirty yards from the market stalls and perhaps forty yards from the village pump when Terrance saw Levin's back. Levin was squatting next to the pump with a crowd of five- and six-year-olds in front of him.

"There's Levin" Carl said. "I know that pump. It's got my hand-print in concrete at its base. But watch it. Trouble. Damn it, Levin."

Terrance then saw what Carl saw. Two men in fatigues were picking their way through the crowd, headed toward the pump and toward Levin. They were naked from the waist up, with ammunition belts crisscrossing their glistening dark brown chests.

The two men carried AK-47s. Levin's back was turned to them. They weren't rushing. They walked confidently, ready to check this strange thing out, this white man in their midst, ready for anything and everything, the way Terrance had once been.

Then Carl saw a flash of sudden movement to his right. Terrance. Terrance was moving. Moving fast. He hop-scotched through the sea of people, headed for those two men.

Two battered white pickups were parked to the right of the market stalls, nearer the river.

A cluster of fighters milled about the trucks. The fighters were thin and muscular but not fully grown. Most were stripped to the waist and had AK-47s and Uzis slung across their backs or held in one in their hand. They had shaved heads or wore baseball caps backward and held their fatigues up with cartridge belts, most of which had bones, the heads of chickens, or yellow and blue feathers hanging by strings from the belts, as well as knives and pistols.

"Muthafuckas!" Terrance yelled, and the men near the truck turned to look at him as he ran toward them. Some of the men raised their guns. Others squinted. Still another put his hand to his brow, so he could block out the glare of the last sunlight.

"Ti-*Bone*," a man yelled.

The men walking toward Levin turned. Then both men spun and began to move fast, weaving through the crowd, almost running toward Terrance. Levin, hearing the voices, stood and turned toward the running men.

Chapter Twenty-One

Terrance, Carl, and Levin. Grand Bassa
County, Liberia. August 20, 2003

THE WROUGHT IRON BRIDGE OVER ST. JOHN'S RIVER IS OLD AND RUSTED. IT IS NARROW and long. From the air it looks like a wheat straw between the trunks of two fallen logs—not like anything meant to carry weight. But when you get close to it, you see the heft of the iron from which it was made, many years ago. You can see the tresses and the girders and the bolts, as thick as a man's wrist, that hold the bridge together. The roadway itself is half-inch steel plate, laid unfastened on those girders and tresses. The steel plates clatter when your car or truck goes from plate to plate. But the bridge itself doesn't shift or move when your car, or even a goods lorry, drives over it. And so you learn this is a bridge that will withstand both man and nature; a bridge that has seen storm, flood, and war and still stands.

They were the last vehicle in a three-vehicle caravan that crossed the bridge at daylight—two battered white pickup trucks and their green RAV. The first pickup truck was filled with booty—bananas, pineapple, dried fish, and gasoline in five-gallon glass jars. The second truck carried six armed young men sitting on benches in the bed. Both pickups had gun racks with guns hanging from them silhouetted across their rear windows, and both had bed-mounted heavy machine guns. There were no other vehicles on the bridge yet, and the people walking on it were walking alone or in groups of two or three people. The women walked single file and carried big multicolored plastic tubs on their heads.

The road on the far side of the bridge was better than the road leading from Harbel to St. John's. The country was flat there, and the road decently wide, and though the pavement was as often broken as it was smooth, there were no washouts and no ravines, so you could drive twenty-five or thirty miles an hour for minutes at a time, and the plain on the other side of the bridge was broad enough so that the crowd of walking people could walk next to the road. A good number of the cement block houses that stood next to the road were still standing, and a number of those houses had big garden plots. The few compounds of mud houses were well cared for, with whitewash handprints carefully arrayed on the red mud walls and roofs that had been recently thatched and looked able to withstand the hardest evening rain. The yards of red earth between the houses were swept every day so a person walking would not surprise snakes, because the brush had been cleared away.

They weren't even ten miles from Buchanan.

Then they were on the outskirts of Buchanan, and the road was lined by empty shops, ruined houses, and burned-out churches; the air smelled of burned rubber and rotting flesh and the sky was filled with smoke. They came to the Y-junction that Carl had driven through just thirty-five days earlier, when he had come in with David and the two women and the sick kid stuck in the back, just after they had seen Julia's Land Cruiser on its side on fire.

The trucks turned north, not south, into the country where Julia had disappeared.

After a few minutes, the lead truck dropped back, and the second truck shot in front of it. The second truck ran fast for half a minute, and then spun to the left, raising a cloud of orange dust as it stopped short.

"Down-down," Terrance said. "Quick-quick. Now."

Then the guns exploded. The pop, boom, and rattle of gunfire was right there. They were in it. The men and boys jumped from the back to take cover behind the truck. The other truck spun around and stopped, and the RAV took cover behind that truck. The men in the truck in front of them popped out of the cab and crouched as they ran with an RPG, taking cover behind the first truck.

With gunfire came the whizz and plink, plink, plink, plink of bullets into the truck in front of them. The air hissed as bullets flew by them.

There was more gunfire. They heard a short burst, and then four long rumbling bursts. Metal crunched. Bullets sprayed the dirt and whizzed through the trees. They whopped into cardboard and fruit in the bed of the first truck. They sizzled into flesh and cracked bone. A man called out. Another cursed and grunted.

Terrance saw a gun on the rack on the rear window of the pickup they took cover behind. *In case. Just in case. I'm ready*, he thought. *Alive again. Tastes good. My boys can carry this one. I'm backup. Levin and Carl don't know how to fight enemy. I'm with them. Until I'm not. I ready.*

Carl kept down. *We're close*, Carl thought.

Their guys got off another burst. Machine guns pounded and rattled, low-pitched and high-pitched at once. Three times there was a sizzle, a pop, and then a boom that shook and rattled the earth. Three RPGs shells whooshed and exploded. Carl felt the heat before he saw the flame and smelled the fire.

The firing stopped. The air was filled with shell smoke and smelled of burning rubber.

"Clear," Terrance said. He started the engine.

Then the little convoy of three vehicles rolled through the road-block, which was a downed tree. There were three dead men on the other side of the tree, the blood soaking their fatigues and pooling in the red dirt of the rutted road. Their truck was on fire.

Terrance looked at Levin and Carl. Terrance was boss here. They are in a war now. No theory here. Kill or be killed. No world to repair. Only firefights to survive, one at a time. His boys had become their boys, wilding down thunder road, playing for keeps.

"Where the hell are we?" Levin asked.

"We're on our way to where Julia is," Carl said. "We just finished the easy part."

Chapter Twenty-Two
Carl, Levin, and Terrance. Grand Bassa
County, Liberia. August 20, 2003

THEIR LITTLE CONVOY TURNED INTO THE ROAD TO THE CLUB.

"I know this place," Carl said. "Sundays. We'd come here Sundays."

The palms of Carl's hands got cold and wet, and then his neck and brow and the small of his back got cold and wet as well.

They passed the wrecked guardhouse. All that was left was a burned-out shell. The shards of glass that used to be windows were streaked with dried brown blood.

The convoy slipped through groves of rubber trees planted in straight rows. The sky had grown dark with the late afternoon rain, which started to fall hard as they climbed a gentle ridge. There was a field that had been cleared of trees, the stumps in rows like gravestones. In one place a bulldozer had uprooted the stumps and created a huge mound of stumps and roots waiting to be burned. The plantation managers had been getting the field ready to be replanted, which is what you do after rubber trees reach a certain age and stop making sap. But the managers ran away when the war started up again.

There was a fenced green field off to the right and a distant red barn where the concessionaires once raised cattle. The land was open and quiet. The only sounds they heard were the drumming rain and the hiss of tires on wet pavement.

They turned left and climbed a hill. The little sign that said "Members Only" remained where it had always been, stuck near the ground, the words formed in a proper, precise cursive font in a place that was anything but proper or precise.

"It was a funny kind of place," Carl said. "Mixed crowd. Hustlers, do-gooders, smart Liberians, everyone together. We'd drive out on a Sunday afternoon. There was a pool out back and a great view of the hills to the north and west. We'd swim or sit by the pool or play ping-pong. People would sit at the bar and watch football on TV."

Carl suddenly realized he remembered every word Julia had said to him and every moment they had spent together.

He was the one who held back, who disappeared in the morning, who would go days or a week without making contact. He was the one who needed space, who kept a part of himself closed off. Now he remembered the pores on her skin as the red light of the setting sun showed each angle, curve, and shadow of her face—her eyes and her cheekbones, her nose and the two ridges below it, and the rising up of her skin to make the redness of her lips. He remembered her green eyes and the jet-black hair that fell on both sides of her face, and he even remembered the clean smell of being near her, as though she had just showered after playing tennis.

Julia had been there. Carl could feel her. But she had moved away from Carl. Close and far at once. That was who they were. Not ever an item. Close but no cigar. Thirty-five days. A swing and a miss.

The first truck stopped at the checkpoint at the top of the hill. They waited for just a few seconds, as voices called out to one another. There wasn't any hurry in the voices. No urgency. They knew and were known. Part of the crew. Okay to pass.

There were two helicopters on a flat area of tarmac to the left, one blue and one camouflage green. The parking lot in front of the clubhouse was crowded with trucks, SUVs, and Land Cruisers. There was a white UN truck, the letters UN blue and as big as the lettering on a billboard, simple and clear on the white doors and on top of the cab, so it could be identified from the air. *You can't tell who is who,* Carl thought. *You aren't meant to.* There were two tan troop carriers parked on the edge of the tarmac and a number of pickups with mounts for machine guns rising from the middle of each bed.

The clubhouse was filled with young men—perhaps 50, perhaps 100, perhaps 150—who had come in seeking shelter from the driving rain. The men were standing at the bar, sitting on the floor, and squatting against the walls. Some were stretched out on the couches that were grouped together in front of the huge bay windows, which looked out on the swimming pool and the vistas to the north, east, and west.

She had been here. She was close.

Carl and Levin and Terrance heard the din of voices, the guttural talk of men needling one another and the booming of their confident laughter, but mostly they smelled the stink of men's sweat, sharp, sweet, and insistent, like the smell of old wet leather, as they came into the room.

No one looked at them. They walked in with the men from the trucks. Just one more band. One crew. Fighters. There was light in the clubhouse, fluorescent light, and you could hear the low puttering of the generator just outside.

One of the men from the trucks and Terrance walked across the room to where a thin dark man with large bright eyes was sitting on a desk that was set up surrounded by chairs in a way that suggested an office.

Terrance and the man on the desk high fived. They hugged. Then they talked.

Terrance came back alone.

"She wa he," he said. "She gab na. Tree o fo da, mabe we. Mabe to. Ga na. Drop a into de bush. Drop a da bi moon." *She was here. She's gone now. She's been gone a few days, maybe a week, maybe two. She drove off into the bush. Drove off with the big man who runs this unit.*

"They tell us where to find her?" Levin said.

"He na wa be found. Bi mon ca in. He na say whe." *He doesn't want to be found. The big man calls in. He doesn't say where he is.*

"Goddamn," Carl said.

"She's alive," Levin said. "And close."

"What kind of shape is she in?" Carl said.

"She woman," Terrance said. "She strong."

"We're not going to find her tonight," Levin said.

"We need to stop for the night. The roads up here are no good at night," Carl said.

He looked around the room.

"We sleep here," Terrance said.

"Tomorrow we go north," Carl said. "I know these roads. Not as well as I should, but at least I've been here before. I may not know where to find her, but I know where to look. There are a couple of health centers north and west of here. We'll start with those in the morning."

They settled in a spot near the bar, near the door that led from the bar to where the kitchen used to be.

The rain stopped. The cloud that had enveloped the hill blew off to the southeast. The setting sun emerged above the mountains in the west as it dropped, and its light slipped between the cloud cover and the earth, illuminating the grand sweep of plain and mountain, of lime green farmland and dark green forest beyond, the light spreading over the land the way honey or maple syrup spreads over a slice of toast, just before the sun sank behind the mountains.

Then it was dusk, and the land, the mountains, the plain, the farmland, and the forest slipped into the dark blue of the early evening, and then it all disappeared.

The three men lay down, their heads next to the wall, their feet pointed into the middle of the room, and in a few moments all three fell asleep.

Chapter Twenty-Three
*Julia Richmond and Jonathan. Grand Bassa
County, Liberia. July 31–August 20, 2003*

JULIA AND JONATHAN SET OUT AT NOON IN A WHITE FOUR-WHEEL DRIVE EXTENDED CAB Dodge Ram 2500 pickup in the sharp equatorial sun; a sun that was so strong you could feel it burn your skin the moment you stepped out of the shade. Knots of soldier-boys and soldier-girls squatted or sat in the shade of camouflage tarps or nestled against the clubhouse walls. The boys didn't get up when Julia and Jonathan walked out. The boys didn't wave, or even grin.

"Drive," Jonathan said.

Julia drove. Jonathan sat in the passenger seat—a big sweaty man wearing mirror-lens aviator sunglasses, a khaki shirt, a white beret that made no sense to Julia at all, a handgun and a white satellite phone holstered on his right hip. Three expandable black suitcases had been placed between the driver's and rear passenger's seat so Jonathan could swing around while Julia was driving and get what he needed without her having to stop. There were other weapons in those suitcases, Julia knew. At least Jonathan wasn't holding a gun on Julia as she drove, so she could pretend to keep her eyes on the road.

Julia hadn't driven at all in seven months. You don't think about it. In Liberia, there is always a driver. Often a guard. Didn't matter. Driving now was no delight. There was none of the wild freedom, none of the illusion of power, of putting the top down and hitting the gas, that you get when you drive on the highways of the U.S. of A. The white Ram was big and slow-moving. Its engine spit and rumbled when Julia turned the key, resisting life. It had a heavy floor shift that was hard to move and was designed for a shoulder and an arm that was much bigger than hers.

"Down there," was all Jonathan said.

Jonathan did not direct Julia after that. She drove out the way she knew to come in—down the hill, right, past the "Members Only" sign. The air under the rubber trees looked cool and quiet. Looking, you sensed a soft breeze even if you couldn't feel it.

At first Julia thought that Jonathan was taking them to Buchanan, and she started to turn left after they passed the burned-out gatehouse.

"Go right," Jonathan said, and Julia turned toward Bong County and either Guinea or Ivory Coast, depending on whether you went east or west as you drove north. The truck lugged and trembled, shaking over the road, which had become gravel and would soon be the scalloped, rutted red dirt of the government roads.

"Right," he said, after a few miles, as they passed a village where there was a market of between twenty and thirty stalls, a village that looked deserted. "You said the health center was north."

All the villages they passed were deserted. There was no smoke from the cooking fires. No women squatting or sitting next to the stalls. No one at the village pump.

After three or four miles the air thickened and began to stink. Julia felt the smell in her eyes, and she knew that the air would make her cough if she inhaled it, so she didn't breathe.

Julia's Land Cruiser lay blackened on its side. The driver's side rear wheel was off. All you could really see was the undercarriage. It hadn't been stripped yet—which meant people were still hiding, and there was likely still plenty of trouble on the road.

There were two bloated bodies lying on the embankment. Someone had moved Charles off the road.

Julia didn't turn to look. She didn't let herself feel what she felt.

The Land Cruiser was a historical marker, a sign marking the site where a battle had been, marking a road some pioneer in the distant past had traveled.

Jonathan didn't know one burned-out truck from the next. He was just watching the road, although you couldn't see his eyes under the sunglasses. He put a bandanna over his nose and mouth.

Julia saw and didn't see the sign to the District #4 Health Center, a white sign with blue and green letters that was covered with a patina of red dust. Jonathan saw it.

"Left," Jonathan said.

The road was the same bad one-track road she had come down two weeks before. Twenty kilometers through the woods. Potholes with red water from last night's rain. Furrows, not ruts, some so deep that they would bottom out the vehicle if you slipped into one, some that were deep enough to flip you on your side if you hit it wrong.

You could call the woods jungle if you wanted, but there was nothing particularly deep or frightening about these woods, except that they were so isolated, with no sign of animals, people, or civilization. Massive trees stood right next to the road—huge white trunks with crowns that were so tall you couldn't see them. But there was quiet in these woods, the same still and peace Julia knew from the thick woods of Northern California and the great forests of North Carolina —both places where lush vegetation overwhelms the red earth.

They drove for hours, deeper and deeper into the isolated bush, until they came to a deep ravine crossed by a bridge that that looked impassable. Julia stopped the truck and turned off the engine.

The ravine was a slash of darkness, a deep pit that cut the road in half, an abyss. The red dirt ended on the near side of the ravine and started again on the other side, five car lengths away. There was a quickly moving stream fifty feet below that Julia could hear but couldn't see. A few black logs and two or three iron girders had been rammed into the walls of the ravine, connecting the two edges but not bringing them together. No reasonable person would ever drive on this, Julia thought, remembering that she and Sister Martha had always gotten out and walked across after Torwon had somehow gunned the engine and bounced the Land Cruiser to the other side. Even walking across was scary.

"Cross it," Jonathan said.

"I know this bridge," Julia said. "I'm not sure it will hold the truck."

"You've crossed before," Jonathan said.

"Local driver. It's a long way down."

"But you've crossed before. In that Land Cruiser. At least twice."

"I'm not the world's best driver."

"You will be a good enough driver today," Jonathan said. "I will be cheering from the side."

Jonathan got out, taking the smallest black suitcase from behind his seat. The truck listed to the side as he shifted his weight, and then it rose again as he stepped down and slammed the door. He stood off to the right of the bridge in the shade. He didn't even say good luck.

I could leave him here, Julia thought *I could just pop it into reverse, hit the gas and not stop.* Until the impossibility of driving backward for miles struck her.

She started and gunned the engine once, just to hear it respond. She backed the truck up twenty feet. As Torwon had done. Then she threw it into four-wheel drive low and hit the gas.

The girders and the logs slanted down and to the left, but the near side was a few inches higher than the road. The front end rose and mounted the bridge, a rider on a skittish horse. The wheels bounced and slipped over the girders and logs. The steering wheel jerked and shimmied. The chassis shook. The rear wheels came onto the bridge. The undercarriage twisted and groaned on the uneven surface.

The bridge surface dipped sank and swayed with the truck's weight. It grunted as the truck slipped to one side.

Julia gave the truck more gas. The front wheels headed right, while the rear wheels slipped left. More gas. Pulling left, toward the drop. Straighten it out. Fast. More gas.

Then nothing. The left rear wheel wedged against the last girder—all that was between the truck and the drop— and hissed for a moment, spinning, and the truck drifted forward and started to lean into the abyss. Then the right front wheel found the far side of the bridge and the hard red soil of the far bank. More gas. More gas.

Julia stood up in her seat. She twisted the wheel with everything she had and slammed the gas petal to the floor.

The engine roared. The front end rose. It teetered on edge for an instant. Then it came onto the bank and its weight secured the traction of the front wheels. It pulled the body of the truck onto the far side of the ravine.

The truck stopped and stood white and shimmering in the midday heat, its fenders covered with red mud, the diesel humming and rattling like the top of a pot of simmering water.

Jonathan walked slowly on the bridge over the ravine.

He opened the door and put the heavy small black suitcase he was carrying on top of his other luggage. Then he climbed in.

He closed the door and sat looking straight ahead.

"You do know how to drive," Jonathan said.

"I could have kept going," Julia said. "I should have left you standing there."

"I'm sure you'll have other opportunities to test your luck. Which appears to be holding."

"Not even you," Julia said.

"What did you say?" Jonathan said.

"Not even you. I don't leave human beings stranded in the middle of the jungle," Julia said. "Not even you."

"Nonsense. You are talking to yourself," Jonathan said. "*You* don't leave human beings stranded in the middle of a jungle. *I* do what I need to do, before it gets done to me."

"Even so," Julia said. "I'm driving this truck."

"You're driving a truck I gave you because I asked you to drive it. You're only alive because I have use for you alive. Today. Don't forget that."

"Fuck you," Julia said. She shifted the truck into four-wheel drive high. The truck jolted, heaved, and shuddered down the rutted red road.

The District #4 Health Center sits at the top of a rise in a clearing of perhaps three acres and has dark green walls. It has a corrugated iron roof but no real doors—there is a dark open porch lined by rough cut wooden benches, their surfaces polished by years of use. The porch opens into dark hallways. The hallways connect to vestibules, also dark. There is no electricity at the District #4 Health Center. The only light is sunlight, filtering through the windows of some of the rooms or down the hallways from the outside.

A number of rooms open off the vestibules—examination rooms, supply rooms, and a medical record room, so-called, which holds shelf after shelf of soiled, dog-eared green folders, folders that sit on the shelving in considerable disarray. The room for laboring women has three or four beds jammed together at odd angles, as though they had been pushed from one place to another in a hurry. The infirmary room has four beds lining the walls. It is used for infants with diarrhea or for children listless or shaking with malaria. There are three examination rooms, each with a wooden desk in front of a large screened window, with a chair next to the desk.

All the rooms were empty. Julia parked the truck and checked them all. The place looked abandoned.

Jonathan looked both bigger and smaller than before when he swung down from the truck. Bigger, because he was a big man dressed in sharp clothes and carried himself as if he owned the world, and also bigger because the District #4 Health Center was a place where small people lived close to the earth, and he was so much bigger than they were. Smaller, because there was no wind in his sails. No one knew him here. Here, there weren't people to take his orders or cluster around him. He was just a big dark man with a gun on his hip who dressed too well for the bush and was traveling in a truck with a white woman.

Julia sat on the steps of the empty health center, ignoring Jonathan. The mud houses down the hill and further back to the right and uphill were just as she remembered. There was smoke rising from kitchen fires in both compounds. She felt oddly, unexpectedly, at home.

What a strange place to hide from the ravages of a war men like Jonathan had brought on, she thought, as Jonathan climbed the steps carrying his own suitcases. Strange and logical at the same time. Men like Jonathan make wars. Women allow the wars to go on. The wars are like fires that burn as long as there is fuel, and then burn themselves out. The fuel is the extra, the fuel is the excess. As long as we have more than we need to live on, we will live to see both the good that is in us as people together and the evil that sits alongside it and that resides in each of us alone. In abundance, we see the good that has come from being together, the miracles we have made by learning from one another and working together. And out of that same abundance comes greed and violence, as some of us, the men who think themselves big, use what we have made together to try to realize their insane dreams, to satisfy insane lusts.

The people in the bush, the people the clinic served, thought they had nothing to spare, like the birds in the trees and the insects whirling in the bush. But even people in the bush have something to trade, and no one lives in isolation. Medicine comes from away. The tee shirts come from away—they were made in Bangladesh. The machetes that some men use to cut brush and other men use to cut off arms and legs come from China, as do the cheap metal pots. The marbleized plastic bowls that women use to carry water on their heads come from Nigeria, as do the soldiers who had landed in Monrovia. The trucks and guns came from Japan, Korea, Israel, Russia, the U.S., and Azerbaijan. Even in the bush, there was excess; excess that flowed out of the industrialized world and into every nook and cranny of the ancient low-to-the-ground world, like hot lava flowing down the side of a volcano. Together we make abundance, even as this abundance fuels the fires that tear us apart.

Carl is dead, Julia thought again. *Lord only knows what's left of Buchanan. Zig, Sister Martha, all dead. The hospital, Lord only knows. How I wish Carl wanted more than he wanted. How I wish he and I hadn't been so afraid. It was good. Sweet. Real. I got him, I think, and I think he was starting to get me. He had a hard enough time stopping by once a week or thinking that being together mattered. And yet sometimes he wanted me to talk. Sometimes he wanted me to push and probe and pay attention to him and take care of him. He was starting to listen. And even to know me.*

But no one is coming. Carl is dead. I'm on my own. Stuck here giving this monster cover.

Jonathan stood next to the first step, with his arms crossed on his chest. It is difficult to be in charge when there is no one to be in charge of.

We'll be safe here for a while, for a few days or perhaps for a week, while the fires of hell are burning all around, Jonathan thought. *Know when to hold them and know when to fold them. Know how to strike when the iron is hot.*

The next day some women came back to the health center. The following day even more women came, bringing with them their babies and all their problems. The doctor was back. Still no nurses, no PA, little in the way of medicines or supplies. But the doctor was back, so the people came.

Jonathan took over one of the exam rooms. He stayed out of Julia's way, which was a good thing, because she couldn't bear to look at him. He talked on the satellite phone until the battery ran out, and then used the battery of the truck to recharge it. Sometimes his voice was raised. Other times his voice was quiet and sounded almost contrite. *Just a few days,* Julia told herself. He will arrange something, mount the driver's seat of the truck, and drive away, leaving Julia and the health center alone. *No war here,* Julia thought. *Please God, do not let him bring the war here.*

She worked as she always did, but it was more difficult without Sister Martha. She did what she could with her crappy Kreyol. She could look and feel. People could point and find a few words, whether Julia understood them or not. Everyone had plenty-plenty and small-small. It wasn't much, but it was a place to start.

She dug a new pit for the latrine, and the PA returned and helped her move the latrine over the pit. Every morning she filled the yellow and red water coolers from Carl's pump and brought them to the clinic before seeing patients, one after the next. They filled the water coolers when she wasn't there, Julia told herself. They washed their hands when she wasn't there before and after each patient. They used the latrine. Of course they did. But the water coolers weren't filled each morning unless Julia filled them, so every morning she went out, just after she awoke.

At first there were many patients, who came because they heard the woman doctor was there, and the people in the villages were used to coming all at once every time word spread that the woman doctor was at the health center. Then word spread that the woman doctor was sleeping in the health center, not going and coming. So people came when they wished and didn't rush, and the number of people who came each day fell off a little. And Julia would sleep for a little while in the late afternoon, when the rain came.

One day, a few weeks after they arrived, Jonathan began to shout. It was late in the afternoon, almost evening, and most of the patients were gone. His voice grew loud and echoed in the walls and the wooden floors, shaking them. Julia went to sit with the three women who remained on the porch, sitting on the benches with their children. The children suspended their playing on the porch when they heard Jonathan shouting. They came in from the garden in front of the health center, where the white truck was parked just down the steps. You could hear Jonathan's voice in the village, Julia thought, and she was embarrassed because this was a quiet place, where the loudest sounds people ever heard were the crying of a baby, the crowing of a cock, and the evening thunder, and even that was simple, muffled, and wise.

Then the shouting stopped. Julia stood. The women on the benches raised their eyes to one another and their children began to play once more.

"Dr. Richmond," Jonathan said, loud enough so that the whole clinic could hear and the sound carried to the village, but not as loud as his voice had been when he had been yelling.

Julia walked into the clinic. Jonathan stood at the door of the exam room he had expropriated, the room she and the others now avoided.

"There are three men at The Club with our boys," Jonathan said. "What do you know about this?"

"I didn't know you still had The Club," Julia said.

"That isn't of any concern to you. Those three men. Will they come here?" Jonathan asked.

"I don't know what you are talking about," Julia said.

"Are there people looking for you? Does anyone know you are here?" Jonathan asked.

"If I knew that, would I tell *you*?" Julia said.

"Thank you for answering my question," Jonathan said. "We will send them away. And I may have found us a tunnel out to the north. I'll know tomorrow. Don't get your hopes up."

"Us?" Julia said.

"Us. You're still my ace in the hole. And I'm still in the game, as long as we've got the boys at The Club. Thank you for your hard work and continuing support," Jonathan said.

"Fuck you," Julia said, and she turned and went back to the porch.

The women and their children were gone from the benches. It had rained and the air was clean now. The ruts on the red road that came from the bush and came toward the health center were filled with water, and in the water was the reflection of an orange sky, lit by the setting sun.

Three men.

Julia went to the exam room and lifted the red and yellow water coolers from where they sat in her examination rooms. She brought them out to the porch and emptied the remaining water onto the garden she had started. Then she took the water coolers down the hill to the pump and filled them, and she cupped her hands, filled them with water, and splashed it onto her face, onto her eyes, and behind her neck.

She could not think. She could not hope. She could feel, and now there was too much feeling. There were chills and a shaking in her shoulders and in her spine coming up into her head and her eyes and a dropping pit in her pelvis and her gut. She splashed more water on her face to wash the feeling out of her eyes. Too much feeling. She didn't know how to pray, but she was praying nonetheless in every ganglion and muscle fiber, in every cell and synapse.

He did feel what she felt. He did know what she knew. Carl was alive and he was close, and he was coming, and she was not alone.

Chapter Twenty-Four
William Levin. Grand Bassa County,
Liberia. August 21, 2003, 4:00 a.m.

IT TOOK A FEW MINUTES OF WAKING AND THEN FALLING BACK TO SLEEP BEFORE LEVIN understood that the need was real and he would have to get up.

Old white man's bladder again. Damn. Old white man's burden.

He was alone, a white man in a room of black men with guns, in a country at war, a zillion miles from home.

But he was not alone. He was in Liberia, as distant from the rest of his life as it was possible to be. They were close to Julia. He had never been in a place like this. He was surrounded by war, guns, ammunition, and soldiers, by everything he hated. They had come together, the three of them, as different as three men could be. They had one purpose, one goal. Only that goal mattered. Levin knew how to send out a call, how to organize demonstrations, and how to go to meetings. He knew how to sink an endotracheal tube, how to throw in a chest tube, and how to run a code. But here he was just one of the boys. Bigger and smaller than himself.

Levin felt his way along the wall into the empty hallway. He tried each door that opened off the hall as he came to it, the cool metal of each door handle an island of certainty in a sea that was dark and indistinct.

The first two doors were locked. The third door was already open. He stumbled into the kitchen. Four tiny blue pilot lights burned in the darkness but cast no light, glimmering where the big cast iron cook stove had to be.

He turned and felt his way back to the hall. The next two doors were locked.

The third door was closed but opened easily when he pushed down on the cool metal handle. He saw the sign on the door in the dim reflected light as he opened it. Women's. No reason to care.

He found a toilet and his bowel and bladder emptied. He sat longer, listening, thinking, almost wanting a cigarette, although he never smoked.

He heard the sounds of night before dawn—the whirring and humming of insects in the low branches of trees and the hooting and calling of the night birds. Then there was movement in the night, under the birds, and sound. Sudden, muffled movement. Hard metal sounds. The sticky hiss of tires moving slowly on pavement. Many tires, on trucks running without headlights, on a night with a waning three-quarter moon. Enough light to see by without being seen. The quiet groaning of springs as weight shifted in trucks that moved uphill. The low shudder of gears driving an axle. The click of doors being opened and then eased closed again, eased closed without slamming, so as not to be heard.

The soft thud of a bullet being slipped into a chamber.

The almost imperceptible click of safeties being slid off in the night.

The quiet crunch of tires on gravel as a 105mm howitzer is moved into position.

The click, click, click, click, click of targeting gears as the howitzer was aimed and locked. The squish and thud of a shell as it is jammed into the breech. The clunk of the howitzer feed door jammed shut behind a 105mm round.

The click of the firing button. The almost imperceptible thump of machinery just an instant before the powder explodes. The boom and swoosh as the shell rockets toward the wall of a building, which it will destroy. The explosion, the flash of light and hot wind and the shock wave.

The first shell to hit the front wall of The Club slammed Levin across the room and into a wall. The front wall collapsed, crushing the men beneath it. There was fire, smoke, and dust. And dark. And blindness. There was a horrific buzz, a loud ringing in his ears. Levin couldn't hear a thing. What? So confusing. He couldn't breathe

Carl. Terrance. Under the rubble. Gone.

Chapter Twenty-Five
William Levin's AOL. New Mail.
December 31, 2003–March 2, 2006

From Julia15@gmail.com
Subject: Happy New Year
Date: December 31, 2003
Happy New Year. Alive and well.

From doctor1pumphandle@aol.com
Subject: Re: Happy New Year
Date: December 31, 2003
Julia! My God! Where are you? Are you okay?

From Julia15@gmail.com
Subject: Re:Re: Happy New Year
Date: April 27, 2004
Still in Liberia. Safe and sound. Only occasional access to e-mail. I know about Carl. Love that he got to meet you.

From dr1pumphandle@aol.com
Subject: Re:Re:Re: Happy New Year
Date: April 27, 2004
Where in Liberia? Can I call you? How much do you know? How much do you want to know? Are you safe? Do you know how much Carl loved you? How much we all love you?

From Julia15@gmail.com
Subject Re:Re:Re:Re: Happy New Year
Date: December 31, 2004

Happy New Year again. I thought maybe. We weren't an item yet. No cell reception where I am. Good work though. Immunization rates better. Improved infant and maternal mortality numbers. Malaria, TB, typhoid, meningitis, and HIV overwhelming. Good village pump. Clean water so little infant gastroenteritis death. Moms breast-feed! I still want to grow up to be like Carl. And you.

From dr1pumphandle@aol.com
Subject: Which Village?
Date: December 31, 2004

Tell me where you are so I can send you equipment and meds, whatever you need. There's a boat that goes from the Port of Providence to Monrovia every two weeks. Can I send you a satellite phone? That way we can talk. I'm the one who wants to grow up to be you. Carl and I only knew each other for thirty-something days. It happens fast when it happens. There were three of us. We got to be a tough little unit. Saw Liberia, out there looking for you.

From Julia15@gmail.com
Subject: Re: Which Village?
Date: February 23, 2005

Village is about thirty kilometers from where you got jumped. We just missed. Have access to a satellite phone. But I can't talk about it yet.

How did you meet Carl? Tell me what you remember. I want to hold on to as much as I can. Why is that? Okay to sell the car.

From dr1pumphandle@aol.com
Subject: Re:Re: Which Village?
Date: February 23, 2005

Memory is dumb luck. And the grace of God. And I don't do God. Carl called me as soon as he got home from Liberia after the marines pulled him out. Kind of desperate to find you. We met in a Liberian restaurant. Both of us were trying to figure out a way to help. Then we spent four weeks together on a boat and another week driving through a war looking for you.

Carl said he could picture you and thought he knew what you were feeling every minute of every day. Knew without thinking about it. Just always knew. He said you had become a part of him, and didn't realize it until you disappeared. That he had to go back, because he was looking for a part of himself.

You were lucky people. Most of us spend our lives looking for that.

The car is probably worth $8,500. Not sure I can sell it, though. It's all I have of you. And Carl. And Terrance, who you never got to meet.

From Julia15@gmail.com
Subject: Re:Re:Re: Which Village?
Date: September 16, 2005
How did he die?

From dr1pumphandle@aol.com
Subject: Re:Re:Re:Re: Which Village?
Date: September 18, 2005
In his sleep. With his boots on. We were with a militia allied with Taylor at an old country club on a hill. Carl said you had been there together a couple of times. The boy soldiers said you'd been there and left a couple of days before we got there.

MODEL hit us in the middle of the night. Some kind of artillery. It knocked the outside wall over and buried Carl and Terrance. They were killed instantly, along with about a hundred others, mostly kids, sixteen, seventeen, fifteen, twelve. Kids. I was in the bathroom, away from where the artillery hit. Saved by an aging bladder. I think I was the only survivor. MODEL would have killed me too, but I talked American English at them until they got a look and saw I was a white guy. I was not myself for a while. Dazed. PTSD. MODEL brought me to Buchanan and then to the airport. The marines brought me home.

I should have kept looking for you. The boys said their boss was taking you to trade for arms. I didn't think I could find you on my own. I was pretty gone.

From Julia15@gmail.com
Subject: Carl's Sister
Date: March 2, 2006
I think Carl had a sister in Rhode Island. Does she know?

We met March 2, 2003. I guess we were something of an item after all.

Chapter Twenty-Six
Yvonne Evans-Smith. Pawtucket, Rhode Island. July, August, and September 2003

At first Yvonne thought Terrance was dead. Then she thought he was alive. Then she hoped. Then she prayed. Because she knew he was alive at first. Then she knew he had died.

That's what you think when your child isn't home asleep on the couch or isn't laying there sprawled out, watching the TV, the soda cans and empty Cheetos bags spread over the floor like leaves from a tree that has died. That he's dead. Why else would he have not come home? You think he went out and did something to somebody and got himself shot. Or that somebody gave him something bad, and that he's lying dead in a crack house, and that someone torched that house so no one ever finds out. That he took a car or someone else took a car, and they were running down I-195 at 80 miles an hour when a cop came up behind them, and they tried to outrun the cop and drove the car into a bridge abutment doing 110.

So she didn't sleep at night.

It doesn't make sense. Your children should bring you only peace. Your children should be good to you, every day, and you should be good to them, because your children are you and you are them. All Terrance did was lie about the house. Night watchman at night. He barely spoke. Never said anything about his days or nights, about who he hangs with or what else he did on his days free or at night when he was home. Yvonne didn't want to know what he did when he went out. With whom. To whom. Wasn't going to school. No one was ever going to hire him—no skills, on a visitor's visa, never worked a day other than playing security guard. After all that time in the bush being hopped up and gun-mad, he didn't know what work was. It still made a difference to her to have this one here, safer, sleeping under her roof each night, with a life today and, who knows, maybe a way to build a life for himself here once he figured things out; once he got tired of the couch and work at night and going who knows where during the day.

"Listen to Dr. Levin," she told him. "Go to school. Go to learn. You can do that. At least that."

Yvonne hadn't ever really slept in her many years of no one. Then Terrance came, and she could sleep again sometimes once she heard the broken screen door banging on its frame, once she heard the wall shake when the house door shut, when the door lock's tumblers clicked, snapped, and then thudded closed.

Terrance could be anywhere. The first day, unable to settle, she checked her cell phone for voice mail. She checked the answering machine at the house. She checked her voice mail at work. She checked and checked again. There was nothing.

The second day she tried to call Terrance's father and her second man in Liberia, and then her sisters and a niece, but only got busy signals from home. She turned on the news and looked at a newspaper online. There was just chaos in the streets. It shamed her, so she turned it off. At least Terrance was here and not there.

The third day she called her pastor, who said he would ask others if they had seen Terrance. He came to her house that night to pray with her.

Yvonne cleaned under the in-boxes and the paperclip dispenser and the telephone on her blond wood desk, cleaned that desk three or four times, and she answered the telephone before it finished the first ring, every time.

On the fourth day she called her brother in Philadelphia and her half sister in Minnesota. They did not usually talk. She did not want to tell her troubles. They had lives and troubles of their own. They listened. He was not at their house either. They barely knew him. He did not remember life with them. We will call if we hear any word.

She began to look for signs, to see if he was dead or alive. The signs were small ones here, where people were well-fed and well dressed and just shuffled from place to place. The screen door stayed on its hinges. (If it had come off the frame, it would have been a sign he was dead.) The buses kept running on time. (If the buses had stopped working, it would have been a sign he was dead.) The bland pictures—of bridges and boats in the harbor, of wooden chairs set in the sand of a beach—that hung on the walls of her office were hanging square, as they always had.

Yvonne was sure Terrance was alive somewhere. He had to be.

But she also couldn't pick up the telephone and call the police. He was over on his visitor's visa. Not a citizen. There were hard stories about back home but not hard enough to qualify him for asylum. Not persecuted on account of race, religion, nationality, political opinion, or for being part of a particular social group. Persecuted by memories and dreams. She thought about Temporary Protected Status. Liberians could get that. But if he applied they might learn something about who he'd been and what he'd done, and then he'd be deported without question.

Terrance was the flesh of her flesh. When she left home to come to America, she intended to find a way out for all of them. When she brought him over, she thought he would be safe, and then, one by one, she could bring the others. Then the war started up again, and she couldn't bring the others. Now home was gone. There was no way back to the home of school uniforms and swimming in the ocean or to the home of sitting with her aunts and cousins around a charcoal fire or the home of six-year-olds making trouble near the village pump. Terrance became the only home she had left. Even if all he did was sleep all day on her couch and prowl the streets at night when he wasn't working.

On the fifth day, when she couldn't bear it any more, she straightened the pillows on the couch and went to pick up the soda cans and the junk food wrappers from the floor and the coffee table.

Then her pastor came back to her house to pray with her again. There might be a man. The man might sell used cars. The used cars might be shipped from the Port of Providence. Three men might have left on a boat.

Six weeks later, Dr. Levin called. He wanted to come to see her. He remembered where she lived.

Chapter Twenty-Seven
Naomi Goldman. Lincoln, Rhode
Island. July and August 2003

IT WAS NOT LIKE CARL TO DISAPPEAR WITHOUT WARNING.

They were close. He was all she had. She was all he had. They understood one another without having to speak. Carl understood that Naomi was always afraid, and he knew what she was always afraid of. Naomi knew what Carl had seen and what he remembered.

They were both good at ducking questions. Their father was in the Plymouth County Correctional Facility in Plymouth, Massachusetts, for the rest of his natural life and their mother was dead. That's all she wrote.

Of course, Carl was a better person than Naomi was. He had a purpose in life, and he had a goal. Vision, values, mission, goals, even strategies and tactics. International development. The empowerment of the Third World. Hope and progress through local economic development. Democracy that would come through skills and tools and training. He went from place to place, looking for ways to set people free.

Naomi spent her life in hiding. She hid in the trees. She hid in the boxwoods and Japanese yews in front of the houses where they had cut the lawns and trimmed the edges and shoveled the snow. She hid in the sheets of water that ran down the street after a hard rain. She hid in the dead-end streets and the fences that marked the property lines of quarter-acre yards, in the baseball diamonds next to the schools, and in the school crossing guards who raised their hands to stop traffic for schoolchildren, even though Naomi herself never walked to school. She hid in the yellow school buses with the strange gates that swung open when the buses stopped, even though she was never allowed to take a bus to school.

The trees, the shrubs, the sheets of water in the streets, the bright yellow school buses with flashing red lights were the places she hid herself when he father touched her. She hid in the nooks and crannies where a bad little girl could hide and not be seen, places she could go in her imagination when she had been bad and her father took her to the truck for instruction and reeducation.

Carl didn't know her places. He hated the trees and the lawns and the cul-de-sacs. He hated Lincoln and Pawtucket. He hated Rhode Island and everything that had happened to them here. The moment he came back, he wanted to run away again. Naomi was used to Carl's comings and goings, of course. She was used to his calls at 3:00 in the morning because he couldn't keep the time difference straight and to his sudden unannounced arrivals and similarly sudden departures.

Carl always warned her he was about to vanish. He disappeared when Lincoln got to him, when the streets empty of people and the perfectly manicured lawns and the perfectly square hedges made him remember too much of what he had suppressed.

Naomi lived in Rhode Island now. She would always live here, because her hiding places were here. She was safe here, in her unsafe way. She knew where to hide the next time she failed.

There were keys under a fake rock near the front door. Carl let himself in when he came home. He could come and go as he pleased. Naomi got him. She understood.

But this time was different. He disappeared with no warning whatsoever.

When Carl vanished, Naomi wondered for a day, and then suddenly she knew he had gone back to Liberia. He didn't tell her, because he didn't want her to stop him. Damn him. He didn't know that she wanted to go. The hell with the chaos and the danger. She wanted to be like him. Carl had freedom. Carl had Africa. Naomi had an apartment in Lincoln in a gated community. She wanted him to take her along this time, to experience a life of no hiding places, so she could stop hiding once and for all.

Carl had set her free once. He had set them both free.

Naomi was in the trees, with her boxwoods, in the sheets of water that flowed over the windshield when Carl opened the door to the truck. It was winter and Carl had been shoveling. The sun had set, and the night was cold. The heavy snow made his gloves, hair, eyebrows, and neck wet. Carl had been working alone, shoveling. He was shivering, and he was desperate for a toilet. The truck's engine was running, the heat was turned up, the windshield had fogged, and the windshield wipers were slapping from side to side. He didn't knock and ask for permission the way he and she had been told, had been taught, had been instructed. He defied orders. He was cold and tired, and he had to pee, and he was only twelve. He just opened the door. And he saw.

DaddySir shouted, and Carl closed the door, and then DaddySir was outside. Pushups! DaddySir said! A hundred pushups! Naomi stayed in the truck. She was also shivering. She was in her hiding place, though she was crying because of what DaddySir would do to Carl now, because she had been bad, and because she always cried when DaddySir was angry, because she was afraid. Carl couldn't do a hundred pushups. Carl wet his pants, and you could smell the pee. They were bad, bad people, Naomi and Carl. Bad things happen to bad people.

The next morning Carl had a fever of 103.

Brenda sat with Carl while DaddySir took Naomi out to plow with him. Carl told Brenda as soon as Naomi was out the door. Naomi never knew what words he used or what words he knew. But Brenda understood. Even Brenda. Somehow she had always known, the way their Mama had always known. DaddySir was out of the house, and even Brenda knew how to pick up the phone.

It was not until the trial that they learned that he had also killed their mother. But they both had always known. Even Brenda knew, someplace inside her.

When Carl disappeared Naomi called a woman she knew, a Liberian woman from the African Association of Rhode Island, and two friends from Princeton—one who worked in USAID and one who worked in the White House—but they didn't know anything about Carl or what was happening in Liberia. They made a few phone calls for her. Not much information available. Sketchy situation on the ground. The State Department has travel restrictions in place. Hard to get in and out. Americans have been evacuated.

Then a letter, a good old-fashioned letter, handwritten on a plain sheet of paper, showed up two days after Carl disappeared. It was vague and clear at the same time, mailed to slow down the transmission of information, so it would get to her after he was clear. Carl's handwriting was strong and precise. He printed, and his letters were straight, the lines square across the page, the pen strokes thick and deliberate.

Thanks for being his safe harbor one more time. Sorry he had to cut the visit short. He was headed back. He had found a way in. Yeah, Dr. Richmond. LIBERIA IS NO PLACE FOR YOU, NAOMI. YOU ARE THE BEST. He wasn't going alone. Hoped to be back in a couple of weeks. Might be out of cell phone range for a while. I'LL CALL OR E-MAIL AS SOON AS I CAN. YOU KNOW HOW MUCH YOU MEAN TO ME. Hoped to be back soon.

And then it was back to the half-life Naomi had before. Drive to work. Wave at the guard in the guardhouse. Sit at a desk. Be pleasant at meetings. Give presentations. Wave at the guard in the guardhouse. Drive home. Go to the store. Wave at the guard in the guardhouse.

Not even half a life. Carl never knew that half-life she led was for him so he would have a safe place to come home to when he was ready to come home. So he would also have a place to hide.

Damn Dr. Richmond. Whoever this Dr. Richmond was.

Everyone at work thought she had another more glamorous life, but acting out the character she was supposed to be was as much as Naomi Goldman could manage. She was partial to a blazer, a silk top, and a string of pearls. Naomi wore her hair down, and she had it done every week. It was all smoke and mirrors, an illusion, a distraction that kept people from seeing the lonely and stunted human being inside.

One Monday morning at the office about ten days after Carl left, Naomi Goldman looked up from her computer and closed its case. She made three phone calls, one right after the other. She squared her shoulders, looked straight at the poster on the wall across from her, a reproduction of a quilt that depicted a family picnic, and then she sat completely still for three or four minutes. Then she opened her computer case again, waited for a moment until it came back to life, drove it, with a few clicks, to where she wanted it to go, typed for a moment, and then closed the case again. She turned her attention to the telephone on her desk. She worked its buttons for a moment, spoke into the receiver and worked a few more buttons to play back what she had just recorded, tapped a few more buttons yet, and replaced the receiver.

Then Naomi stood, gathered a few things—her keys, her glasses case, her cell phone, and the cell phone charger from her desk and put them into her slim brown leather pocketbook. She opened a drawer of her desk and extracted a few more items—a letter opener and two pens she had received as gifts—and put them in her pocketbook as well. There was a small three-part picture frame on her desk, which held pictures of two men and a man and a woman standing together on a rocky shore in front of an ocean with the sun setting and an island in the background. She started to reach for the picture frame, but then stopped her hand in midair. She looked around the room the way a traveler looks around a hotel room one last time to be certain nothing has been left behind.

And then she left.

Carl had chosen of his own free will. He had chosen where to go. How to live. What to live and what and who to die for.

There would be people coming from Liberia, fleeing the war, coming out through Ivory Coast, Sierra Leone, Senegal, Ghana, and Nigeria.

The immigrants would need clothing and a place to stay, and they would know more about Liberia than any reporter for the *New York Times* and the *Washington Post* or *Time Magazine* knows. Naomi knew the pastors of three Liberian Churches. She had worked with the International Institute, where refugees came. The refugees would be coming from where Carl was. They would be bringing news. News about Liberia. News about the part of the country where Carl was. Maybe even news about Carl. When they came out, they would be bringing Carl out with them.

Doesn't matter where you sit if all you are going to do is go to meetings and give presentations. You might as well sit among people who want to learn. You might as well teach and see what you can learn from people who know how to be together and find freedom together despite their fears. You might as well sit among people you love.

Chapter Twenty-Eight
William Levin, MD. Providence,
Rhode Island. March 15, 2006

GEORGE W. BUSH WAS THE PRESIDENT OF THE UNITED STATES IN 2003, WHEN LEVIN AND Carl and Terrance set out for Liberia, and he was still president of the United States when Levin returned home alone.

Bush stayed president. Then there was an election that Levin barely noticed, because he submerged himself in work.

Levin didn't do anything to get home. It just happened. MODEL found a dazed white man digging in the rubble. He was digging with his fingertips, desperate to get the crushed cinderblock wall off Carl and Terrance, as the light was just starting to show over the eastern hills, digging frantically until the skin came off his fingertips and his hands were covered with his own blood.

Levin couldn't remember what language they spoke, thinking back on it, when they told him to stand and put his hands on his head, or at least that's what he remembered them saying, later. First put your hands over your head. At least they didn't shoot him on sight. Perhaps it was better. Perhaps they spoke Kreyol, and he understood them because he had learned some Kreyol by living for three weeks with Terrance, but perhaps they spoke English. They would have asked him for papers and looked for a dog tag. Someone hit him about the head when he didn't respond. He was just at the beginning of his submerging, the long period in which he wasn't able to respond to that or too much else, the period of living in a mist, in the shadow of a life.

They took him to Buchanan first. He must have said something in American English. They must have recognized from that and from his name that he was an American citizen.

In Buchanan there were State Department types and military who didn't believe him at first. The whole story was just too incredible, just too incredibly naive and stupid to be true. But then a guy talked to another guy who talked to another guy, and someone turned up the marines they had met that night at the hotel restaurant in Monrovia, who told them, yes, there were a couple of dimwits who tried driving through Monrovia in the days just after Taylor blew town, and we told them they were going to get themselves killed, and we told them they were proceeding at their own risk. There were some raised voices on the phone, something about you can't just let Americans wander about a war zone on their own without passing it up the chain and something else about letters to go in someone's file. It didn't matter. They had come and gone on their own. Now Carl and Terrance were dead. It wasn't anybody's fault but their own. They still didn't have Julia back yet.

The embassy people looked him up on the internet. They called the hospital and Judy, who had not reported him missing, according to the precise instructions he had given her the night they left, and who confirmed that yes, Dr. William Levin was who he said he was. But they kept going around and around, because they couldn't believe it was just as he said it was—three unarmed men in a used Toyota RAV on their own in Liberia in the middle of a war.

But despite their going round and round, that's all there was. Nothing about his travel history raised any red flags other than Nicaragua in the 1980s, but that was old news, and no one took Nicaragua seriously anymore, not even the good old CIA.

Yes, there was the Cuba trip in the late '60s, and they knew all about that, but even that didn't really excite them. The Russians weren't players in 2003. The international Marxist conspiracy had proven to be nothing more than a false start, nothing anyone had to take seriously anymore, communism having come apart fifteen years before. Al-Qaeda was where the action was in 2003. Not world social-ist revolution.

So they bundled him up and sent him home. They flew him through Accra. They put him up at a cheap airport hotel, and then charged his credit card for the flight home through London. Judy met him at the airport.

And then Levin disappeared.

He didn't disappear by running away. He didn't drop out of sight or move to the mountains of Mexico to live with the rebels in Chiapas. He didn't try to go to Syria or Jordan to work with the Iraqi refugees. No, Levin disappeared by going back to work every day. He showed up for his shift whenever he was on the schedule. He volunteered for double shifts. He worked holidays. He went back to teaching the same classes he had always taught. He even went back to going to meetings of the same organizations that had failed to achieve anything in forty years, meetings he knew were pointless, that he had always known were pointless but could never admit that to himself.

But his hope and his energy were gone. He walked through his life like a zombie, like a man who had already died but hadn't been told that it was time to lie down in his grave. Levin even went back to running, or at least his body did. Same house. Same car. Same wife. Same job. Nothing but a ghost in the machine. He disappeared back into the life into which he had submerged himself in the first place. In Liberia, he had a brief moment of real life when he drove though the streets of Monrovia with those two crazy-crazy motherfuckers while Liberia was trembling with war. Now he was alone. The Levin who had lived for one brief instant was gone.

George W. Bush was still president of the United States of America.

When the first e-mail came from Julia, Levin got stirred up for a few days, but when weeks went by and he didn't hear anything else, he submerged again. The same thing happened when the second e-mail came. The third e-mail barely roused him. He was in a permanent vegetative state. There was no evidence of cognition, of brain function, of feeling. *I should go back to Liberia*, he thought, *and try to find Julia on my own. But Julia doesn't want to be found. So just let me go back into my little spider hole. I'm an old guy,* Levin thought, *full of stupid impossible ideas. Time to give it a rest.*

But then the e-mail came about Carl's sister. A sister. Carl had a sister. In Lincoln, Rhode Island, maybe six miles away. How could he not have known, not have remembered? All that time he had been thinking only about himself. How could have he failed to think about Carl's family?

He had called Yvonne, of course, the moment he landed. She was the first person he saw after Judy. The drive to Yvonne's house in Pawtucket was one of the hardest things he ever had to do. But he did it right away, because he felt that he was responsible, and he needed to own up He had told people about losing a loved one a hundred times. Telling Yvonne was different. This was family. Who knew? *Family is funny,* Levin thought. *It chooses you. It's not a genealogical chart. It's an emotional landscape.*

Carl had a sister.

Levin went for a run.

Levin changed his route after he came home. He didn't want to run in the cemetery anymore. Couldn't. Just couldn't. Only the living now. Too many dead.

It was March again. It had been March after the Station fire when Terrance broke into Levin's car, when he had chased Terrance down Chestnut Street, yelling, "Car thief! Car thief!" at the top of his lungs. The light was back in the early mornings and late afternoons—clean, strong, beautiful light. The snow had melted from the sidewalks and streets, but the pavement was still wet and ice-encrusted in the mornings, and you could still see your breath if you ran early.

Now Levin ran in neighborhoods and in mill villages, among the bars and the bodegas and the fast-food joints so he could be with people and always see signs of life. He ran in Pawtucket, in Fairlawn and in Woodlawn, and to North Providence. He ran in Central Falls, where the triple-deckers were packed like cards, and there weren't any lawns, let alone trees, but there was still life everywhere—strange little businesses, little upholstery shops, auto glass shops, barbershops and hairdressers. Levin remembered when Central Falls had the most bars per square mile of any place in the U.S. Now it had the most culture of any place in the U.S. Columbians, Guatemalans, Liberians, Syrians, Poles, Irish, Ukrainians, English, and Swedish, all living together in this tiny little place without trees.

Some days Levin ran down Smith Street, past the General Assembly—the great marble monument to the people's voice sitting there on Smith Hill, corrupt and manipulated, a lonely place, crying out for the people's attention. Then he'd run through Capitol Hill to LaSalle and Rhode Island College, the streets leafy in the spring and summer, the houses well-kept and unpretentious, and the bakeries so inviting. Some days he ran to Olneyville, which was all Spanish-speaking now, past an old lumberyard where he could smell the saw-dust of fresh cut boards of oak, pine, and cherry.

He avoided South Providence. When he ran there, he didn't see streets or people. All he saw was Carl that day in July, chasing Terrance in the red RAV4, racing down Broad or nosing through the backstreets, and Terrance when they trapped him near the port, in the chop shop with that big, smug Liberian guy.

A sister. In Lincoln. It was Lincoln. Why had he repressed that memory?

Levin ran south on Pawtucket Avenue. His knees were stiff. They weren't going to hold for fifteen miles today. He'd be lucky to get six. Down Pawtucket Avenue. Past the drug rehab place, the chain drug store, the auto parts stores, and the tire stores. Past the hip-hop joint and the tropical fish store. The Old North Burial Ground was across the street, but he didn't cross, and all you could really see from the street were the greenhouses where they raised lilies to put on the graves at Easter. Levin's knees were starting to hurt now, but he didn't slacken his pace. *Let's see how much these old knees can take,* he thought. Past the map store and the shopping plaza. Down the hill. Along a mossy drainage ditch. Past the Roger Williams Memorial. Old Rog, old rebellious spirit, never comfortable with any one religion or anybody's rules, who gives a little antiestablishment juice to this stuffy old town. Over to Burnside Park and around the statue of the general sitting on his horse. Good old Ambrose Burnside. General who almost lost the Civil War. Governor. First president of the NRA, the organization that taught America the freedom to sell counts more than peace, security, and the lives of kids, the organization that made a fool out of democracy. Lots of ghosts in this little town.

Levin's knees hurt now. He needed to take a break. He walked to City Hall, slowly, letting his knees recover, just quickly enough to prevent the muscles of his calves from spasming up.

And then he headed home. *My knees are better*, he thought. *I ain't dead yet.*

He walked up College Hill and started jogging. *I'll run home on Blackstone Boulevard. I can run on grass instead of pavement and be a little nice to my knees.*

But there was still snow on the running path of the Boulevard.

The morning was still clear and bright. There was now steam rising from the black pavement where the sun fell on it. The other side of the street was in the sun. He was running in the shade. He crossed over.

A woman in a fur coat driving a big yellow convertible with the top down passed him from a side street and turned left onto the Boulevard.

In the back of the convertible was a big brown dog with its head over the side of the car. The dog let its tongue hang down with evident pleasure.

When the car slowed to let a pedestrian cross, the dog hopped out of the car, trailing a long lead rope that was tied to a door handle.

Then car started moving again. The dog began to run to keep up. The dog ran on the sidewalk, behind the car and keeping pace with it, the long lead jostling and waving as the dog ran.

Levin shouted to let the driver know that the dog was out of the car.

Then the car gathered speed. Levin shouted again. The driver hadn't noticed that the dog was out of the car.

The car accelerated. The dog ran behind the car on the sidewalk, the driver unaware that her dog was running next to and behind her.

Levin shouted one more time.

Ahead of the car, a plainly dressed woman walked on the sidewalk. Many domestic workers—all immigrants—walked from the bus stop on Wayland Square to work on the East Side.

The woman walking on the sidewalk was of average height. She was simply dressed and was walking away from Levin and from the car. That was all Levin could see. She didn't turn when Levin shouted.

The car drove along the street. The dog ran on the sidewalk. The woman walked on the sidewalk between the dog and the car. The rope which tied the dog to the car came up very fast behind the woman who was walking. There was slack in the rope but not much.

He shouted again. No one heard.

The rope hit the back of the woman's legs. It went taut and threw the woman into the air. She fell backward onto her head.

The rope broke. The dog ran free. The yellow convertible drove away.

By the time Levin got to her, the pupils of the woman in the simple coat were fixed and dilated. Her eye's looked like a doll's eyes, the pupils huge and not reacting to light. They looked straight ahead. They kept looking straight ahead when Levin moved the woman's head. There was a trickle of blood and clear fluid coming from the woman's nose. She had a pulse and was still breathing on her own, but Levin knew the score right away. Fixed and dilated is fixed and dilated. Brain dead. Brain dead in fifteen seconds. The woman in the simple coat went from walking to work on the public street to functionally dead in an instant. No warning. She never knew what hit her, or even that she had been hit. Perhaps she felt something tug at her knee and felt herself falling and that was it. Lights out. No one home. Done deal. Dead and gone.

Levin called 911 on his cell, his hands shaking. She had a pulse and she was breathing. No need for CPR. There was nothing for Levin to do but be there on his knees next to this woman and wait for Rescue to arrive.

He raised her eyelids. Her pupils were big and round, but there was a rim of faint green around the pupils. She had green eyes, like Sophia Lauren. She wasn't beautiful. Her features were plain like the way she was dressed, in a domestic's uniform, and her skin was tired out, thick, and grainy. She was in her forties. Maybe fifties. She was dressed in a white frock because she was on her way to spend the day in the house of a rich woman, slowly cleaning it, moving from room to room. One moment she was a living human being, and the next moment she was brain dead. All Levin could do was to be with her, to kneel on one knee at the side of her head as she was dying, so she didn't have to die alone. To put his hand on her cheek and forehead. To wipe the blood and trickle of clear fluid from her nose with a tissue.

They sent two police cars, two Rescues, and a fire truck. Levin identified himself and told them to scoop and run. Just get her into the ED, he said. There's nothing to be gained by treating her in the field. He thought of going in with her, but there was no point to it. The game was over. He called the Emergency Department and let the attending on call know the scoop.

Then he went to the police station to give a statement. It was a simple statement, just one and a half pages. He wrote it out himself and made a very nice diagram, describing what had happened and how it happened. He thought he remembered two letters off the license plate, and that it was a yellow Cadillac, but it could have been a yellow something else. Levin didn't know the names of cars. Maybe it was some kind of Chrysler or a Chevy Impala.

And that was that. All over in an instant, though the paperwork took hours. He'd never know if the woman in the car ever found her dog, or whether she would understand that, in her own way, she had contributed to death of another human being. Or not. Maybe it was just bad luck.

It was 3:00 in the afternoon by the time Levin got home. He was working an overnight shift so he needed to lie down for a little while. But he couldn't sleep.

A sister. Carl had a sister. Carl said something that first day, something about driving home to get his things from his sister's house. Something about Lincoln or Cumberland.

The internet, Levin told himself. *If she's out there, I'll find her. We'll find her together.*

Carl had a sister. You live with others, but you always die alone.

He called Yvonne. Maybe she'd come with him. He wanted someone with him when he went to see Carl's sister. You die alone, but you don't have to live alone.

Chapter Twenty-Nine

*Naomi Goldman, Yvonne Evans-Smith, and
William Levin, MD. Lincoln and Providence,
Rhode Island. March 18 and 20, 2006*

It was Saturday, but Naomi didn't sleep late.

They knew something about her brother, these people. The news wasn't good news. You always believe, you always hope, even if your better judgment tells you not to.

She hadn't heard a word from Carl in almost three years. Naomi knew he was dead. He had gone back into a war. She hadn't heard a word from him since. The State Department people came, but she didn't believe them. Even if your better judgment tells you to you don't believe it. You don't let yourself think it. You never say it to yourself. You don't want to touch it, know it, or feel it. But you know anyway and always want to know how and when and with whom. You want to know that he wasn't alone and didn't suffer. In any news there is hope. You can argue with information, with its source, or with its logic. You can deny it. But you can't argue with silence, with absence, with disappearance. The when and how gives you a kind of hope, however vain. You can't prepare yourself for the pain that comes after.

Naomi had spent three years with the Liberian community, hoping for some word. She worked with other communities as well. Teaching, listening, and learning. "Where are you from," she'd ask. "No, where in Liberia," she'd ask, as she taught simple things. Basic English and math. How to balance a check book. How to make a resume. How to apply for a job. How to hold and keep a job. The rights and responsibilities of being a tenant. How to apply for a mortgage. Basic banking. High school equivalency.

They assumed she was Liberian or part Liberian. She went to Liberian churches on Sunday. She didn't look Liberian, and she didn't talk Liberian, but they took her in anyway. She loved those churches—the music, the electric piano, electric guitar, and the drums—the way everyone stood together, prayed together, hoped together, believed together, and sang together. If there was a god, God was on earth in those churches, and she could feel that presence, the presence that she did not believe in. But there was no god. If there was a god, Carl would still be alive and would have come back or would e-mail, write, or call.

No one wanted to talk about the war. No one even wanted to talk about Liberia. No one knew Carl.

If he *had* come home, Carl would not have recognized Naomi's life.

Naomi now lived in an old house off Broadway, and she had neighbors, real neighbors. She had a big garden that filled her bright kitchen with lettuce and asparagus in the spring, tomatoes, squash, and peppers all summer long. Her hair was natural now, thick and wavy, and she wore dresses and tops made of natural fibers, woven in bright colors—not African cloth but other clothes from around the world, soft to the touch, and she often worked in jeans.

No more pearls.

Yvonne wore a green blouse, a black skirt, her tan coat and orange silk scarf, and black gloves.

It wasn't quite raining but it wasn't dry either. Yvonne put her scarf over her head so she could keep her hair dry. Her face was carefully made up—careful eye liner, a smooth, almost undetectable foundation that gave her the appearance of perfectly smooth skin, and purple lip gloss that picked up the purple of her eyeliner. No reason anyone had to see all the lines and creases.

"Will you come Monday?" Yvonne said when Levin picked her up. "Turnabout being fair play. I took the whole day off. I wouldn't miss it for the world! First woman president in Africa! President Ellen Johnson Sirleaf. Here, in Providence, Rhode Island. People in all the churches and community organizations are getting ready. There will be flags, and there will be speeches."

"I'm not working until later," Levin said.

"So you will come! You must come!" Yvonne said.

"I've seen politicians come and politicians go. The president used to work for the World Bank, didn't she?" Levin said.

"She has the best credentials. She is a graduate of Harvard University," Yvonne said.

"And the World Bank and Citibank," Levin said. "It's okay. Some days I can't find a good word to say about anyone. I'll come. Anyone has to be an improvement over Charles Taylor."

Levin paused. "I don't know what I'm going to say to Carl's sister. I'm ashamed. That it took me all this time to find her. That I lived and he died."

"You'll tell Carl's sister what you told me," Yvonne said. "You'll tell her when and how her brother died. And where. You have nothing to be ashamed of. You were a good and loyal friend. Her brother died honorably. You are doing this woman a kindness."

"I'll go with you on Monday," Levin said. "Thank you for coming with me now."

They had arranged to meet Carl's sister in the lobby of the Biltmore Hotel. They were early. Levin dropped Yvonne, and then parked the car.

In two days, the president of Liberia would be standing a few steps away, on the steps of City Hall. *If only women could do what men had failed at so miserably*, thought Yvonne. *If only she can bring us together, stop the violence, end the poverty, and make us whole. Make Liberia one place. Let us be together and strong. Whatever else you say or think about life in America, America is one place, one people, who don't murder one another for power. Most of the time.*

Yvonne saw a thin white woman in her late twenties browsing in the hotel gift shop. The young woman had fair skin and was dressed for business in a sweater and a skirt and pearls, and she appeared to be waiting for someone. *Carl ran some kind of organization in Liberia that built village pumps. A white man*, Yvonne thought, *and that is his sister standing there.* But she didn't approach her. Instead she waited for Levin.

Levin came into the hotel lobby. There was another woman standing near the door, a women with dark tan skin wearing a multicolored woolen poncho.

Levin walked past her, toward Yvonne. Then he turned suddenly to look at the woman in the poncho. Their eyes met and all the color drained from Levin's face.

Levin staggered, as if he might fall or faint. Yvonne and the woman in the poncho both moved to catch him. But then Levin put his hand on a marble column.

"I'm Naomi," the woman said. "They always said Carl and I look alike."

"Bill Levin," he said. "You look . . . This is Yvonne Evans-Smith."

Naomi held out her hand. But Levin threw his arms around her. He pulled Naomi to him. Naomi's looked uncertain, unsure. Then she held Levin and started to cry. Yvonne held her and Yvonne started to cry. And then Levin held Naomi again.

A beautiful woman, Yvonne thought.

The story was different from the story Yvonne thought she knew.

Carl was a man of color.

Terrance didn't die alone.

Starbucks was two doors down. They sat in the big club chairs. On the edge of those chairs.

Levin told it all, from the day Terrance tried to steal his car to the day he met Carl at Sally's to chasing Terrance to the chop shop. About the days across the ocean, about the harbors in Nigeria and Ghana and Ivory Coast and waiting at the port. About Liberia. About Carl and how he calmed them, about how he drove them and kept them focused. About his courage. About his kindness and strength. About how close they had actually come to Julia, and how they would have found her the next day or the day after that. About the night Carl and Terrance died, and how they died, and about how Levin went a little crazy digging in the rubble for them.

"So you never found Julia?" Naomi asked.

"Not then," Levin said.

"What happened to her?" Naomi said. "Isn't that all that matters now?"

"I hear from her once in a while," Levin said. "By e-mail. Once every couple of months. She's in a village, working as a doctor. She never got over Carl, as far as I can tell. She isn't ready to talk to me about him yet. She e-mailed me last week about you. Carl must have talked about you, and she remembered. She asked about you, and that got me to track you down."

"We're going. I'm going. How can you be sure she's okay?" Naomi said.

"Going where?" Levin said.

"To Liberia," Naomi said. "To find Julia. I want to see Liberia. I want to see the place Carl died. It won't change anything. I want to walk where Carl walked. I want to meet Dr. Richmond. And I want to bring her home."

"Come with us Monday," Yvonne said. "Ellen Johnson Sirleaf, the new president of Liberia, the first woman president in Africa, is coming to visit Providence. Taste Liberia on Monday. And then perhaps later, when things improve, we will go to Liberia together. You want to meet Dr. Richmond. I want to go home."

Chapter Thirty
What Happened Next to Charles Taylor

IN AUGUST 2003, CHARLES TAYLOR AND HIS FAMILY WERE WHISKED TO A SEASIDE COM-pound of villas in Calabar, Nigeria. He brought with him three wives, a flotilla of expensive cars, twenty-three armed security guards, and many, many others, including twenty-seven teenage girls who were said to be the daughters of his fallen comrades-in-arms, orphans he was caring for because of his commitment to justice and mercy, in order to honor their fathers' memories.

There was, supposedly, a deal.

The deal Taylor says he made with Presidents Obasanjo, Kufour, Mbeki, and Conté was that he would leave Liberia and go into exile in Nigeria. President Obasanjo said the deal depended on Taylor staying out of politics in West Africa and living quietly without causing any further mayhem. The deal also seemed to involve a "gentleman's agree-ment" that Nigeria would not extradite Taylor, despite the indictment of the Special Court for Sierra Leone and the Interpol warrant that was out for Taylor's arrest.

In any case, nothing was ever written down, so no one will ever know who said what to whom to get Charles Taylor out of Liberia and bring fourteen years of civil war to an end.

But Charles Taylor did not keep his hands off West Africa.

By October 2003, Taylor had figured out how to move money around. He got himself a secure private telephone line and a satellite phone, the tools he had used to wreak havoc on West Africa for many years, and he worked those phones the way a carnival barker works a crowd. Taylor left Liberia with something like two hundred million dollars, money he kept in twenty or thirty shell companies in Liberia, other West African countries, Europe, and the U.S. This was money that could be used to buy and trade companies, money that could be used to keep supporters loyal, money that could be used to buy guns and favors and to position Taylor for an eventual return to Liberia.

Taylor did everything he could to influence the October 2005 presidential election in Liberia, channeling money to nine of the eighteen parties, fielding candidates, and spreading yet more money around, but he apparently failed to be a major player in the face of huge international and UN supervision of that election. Taylor's ex-wife, Jewel Taylor, who had divorced him earlier that year (leaving him with just two remaining wives, to say nothing of the twenty-seven female teenage orphans he was looking after out of the kindness of his heart) was elected a senator from Bong County—and many other associates were carefully being moved into positions of power and influence.

At the same time Taylor sent hundreds of thousands of dollars to two loyal but small-time warlords, who used the money to train and equip small armies of several hundred combatants each; armies that would be in place and at Taylor's beck and call to be used when the time was right. Taylor was involved in and likely funded a January 2005 failed assassination attempt on President Lansana Conté in Guinea. (Conté was one of the African presidents who had pressured him into leaving Liberia in 2003.) One can only wonder just how much more havoc Taylor would have created if President Ellen Johnson Sirleaf hadn't requested Taylor's extradition to Liberia in March of 2006, just three months after she was installed as Liberia's new president.

President Obasanjo of Nigeria declared he would allow Charles Taylor to be arrested only if Taylor's arrest was requested by the new government of Liberia—a clever test of Taylor's remaining power and influence in Liberia—and that he would extradite Taylor to Liberia in the event Liberia requested Taylor's extradition, but he would not respond to the indictment of the Special Court for Sierra Leone.

After her election and installation in January 2006, President Johnson Sirleaf, who had once been a supporter of Taylor's (but later disavowed that support), declared that the extradition of Charles Taylor was "low priority"—that other national rebuilding work was much more urgent. There was then protest and an outcry from people in the international human rights community, and that outcry was heard in the U.S. Congress, where there were members who advocated cutting off aid to Liberia if Taylor was not brought before the Special Court in Sierra Leone.

Lord only knows what strings were pulled behind the scenes in March 2006, how much telephone and satellite phone traffic the Liberian request to extradite Taylor generated, or how many private armies were moved from one place, one diamond field, and one border, to the next. Both Presidents Sirleaf Johnson of Liberia and Thabo Mbeki of South Africa visited President Olusẹgun Obasanjo in Nigeria in the two weeks leading up to the request for Taylor's extradition.

Reluctantly, but at last, the new government of Liberia requested Taylor's extradition on March 17, 2006, two days after President Johnson Sirleaf addressed a joint session of Congress (and likely consulted with members of the Bush State Department and others in the U.S. government); two days before President Ellen Johnson Sirleaf visited Providence, Rhode Island, and four days before she addressed the UN Security Council.

Nigeria announced it was "releasing" Taylor—but not arresting him—on Saturday, March 25, 2006, because the government of Nigeria had suddenly discovered that there was no extradition treaty between Liberia and Nigeria.

On March 27, 2006, Taylor disappeared from the compound in Calabar.

President Obasanjo left for Washington, DC, on March 28, 2006, on his way to see President George Bush in order to build support for a permanent seat for Nigeria on the UN Security Council and for his own attempt to rewrite the Nigerian constitution to allow him to run for a third term as president. By the time Obasanjo took off from Abuja, Taylor had disappeared from his compound and suddenly was nowhere to be found. Obasanjo's plane landed at 9:30 p.m., March 28, 2006, U.S. time, which is 3:30 a.m., March 29 local time in Nigeria. The president of Nigeria was met in DC by representatives of the U.S. State Department, just as his foreign minister was meeting with Bush's National Security Advisor Stephen Hadley in what must have been a very interesting meeting indeed.

Taylor and his retinue of three Land Rovers with diplomatic plates was cleared through Nigerian immigration at 7:30 a.m., March 29, 2006, at Gamboru-Ngala, on the Nigerian border with Cameroon. Taylor was traveling in a flowing white robe but on a fake passport. His retinue was held up at Nigerian customs, however, when a customs official noticed that there were several million dollars and euros in cash, all in two 110-pound sacks, as well as bricks of heroin and packets of diamonds and gold.

On March 29, 2006, at 7:30 a.m. local time in Nigeria, 1:30 a.m. U.S. time, or about four hours after President Obasanjo's plane landed in Washington, Charles Taylor was arrested by Nigerian police.

It is very unusual for customs officials to inspect the luggage of vehicles bearing diplomatic plates, because such inspections represent a violation of international law.

One never knows exactly what transpired in meetings like the one between Obasanjo and Bush. They met at about 10:00 a.m. on March 29, 2006, about seven hours after Taylor's arrest. According to press releases and news reports they talked about West African politics, about Taylor and Liberia, about the discovery of oil in Guinea, about the situation in Darfur, and about political instability in the oil rich provinces of Nigeria, where U.S. and other foreign oil companies have major investments.

U.S. aid to Nigeria in 2006 included $45 million in humanitarian and development aid from USAID, about $170 million in military aid, and some $19.2 billion of "exceptional debt relief" from the World Bank, which is technically not U.S. aid at all. Technically.

A year later, U.S. military aid had grown to $330 million, almost doubling.

President Obasanjo failed in his attempt to change Nigeria's constitution and left office in 2008. Nigeria was unsuccessful in obtaining a permanent seat on the UN Security Council. No African country has ever held a permanent seat on the Security Council. The population of Africa is close to one billion people, or about one-seventh of the world's population. The land mass of Africa is one-fifth of the total land mass of the earth.

Charles Taylor was sent home to Liberia in chains, and then was shipped to Sierra Leone, and from Sierra Leone was shipped to The Hague to stand trial—the first head of state to be indicted while in office; the first former head of state to stand trial in an international court for his crimes but very likely far from the last head of state to have murdered and tortured his own people, driven by his own lust for money and power, and egged on by the lust and greed of people who lack the capacity for remorse.

Chapter Thirty-One

Naomi Goldman, Yvonne Evans-Smith, and
William Levin. Monrovia, Liberia. May, 2007

THERE WAS NO JETWAY. THEY STUMBLED DOWN THE STAIRS OF THE HOT ALUMINUM GANG-way into the blinding sun, stiff in their knees and shoulders and lower backs from sitting, despite having spent the night in the airport hotel in Accra.

Everyone who came off the plane crowded into a room the size of a small post office. A woman in a green uniform stood at the door. Three immigration officers in blue uniforms sat in Plexiglas booths on the right wall. The passengers from the plane crowded around each booth, jostling for position. The immigration officers sat on tall stools and looked down on the people who jammed before them so that their voices were both amplified and muffled by the booths, which made the booths vibrate when the people inside spoke.

Then suddenly the three friends were in the hot sunlight sur-rounded by thin dark men in torn tee shirts offering to carry their bag-gage. If Yvonne had not been there, they might have been swept away.

Yvonne became their protector. Her back straightened, her voice hardened, and you could feel the hair on the back of her neck stand up as she snapped at the thin young men who clustered around each traveler, speaking harshly the way a school teacher addresses an unruly class, speaking in a guttural language that sounded like English but that neither Levin nor Naomi understood.

"Ga wa! Na tou. Na carry," she said. *Go away! Don't touch. We don't need help carrying the luggage.*

A woman in a brown and green lapa came from nowhere and threw her arms around Yvonne, who became herself again for a moment, and then she became someone Levin and Naomi had never met; someone with moist eyes and the excited voice of a young girl come home to her family. There was a man there too, and then two men in dark suits wearing shirts with open-necked collars, and then another woman. They had come together in two cars. Room for everybody.

The cars were small Japanese station wagons, one red and the other black, both dusty and dented. There were introductions: the men were called John and James; the women Gladys and Nowei; Gladys was Yvonne's niece and was married to John; Nowei was John's sister and was married to James; they were all Christians, and the men were deacons in a church in Monrovia. They had come to drive Yvonne and her friends to Buchanan and to find Terrance, because Terrance had disappeared without a trace. The story that Levin told—that Terrance had come back to Liberia, had died at the camp of a band of Charles Taylor's men when MODEL moved on it in the middle of the night, attacking with night vision goggles and RPGs and destroying the clubhouse of the LAC—all that seemed too unbelievable to Yvonne's sisters to be true. Even in Liberia. Even though Yvonne knew it was true after all.

It was almost 3:00. The men packed the luggage as the women arranged themselves in the cars: Yvonne and Gladys in the back seat of John's car, with Levin in the passenger seat; James driving Naomi in the second car, with Nowei behind. They would drive to Buchanan that night and go tomorrow to The Club, and then go to find this Dr. Richmond, once and for all.

There were just three hours before dark. They needed to be in Buchanan before the sunset.

The UN was all over the airport. They passed a white UN jet on the tarmac and four UN helicopters on the grass outside the passenger terminal. A fleet of white UN Land Cruisers were driving back and forth, buzzing around the airport like flies.

The two cars headed south. Just past the airport there was a UN checkpoint, a guard post manned by Thais with two machine guns trained on the road from behind a wall of sandbags.

They passed the Firestone plantation. Levin remembered the fields and cows and the row of big black tanks spelling out F-I-R-E-S-T-O-N-E.

Suddenly Levin was short of breath, sweaty and nauseated at the same time. Suddenly he was in the back of the RAV, nosing through crowds of people. Suddenly he heard the blast and smelled the dust and gunpowder as MODEL moved in, destroying everything and everyone. Suddenly he was digging, his fingertips raw. He wasn't listening. He was pale and sweating and his shoulders began to shake.

They went over a rise, and the moment passed.

The pavement was smooth in the plantation. They swept through the lines of pale green-barked rubber trees and through their thin shadows. Sunlight flickered in the cars in a way that, had it been sound, would have been the sound of a train, clattering and ticking over the rails, as the cars pierced the lines of light and dark, of sunlight and shadow, in a way that was mesmerizing and nauseating at once.

Yvonne sat in the back seat of the first car. Gladys was a niece but was as good as a sister. She was the niece and sister and aunt who kept track of who was who, who was close, and who was having problems. They would to stop in St. John's River. Two sisters and a brother there. Then they'd go on to Buchanan, where there was a hotel for Naomi and Levin. Three sisters in Buchanan. More nieces and nephews than you could count. Everyone was all stirred up. Everyone wanted to see Yvonne. She hadn't been home in all these years. People would gather as soon as Yvonne came back from the bush. Everyone would come and visit and eat together. Everyone was talking about the big visit. There hadn't been a big visit like this in years.

Gladys had news. Gladys's father, Yvonne's sister's man, same ma different pa, was safe in a village in Bong County, but three of her brothers had disappeared from Monrovia during the war, one into Sierra Leone. Yvonne had news one sister was in Ghana, and that sister had a daughter in Philadelphia and another daughter who was in college in St. Louis on a full scholarship and was headed to law school.

Yvonne listened and found herself overwhelmingly proud of this land and her people. Her people had dignity. They fought, yes, and the fighting was terrible. But they didn't complain. They fought, they loved, and they worked. Their faith was strong. God was everywhere in Liberia. Liberia was her home. She loved it here, and she felt kissed by the blood-soaked ground as they drove over it.

Naomi sat in front in the second car, next to James.

It had been a hard, sad year for Naomi. Her work at the Institute kept her sane. Levin was a good man who had been kind when he brought her the news, and then patient with her questions. The story was unbelievable at first, even absurd. Americans don't leave the country in ships full of stolen cars bound for Africa. Or get themselves killed in other people's civil wars. Naomi knew Levin was telling the truth, and that Carl was dead, but she also didn't believe any of it— both at the same time.

But Yvonne, the woman with Levin, had been Naomi's salvation. Yvonne took over Naomi's life while Naomi grieved. She cooked for Naomi and filled her freezer with food. She came by the Institute when Naomi was teaching at night. She taught Liberian children's songs to the kids of Naomi's students and finger painted with them as their parents learned. You do not see Yvonne's inner life. They walked out of the Institute together every night but rarely spoke.

"It is better than it was," Yvonne said one evening, when they were alone. "Not good yet but better. Okay to travel in the day. Women back in the markets. Dried fish coming from the river again. Schools opening."

"Safe enough to go?" Naomi asked.

"If you wish," Yvonne said.

"Will you come?" Naomi said.

"I will. I'm not sure I should have ever left," Yvonne said.

"Dr. Levin?" Naomi said.

"Dr. Levin will come. We need him to show us the places and he needs us to hold him up," Yvonne said. "We will go together, the three of us."

The road swung past a cluster of buildings: the plantation store, the plantation school, and the plantation hospital. Then they passed the houses of the rubber workers—neat lines of square four-room concrete houses, with metal roofs that looked like the little green houses from the game of Monopoly.

But here the rows of little houses suggested liberation, light, order, and progress. The rubber workers' houses, each with a green lawn out front and a banana tree in the back yard, were a huge step up from what Carl had described when he talked or wrote about life in the bush. Naomi imagined that all the houses had running water, neat little white enamel electric stoves, and flush toilets. Carl had said people lived in huts made of mud and sticks with hard dirt floors, wooden sleeping benches, and a cooking fire outside. This was different from what Carl described and different from home as well.

The road left the plantation, and they entered the real Liberia for the first time.

On the side of the road were market stalls and a gaggle of the mud houses Carl had written about; mud houses framed by wooden poles, which had roofs thatched with leaves from the forest. The air was hazy with smoke from cooking fires. The roadbed disintegrated. They were driving on broken pavement now, with patches of road that were just red dirt, rutted and uneven. The car bottomed out and jolted as they drove, its old suspension unable to support the weight of the people inside on the uneven ground.

In the next village there were people everywhere. People in the market stalls, sitting on the ground or on low benches, people next to the village pump, which was set in concrete—a pump like the pictures Carl had sent her after each was finished. People, mostly women, walked next to the road, carrying bundles or baskets or those multicolored bright green and red and purple plastic tubs on their heads.

But what Naomi saw in the villages was life and dignity, not poverty or squalor, and she began to understand Carl, perhaps for the first time. When Carl had told her about the complex and beautiful world of the country people in the bush, Naomi imagined a world that was primitive, that was dirty and diseased. When she heard stories about the headmen and their wives, she imagined a place where people were downtrodden and suffering. When Carl had talked about the elegant way people lived and died, how people appeared to live without fear until the wars came, about how their lives were transformed by something as simple as a village pump, Naomi imagined that Carl was their savior and not the other way around. He had tried to tell her. She had listened, but she hadn't really heard.

Naomi had her own beliefs about what was ordered, stable, and good. But as she looked at these people and their villages, everything she thought she believed about Liberia and its people changed. There was order here. Dignity, but different dignity. A different order. A different way to think.

It didn't matter much. Because Naomi was still alone. More alone now than ever.

The huts and people disappeared. The road got worse. It was pockmarked by potholes that looked like small lakes and creased by ruts that were as deep as a strong man's arm and ten car lengths long.

The evening rain was short that day. Just enough to moisten the dust. Not enough to send rivulets across the road.

The two cars pulled over next to a market and across the road from a field ringed by mango trees that looked down on a broad river crossed by a thin iron bridge. The sun found its way out between the clouds just over the horizon. They were beginning to lose the light, which cast long shadows. One of the stalls had tables piled high with dried fish. Another had a table covered with withered green oranges.

Gladys and Yvonne opened their doors and Naomi came out of her car.

"This is my home," Yvonne said. "I have to stop for a few minutes. I won't be long. We need to be in Buchanan by nightfall. We will come back in a few days, and I'll have you meet my family then."

Yvonne walked between two houses. She took Gladys' arm to steady herself. Two old women waited in the yard of a house Yvonne remembered as she walked toward the river. Old women in green and blue lapas, their withered brown skin hanging on their faces. Trudi and Henri, hiding in the bodies of these old women, their voices now deeper and subdued.

We are old, Yvonne thought as she embraced these women who were hiding the young girls who were her sisters. So old. Life has come and is going away.

Then they were on the bridge and rattling over the iron plates. There was still light but no sun, so the countryside was blue and hushed. The road was better on the far side of the bridge, and they passed concrete houses with neat yards on both sides of the road.

Levin remembered the sensation of speed as they flew through that place behind the two militia pick-up trucks, before they all turned north. He remembered that they thought Julia was close, was almost in their grasp. He listened to the murmuring of the women's voices in the seat behind him. He kept one hand on the dashboard in front of him to brace himself as the car lurched side to side and bottomed out, and to protect himself from what he was feeling and would feel.

It had all seemed so simple. They would come to Liberia, find Julia, and bring her back. Get in, get out, and get gone. They did what appeared impossible. They got to Liberia while there was a war on. They drove through its streets. They got into and talked themselves out of trouble. They were close to Julia, about to find her. They had become one, the three of them. You live together. You die together. You do what needs to be done.

And then disaster. And then nothing. This endless, empty, painful nothing.

Lord only knew what Julia saw, felt, knew, or understood.

You save one life, you save the world. What kind of idea was that? What does it mean, to save a life? What arrogance! To decide who needs saving and what life means. Repair the world? Who says the world is broken, and who asked anyone to fix it?

But Levin was obsessing again. Back to living only in his own head. Endless obsession. No action. No justice. No peace. No change.

So the hell with all the degrees and the certificates on the wall, Levin thought. *Forget meetings and movements. There is no purpose in this. I'm just one incredibly stupid, lonely old man.*

Chapter Thirty-Two
Yvonne, Naomi, Levin, and John. Grand Bassa County, Liberia. May 2007

THE JUNGLE HAD GROWN BACK THROUGH THE BLACKENED GROUND. THERE WAS GREEN everywhere, green underbrush, green saplings, and dense green vines. Some of the saplings were six, seven, even nine feet high, so eager is the jungle to regain its ground.

Trees are different than men. A man's arms are spread farthest high up, so that he can pick the fruit of the trees. Most of the greenery was at knee- and thigh-level, broadleaf plants with bold, wide, undulating leaves to catch every photon of available light. Lithe grasses that reached upward are different yet, thrusting themselves as high as their green skeletons allow and then bending to catch more light. The broad leaves of the young trees each looked like the map of a great virgin country with an irregular shore and rivers. The spiked grasses bent over from their own weight as they grew tall and waved and swayed in the gentle midday heat. Men bend over as we age. Trees stand up and insert their narrow tops into the sky as high as they can get, where the air is clear and the sun in strongest.

They had come out from Buchanan that morning in one car. John driving, Levin in the passenger seat again—men in the front and the women in the back. They drove to the plantation. There was still a sign, but there was no guard station anymore. They drove through the rubber trees, and then turned left at the road to the country club.

Some of the walls of The Club were still standing, but there was now a green and yellow thicket where the floor had once been. The wrecked grey-black cement block walls were covered with mosses and molds that snaked through the greenery as if it were camouflage, meant to blend into the shadows and streaming light. The burned-out trucks lay on their sides and were now brown-red, as they rusted. You could still see slivers of chrome as you walked from place to place.

The walls of the swimming pool had started to collapse. Where there had once been smooth pale blue tiles there was now a falling-in mound crusted with blue-green algae, and though there was still water in the pool, it had blackened, and there were water plants and marsh grasses growing in the water that had once been clear and sparkling.

The black tarmac in the parking lot and the cement of the helicopter landing pad had cracked, and there were weeds and grasses and even a few small saplings growing out of each crack. It would be many years before the asphalt and concrete could be digested by the earth, but the earth had begun the slow process of returning the asphalt to dust and allowing bush and jungle to replace that dust.

Levin didn't see the brass shell casings at first. He could feel them under his feet as he walked. Half buried in the red earth, under the grasses and the moss, they crunched and clinked as he walked from place to place and made the footing tricky, like walking on clam shells left on a rocky beach by the retreating tide. There were still weaver birds making mud nest colonies in the ironwood tree, just beyond where the changing rooms had been.

There really wasn't much to see. There was a place under a mango tree where the earth rose a little and another place on the other side of the swimming pool where a depression had become marshy with time. Perhaps the dead were buried in those places.

John stayed in the car.

Yvonne and Naomi picked their way across the site. Perhaps it gave them some comfort to be there. To walk where Carl and Terrance had walked. To stand where Terrance and Carl had died.

For Levin there was no comfort. No comfort now. No comfort ever. They had been one body—Carl, Terrance, and Levin—and for one brief moment, once in his life, he had been part of something bigger than himself, however doomed. This was the place where it ended.

Levin walked inside the ruins of the clubhouse. Was this the wall they slept next to? Were the cement blocks on the ground the cement blocks that had buried Carl and Terrance? The women followed Levin as he walked, even though he wasn't able to say what he was thinking. The bar had been over there. The hallway here. The toilet, down the hall where the kitchen once was. What we should remember? How we should feel? What do we know? How can we ever get back what we have lost?

There is no proper trinket, Levin thought. *No souvenir. No appropriate memento.* They did not find a keychain or a pocket knife or a wallet or a necklace or a hat. There were the shell casings, of course, but they left the shell casings alone, and ground them deeper into the earth as they walked. There was just the thicket, the jungle, the undergrowth Levin felt around him, the dense green carpet that digests hopes, courage, dreams, sins, and failures; inhaling the people we are, the people we've been, and the people we love, after we stand up together to love and then lay down together under this warm green crust. Our bones, our carcasses—they are the only souvenirs, but who needs them? The green earth, the thicket, the jungle, growing back through the cracks in the asphalt is enough, is what we together become.

Then the women were in the car, waiting for him. John started the engine. It was time to go.

One foot after the next. One step at a time.

Chapter Thirty-Three
*Yvonne, Naomi, Levin, and John. Grand
Bassa County, Liberia. May, 2007*

THE DUSTY SIGN POST ON THE BONG COUNTY ROAD WAS BENT AT THE TOP. THE SIGN THAT
had once been white looked like it was had been left behind, marking a
place that had closed long ago. You could make out the blue and green
lettering if you stopped the car and got out to look. The sign marked a
rutted one-track road that led into the bush.

John turned onto that road.

The forest was empty there. No people walking. No huts or villages. No animal scat in the road. Nothing moving—no birds, no dogs,
no goats, no chickens, no lizards or even any snakes sunning themselves on rocks. Only the huge trees with smooth bark and trunks so
tall that the first branches were too high to cast any shade on the road.

The road was difficult, but John kept going even after it felt like the
jungle had swallowed them whole. The car skidded as John fought his
way from place to place, dodging potholes, some of which were filled
knee-deep with red water from the previous night's rain, or jolting
through them, speeding up and stopping, lurching from side to side.
Levin, Yvonne, and Naomi were thrown about the inside of the car, their
heads grazing the roof and their shoulders banging against the doors.

They should have turned back. If the car broke down, there was
no one they could look to for help.

They stopped at a little log bridge. John and Levin got out of the car.

The bridge was just wide enough for a car but it didn't look at
all reliable. Thick black logs lay between two steel girders, bridging a
fifty-foot drop. The logs were wet and had lime green moss growing in
the grooves between them. There were open places between some of

the logs, and if you looked down you could see rays of sunlight playing on the rippling water far below, and you could hear the water murmur and gurgle.

You could walk across the bridge if you kept one foot on each of two logs, as long as you stayed in the middle so there was a place to fall if you stumbled.

There was a bad list to the bridge, which tilted down and to the left. There were enough spaces between the logs for the tires of a car to get wedged between them. But the tire tracks on the near side of the bridge, on the black timbers, and cut into the embankment on the far side proved that people drove across this bridge.

The men returned to the car.

"John can get over the bridge," Levin said. "We'll walk across. The bridge is actually pretty good."

"Doesn't look like a bridge to me," Yvonne said.

"Tire tracks," Levin said. "You'll see. Looks like people are driving on it all the time."

Yvonne looked at him over her glasses.

"People drive on it. See for yourself," Levin said.

Yvonne and Naomi got out. They walked to the embankment. They saw the tire tracks, and that strengthened them some. Then they walked onto the bridge and crossed to the other side.

Levin stood next to the car on the near side of the embankment. John let the car creep forward. He gave the car a little gas, so the front end rose onto the bridge, like a boat next to a dock rising with an incoming wave. The bridge itself was only five car lengths long and wouldn't take long to cross.

Then the car was on the bridge. The bridge sank a little with the car's weight, and the tires thumped on the roadbed timbers as the car began to cross the ravine.

As the car inched forward, the rear end slipped on the wet logs. Then the rear wheel on the driver's side, the driving wheel, wedged between two timbers and began to spin.

The car stopped.

The front end slipped down, leftward, toward the gorge. John hit the gas. The rear wheel hissed as it spun in place.

Then John threw the car into reverse. It leaned backward, but the left rear tire remained caught between two logs.

John threw it into drive again and turned the front wheels to the right, away from the edge and the drop into the gorge. Now both rear wheels spun, sizzling and hissing as the car snaked forward a few inches, then stopped again. The burning rubber stank.

The bright morning sun became hotter. John turned the engine off and opened his door. "Stuck, boss," John said.

"Don't call me boss," Levin said.

Levin came onto the bridge and stood behind the car.

"Give it a little gas," Levin said, "and turn the wheel."

John started the car. Levin put his weight behind the rear bumper and pushed as the engine revved. The rear wheel shrieked in its new home, smoking and stinking as it turned.

Yvonne and Naomi came onto the bridge and stood at the front of the car.

"You men push the car, and I'll run it," Yvonne said.

"I'll help push," Naomi said.

"Your call," Levin said, sweating.

Yvonne and John changed places. John stood behind the car, his back and right shoulder against the rear fender. Levin opened the passenger side door and window so he could push on the doorpost and talk to Yvonne at the same time. Naomi stood next to John.

"Ready?" Levin said.

Yvonne nodded and stepped on the gas. The engine roared. The rear wheel edged forward a quarter turn.

"Push!" Levin yelled.

The car slid forward a few more inches in the groove between the wet black logs.

The engine revved. There was more white smoke from the tail pipe. They all pushed together. Then the tire came out of the groove.

The rear end of the car rose and rested, for an instant, on the top of the log that made the groove, just two fat logs and a steel girder over from the drop into the ravine.

Then Yvonne, feeling the car lift, came off the gas.

"Gas! Gas! Gas!" Levin yelled, as the left rear tire started to slip to the left, toward the edge of the bridge.

Yvonne pushed the accelerator hard. Both rear wheels spun and slipped off the bridge together which lifted the front end into the air. The passenger side front wheel was a few inches off the surface of the bridge. The car tipped toward the gorge, hanging in the air.

Yvonne was thrown against the driver's side door. That tilted the unbalanced car more.

The passenger side rear wheel came off the bridge.

Yvonne looked out on the drop. She saw the darkness and could just make out the stream far below. Had there been luggage on a roof-top carrier, its weight would have flipped the car into the ravine.

Naomi threw her whole weight into the bumper and prayed.

"No gas!" Levin shouted. "Come off the gas! Stay calm!" he shouted.

John pushed and pulled as hard as he could on the open window of the passenger side door, using his dead weight as ballast to pull the car away from the drop.

Yvonne tried her door. The latch clicked but the door barely moved. It was wedged closed, stuck against a log.

Levin pulled on the passenger side rear tire, hoping against hope they could keep the car from tipping over.

The car didn't move. Then John reached into the car with his right hand.

Yvonne grabbed John's wrist and pulled on it, lifting herself out of her seat. She climbed, one of her hands clasped to John's hand, the other first on the steering wheel, then on the rearview mirror, then on the glove compartment door, and then on the window itself; one foot on the steering wheel and then the other foot on the console between the seats, where people in Europe and the U.S. put the hot drinks that they buy from fast-food restaurants so they can have hot coffee and fancy lattes as they drive to work in the morning. The car shook as Yvonne's weight shifted from one side to the other.

Soon she was standing inside the car, her feet on the driver's side door, and her head now out the passenger side window.

Yvonne was a strong woman, but she was not thin. As she climbed through the passenger side window, Levin and Naomi felt the passenger side rear wheel and the rear back part of the car shift back toward righting itself. They pushed even harder, feeling the shift, hoping they could flip the car back onto four wheels.

"John!" said Levin.

John did not turn or speak. He let go of Yvonne's hand, grabbed the window, dropped his bottom and grunted again, pulling the car back toward the bridge with every ounce of strength in his thin body, still trying with Naomi and Levin to tip the car back toward the bridge.

Yvonne's head came through the window. Then her arms and shoulders came through.

The car wavered back and forth around its tipping point, uncertain which way it would fall.

Then Yvonne put her left foot onto the dashboard, her right foot onto the passenger side head rest, and pushed her chest through the window.

The car shuddered. Yvonne twisted. Her hips came through the window. She bent her body at the waist, lunging for the ground. John let go of the window-sill and grabbed for Yvonne as she grabbed for him. They locked arms around one another's chests.

Yvonne's center of gravity shifted from the car to John.

The passenger side of the car rose as Yvonne's legs came through the window, and Yvonne and John fell onto the bridge.

But the center of gravity of the car shifted backward, away from Yvonne and John and back toward the ravine the instant Yvonne was free of the car.

There was a crunch as the car tipped toward the ravine and its weight collapsed the sheet metal of the driver's side doors. For a moment all the wheels were off the ground, facing away from the drop.

Then the wheels rose higher.

The car rolled onto its roof, collapsing it. Then the car hesitated again. The wheels pointed into the air like the four paws of a dog scratching its back in the gravel. Then the wheels drifted to the left, leaning into the drop.

And then the car disappeared. A moment later there was a crash, which was not as loud or long-lasting as you might have expected.

And then there was quiet. Water gurgled in the brook, making sounds like a happy baby makes.

Only Naomi was still standing, her face smudged with the black soot from the undercarriage of the car.

Yvonne and John rolled onto their hands and knees. They stood slowly, holding on to each other a few feet from the edge of the bridge. Yvonne's shoes had come off, and the back of her legs were bleeding.

Levin was on his back. He rolled onto his side and stood up.

Chapter Thirty-Four
District #4 Health Center. Grand Bassa County, Liberia. May 2007

But for the white man, they looked like Liberians. With his clothing torn and baggy and his skin thick with red dust, even the white man fit in. They were four people walking down the road.

The District #4 Health Center sits on a low hill. It looks down on the forest and the road that comes through that forest. There is a village just a few hundred yards beyond the health center on the road, a village of red mud-walled huts covered with thatched dried tan leaves gathered from the forest. When you are sitting on the porch of the health center, where the people sit when they come to see the doctor, the village is just behind you, and you can smell the charcoal fires and hear people talking, babies crying, and children being spoken to severely by their mothers.

The four people climbed the hill as the road rose in front of the health center. One, an old woman, leaned on a stick to help her walk. The dusty white man with the beard carried a dirty rucksack. The thin dark man carried a pale blue suitcase that had seen better days. The thin tan woman walked under an umbrella to protect herself from the sun. She pulled a dusty red suitcase on wheels that left a track of two pencil-thin parallel lines in the dust of the road, a thin track that looked like the mucus track left by a snail or the vapor trail left by a jet—two straight lines that ran behind her as far as the eye could see.

It was just past mid-afternoon. The sun was still strong, and the day was still hot. People were better off in the shade.

Ten people sat on the porch. They were mostly women. Two with bellies were there for the big belly clinic, and three had young children, one of whom was at the breast, while other children bounced like crickets on and off the porch and on and off their mothers' laps. There was a man with a bad eye who had a peg where his right leg belonged. Some of the people on the porch had come from the village. Others had come from villages and compounds deep in the bush. Some had walked for four hours to come to the District #4 Health Center. Some had walked eight.

The four people walking together paused at the base of the little hill and looked at the people on the porch who looked back at them. Then the four people began to climb the rise that led to a concrete staircase.

There was an old white extended-cab Dodge Ram parked off to the right. It was missing one wheel and was jacked up on wooden blocks.

The dusty white man with the beard came first to the top of the stairs. Then the woman with the stick came up and the stick thumped on each stair. Next, the thin man carrying the suitcase came up, followed by the woman, who was now carrying the umbrella, which she had folded before she climbed the stairs. The dusty red suitcase she was pulling hummed and thudded at the top of each stair.

When they had all reached the top step, the two women looked at one another. The thin man looked at the posters on the walls, one of which showed a woman with a big belly, one of which showed a mosquito drawn much larger than life next to a picture of a bed net off and then over a bed, one of which showed a man and a sitting woman together with a picture of a bed and another picture of a condom in between them, and one of which showed a crying baby that was way too thin, with a tan-green patch that you were meant to think was liquid beneath the baby's buttocks. The people in the posters looked flat, like pancakes, instead of people with depth and shadow, which made the illustrations look primitive. But the posters were printed in bright colors—reds, blues, yellows, browns, and oranges—and the meaning of the posters was clear even if you were not from the village, from Grand Bassa County, from Liberia, or from West Africa at all.

The white man looked at the people sitting and standing on the porch as if he was waiting to be greeted by them, but no one said a word. Everyone paid attention to the four newcomers, but no one looked at them, because it is not polite to look at those you do not know. It was also not the place of patients and people from a village or the bush to speak to newcomers in someone else's house or compound or clinic without having been introduced.

A thin brown middle-aged woman with a wrinkled leathery face and wearing a tan smock emerged out of the shadowy hallway of the health center holding a tattered pale green file folder. She was about to call the person whose name was written in block capital letters at the edge of the folder when she saw the four people standing together on the porch just a few feet away.

"Hallo," she said after a moment's hesitation and with an intonation that made the word more a question than a statement.

Before Levin could speak, Yvonne took a step to her left, so that she stood in front of him.

"Whe Docta?" Yvonne asked. *Where is the doctor?*

"Docta he," the woman in the tan smock said. *The doctor is here.*

"See docta?" Yvonne said. *Can I see the doctor?*

"Na na. Wha trobel?" the woman said. *Not now. What's wrong?*

"She's hurt," Naomi said in American.

A large bald man who was darker than the woman stepped from the shadows to see for himself. The larger man was more than twice the size of the woman with the tan smock and his form filled the doorway in which he stood. The bald man was wearing a green camouflage shirt and new blue jeans. There was a pencil behind his ear. His body blocked the light coming from the inside windows to the west, his big doughy hands holding a clipboard in front of him as if it were a weapon or a shield.

"How can I help you?" the big man said in perfect American English with a Midwest accent, an accent which took the Americans by surprise.

"She's hurt," Levin said, before Yvonne could respond. "Car flipped over."

"Let's sit her down on one of these benches and we'll take a look at her," the big man said. Levin turned and took the handle of the dusty red suitcase from Yvonne's hand and helped her to settle on one of the smooth wooden benches against the wall.

The big man dropped to one knee and lifted Yvonne's pants leg so he could see the cuts on the back of her calf, which were swollen and red. He turned the leg from side to side so he could see better.

Levin started to go into the clinic.

Then a slim white woman with grey streaked black hair came out of from the darkness. Her hair was pulled into a pony tail from which wisps of hair escaped.

"Dr. Levin, I presume." Julia said. She stepped out onto the porch, into the bright daylight.

"Dr. Richmond," Levin said. "Oh my God, Julia." Levin threw his arms around her. He lifted her off the floor as he held her to him. "You are alive and well. You look so good."

"I am alive and well," Julia said. "You don't look too much the worse for wear yourself. Except for how you look. How was your trip? Introduce me."

Then there was a woman standing next to Julia. She was tall and dark tan, and she had wavy black straight hair that fell to her shoulders and that she pulled out of her face with an unconscious movement of her hands, something she did whenever she wanted to be sure she could see.

And then Carl was there. He was right there with Julia. Alive again. Tall and quiet. The orangey sweet smell of his skin. How it felt to have his skin on her skin. Julia felt heat and then cold, terrible cold, in her chest and lower back. It came up fast and grabbed at her throat and at her eyes.

When she came to, Julia was lying on a bench. Bill Levin was there. Chirelle, her new PA, was there. Jonathan was there also, standing against a wall, watching but also ready to help. And the new woman was there kneeling next to her, holding a cool cloth on her forehead and wiping her eyes.

"I'm Naomi. Carl and I looked a lot alike. I should have warned you."

"Julia. Not much of a hostess though. I thought I had more self-control."

"I don't need a welcome," Naomi said. "I just wanted to meet you, to see what Carl saw and to thank you."

"Thank me?" Julia said. "I don't think so. Carl got killed because of me. I'll never forgive myself for that, and you shouldn't ever forgive me either."

"Stop that," Naomi said. "Carl was a free man. He made his own choices. He wasn't so easy to know. You gave him a kind of freedom he had never known before. He felt loved, Julia, if only for a little while. I hate that he died. I hate that he died looking for you. But I know my brother. You were the best thing that ever happened to him, even it took him too damned long to figure that out."

"I don't go there," Julia said. "I can't."

"It's okay," Naomi said. "We're there with you—me and Dr. Levin and Yvonne. Yvonne never knew Carl, but she's still part of this strange crazy bunch. You don't know her yet. You will. Her son Terrance was the third guy, the other guy who died with Carl. Let's get you on your feet. Yvonne's on the porch. She wants to meet you, and she also needs the benefit of your skill and expertise right now. She's got a cut leg."

Julia stood and they walked together onto the porch, where Yvonne was sitting.

"Yvonne, this is Dr. Richmond. Dr. Richmond, Yvonne Evans-Smith of Providence, Rhode Island, once of Saint John's River, Liberia, the mother of Terrance Evans-Smith, who came with Carl and Dr. Levin and was their friend and their guide."

"Dr. Richmond. It is good to know you at last. Thank you for your service," Yvonne said.

"What is everyone thanking me for?" Julia said. "I'm the cause of all this kerfluffle. Now let's get a look at that leg."

Jonathan knelt down and held Yvonne's right leg and calf in the light for Julia to look at. Julia could see laceration in the calf and how it had become infected.

"Decent size lac," Levin said. "Too late to sew it though. It will have to heal up on its own. It'll leave a scar, but she's got a little cellulitis. Nothing that a little Keflex can't fix. Got any antibiotics in this place?"

"Not much Keflex in Liberia," Julia said, as she looked at Yvonne's leg and shook her head.

"Got Betadine, though," Jonathan said.

Chapter Thirty-Five

Jonathan Crossman. Grand Bassa County,
Liberia. August 2003–May 2007

Jonathan had not intended to stay. He called people who knew people in Calabar, Lagos, Tripoli, Joberg, London, Paris, and Washington. The situation was fluid. No promises could be made. Best to lay low and play your cards close to your vest. Keep your assets close at hand. Keep that woman safe. Talk in a few days.

He took a suitcase out of the truck and took over one of the examination rooms. They brought in a cot from one of the overnight rooms for him. Primitive but adequate. During the day the desk in the exam room had dim but adequate light. Jonathan had a cable he could hang off the truck battery and solar recharger for the satellite phone, so he was ready for anything. They didn't know who he was at the clinic, so they left him alone. The clinic was safe for him because it was so far off the beaten path. For a few days. Until something jelled. Just a few days. Perhaps a week.

All day long, they brought in children who needed shots, those who were dying, and young girls with big bellies.

Julia sat with each one. A complete waste of time. *The fit will survive. The others will die anyway. We make a load of babies to replace those that die, and we get a few good ones. Not an efficient process, perhaps, but an effective one.*

One morning Jonathan began to yell into the satellite phone. The clinic was a quiet place, and its walls shook when Jonathan yelled. MODEL had hit The Club. They were saying no survivors. Jonathan yelled louder. An American who was there got pulled out alive, but none of his boys made it. One of those three men looking for Julia. But the hell with that. His boys had taken an incredible hit. MODEL brought up a big gun and blew the place to smithereens. They'd cut Jonathan's legs off at the knees and his arms off at the chest. The boys at The Club were his leverage. He was going to make a deal, pass them to someone else and use the girl doctor as protection while he was crossing borders. Now he was stuck, abandoned, and alone. MODEL was now in Bong County. South, north, and east. LURD was to their west. No tunnel out. Jonathan was fucked.

Julia heard Jonathan yelling. Inside the shouting voice were words distorted by fast talking, walls, and the closed door. Words that could be assembled into phrases.

"Only a white man?" Jonathan said. "Who cares about a goddamn white man? No other survivors? A howitzer? How the hell did they get a goddamn howitzer up here and into position? The damn building fell in on them in the middle of the night? What did they think they were hitting? The Pentagon? Everyone else is *gone*."

Julia waited. She waited for Jonathan to say that they had another American, and why the hell did only a couple of Americans survive. But Jonathan said nothing more. A white man. The only survivor. They had come looking for her. Bill Levin? Impossible. But nothing else. No one else. Carl had come for her. Carl was there for an instant. Now there was nothing where Carl had just been.

Julia turned her face to the wall. She was still for a few moments. Then she turned back and walked into an examination room to see her next patient. She saw patients the rest of the afternoon. Slowly. One after the next. That's what they teach you in doctor school. You put yourself and your emotions aside.

Jonathan came to the door an hour later and saw Julia weighing a baby on the vegetable scale. She knew. No need to rub it in. The men who were looking for her had died. Maybe the white guy was in that group, maybe not. He had been taken back to Buchanan and was about to be interrogated. They were done here now.

Now Jonathan needed real cover.

He changed out of his khakis. They had to search, but they found scrubs that fit him. He could sit in scrubs and still work the phone. The phone rang for a few days, and then it stopped ringing.

Jonathan watched Julia from his chair behind the desk in what used to be an exam room as she moved from place to place in the clinic.

Three days later, Jonathan got the last two suitcases out of the truck.

Those kids would come in, their heads flopping on their short necks as if attached to their bodies by string. Julia looked at them all. She'd praise the mothers for bringing their kid to clinic, even when she knew and the mothers knew that the child was dying. All Julia could hope for was that this mother might wait before having the next child, and when that next child arrived, perhaps the mother would come to clinic when the child became sick and before its death was a certainty. Sometimes the people from the bush brought in men or girls with rabies, their eyes wild and disorganized and their limbs stiffening up.

Sometimes Jonathan would go with Julia and a PA or a community health worker when they walked out to a village, to an old woman or an old man near death with a fever who was too weak to travel. There was usually nothing Julia could do. They rarely had morphine, so she would cover the woman or the man with a blanket so she or he didn't feel cold, and then she would wipe the person's forehead with a cool cloth as she or he died, hot and cool at once.

At first all Jonathan did was watch Julia as she moved about the clinic, walking stiffly from room to room, from patient to patient. He sat in scrubs at the desk in the main clinic room as though he were in charge, while he waited for a white pickup, its bed filled with armed men, that he believed was coming for him. When it came he knew his life would end. He was ready. If you live by the sword, you perish by the sword. There was nothing grand or romantic about this life. You do the best you can with what you have. Jonathan had done pretty damn well, given where he had started and what he had started with. He wondered sometimes whether he'd die in the village or whether they'd take him out into the bush to kill him, but he didn't dwell on it. You pays your money, you takes your chances. No one in the clinic actually paid him any attention. Everyone else had a purpose and a job to do or a sickness that needed healing. It is hard to be in charge when there is nothing to be in charge of.

But no pick-up came. MODEL thought he had died at the club.

Then, bored as the days progressed, Jonathan began to help. It was silly and a waste of his time, but there was nothing else for him to do and nowhere else for him to go. He could keep his head down and live. Or he could raise his head up and have it cut off. Overall, living was a better choice than dying. It was different, thinking about living. Jonathan had always thought death was just around the corner and his job was to stay one step ahead of it, doing whatever he needed to survive. You think differently when there is no one trying to kill you. Your brain slows down a little. You see things. You hear things. You have ideas.

Jonathan learned to weigh babies. He learned to draw the shots. He learned how to take a temperature and blood pressure for the old people.

Then he learned what to look for when the children with sick mouth opened their mouths and pushed out their tongues, when the tonsils were cherry red and covered with white-green pus. He learned how to feel for lymph nodes under the necks of the seven-year-olds, and eventually he even learned how to give the children their shots. He learned how to distract the kids by looking to his left while his hands were moving to his right; by touching a shoulder when he was aiming for a thigh, and or by moving so fast with a needle that the kid didn't see or feel the needle until after it was pulled out and the shot was done.

Julia ignored Jonathan at first. He was a burden, an unneeded distraction, a liability. He might attract attention to them, and attention meant blood and death. He knew all Julia wanted was for him to move on into the bush toward one border or another and take his guns with him.

They slept in different exam rooms, and they cooked what the country people brought them—cassava and bush meat, bananas, mangoes, pineapple, and dried fish from a river that was half a day's walk. They cooked in the little cooking and laundry shack that had been built behind the clinic on the edge of the hill nearer to the village. Julia made a garden next to the cooking shack and grew maize, beans, tomatoes, peppers, and squash.

Julia rarely spoke. She looked away when Jonathan came into the room.

One day, a seventeen-year-old mother brought in one more baby nearly dead of malaria, its head and arms limp, its eyes dull and yellow, its nostrils moving just a little as it grunted to breathe—the last patient of the day, to be looked at in the quick red light of the evening that angled through the windows as the sun set. Julia told the mother to take the baby home, and she even gave the mother a little medicine, though she knew and Jonathan knew and the mother knew that the medicine wouldn't work. Julia told the mother that she must wait for a year before having the next baby, and she told the mother to bring a baby to clinic the moment it got sick, hoping, probably vainly, that the next baby would be one she could save.

The young mother stood and wandered out of the room. They cleaned the clinic at the end of the day. They wiped the surfaces with bleach, and Jonathan brought the yellow plastic water tanks to the village pump on an old rickety wheelbarrow so he could fill them, so they would have water to wash their hands at the next day's clinic. Then Jonathan swept the floor as Julia made her last notes in patients' charts. He filed the charts in the file room as the last light left and the clinic slipped into darkness.

As he swept the porch, Jonathan found the baby, not breathing, still and cool but not yet cold on one of the shiny wooden benches on the porch.

There was a shovel next to the cookhouse that they used to turn over ground in the vegetable garden and to dig a hole for the latrine that they moved from place to place. Jonathan lifted the baby as if she were still alive and held her to his chest as he carried her to the cookhouse; as if she had been his own child. And then he placed the baby on the ground and walked twenty paces to the edge of the forest. He dug a hole for her that was three feet deep.

Julia came out to the cookhouse as he was carrying the child to the hole he had dug. She watched as he placed the baby in the hole and filled it with dirt.

It was not that night, and it was not the next night, but it was the night after that Julia came into the examination room in which Jonathan slept and joined him as he slept on the low bed that was used during the day as a place for women to lie down when they were being examined, although there was not really room for two people in the bed. And it was perhaps a week later that Jonathan found himself thinking about how the clinic could run better, which for them meant how they could stop running out of malaria medication and antibiotics and oral rehydration solution—supplies that Jonathan should have been able to command with the flick of a finger, an order to an underling, or an agitated phone call, but now he had to think through the process more carefully, as it was wiser to extract promises and then the supplies themselves without making clear who was who, who was here and who was there, and who was steering this ship after all.

White people come and white people go. The Americans are here one week and gone the next. The white guy who knew Julia worked with them for a few days and talked to Julia long into the night, but he would soon realize that there was no work for him here, not really. Julia was covering the work. They could take care of their own. The people would come in from the bush too late. The clinic needed supplies, which were always short. There are plenty-plenty people to do the work once those people remember to pitch in and get the work done together.

Chapter Thirty-Six
Yvonne Evans-Smith, Naomi Goldman,
Julia Richmond, MD, William Levin,
MD, John Goh, and Jonathan Crossman.
District #4 Health Center. May 2007

No GOODS LORRY CAME AS FAR AS THE DISTRICT #4 HEALTH CENTER. EVERY FEW DAYS A
car or a small beat-up pickup truck came down the road. The County
Health Department sent out a Land Cruiser with supplies once a
month now that they didn't need to send a doctor every week or two.
The Health Department could have carried the Americans back to
Buchanan, but it was against regulations for its Land Cruiser to carry
passengers, so Jonathan ordered a tire and wheel, a hand pump, and a
red five-gallon gasoline can filled with diesel fuel to be sent on the next
trip of the Land Cruiser. Those things arrived about a week after the
Americans hobbled out of the jungle on the red dirt road. Jonathan
lent them his solar battery recharger, which they jerry-rigged to the
terminals of the extended-cab white Dodge Ram. John and Levin
spent the better part of a morning putting the new tire on the truck,
inflating the other tires, filling the tank with diesel fuel. No one was
more surprised than the two men when Levin turned the key and
the truck turned over very slowly twice, paused, and then caught, its
engine rumbling back to life, as thick black smoke poured out of its
tailpipe.

They had spent their evenings together on the porch that week,
and it felt to them like being at summer camp or at an extended family's once-a-year week at the lake cabin built by their grandparents and
inherited by five cousins. They sprayed themselves with mosquito
repellant, sat on the benches, and talked.

Levin and Julia talked most. "I don't understand you staying here," Levin said.

"It's good work, the work we always talked about me doing," Julia said.

"But Julia, you're in the middle of no place. No colleagues. No new ideas. No journals or meetings. We've finally given up treating otitis media, for God's sake. You're going to wither and rot."

What Levin knew but didn't say was that the light had gone out in Julia's eyes. Same shell. Same skin. Same hair. Same face. But no hope and no spark now. Africa and the damned war had done to Julia what eighteen years of growing up in America, four years of college, four years of medical school, and four years of residency had failed to do. Julia's soul had disappeared, and all she could do was see patients all day long, one sad story after another.

When Julia heard Levin say come home now, she didn't think, *this is my home*. She didn't think about Jonathan and whether or not she loved or even liked him, though she had started to trust him a little at last. She didn't think about the calling of the pepper-birds or the murmured voices from the village in the morning or the backyard barbeque smell of the charcoal fires or the cleansing beauty of the evening rains or even about the feel of washing herself under the village pump after dark when the village had gone to sleep. In some hidden place, Julia thought only about Carl, about her own awkwardness and failures that had brought her here, where she probably deserved to be, the awkwardness that had killed Carl, because she had been careless and made something happen between them that brought Carl back to Africa to die, and now all she wanted was to stay here where no one could see her or her mistakes. There was no value in going anywhere. The world is as the world is. It cannot be repaired. If you lift your head up, someone will certainly cut it off. If you hope, those hopes can only be dashed. If you let yourself feel, you will make a mistake and only feel heartbreak and shame.

"I'm going to stay here and keeping working." That's what she told Levin. *The need is great. There's nothing left of me to try again*, she told herself. These people were good to come, but Julia was anxious for them to go so she could crawl back inside herself again.

It was about the middle of the day and hot-hot when the Dodge Ram roared back to life. The Americans and John had been at the health center a week, each sleeping in an examination room or in the records room. They had all gone through their changes of clothes and had washed their things out once in a big plastic tub with water from the village pump, and then left their clothes hanging on the benches of the health center overnight to dry. It was time to go home. They could easily make Buchanan by nightfall if they left soon after Levin and John got the truck running again. Julia could come in after the next Health Department Land Cruiser visit and drive the truck back to the health center. They'd be in Buchanan by nightfall. Monrovia the following day. The twice a week flight out through Freetown, Casablanca, and London two nights later, and then home two days after that. They would be back in Rhode Island before the end of the week.

When the truck started, the growl of its engine alerted the village to an event happening in their community. The white truck was running. It would move from its place next to the health center, where it had rested for a number of years. The Americans and John went to pack their things.

Julia was in big belly clinic when she heard the truck turn over. Her spirit soared for an instant, and then fell back. There was something inside her that still hoped for escape, a part that was formed when she was imprisoned at The Club and resisted, a part that wanted to preserve her own life and make it better, a part that had been buried for years but hadn't quite died. *There is a way out*, she thought for a moment. But then her reality set back in. *I cannot leave this place*, she told herself. *This is the life I deserve.*

So when Levin, Naomi and Yvonne came to stand outside her examination room waiting for her, Julia was ready to push back against them. They aren't carrying their bags, she told herself. They are going today but not quite yet. There is more business to transact. Jonathan was sitting at his desk, a pencil behind his ear. Julia didn't know what he thought about the Americans, and frankly she didn't care. This was her fight not his.

"It's time," Levin said. "Truck's running."

"I heard," Julia said. "Safe travels."

"Why don't you come?" Levin said. "There's room for five. The back seat is tight but we can squeeze."

"Don't be silly," Julia said. "My work is here."

"Call it time off," Yvonne said. "Everyone deserves a little vacation now and then."

The sun was high but light in the main clinic room was muted. Jonathan sat next to a window across the room. Sunlight fell on Jonathan's back as he tipped his chair backward on its two rear legs to listen.

There was little sound coming from the village. The people and animals knew to rest in the midday heat. The smells in the room were human smells—sweat and a hint of baby's urine and the sweet smell of seedy yellow newborn stool, which smells like apricots, set against the tang of rubbing alcohol, which was strongest in the examination rooms, and the dry powdery pharmaceutical smell and taste of antibiotics and acetaminophen, which was strongest in the drug room.

Jonathan did not think these people were trouble. They were unable to get a car across a bridge, and then they stranded themselves in the village and had to beg for car parts. For a day or two Jonathan wondered if they were something different then they appeared, if they were after information, if someone had heard a rumor and wanted to quietly check it out. But no, these people where exactly who they appeared to be, which was next to nothing.

Jonathan learned from Julia, little by little. She kept his bed warm at night, and she didn't challenge him when he began to build again, little by very little in the clinic and the village, not that there was very much yet. Julia taught Jonathan to listen and that got the village to trust him, and Jonathan for himself found a kind of place and a kind

of trust in the village and in village life. They were his people. They
shared food with Jonathan and Julia. He enjoyed walking to the village with them and squatting with the men to hear stories about the
headmen of other villages, their sons and their wives, about feats of
strength performed in the jungle, and about the amazing abilities of
men with only one arm or only one leg or of one man with no legs at
all.

No one talked about the war, about what they did in the war or
what was done to them.

Julia taught him to lift the children into the air, and she taught him
how to tickle them. He was amazed to discover that the delight those
children exuded brought delight to him as well.

But there wasn't anything between Jonathan and Julia, not really.
She was cold to him, even when they were together. She tolerated
him. To a certain extent, she used him for protection, for warmth,
and for release. There was nothing beyond that. Jonathan used her as
well. She had been his life preserver, his ticket out. They understood
one another, and both understood the rules of the game. There was
nothing beyond that for him either. So when the Americans cornered
Julia, Jonathan knew the game was over. No regrets. They had gotten
plenty of mileage out of each other. Jonathan was still alive, which
was more than he thought would happen. The men in the white
trucks had never come to take him away, shoot him in the jungle, and
leave his body to rot. Know when to hold them and know when to
fold them.

"Just a little R and R," the white man said.

"I don't need anything," Julia said. "Send us antibiotics and aspi-
rin. Ship them over once a month."

"Julia pack your things and get into the truck with us. Do it now,"
the white man said.

"Screw you, Bill. I'm not your resident. This is my life now. You
don't get to tell me what to do anymore," Julia said. She stepped
through them to clear a path for the patient, a thin dark woman standing behind her.

"My boy came to see you home," the older woman said. Jonathan knew her type. That woman had gotten out. She built herself a new life in the U.S. Now she was better than Liberia. She had come back to teach Liberians, and everyone else, how to live.

"I'm so sorry about Terrance," Julia said. "I know I am responsible for his death. But I'm part of something here. I can't just walk out on these people. They depend on me."

"That something survived for thousands of years without you," the older woman said. "And people will get by whether you are here or not."

Julia walked onto the porch and the Americans followed her. She wanted to lead them away from the place that she felt was hers, the place they were invading, and closer to the truck that would take them away from her and the health center and her village, to help them put this silliness to rest.

"You're not thinking straight," Bill Levin said.

"I'm a consenting adult," Julia said. "I'm a free woman, and I can make my own choices, thank you very much."

It's not working, Naomi thought. *Nothing Dr. Levin says will get her to come home with us. It was all for nothing. Our coming here. Carl and Terrance. The whole thing. Julia will never move. She's hiding. Carl died, and she blames herself, and she's buried her life. This place lets her live without feeling, without love, without risk, without herself. I know this place. I used to live here myself.*

What did Carl say about Julia? Pie in the sky. Likes saving little kids. Who was going to save this woman from herself? And what did Carl say about Naomi? About her sitting inside of him as if she were a part of him? If Julia was a part of Carl and Carl was dead and Carl was a part of Naomi that made Julia a part of Naomi, and Naomi couldn't live with being split up any more. *No more hiding in trees. Not more hiding. We are one people*, Naomi thought. *One body.*

"Come in the truck with us," Levin said. "You can always change your mind when we get to Buchanan."

"No. I'm staying here. That's final," Julia said. "Have a safe trip."

"We're done here," Levin said. "I'm going to get my things." He nodded at John. "Let's get the things and pack the truck. Luggage in the bed. Back seat is going to be tight, and I think we can make Buchanan before the rain, if we haul some ass." Levin paused. John was a churchgoing man. "Sorry man. If we get a move on."

John stood and began to walk with Levin back inside.

"No, we're not done yet," Naomi said. She stepped next to Julia and put her arm around Julia's waist.

"We're taking you home, hon," Naomi said, and she held Julia tight to her, Naomi's body warm and strong. Carl.

"Don't call me hon," Julia said and she started to twist away.

Yvonne came and stood on the other side of Julia. She put her arm around Julia's waist so they were standing arm in arm. Julia was angry and proud and twisted away as she turned to look at Naomi who she was going to tell to go fuck herself.

"Go loose. Let *us* carry *you*," Naomi said.

It was Naomi next to Julia, not Carl.

Suddenly Julia was under water. Couldn't breathe. Sucked away by the current. No air. Drowning. Cold. She didn't know which way was up.

Then she felt was something warm and strong. A body. Bodies. They were holding her. They lifted her. Carl was there. Then he wasn't.

Then Julia was Kim, bending over in the garden, hoeing someone else's farm. Let me swim for you, Carl said. Go limp. All Julia wanted was Carl, who was strong and warm and good and now was gone because she was awkward and disconnected. Naomi and Yvonne held Julia around the waist as they walked her down the steps. Jonathan came down the steps and opened the rear doors of the truck's cab. He lifted her into the rear seat.

"Farewell," Julia said to Jonathan just before he closed the door.

"Take care of yourself," Jonathan said. "No one else will."

"You not even close on that score, brother," Naomi said. "We take care of our own."

John and Levin got in and slammed their doors. The big engine turned over three times, and then caught. John backed the truck up a few feet and put it into first.

They drove down the little hill to where it meets the red road in the jungle, and they drove off down the red road they had come on a little more than a week before.

The truck raised a cloud of red dust, which settled on the grass of the field and the leaves of the trees adjoining the road, and which would be washed away by the evening rains.

The sun was strong and hot, and the hot air wavered under the green trees.

Chapter Thirty-Seven
Naomi Goldman

IT WAS GOOD TO BE IN AFRICA, TO FADE INTO THE BACKGROUND AND LET THE BOUNDARIES dissolve, to be part of all that is great and pulsing.

But Naomi still came home to Rhode Island, because it was the only home she knew. Home with its racism. Home with its greed. Home with its commercialism, the bright colors dancing on billboards and across the television screens in all the living rooms in America, as people sat before them, transfixed, all day long and late into the night.

Julia came to live with Naomi in West Providence, near Broadway, where all sorts of people live, where you could hear the car radios and the boom boxes blaring late into the night. Julia stayed in the extra bedroom Naomi thought would be Carl's. Naomi thought about it that way even though Carl had never seen this house, and she kept thinking it was Carl's even after she knew Carl was never coming home, because even though she knew Carl was dead, a part of her never believed it.

Julia sat and stared out the window most of the day for the first few months. People came to visit—mostly friends from the hospital and Levin, who brought his political people. Sometimes Julia went out for Levin's demonstrations or to see a movie, but her heart wasn't in any of it. She sat and looked out the window and, like Naomi, she was waiting for Carl to come home.

Levin brought Julia's car back, and she started to drive. One day in the early spring she said she was going to take a road trip and see family in California. Naomi knew she'd never be back.

In a sense, Naomi was now alone. Her father was still alive, still in the lockup from which he would never emerge, but then he had been dead to her from the moment they had escaped him. Carl was gone. Her mother was gone. Her grandparents were gone.

Naomi's friends called her on the phone and stopped by the Institute, and they went for lunch, sometimes even to Sally's. She would tell them about the trip, sometimes, and sometimes she would just listen to the stories of their lives. She talked about Carl when they asked, and she could now tell other people the truth about his strengths and weaknesses, about his brilliance and kindness and love, and also about his reckless abandon, about why he ran away, about the brave thing he tried to do and failed at, about the woman he loved who survived him, and about how strong he was to have cared for Naomi when they were children and what they endured together growing up.

These were the stories she would tell her children. Her children would live in these stories, and through those stories Naomi hoped her children might be able to see through the racism and the lust and the greed and understand that they too are part of a people and part of a place that is great and pulsing, and through the stories she would tell them and the stories they would tell one another they would discover the freedom to find what is great and pulsing within themselves and their people and their world.

America is freedom, she would tell them, despite the war and the madness. Sometimes America is the freedom to buy, the freedom to sell, and the freedom to bribe. But America is also the freedom for people to take care of one another, to listen, and the freedom to tell the difficult truth about who we have been and what we have done; about both the successes and the failures, about the strengths and the weaknesses, about the kindness and the greed. In America Naomi's children would still perhaps have the freedom to experience the world in all its grandeur, the freedom to be together, the freedom to talk and listen, and the freedom to tell stories about who we are and who we can become.

Perhaps they will be better people than we are, Naomi thought, *though probably not. Perhaps our children will find the right balance, the right combination of kindness and striving, of selfishness and selflessness, of* ego and humility, of lust and love, of freedom and democracy, of justice and of peace. Perhaps they will be better than we are and will succeed where we failed and find a way to move forward in the richness and abundance of the world, without stupidity, violence, war, and greed. Probably not. They are our children, the flesh of our flesh, the bone of our bone, and they will stumble forward in time the way we do, one step at a time, one step forward and two steps back; and then, sometimes, rarely, perhaps once in a generation or two but sometimes not for a thousand years, one step forward again.

I miss him, Naomi thought. I miss Carl. I'll always miss him.

He's gone now, she thought. But at least he taught me how to love.

Chapter Thirty-Eight
Results

ABOUT 2 PERCENT OF THE POPULATION, OR 618,000 AMERICANS, DIED IN THE U.S. CIVIL War, or War of Rebellion, or War of Northern Aggression, or War Between the States, at a time when the U.S. population was more than thirty-one million. About three hundred thousand Liberians, or 10 percent of the Liberian population, died in the long period of civil strife associated with the rebellion and then the reign of Charles Taylor, from 1989 to 2003, which occurred when the Liberian population was about three million people.

Charles Taylor stood trial in the Special Court for Sierra Leone, but the trial was moved first to The Hague, and then to Leidschendam in The Netherlands, because everyone knew it was too dangerous to try Taylor in Sierra Leone itself. Too many of Taylor's friends were still active in Liberia and Sierra Leone, places in which the rule of law is more hope than reality. The trial began in 2007 and judgment was rendered in 2012. The trial was conducted before the Special Court for Sierra Leone but under the auspices of the International Court of Justice, itself a court of the United Nations, which was created to hear accusations of crimes against humanity.

The legal status of crimes against humanity is unclear and represents an evolving body of international law. Charles Taylor was charged only with his activities involving Sierra Leone. He could not be charged in an international court with crimes committed in Liberia while he was the head of state because of a principle called sovereign immunity, which means that a head of state cannot be charged with a crime in his or her own country while serving as head of state by anybody other than the country itself.

Taylor is reputed to be a very wealthy man who still has considerable influence in Liberia, where it is claimed that he still has friends and associates in his employ. He is also reputed to control considerable assets in Liberia—timber, iron, and diamonds—through those friends and associates.

Final arguments in the three-year trial were heard on March 11, 2011, almost eight years after Taylor fell from power and almost five years after he was turned over to the International Court of Justice and the Special Court for Sierra Leone.

On April 26, 2012, the Court found Taylor guilty of aiding and abetting eleven crimes, including murder, rape, sexual slavery, and forced labor. He was also convicted of conspiring with the Sierra Leonean Revolutionary United Front to plan attacks in three different areas of the country, including the capital, Freetown, and diamond-rich district of Kono.

The civil war in Sierra Leone claimed some fifty thousand lives. Thousands more Sierra Leoneans were forced to serve as child soldiers and sex slaves. Thousands more yet had limbs amputated.

On May 30, 2012, Taylor was sentenced to serve fifty years in jail for his crimes. That sentence was appealed by both prosecution and defense and was affirmed by the International Court of Justice in 2013.

Taylor was never indicted for his role in the rape and destruction of Liberia itself. If found innocent of charges in Sierra Leone, Taylor would have returned to Liberia a free man.

Chapter Thirty-Nine
Summary and Conclusions

William Levin retired from the practice of Emergency Medicine at the end of June 2008. He moved to San Juan del Sur, Nicaragua, where he lives near a beach. He is writing a memoir about his time in Liberia. He writes in the morning, works in the public clinic for a few hours in the afternoon, and then walks the beach each evening as the sun is going down.

Yvonne Evans-Smith stayed in Liberia. She lives in Sinkor, teaches accounting at Cuthington College, and makes dinner for her brothers and sisters, her nieces and nephews and their children every Sunday afternoon.

Ellen Johnson Sirleaf finished her second term as the president of the Republic of Liberia on January 18, 2018. George Weah, a former soccer star, was elected to replace her. His vice presidential running mate was Jewel Howard Taylor, senator form Bong County and the divorced wife of Charles Taylor.

Julia Richmond lives in Bolinas, California, in a little walk-up apartment near the sea. She works at San Francisco General Hospital three days a week in the walk-in section of the pedi-ER. She sees coughs and colds and sore throats and kids with constipation, and she has all the Keflex and Betadine she needs. She's trying to learn medical Spanish. There's a psychologist she knows who writes poetry and who drives over the Golden Gate Bridge on a beautiful red 1964 BSA Lightning every other weekend, and who doesn't need to crowd her space, and that is pretty good. But she knows and he knows that she is always looking for the brilliant eyes of someone else when she looks into his.

And she knows and he knows that the clock is ticking, and that before long she will have his child, and they will move in together and love the child and each other in a different way, and that she will always remember the time when she loved with all of herself, and not just with her daily routines, not just by being there in body. Then the man she is with will love her by being patient with her absences and will love her by being willing and able to find her in the places she is hiding. One day soon she will let that man come to find her more often when she is buried in her thoughts and memories, and she will let him bring her back to the present from time to time and throw her arms around him and feel the warmth of his body and feel him flow into the empty spaces inside her. And being back in the present with him will give her some pleasure and even a little joy.

That time is coming. Just not quite yet.

Appendix
Charles Taylor. Rhode Island and
Liberia—An Implausible but Real History,
with a Little Conjecture Added

PEOPLE IN RHODE ISLAND SAY THAT CHARLES TAYLOR ONCE LIVED IN PAWTUCKET, A working-class city just north of Providence, the state capitol, in a place then called Crook Manor. Crook Manor was a public housing development on Weeden Street, Pawtucket, and has been renamed Galego Court, although everyone in Pawtucket still calls it by its original name.

There's no proof that Charles Taylor ever really lived in or even visited Rhode Island. He lived in Dorchester, Massachusetts, and attended a now defunct community college, and then Bentley College, now University, in Waltham, Massachusetts (also the home of Brandeis University), and graduated from Bentley with a BA in Economics in 1977. While he lived in Dorchester, Charles Taylor worked as a security guard, a truck driver, and a mechanic. He worked at Sears and Mutual of Omaha. Taylor was in Liberia from 1979 to 1983, as part of the government of two Liberian presidents, and then returned to the U.S. in a hurry once he was accused by then president Samuel Doe of having embezzled one million dollars.

Taylor was arrested in Massachusetts after the U.S. received an extradition order from the Republic of Liberia. He was imprisoned in the Plymouth House of Corrections, a maximum security facility in Plymouth, Massachusetts, until 1985, when he escaped, though he now claims he was released by the CIA. Released or escaped, he is the only prisoner ever to have escaped from the Plymouth House of Corrections and remained at large.

Although there is no evidence that Charles Taylor ever lived in Rhode Island, there is plenty of reason for thinking he spent time there and got to know the place pretty well. Rhode Island has the largest Liberian population per capita in the United States—some fifteen to seventeen thousand people—mostly Krahn, Bassa, and Gao people, some of whom lived in Crook Manor in the 1970s and 1980s and some who still live there now that it is Galego Court. Perhaps the existence of this population led people to speculate that Taylor likely visited Rhode Island now and then. Perhaps Taylor really lived at Crook Manor in the early 1980s when he was in the U.S. as a fugitive, fleeing Samuel Doe. No one—other than the people who lived in Crook Manor then, who either did or did not have Taylor as their neighbor, and Taylor himself—will ever know for sure.

After Charles Taylor disappeared from the Plymouth House of Corrections, he found his way to Libya, where he was trained in guerilla warfare. With support from Colonel Muammar Gaddafi, he went to Ivory Coast and founded the National Patriotic Front of Liberia. In 1989, the National Patriotic Front of Liberia fomented an armed rebellion in Liberia, aiming to overthrow then president Samuel Doe. Taylor invaded Nimbi County from Ivory Coast with a hundred armed fighters and quickly attracted the support of the local population, which had been brutally attacked by the Armed Forces of Liberia in 1985.

This armed rebellion marked the beginning of the First Liberian Civil War, which would degenerate into a brutal ethnic conflict among seven different armed camps, first leading to Doe's overthrow and televised brutal murder, and then to five more years of murder, rape, dismemberments, and chaos. More than three hundred thousand people were killed and more than a million became refugees, as whole populations were raped and savagely murdered, often by child soldiers who were drugged and forced to commit atrocities, and who were ordered to rape and kill their own families and communities. After five years of fighting, Taylor, backed by Gaddafi and other international friends and coconspirators, emerged as the strongest and most brutal of the warlords. The war lasted until 1995, when a peace agreement brokered by the president of Ghana and facilitated by other African states, the UN, the U.S., and the European Union led first to an uneasy cease-fire, and then to elections.

In 1997, in an election most people thought was free and fair, Charles Taylor was elected president by the people of Liberia, with 75 percent of the vote. Many people voted for Taylor because he appeared strong enough to stop the bloodshed that had been ravaging the country and had wrecked its fragile institutions. Many more voted for him because they feared he would continue the war and bloodshed if he lost. His supporters ran through the streets, singing, "He shot my ma, he shot my pa, I will vote for him."

The Second Liberian Civil War began in 1999, when a group called Liberians United for Reconciliation and Democracy, supported by the governments of Guinea and Sierra Leone, invaded Liberia from Guinea. To be fair (if that word is relevant at all here) there is evidence that Taylor was involved with rebel groups or parties in both countries and so the governments of Guinea and Sierra Leone might be thought of as trying to keep the playing field level, although it is not possible to know who did what to whom first and when.

Sierra Leone, Liberia's neighbor to the west, had its own history of civil strife and bloody, maniacal civil war. Sierra Leona was a British colony until 1961 and was partially populated by a group of imported ex-slaves from Britain and the U.S. who turned themselves into a ruling class, very much like Liberia, though Liberia became independent more than a hundred years earlier. Sierra Leone's politics are made more complex by the existence of diamond mines near its border with Liberia, which produce over three hundred million dollars worth of diamonds a year.

The Special Court for Sierra Leone where Charles Taylor would be tried and eventually convicted was established in 2002. Ahmad Tejan Kabbah, the president of Sierra Leone, wrote United Nations

Secretary General Kofi Annan in July 2000 asking for UN help prosecute those responsible for war crimes during the ten-year civil war in Sierra Leone. Many of those atrocities had been committed by the Revolutionary United Front, the Sierra Leonean rebels and Charles Taylor's allies—an organization known for using child soldiers as young as five, ordering children to kill their parents, practicing cannibalism, using rape, and amputating the limbs of people who were going to vote as routine methods of instilling the fear and obedience of the population. The government of Sierra Leone asked for UN help, because it was not strong enough on its own to hold and try Sierra Leoneans in its own court in a region where Charles Taylor, the president of the nation that comprised Sierra Leone's eastern border, held sway and was thought to control militias and armies inside Sierra Leone. And Sierra Leone was certainly not strong enough on its own to bring Charles Taylor to justice.

The president of Sierra Leone's letter was quite specific, proposing clearly delineated powers, many of which are contained in the final agreement creating the court, suggesting that much of the text of that letter was prenegotiated. UN Security Council Resolution 1315 of August 14, 2000, directed the Secretary General of the UN to negotiate with the government of Sierra Leone to create the requested Special Court. The Special Court came into being two long years later, in late 2002, after countless more atrocities were committed by all parties involved. The Special Court was a judicial body established by the government of Sierra Leone and the United Nations to "prosecute persons who bear the greatest responsibility for serious violations of international humanitarian law and Sierra Leonean law" committed after November 30, 1996, during the Sierra Leone Civil War, with which Taylor was deeply involved (http://en.wikipedia.org/wiki/ Special_Court_for_Sierra_Leone - cite_note-2).

The Special Court for Sierra Leone had no real precedent in international law. It was not a Sierra Leone court. It was not a United Nations court or part of the International Criminal Court, the usual tribunal for acts committed in violation of international law. The

Special Court for Sierra Leone had both international and Sierra Leonean judges but did not have the power to oblige the extradition of accused persons from another nation. It was a compromise, made in a dangerous, difficult time, and was the best the international community could scrape together in a difficult and dangerous part of the world without committing much in terms of resources or political capital. But it was a pathway to end the war and bloodshed in that region, and, however incomplete, and however hypocritical (because it did not hold the U.S or Britain to the same standards of accountability for atrocities and war crimes), it was a pathway that worked.

Security Council resolution 1315 was a complete reversal of resolution 1260, from August 20, 1999, which was strongly supported by the U.S. and Britain and committed the involved nations to amnesty for all military combatants. Now, no more amnesty.

Something had changed between 2000 and 2002, and that something was 9/11.

For a decade, the U.S., Britain, and the world had responded slowly to the war and atrocity that reigned in West Africa, to the extent it responded at all, and as it responded slowly to genocide in Rwanda.

But after al-Qaeda attacked us in 1998 and 2001, and after we realized how al-Qaeda and others were using diamonds to fund terrorism in a way that could evade detection, we acted. Finally, greed and mayhem are like infectious diseases. They spread. We acted when the greed and mayhem that have been destroying West Africa was infecting us as well. And only then.

Charles Taylor was deeply involved with al-Qaeda, and his deepening interest in Sierra Leone most likely had to do with obtaining control over its diamond mines in order better serve his customers. Diamonds can move across international borders easily without detection, since they are small and easily concealed on the bodies and in the body cavities of human beings, are easily converted into cash, can't be traced, and don't trigger metal detectors. Taylor's control over the Sierra Leonean diamond mines meant he could trade diamonds for weapons and use those weapons to control West Africa. Al-Qaeda and other international terrorist organizations wanted those diamonds because they were an untraceable way to move money around the world and fund its war against the West.

The Special Court for Sierra Leone was financed by voluntary contributions from individual countries, mainly the U.S. and Britain.

On March 3, 2003, Charles Taylor was indicted by the Special Court for Sierra Leone, sitting in Freetown. The indictment was unsealed on June 4, 2003, when Taylor was in Ghana for peace negotiations with LURD and MODEL. John Kufuor, president of Ghana, declined to extradite Taylor to Sierra Leone, and Taylor fled home to Liberia.

On August 11, 2003, Charles Taylor, his troops surrounded and his international support gone, resigned and was immediately placed on the personal jet of Olusẹgun Obasanjo, president of Nigeria, with his family and President John Kufuor of Ghana. He had been granted asylum by Obasanjo and would live in luxury in Nigeria for three years.

On the same day, on August 11, 2003, three U.S. warships showed themselves off the coast of Liberia, where they had had been lurking out of sight for over a month, and the Liberian people lined the shores and cheered. "Feed us!! Save us!!" people cried, for those warships were the first hope people had that the long nightmare of Charles Taylor's reign might finally be over.

The U.S. landed an expeditionary force of 150 marines at Robertsfield Airport, and about 30 marines at the port at Monrovia. Nigeria brought in 6,000 men under the UN flag as peacekeepers. That was all it took to end 14 years of devastation, which followed on 8 years of dictatorship, which followed on 140 of oligarchy and rule of one people over another—an oligarchy that itself started as a way to end slavery in the U.S.

The story of Charles Taylor in Liberia appears to be the story of the havoc, murder, and mayhem one man can wreak on a people, a nation, and a region. Taylor was associated with at least three civil wars (two in Liberia and one in Sierra Leone), political instability in at least three countries (Liberia, Sierra Leone, and Guinea), the deaths of at least 350 thousand people (in Liberia and Sierra Leone) and the displacement of more than one million.

But Taylor did not act alone. Many people profited from Taylor's reign of terror. Many people helped or supported him. Too few resisted. Taylor inserted himself into a culture that was already lawless and divided, into a place where people had already let big men, big money, and big countries have their way. Liberia already had a culture of obeisance to power before Taylor built himself an army, instead of a culture that valued each person and each community and encouraged each person and community to stand up for themselves and work together in mutual defense.

There is no science that tells us how to balance the needs of the individual, the ability of people to collaborate and cooperate under the rule of law, and the importance of domestic tranquility against the desires of a few greedy men or the actions of a few greedy people, acting together. But there can never be enough vigilance, never enough engagement, and never enough emphasis on what we have built together. Never enough mutual defense. Never enough democracy. Never enough peace. Never enough justice. And never enough resolve to protect the bounty that our ability to be and work together has created for us.

An injury to one is an injury to all. We can only survive as individuals if we stand together and act together as a people. Democracy works but only if we make it work to create justice, and by creating justice, create and sustain peace.

Glossary

ATU—Antiterrorism Unit. A paramilitary Force of the Liberian Government established by President Charles Taylor in 1997 to guard government buildings. It was made up of foreign mercenaries from Burkina Faso, the Gambia, Sierra Leone, South Africa, and other nations and was implicated in murder, rape, and theft and looting in Monrovia in 2002.

Congo—A sometimes pejorative way to describe Americo-Liberians, used by other Liberians.

Congoman—A man of Americo-Liberian descent.

Congotown—A community in southeast Monrovia.

Copper—Small amounts of money. Often used to mean money or payment in any amount.

Dash—A small payment, a tip, or a gift. Does not imply anything like the word bribe, but rather indicates reciprocity, recognition of a favor or service done, or the worth of the person.

ECOMIL—Economic Community of West African States Military Command, formed in 2003 by ECOWAS, with the support of the U.S., to halt the occupation of Monrovia. It was succeeded by UNMIL.

ECOMOG—Economic Community of West African States Monitoring Group. A multilateral armed force established by

ECOWAS in 1990 to intervene in the first civil war in Liberia (1990–1996). It included armed forces from Nigeria, Ghana, Guinea, Sierra Leone, the Gambia, Liberia, Mali, Burkina Faso, Niger, and others.

ECOWAS—Economic Community of West African States. A regional group of fifteen countries founded in 1975 to promote economic development and integration, which has at times functioned as a political and military entity.

Goods Lorry—A truck, usually with side walls but an open top and back, used to transport people and materials in rural Liberia.

Grand Bassa County—The Liberian county in which the town of Buchanan is located.

Jitney—A shared taxi, usually a minivan able to carry six to twelve people, widely used in West Africa in place of public transportation.

LAC—Liberian Agricultural Corporation, the second largest producer of rubber in Liberia, which employed as many as three thousand workers.

Lapa—A large bolt of brightly color cloth used to make dresses and other clothing in West Africa. Often used to refer to a dress made from that cloth.

LD—Liberian Dollars. Worth about 0.012 U.S. dollars, or about 1.2 U.S. cents.

LURD—Liberians United for Reconciliation and Democracy. A rebel group active in north and west Liberia from 1999 until 2003.

Merlin—A British NGO that has provided public health support for Liberia since 1997.

Mittal—Now, Acelor-Mittal. A steel and mining company that once operated a large iron smelter in Buchanan, Liberia. Mittal's smelter was said to have been stripped of all its operating equipment when Buchanan was occupied by ECOMIL in 2003.

MODEL—Movement for Democracy in Liberia. A rebel group active in south and east Liberia in 2003.

Montserrado County—The Liberian county where Monrovia is located.

MSF—Médecins Sans Frontières (Doctors Without Borders), an international medical aid nonprofit that brings clinicians to care for populations suffering from the consequences of war and natural disasters.

Night Soil—Feces. A description used in places without latrines.

NGO—Nongovernmental organizations, usually private aid organizations like MSF and Merlin.

RPG—Rocket-propelled grenade.

Small Boy Units (SBUs)—Units of forcibly conscripted child soldiers as young as seven. Known for their brutality, the Small Boy Units were used extensively by the Revolutionary United Front during the 1991–2002 civil war in Sierra Leone and were closely linked to Charles Taylor and occasionally used by his forces in Liberia.

SSS—Special Security Service of the Armed Forces of Liberia was a military unit modeled on the U.S. Secret Service. Created by President Tubman and responsible for protecting the president of Liberia, the SSS was blamed for many human rights abuses during the Doe and Taylor presidencies.

UNMIL—United Nations Mission in Liberia was established by Security Council resolution 1509 (2003) of September 19, 2003, to support the implementation of the cease-fire agreement and the peace process; protect United Nations staff, facilities, and civilians; support humanitarian and human rights activities; and assist in national security reform, including national police training and formation of a new, restructured military.

USAID—United States Agency for International Development.

Acknowledgments

MANY PEOPLE HELPED IN THE WRITING OF THIS NOVEL, OFTEN MUCH MORE THAN THEY might suspect.

I had the honor of meeting and knowing many Liberians, Ghanaians, Malians, Nigerians, and other African-born Rhode Islanders when I practiced family medicine in Pawtucket, Rhode Island. *Abundance* was written for them.

Julius Kolawole, Syrulwa Somah, PhD, and Henrietta White-Holder, friends and teachers, provided an early introduction to Africa and African culture. Robert Pierce, Jr. and the Liberian Health Care Initiative funded and David Joseph of Mediators Beyond Borders helped arrange a medical mission to Liberia in 2009 that formed the basis of the descriptions in this book. Gabriel Fine joined me on that trip and provided a thoughtful critique and analysis of the situation in Africa and helped put that situation in the context of international relations. He was also an early reader of the novel and provided a helpful critique of some of the ideas and attitudes in the writing. Torwon Bunnah helped us understand the situation in and around Buchanan. Merlin and its entire Buchanan staff were great hosts. James Tomarken, MD, hosted us in Monrovia, provided useful insight into the government and politics of Liberia, was a helpful reader, and has become a good friend. Jason Montecalvo told me that it was impossible to buy a cheap used four-wheel drive car in Rhode Island, because they were being bought up and shipped to Africa, something that seemed totally improbable but turned out to be true and sparked the construction of the plot. The Open Society Institute webcast the trial of Charles Taylor, so I was able to watch it from my home in Rhode Island.

Kathy Laska, Paul Stekler, Lindsey Lane, and Jane Murphy, and the sorely missed Richard Walton were helpful early readers. Ellen Bar-Zemer, Penney Stein, Sally Rotenberg, Katherine Brown, and Sarah Zacks convened their book group to critique the novel and provided very useful feedback. Ann Hood and Gail Hochman were patient and realistic with me as an amateur and encouraged this unlikely project in spite of its many shortcomings.

Special thanks to Alexandra Shelley and to Tamara Trudeau for their editing and proofreading of early versions. Special thanks as well to Kim McHale for advice and encouragement all along the way, to Celia Ehrenpreis for her support and steady hand, and to Molly Hubbard for her creative approach to reckless abandon.

Terry Bisson provided editing, advice, encouragement, and wisdom. There is more to his quiet heroism that most people will ever know. Michael Ryan is the best copy editor a writer could hope for—precise and objective but also able to see and feel the story while trying to salvage the language and the punctuation. There is no better publisher than PM Press—Ramsey Kanaan, Stephanie Pasvankias, Steven Stothard, and many others—who make books for the right reason, which is protecting our freedom by strengthening our democracy.

I've been supported in every way by Carol Levitt for forty years and by Gabriel Fine and Rosie Fine for twenty-eight and twenty-seven years, respectively, which makes me the world's luckiest man.

About the Author

MICHAEL FINE, MD, IS A WRITER, COMMUNITY ORGANIZER, AND FAMILY PHYSICIAN. HE IS the chief health strategist for the City of Central Falls, RI, and Senior Clinical and Population Health Services Officer for Blackstone Valley Community Health Care, Inc., and recipient of many awards and prizes for his pioneering work bringing together public health and primary medical care. He was director of the Rhode Island Department of Health, 2011–2015.

ABOUT PM PRESS

PM Press was founded at the end of 2007
by a small collection of folks with decades of
publishing, media, and organizing experience.
PM Press co-conspirators have published
and distributed hundreds of books, pamphlets, CDs, and DVDs.
Members of PM have founded enduring book fairs, spearheaded
victorious tenant organizing campaigns, and worked closely with
bookstores, academic conferences, and even rock bands to deliver
political and challenging ideas to all walks of life. We're old enough
to know what we're doing and young enough to know what's at
stake.

We seek to create radical and stimulating fiction and non-fiction
books, pamphlets, T-shirts, visual and audio materials to entertain,
educate, and inspire you. We aim to distribute these through every
available channel with every available technology—whether that
means you are seeing anarchist classics at our bookfair stalls;
reading our latest vegan cookbook at the café; downloading geeky
fiction e-books; or digging new music and timely videos from our
website..

PM Press is always on the lookout for talented and skilled volunteers,
artists, activists, and writers to work with. If you have a great idea for
a project or can contribute in some way, please get in touch.

PM Press
PO Box 23912
Oakland, CA 94623
www.pmpress.org

FRIENDS OF PM PRESS

These are indisputably momentous times—the financial system is melting down globally and the Empire is stumbling. Now more than ever there is a vital need for radical ideas.

In the years since its founding—and on a mere shoestring—PM Press has risen to the formidable challenge of publishing and distributing knowledge and entertainment for the struggles ahead. With hundreds of releases to date, we have published an impressive and stimulating array of literature, art, music, politics, and culture. Using every available medium, we've succeeded in connecting those hungry for ideas and information to those putting them into practice.

Friends of PM allows you to directly help impact, amplify, and revitalize the discourse and actions of radical writers, filmmakers, and artists. It provides us with a stable foundation from which we can build upon our early successes and provides a much-needed subsidy for the materials that can't necessarily pay their own way. You can help make that happen—and receive every new title automatically delivered to your door once a month—by joining as a Friend of PM Press. And, we'll throw in a free T-shirt when you sign up.

Here are your options (all include a 50% discount on all webstore purchases):

- **$30 a month** Get all books and pamphlets
- **$40 a month** Get all PM Press releases (including CDs and DVDs)
- **$100 a month** Everything plus PM merchandise and free downloads

For those who can't afford $30 or more a month, we're introducing **Sustainer Rates** at $15, $10 and $5. Sustainers get a free PM Press T-shirt and a 50% discount on all purchases from our website.

Your Visa or Mastercard will be billed once a month, until you tell us to stop. Or until our efforts succeed in bringing the revolution around. Or the financial meltdown of Capital makes plastic redundant. Whichever comes first.

Damnificados

JJ Amaworo Wilson

$15.95
ISBN: 978-1-62963-117-2
5x8 • 288 pages

Damnificados is loosely based on the real-life occupation of a half-completed skyscraper in Caracas, Venezuela, the Tower of David. In this fictional version, six hundred "damnificados"—vagabonds and misfits—take over an abandoned urban tower and set up a community complete with schools, stores, beauty salons, bakeries, and a rag-tag defensive militia. Their always heroic (and often hilarious) struggle for survival and dignity pits them against corrupt police, the brutal military, and the tyrannical "owners."

Taking place in an unnamed country at an unspecified time, the novel has elements of magical realism: avenging wolves, biblical floods, massacres involving multilingual ghosts, arrow showers falling to the tune of Beethoven's Ninth, and a trash truck acting as a Trojan horse. The ghosts and miracles woven into the narrative are part of a richly imagined world in which the laws of nature are constantly stretched and the past is always present.

> "Two-headed beasts, biblical floods, dragonflies to the rescue—magical realism threads through this authentic and compelling struggle of men and women—the damnificados—to make a home for themselves against all odds. Into this modern, urban, politically familiar landscape of the 'have-nots' versus the 'haves,' Amaworo Wilson introduces archetypes of hope and redemption that are also deeply familiar—true love, vision quests, the hero's journey, even the remote possibility of a happy ending. These characters, this place, this dream will stay with you long after you've put this book down."
> —Sharman Apt Russell, author of *Hunger*

Clandestine Occupations
An Imaginary History
Diana Block

$16.95
ISBN: 978-1-62963-121-9
5x8 • 256 pages

A radical activist, Luba Gold, makes the difficult decision to go underground to support the Puerto Rican independence movement. When Luba's collective is targeted by an FBI sting, she escapes with her baby but leaves behind a sensitive envelope that is being safeguarded by a friend. When the FBI come looking for Luba, the friend must decide whether to cooperate in the search for the woman she loves. Ten years later, when Luba emerges from clandestinity, she discovers that the FBI sting was orchestrated by another activist friend who had become an FBI informant. In the changed era of the 1990s, Luba must decide whether to forgive the woman who betrayed her.

Told from the points of view of five different women who cross paths with Luba over four decades, *Clandestine Occupations* explores the difficult decisions that activists confront about the boundaries of legality and speculates about the scope of clandestine action in the future. It is a thought-provoking reflection on the risks and sacrifices of political activism as well as the damaging reverberations of disaffection and cynicism.

> "Clandestine Occupations *is a triumph of passion and force. A number of memoirs and other nonfiction works by revolutionaries from the 1970s and '80s, including one by Block herself, have given us partial pictures of what a committed life, sometimes lived underground, was like. But there are times when only fiction can really take us there. A marvelous novel that moves beyond all preconceived categories.*"
> —Margaret Randall, author of *Che on My Mind*

Fire on the Mountain

Terry Bisson
Introduction by Mumia Abu-Jamal

$15.95
ISBN: 978-1-60486-087-0
5x8 • 208 pages

It's 1959 in socialist Virginia. The Deep
South is an independent Black nation
called Nova Africa. The second Mars
expedition is about to touch down on the red planet. And a pregnant
scientist is climbing the Blue Ridge in search of her great-great
grandfather, a teenage slave who fought with John Brown and
Harriet Tubman's guerrilla army.

Long unavailable in the U.S., published in France as *Nova Africa*, *Fire
on the Mountain* is the story of what might have happened if John
Brown's raid on Harper's Ferry had succeeded—and the Civil War
had been started not by the slave owners but the abolitionists.

> "You don't forget Bisson's characters, even well after you've
> finished his books. His *Fire on the Mountain* does for the Civil
> War what Philip K. Dick's *The Man in the High Castle* did for
> World War Two."
—George Alec Effinger, winner of the Hugo and Nebula
  awards for *Shrödinger's Kitten*, and author of the *Marîd
  Audran* trilogy.